T0197356

FIVE BENEATH
Philly

FIVE BENEATH

Philly

TOM RICHMOND & SUSAN BANDY

FIVE BENEATH PHILLY

This is a work of fiction. All of the characters, names, incidents, organizations, and dialogue in this novel are either the products of the author's imagination or are used fictitiously.

iUniverse books may be ordered through booksellers or by contacting:

iUniverse
1663 Liberty Drive
Bloomington, IN 47403
www.iuniverse.com
1-800-Authors (1-800-288-4677)

ISBN: 978-1-5320-2734-5 (sc)
ISBN: 978-1-5320-2733-8 (e)

Library of Congress Control Number: 2017913329

Print information available on the last page.

iUniverse rev. date: 09/27/2017

Five beneath Philly is dedicated to Stephanie. Her trusting, enduring, and encouraging spirit made this book a reality.

Prologue

Allen Williams prepared himself mentally for what was sure to come. Strength, speed, and agility were his. He knew all three could spell trouble for the thugs now working his friend over. At 6' 2" Allen appeared intimidating with a build to match. Victor Rubio, his best friend, was in trouble again and for the same reason.

Vic, with the slighter build was excessively over confident. He had brought the beating on himself. He always did. With a few beers under his belt, he became haughty, surly, annoying, even insulting, a poor winner who was getting paid off for being a pompous ass. He just couldn't help himself. Flaunting his prowess at pool was part of the game. The game of 'Scotch Doubles' went long into the night with Allen as his partner. Allen's skill didn't matter. His participation only lent legitimacy to the game while Vic fleeced his marks. Once again, this night, Vic went too far.

Now, Allen was stepping in as Vic's guardian angel. Between gloved-blows to Vic's face, the leader of the losers caught Allen in the corner of his eye.

"Back off, buddy. This ain't your fight."

Allen replied, "I can make it mine or not. That's up to you."

Suddenly, the leader quit Vic and dove headlong into Allen's midriff slamming him hard into the trash cans lining the alley. Allen quickly regained footing on slippery bricks while two of the thugs held Vic like a punching bag and their leader resumed pounding his face.

"That's good, pull his arms back so's I can drill him real good."

They obliged, as he continued pummeling Vic's face. Absorbing the blows, Vic shouted with bravado spitting a tooth in the leader's face."

"Anyone else want in? I ain't goin' nowhere!"

Allen's eyes fixed on the leader's back. Running at him, he leapt into the air delivering a solid kick between his shoulder blades. The shock instantly drove wind from the leader's lungs. He dropped to the bricks gasping for air. His buddies dropped Vic seeing Allen poised in a 'cat-like' stance ready to deliver more blows. They hauled ass down the alley.

On his knees, Vic shouted, "That's right! Undefeated champs of South Philly, that's who you're messin' with!"

Allen's gaze settled on Vic.

"What say we call it a night, Tonto?"

Bending over, Allen put an arm around Vic's shoulders helping him up. Together they staggered beneath murky street lamps penetrating the waterfront mist. A damp chill made them shiver as they weaved homeward through the squalor of South Philly. A full moon's light reflected off the dirty gutters leading their way home. Only a trace of their former presence in the alley remained as the mist closed in behind them.

At daybreak, they arose to attend high school. After the final school bell, they moved on taking up their places alongside the livestock conveyer belts of the Cross Brothers' Meat Packing Plant. Several conveyor belts snaked through Philly's largest slaughterhouse. Here the boys wore bloody, black, rubber aprons as they disassembled livestock just like their fathers before them.

In the break room Vic asked, "Thanks for defending me last night. I continue to wonder where you learned to fight like that, Allen."

Allen replied, "Let's just say I read books, lots of books, something you should consider trying in the future. I'm going to get out of this place someday, just *you* wait and see."

Vic shrugged, "Some are *born* players, like me. I'm a pool shark. So *what*, I show off a little. Someday I'm going to own a pool hall, you wait and see. Maybe two, who knows?"

It didn't matter what they dreamt. Unless something extraordinary happened, their fate was sealed. They would remain trapped in the Cross Brothers' Slaughter House embraced by a community bereft of upward mobility. Working stiffs knew too well the way up was through the union, maybe making foreman and living to see retirement.

Vic's father was closing in on that dream. Sadly, Allen's Dad would never see it. Instead, he'd drop dead from a massive coronary brought on by years of grueling work, Lucky Strikes, and beer-soaked nights.

Nevertheless, Allen managed to cling to a dream. If anyone could slip the surly bonds of the Cross Brothers' monstrous maw it would be him. He was bright, energetic, and quick on the uptake. Willing to rise above 'The House.' His problem wasn't knowing what to do, but how? Often, Allen prayed, *"Hope springs eternal. Where there's life, there's hope...make me an instrument of Thy will, dear Lord. Thy will be done. Amen."*

Chapter 1

I don't mean to sound ungrateful. Dad's done plenty to keep the wolf from our door. It's just his drinking makes it harder on the rest of us to deal with life. I usually study in the cramped little kitchen of our three-bedroom flat while Mom and my grandmother make dinner. They're waiting, as usual, for my dad, Bill Williams. It is payday, which means he'll be home later than usual.

It's good Grandma is here to encourage me. Since I was old enough to read, she has patiently tutored me and challenged me with reading above my level. Thankfully, she's instilled a love of learning in me. Mom wants more for me, too, but Grandma always has time. I love reading, mostly history. My dream is to become a history teacher.

We await dad's return from one of many waterfront bars he frequents after work. There he seeks solace. Tonight, when he returns, he will be somber or glowing depending on which crowd he drinks with.

In South Philly, there are plenty of bars between the Cross-Brothers' Slaughter House and our home on Second and Arch Street. They all share the same neon lit odor of rancid beer and tobacco. Most patrons are as crispy as the bugs lying at the bottom of the yellowed window signs.

I'm an only son in a family of six. My two younger sisters can't work yet, while my older sister, Ginny, works part-time in a candy shop, a low pay passage to an early marriage.

When Dad finally enters, he's got that glow on his face. I tell myself he must have met up with the happy crowd. After all, it's Friday. Reason enough to celebrate, since it's also payday. Dad leans on the doorframe for a moment dutifully handing over the remainder of his pay to Mom. She grimly accepts what she must make do with until next week's offering.

She wears a bandanna scarf hiding her wilted hair. Her apron fits loosely on her narrow middle-aged waist. The scent of flour wafts behind as she moves about cramped kitchen preparing our dinner.

She calls out, "Get washed up, Bill. Dinner's almost ready."

Dad dutifully weaves down the narrow hall. He's already washed in the industrial sink at 'the house', as they call it. He struggles daily to scrape the film of animal fat off his bloodied hands and arms. Now, he'll attempt to wash away the grime of the bar he just left. From the bathroom, he calls out.

"What's for dinner, Betty girl?"

She returns, "Chicken stew and biscuits."

He shakes his head ruefully.

"I could sure do with something besides chicken for a change."

Grandma's eyes narrow, but she holds her tongue as she sets the table.

For the longest time, Mom has watched my dad try to escape the monstrous monotony of 'the house'. Ever since returning from WWII, he's labored there on the line. At first, he took the work there because the pay was good, relying on his youth to withstand the conditions until he bettered himself. Now, as foreman, he's found himself caught in the trap, too old to do better and too many responsibilities to quit.

At first, Mom tried stopping his drinking. Yet, every time she did he would grow frustrated and he ended up going out for more. At first, she resigned herself to making a comfortable place for him to come home to hoping that might somehow make him quit. With no success, she determined, at least, I would never face the same fate.

I'm my mom's last hope, according to her. I am always encouraged, or should I say driven. Mom and Grandmother dream of my making it to college. With their inspiration and my love of history, I immerse myself in studies where the world becomes different. In books, momentous things occur, sometimes tragic, but sweeping after any fashion. People in books do great things or horrendous things, but for me it's always far removed from the grit and grind of South Philly. I cling to my dream of becoming a history teacher just like Mr. Ryan Roberts, my teacher at school. He's my mentor helping me realize my dream. What's more, he promises to help me attain grants and the scholarship I will certainly need when the time is right. If I can just stay the course, I will escape the cycle that's dragging my father down.

Dad returns to the table, sitting down hard reaching for a biscuit. Waving it around, he gains the attention of my sisters and me.

"I've got good news, son."

I try to appear attentive overlooking my stew.

"What is it Dad? Did you get a raise?"

"No, nothing like that. That'll be the day those shysters come over with a raise. Anyway, I was talking to the second shift foreman on the cutting line. He tells me one of his men quit yesterday."

Mom quipped, "Doesn't that sort of thing happen all the time?"

Dad ceded, "Yes, but this guy was on second shift, you know, three to eleven." Still I remained unfazed by this news.

Dad continued, "Allen you've got a birthday coming and since you'll be eighteen, you could land that job on second shift."

For a moment, I was dumbstruck struggling to retain my sensibilities.

I asked, "Do you really think you can get me on at 'the house'?"

Dad reeled backward tipping his chair precariously as he floated his biscuit in the air.

"Hell, yes, and second shift means shift differential, too, you know. That comes to $1.92 an hour. Why, in no time, you'll be bringing home nearly eighty dollars a week! Now what do you have to say about that young man?"

Apparently, the celebration was on without me. Mom's face was aglow. My sisters squealed with delight. Only Grandma and I seemed to ponder the impact of such opportunity.

My first thought was "*how do I work and graduate high school at the same time?*" It seemed my father already crossed that bridge.

"You can still go to school, you know. You'll just have to leave study hall a little early. I'm sure we can work that out, right, Mother?"

His quick glance aside reaffirmed her best wishes. Then, Dad proceeded speaking of the ways this would work.

"First, you can take the trolley near school and be at 'the house' by three. Then, when you get out of school you can take the bus home. I'll be there, at first, to introduce you to the foreman and the rest of the crew. This is it, Allen your first real job. You know this is your shot at saving enough for college. Of course, you'll have to set aside quite a bit for that, you know. What do you say son?"

For God's sake, what could I say? This was it, wasn't it? It seemed there was no other way. I was a foreman's son and would soon take my place on the slaughter house *disassembly* line just as my father before me. Of course, never being the ingrate, I accepted my fate graciously with a smile.

The following day, Mom called arranging for me to leave study hall early. This was no problem as it was at the end of my day. The guidance counselor was familiar with such requests from other working families. Next, my father arranged an interview with Karl Grafton, the foreman on second shift at 'the house.'

We first met in the break room deep within the belly of the Cross Brothers' huge slaughter house. There in a crowded, smoke-filled break room, workers leaned over greasy tables spending their fifteen minutes of freedom pursuing life's simple pleasures. There I experienced my first real job interview.

Karl was a stout barrel-chested man, with Popeye-like arms. His ruddy, reddened face looked plump under his wispy, thinning, red hair pulled straight back over his head. Parts of it sprang out in tufts over each ear where his hat normally held his unruly hair in place. In his fifties, he was pretty much a product of my dad's day only he worked second shift.

Naturally, I was nervous sitting in that ten by twenty room with a dozen men bantering away their moment of escape from the line. Others just sat heads on the table trying to recover from the previous night's drinking. Still others ate voraciously out of brown paper bags while holding up their end of the conversation.

Newspapers were strewn about haphazardly lying in wait for the next set of readers to arrive on break. As I looked around, I studied the long window running full length along the room. I reasoned it was for bosses to spot who was on break. I knew it couldn't possibly exist for workers to view the bloody cutting line they'd just left.

At any rate, I was on time for my interview with Karl. Dad said he would come later to see how things were going, though I'm not sure what he might say or do to make a difference. I knew I must remain attentive looking Karl straight in the eye to make a good impression. I would answer yes sir and no sir and never lie. Besides, he already knew I never had a real job in my life, so what could he possibly ask that would stump me.

Quickly, I learned Karl was more interested in motivation than skill anyway. He started in telling me about the operation in general.

"I know your dad probably tells you what it's like working here, but I should give you the big picture anyway. That way you'll get some idea of where you fit in, O.K.?" I answered firmly, "Yes, sir."

"Anyway, it goes like this," he said. When the product, that's either slaughtered beefs or hogs, depending on what were setup for, arrives by rail they enter a pen for selection. For example, beefs are graded per their weight and body fat content. Later, it gets more detailed like types of meat like prime, select choice, utility, and so on. Anyway, that part doesn't concern you right now, so I'll just tell you how the line works.

"First, the animals pass through a door in single file from the pens. Then at a certain point, they pass over a bar, with their legs on both sides, and the floor slowly drops away. At that point, they are carried on a conveyor belt. They pass through a station where there's a man on the catwalk above. He holds a ten-pound sledge hammer. He's called the knocker man. He slams the beef right between the eyes, and then the brain-dead beef drops to its knees. Now, chains are attached to its rear legs. The chains lift them up and they are attached to an overhead trolley. This is where the animal is bled out. At this station, a man with a long knife will step up and cut the aorta to bleed out the animal."

Karl looked me over pausing a moment checking for any reaction. "It's been said that once an applicant fainted dead away during his initial interview." Looking down, he absentmindedly flicked a piece of suet off his apron sleeve before looking back to determine if I was still with him.

"It's all pretty straight forward if you look at it this way. At a slaughter house, you have big animals entering at one end and small cuts leaving at the other. In between, there are hundreds of workers using saws and wielding long knives. That's what we call 'processing the meat'. Now, the main thing is we want to watch out for contamination of the meat during the whole process. That's why we keep this place at a steady 40 degrees.

"At the beginning of the line it's risky, so that's where our most experienced men are stationed. At that point, a series of stations clean the animal and remove its hide. Then, there's evisceration and the tying off of intestines. These aren't pleasant jobs, I can clue ya. The main thing is we must work fast here. We can't have workers making mistakes. Otherwise, the line shuts down and we all lose money. The owners *really* don't like that either, I'm here to tell ya."

Karl leaned back pulling a crumpled package of unfiltered Camels from underneath his long rubber apron. Lighting up, he waited watching his first puff rise toward the choking layer of smoke already hovering in the room. Then, he leaned forward looking intently into my squinting eyes.

"Do you have any questions so far?" I replied with a respectful, "No, sir."

"Well, like I said kid, it's not a pretty job. Animals come here to die. They get decapitated, beheaded, and eviscerated. That's violent, bloody stuff. For some, it's too difficult to watch. Some even say it's dehumanizing, but the pay is good. That's how we keep our people here. Once you join the union, you'll see. We take care of our own."

By now, most of the men were shuffling out of the stale aired break room. I knew another shift was starting and Karl had to be back on the line. As he pushed back his chair to get up, my dad appeared outside the break room window. His slick, rubberized apron was covered with blood. I watched him step into the room with a limp.

"Hey son, how's the world treating you? Has Karl got you all squared away on our operation here?"

I just nodded allowing the two foremen a chance to confer.

Karl remarked, "Bill, I think your boy will do just fine once we get him trained. He certainly seems strong enough. Anyway, I couldn't scare him out of working here." Dad stepped up slapping me a bit too hard on the back.

"I'm sure he'll be a good worker Karl, and smart, too. Where are you planning on starting him out? Do you think he'll do alright on the line?"

"Yeah, I thought I'd put him in behind Vinny on hind quarters. I figure he can shadow him there 'til he gets the hang of it."

Dad said, "That sounds fine; Vinny's a good cutter. You'll learn a lot from him, Allen. Just don't let him start bulling you about how important it is to be Italian around here."

Karl grinned as he moved toward the door.

"Yeah, well then, I'll see you in here tomorrow at three o'clock sharp, Allen. You can meet me in the locker room when you get here. I'll get you fixed up with a uniform and a locker."

I glanced at Dad then back at Karl. I thought it best to seal the deal with a shake, so I presented my hand. He grasped it firmly. I could feel the strength that comes from wielding a long knife in his ham-fisted hand shake. Feeling relief when he finally relaxed his grip, I assured him I would see him tomorrow.

Dad and I left the break room together. He limped ahead of me on the wooden slatted walk that snakes throughout 'the house'. Where ever workers walk, wooden slats provided footing over surfaces that were constantly being washed down. They allow the clotting blood and cutting debris to flow away from the line into numerous drains in the concrete floor. I wondered, *"Where does it all go?"*

When we reached the double swinging doors to the locker room, Dad immediately started his routine. Cautiously, he removed his heavy, rubberized apron placing it in a large bin where it would be retrieved by clean-up personnel. The bin was nearly full now looking like a slippery twisted tangle of bloody, black animal skins. Next, he tossed his disposable hat in the trash. Plunking down heavily on one of the long wooden benches, he started pulling off his knee-high rubber boots. I could see even this simple act was leaving him winded. After the long, hard day, he appeared thin and worn to me. Maybe it was the florescent lighting that made him appear jaundiced and sallow. Yet, I couldn't help thinking, he looked older than usual.

"You know, Dad, maybe you ought to lay off those cigarettes a bit. They're bad for you. He just looked down at the floor for a moment, and then smiled raising his head to look at me.

"I'm just gettin' old son, that's all. Let me give you some advice. Don't ever get old, now *that's* bad for you."

It was just like him, laughing off his condition. At least he had a sense of humor. After getting out of his black pants and white cotton shirt with his name sewn on the pocket, he shuffled over to the huge, round, concrete sink in the center of the locker room. Around the bottom of the sink, there was a round ring of metal raised above the floor. It was a foot actuated pedal for turning on the water. In the center of the sink, a soap stand held several varieties of used soap cakes. There were gritty bars and soft soap to aid in removing the bloody film of animal fat that stuck to the skin and under the nails. After washing thoroughly, he went to the towel dispenser hanging on the wall and pulled down a fresh length of towel rubbing himself gingerly. The process was complete. He turned to his locker to get dressed.

When he was ready, we waited for the four o'clock bus. Usually, he could make the three-thirty, but my interview altered his routine. As we climbed on the bus for home, I couldn't help wondering if my being there would change his daily routine. Would he get off before Arch Street to join his friends at one of his favorite watering holes? I kidded myself thinking perhaps since I was along for the ride he might forgo his routine and come home.

As the bus lurched forward, he turned toward the window looking at the glass as though it were a page in a book he needed to read.

I asked, "What's on your mind, Dad. You seem preoccupied."

He turned to me blinking his eyes for a moment, then spoke slowly as if he were reciting a passage.

"You never get used to it no matter what you might think."

"What's that, Dad?"

"That smell, I used to think when I got on the bus and headed for home the next day it would be different somehow. That I could go to work in the morning and that smell wouldn't be there. Or, at least, I would get used to it, but it's never happened. For fifteen years now, I've gotten up every day and gone to 'the house' that smells of death. It's not just the scent of the blood; it's the whole lot of it that strikes your senses with a slug all at once. It's death, and there's nothing you can do to change it."

Suddenly, I felt very uncomfortable sitting next to Dad being jostled on the bus. I never heard him talk this way before. It was particularly unsettling hearing this as I was about to follow in his footsteps. Was this

his idea of a pep talk? I tried not to think about what he was saying, telling myself he was just tired. He certainly looked more ragged than usual. Then just, and suddenly, he turned back to the window again.

Under his breath, I could hear him say, "Oh, Jesus, I feel rotten."

Suddenly, a spring shower began splashing the windows of the bus. The steady rain glimmered and whirled down the side of the bus creating a mist that obscured the tenements lining the street. The bus continued weaving in and out through the thick, crawling procession of cars and trucks traveling south on Front Street. The driver constantly manipulated his air brakes as smaller vehicles zipped in and out in front of his bus. It was a worrying task for him just keeping his distance. At one point, a little Rambler cut him off causing him to slam on his brakes and curse.

I watched the sudden forward jolt jerk Dad out of his funk. He turned to me with a smile speaking in a matter of fact tone.

"I'm getting off at the next stop son; tell Mother I'll be home soon." When the bus brakes squealed at the stop, sure enough, he got up and left me. I wanted to shout. Then, I wanted to understand it, or at least feel sorry for him. More than anything, I felt disgust watching him leave the bus in pursuit of his routine.

The ride home filled me with despair. I couldn't get it out of my head. He chose to leave me alone on the bus. It did not frighten me in the least. I'm a big boy. I can take care of myself. It's just that I felt betrayed because he could not love me enough to forgo his habit for even one day. That's just the way it was.

I wanted to tell him when he *did* come home, that I changed my mind. I'd tell him I would make it some other way. My thoughts began to drift toward alternatives. I feared that if I stayed in 'the house' long enough I would turn out just like him. *"If there were just some other kind of work,"* I thought, maybe then I could avoid the trap that awaited me. Sadly, I knew no other job could even come close to paying for what I needed to pay for college.

My lack of experience pinned me on the horns of a dilemma that would not go away. I knew it would take more courage and commitment than I thought I had in me at the time. As I struggled trying to envision another way clear to follow my dream, the squealing brakes abruptly interrupted my thoughts. Wherever my dreams might lead, this was my stop. As I stepped off the bus, I noticed the spring shower had let up; at least I was spared a walk home in the rain.

Instead of walking home, I decided to look up my old buddy Vic Rubio. I felt I could use a little diversion. I had a good hunch where he would be. I headed in the opposite direction of home toward Norm's Pool Hall. It was just three blocks down and two blocks over. Pulling my jacket close around my neck, I kept out the chill wind that rippled the puddles on the broken sidewalk. At the last turn of the block, I could see the warm glow of Norm's picture window filtering light onto the cold sidewalk. That window beckoned people on the pavement making it possible for passersby to see who was inside and how they were faring. It attracted many to stop and warm themselves over a friendly game of pool.

A regular like Vic knew better. To him, pool was anything but warm and friendly. It was a living that should be honed with every stroke of the cue stick. He had this dream of becoming a champion pool player. Not an unworthy dream if only it weren't attached to this neighborhood. South Philly didn't produce champions of anything except prize fighters. In my estimation, his chances of emerging a champ were no better than a knife fight in a phone booth.

I never shared that view with Vic. With friends, some things are better left unsaid. Besides, I figure everyone's entitled to their dream. If you have one you should stick to it, at least until it proves you wrong. For the same reason, I didn't encourage Vic very often. I knew too much about the way he played pool. I could see him right now through the window lining someone up for the hustle. I entered cautiously getting a feel for how things were going before addressing him directly. I noticed two other guys leaning against the wall on barstools near Vic. I didn't recognize them. Though I could tell by their interest in the game, they had a stake in it.

Taking a seat nearby, I pretended to watch until I could catch Vic's eye. He drew back his cue concentrating on the eight ball. It was the last ball on the table. Glancing backward, he winked at me. Then he tapped his cue tip into the cue ball almost imperceptibly. Watching the white ball connect with its target was almost a thing of beauty. I knew from experience this game was over.

As the eight ball plopped into the pocket, Vic looked up in triumph.

He spoke coolly, "That makes it best out of five. Do you want to go double or nothing?"

The unhappy loser replied, "Too rich for my blood. I've had my fill." Reaching into his jeans pocket he scrounged two wrinkled twenties.

Relinquishing the table, his mark walked away toward the bar.

Vic turned to those on the stools.

"What about it? Are you guys up for it?" They just silently shook their heads. From where I sat, I could see they were neither warm nor friendly. It was clear they had enough, but would they want trouble? I decided to back my friend before things got any worse. Hopping off my stool, I came over to the table.

"How much are you playing for buddy?" Vic played along.

"I got twenty says I can take you three in a row."

I answered, "O.K. you're on. I'll rack 'em."

We played until the threesome got bored with our back and forth games split down the middle. So, they left.

Vic laughed, "Well, Allen, my man, what brings you in here?"

"Actually, I was looking for you. I see you're still working the crowd."

Vic smirked. "I hear you're a working man yourself now. My old man said he saw you at 'the house' today."

Somehow, I felt apologetic for selling out on my dream. Vic knew all about me and what I really wanted. He also knew the only way I could get there was to make some sacrifices along the way.

"Yeah, my dad helped me line up a job on second shift. He figures I can leave study hall early and make money for college right away."

"Well, more power to you man. As for me, I'm staying right here where I'm making cash the easy way." I leaned on my cue stick staring him down.

"Now I know I didn't hear you just say that. It seems to me I've seen some hellacious fights break out when your beer gets mixed with your easy ways."

Vic laughed with loudly. The kind of laugh I already knew often covered his fear of losing.

"You do it your way, I'll do it mine; besides college is for ass kissers."

"That's funny. I don't remember kissing any part of yours while I was busy saving your worthless butt just the other night."

Vic stood still trying to think of something cool to say. I laughed and set up another game letting him off the hook.

"Anyway, I came down here to see if you'd like to get a job, too. School's almost out and I know you could use some steady money. We could work the line together. I know your dad could get you a job, too, now that you're eighteen. Vic gave me an even look telling me he might consider it, so I left it at that. We finished our game, and I asked him if he wanted to walk back to the neighborhood.

"Naw, I'm gonna stay here and hook a few more suckers before I call it quits. I'll see ya in school tomorrow."

"O.k. buddy. Just watch your step while you're taking their money."

"Yeah, don't worry. I'll keep one eye on their money and one on my ass."

"Better make it both eyes. I'll see you tomorrow."

I stepped out on the street immediately feeling a blast of cold wind in my face. I couldn't help thinking, *"Why is it so damn cold in April?"* Tramping home, I bounced up our three flights of stairs just to get warm. When I came in, I could tell Dad still wasn't there. Mom and Grandma sat at the kitchen table sewing while dinner simmered on the stove. They both looked annoyed.

Mom said, "I thought your father would come home on the bus with you."

I gave her his message, and she took it in stride. What else could she do? The waiting continued until shortly after eight that night. Suddenly, our vigil at the table was interrupted by the phone in the hall.

Mom answered, "Yes, this is Mrs. Williams… What's that, where, where is he?" By her tone, Grandma and I both knew something was dreadfully wrong.

"Yes, of course, we'll be there right away…" Mother sank down to the bench by the phone in the hall. Her voice trailed off as she repeated, "Oh, my God, oh, my God no… I can't believe it."

I rushed to the hall seeing Mom's face turn ashen.

"What is it, Mom? What's happened?"

Grandma called out. "Is it John? Is there something the matter with John?"

Mom just sat staring wide eyed at the wall across from her. Then she began quoting what the officer said on the phone.

"John has suffered a heart attack. The ambulance came for him, but I'm afraid he didn't make it. He's at St. Christopher's Hospital now." Mom was still holding the phone. I could see she was slipping into shock.

Somehow subconsciously my mind snapped me into leadership. It was as if some unseen mechanism went into action as I digested the news. I turned to Grandmother speaking with a firm air of authority.

Grandmother you must stay and watch the girls. Mother and I will get to the hospital right away. I'll get Mom's coat and we'll take the bus right now.

It was as if my words were springing from another source apart from my lips. Grandmother obeyed as I quietly prepared Mother for the trip. There were no tears, no wailing or gnashing of teeth, just action. In minutes, Mother and I stood at the corner of Arch and 2nd, waiting in the cold wind for the bus that would deliver us to our loved one's side.

What had happened to my father was like no other event in his life. It was sudden, stark, and overpowering. One moment he was laughing and drinking with his friends at Kelsey's Bar, when suddenly the pain overtook him. Radiating from beneath his sternum, it crawled down his left arm. Instantly, he felt the clenching of his heart crushing him from the inside out. It was driving him down to the floor like an unseen force.

When I spoke to the doctor in emergency, he told me Dad was dead on arrival. Of course, they made attempts to revive his heart, but it was just too late. At first, I accepted his explanation with remorseful regret. Then he told me something else, something that flooded me with anger. He explained the ambulance drivers were equipped with a new apparatus on their unit that might have saved his life, but they were unable to operate it correctly. It was called an H.L.R. (Heart Lung Resuscitator). He felt if properly used in time it could have saved my father's life. For me, it was just too much information.

Without my mother knowing, I inquired with the nurse about the names of the ambulance drivers who brought my father in. I lied saying I wanted to thank them for their efforts to save my father's life. She couldn't have known my motive at the time. I had never felt such a sensation before. Wanting to take someone's life for a life (my father's life), in the heat of the moment seemed perfectly natural. If my mother had known, she would never have let me go on thinking that way. She was a sweet, kind, and loving person who learned the first things about forgiveness came from the heart not from the head. But, I was in charge now. I was on automatic pilot. I was the head of the household by default.

The details came clear soon enough. My father suffered a coronary thrombosis according to the doctor. Later, I learned from his friends at the bar he had been drinking shots and beers in celebration of my getting the job. His drinking included something illegal, but not unknown to the patrons at Kelsey's. Kelsey kept moonshine under the counter for special occasions. Knowing it was illegal, he would only give it away to special customers, a status my father had long since achieved. The combination of cigarettes, stress, and highly flammable grain alcohol probably had more to do with my father's death than any incompetent medics on an ambulance squad. But, at the time, no one could convince me of that. You see, grief is never accompanied by clear thinking. Later, I would learn revenge is a plate best eaten cold.

I attended the funeral going through the grieving process like everyone else except for one difference. I knew now I could never leave the family or the job that provided their livelihood. The trap had snapped shut tightly. My dream was dying a slow death in that trap.

Despite Mr. Ryan's efforts to revive my dream, I could still see it steadily slipping away with each day's work. He promised he would still do all in his power to recommend me to the right persons at University of Pennsylvania, his alma mater. But it did not matter now. I was convinced. The only way I would see college was if my family had a visit from that man on the T.V. show, "The Millionaire."

It was hard at first. Nights on the line were like a blur to me. I stood behind on the blood soaked wooden walk watching Vinny transform hind quarters into section cuts of flank, round, rump, shank, short loin, and sirloin all destined for further reduction to a variety of steaks down the line. I found it hard to concentrate. It was difficult to differentiate among them. For me, they were one big mass of bloody cold beef weighing 150 to 170 lbs. with no dotted lines delineating where the cut should take place.

On the bus ride home at night, I would think about all the years my father put into 'the house' dwelling on whether I would have the guts to go through with it or not. I tried keeping my spirits up, hoping I could convince Vic to join me on the line. Selfishly, I knew misery loves company. Then one night I decided I needed to strike out from my self-pity.

It was time to strike a blow against those incompetent ambulance drivers whom I thought were at least partly responsible for my father's death. Whether they truly were or not didn't seem to matter now. It was more a reaction for me from my current woes. Daily, I would spend time on the bus planning vengeance. Soon I arrived at a diabolically simple plan. All I needed was Vic and a ten-foot length of chain. The following day, I met Vic in the school cafeteria for lunch.

I spotted him sitting with his current girlfriend, Connie Warren. I remember it was a Friday when I approached him with my plan. He seemed happy to see me.

"Hey, Allen, come on over. I was just about to tell Connie our plans for tonight. Now, Connie was a junior and not exactly the studious type. You could even say she was not the sharpest blade in the house. But, she was cute enough with shoulder length brown hair, dark brown eyes, ample bosom, and a girlish figure to match. A few facets short of a gem, she was just the way Vic liked them, too. She was loyal as a lap dog only easier to hold.

Vic explained, "Tonight I'm gonna win some rounds of pool at Norm's then me and Connie are gonna meet at Tony's Pizza Palace. I'll treat my baby to pizza with my winnings. Then we head to the movies. Do you wanna join us?"

He knew full well I had to work that night until eleven. I glared at him waiting for his apology.

"Oh, that's right. You're a working man now," returning me a feigned look of sympathy. I seized the moment.

"Actually, I can see you tonight after work if you want. I have a favor to ask." Now the real friend in him seeped forth as I calculated it would.

"Sure, anything at all pal, just ask." I glanced at Connie tilting my head. He got my drift and turned to her.

"Connie, I could sure use some dessert. Get me a cup of pudding. Here's a quarter."

"Sure, Vic. How about you, Allen? Do you want anything while I'm in line?"

"No thanks, Connie. I'm fine." When she was out of earshot, I sat next to him.

"Listen, I want you to meet me after work over on Front and Delaware."

"What for Allen?"

"I got a plan to take care of those jokers that fouled up my dad in their ambulance.'

"Yeah, what's this all about? You want me to help you slit their tires or something"? I shrugged my shoulders giving him a mischievous grin.

"Well, you know, something like that."

I leaned closer whispering my plan. His face lit up when he got the gist of it slapping his hand down hard on the table. He was laughing so hard I thought one of the teachers monitoring the lunch room would ask us to leave.

"Quiet, you", I said. "Do you wanna get us thrown outta here?" He caught his breath answering.

"I'll be there with bells on, buddy. I wouldn't miss this for the world." Then his face took on a serious expression.

"What do you think they'll do to us if we get caught?"

"Not much, I figure, if we share the responsibility, then neither of us takes the whole wrap. Besides, the way I'm gonna do it, no one will ever know."

Since my father's funeral, I did a little research in my spare time. I learned the City Ambulance Company that responded to my dad's emergency stationed their cars in zones. They would wait in these predetermined locations monitoring their radios until they got a call. The same drivers that took care of my dad were assigned to a small parking lot on Delaware Avenue near the Columbus Memorial.

I checked out the location. Sure enough, I found the two of them sitting in a zone near a bus stop on the corner of the parking lot. I came back for a few days in a row making sure these were the same guys and this was where they always waited. I figured, with Vic's help, the rest would be easy.

After eleven forty on Friday night, Vic took up his place in a phone booth just around the corner from the parking lot. His instructions were to call the ambulance company at exactly eleven fifty faking an emergency nearby. I knew the bus stop would be deserted by then, so I stealthily approached the cement supports of the bus stop bench with a hook and chain tucked inside my jacket. Ever so quietly, I slipped the chain gingerly around the bench supports then made my move. Carefully, I crawled on my hands and knees to the back of the ambulance. Then lowering down on my back, I crawled beneath the rear of the ambulance placing the chain around the rear axle locking it there on their limousine style car. The occupants never saw or heard me as they sat listening to music on their radio trying to break the monotony of their vigil.

What happened next will never account for full revenge, but it seemed damned close at the time. Thankfully, enough time had passed for me to reconsider the penalty for murder. I had just ducked around the corner of the building next to the empty lot when the driver heard his radio crackling with the emergency call. In a matter of seconds, his lights and siren came on as his foot slammed down hard on the accelerator. They were off like a shot with tires squealing for at least two seconds. Then they felt a sudden jolt at the end of the chain. It was terrific, but the results were not exactly as I expected. Instead of pulling the axle from the ambulance, the weaker bench went with them up the street.

It was more than enough for me and Vic to see that ambulance racing down the street towing a bus stop bench disintegrating behind them. The fact that they never even stopped once to see what the matter was really made it all worthwhile. Never mind what it said about the attendants' state of awareness. We could just imagine their arriving at the bogus site of the call with an unexplained length of chain trailing behind their ambulance.

After that night, a lot changed in our lives. Vic finally agreed to take a job with me on the line at 'the house'. It was a time for both of us to really grow. I was learning to be the man of the house, while Vic tried hard taking on more responsibility at work. By the time we were ready to graduate, he enjoyed a newfound respect from his father. Also, further adoration came from Connie due to his steady job at Cross Brothers'. Personally, I felt more prepared than ever to take on the everyday challenges before me. Deep inside one thing never changed. My dreams for the future lay dormant, but the memory was still alive.

Chapter 2

In May, most of my time was spent in training standing right behind Vinny. I would listen to him go on about his proud Italian heritage as he hacked away at an endless parade of hind quarters. My training included working every cleanup operation there was on second shift. This, I was told, would help me get the big picture.

In short, I was introduced to steam power sprayers, disinfectants, and the slosh of bloody debris clogged remains in drains of steamed rats. Sometimes there were trapped entrails to be pulled from conveyor belts. One evening I was asked to clean out the sump. Here gallons of filth and rending collected when the floors were washed down each night. Finally, my apprenticeship complete, I was sent to the front office to fill out union membership papers.

With a deduction from my paycheck, I officially joined the ranks of The Amalgamated Meat Cutters and Butcher Workmen of North America, Local 195, A.F.L.-C.I.O. For all that, the paperwork put me in the front office on the last Friday of May.

It was one of those moments you least expect everything in your world to change. That's the way it felt when I rediscovered Amy Martin. Rediscovered because it was not the first time we met. We had dated a couple of times in my junior year. She was out of school now. Right in front of me, she worked as an accounting clerk.

The year before, I remember, how excited she was to be attending Pennsylvania State. Now she was back. I wondered why anyone would return to our neighborhood after gaining a full scholarship. Curious, I asked her that as she handed me my papers.

"It's great to see you, Amy," I said. "But what are you doing here? I mean I thought you had it made at Penn State."

She was beautiful as ever only more mature. Her high buttoned dress and black shoes made her seem so professional. Her black hair was still long but was kept up in a bun. She looked at me quizzically through horn rimmed glasses. Still, they could not detract from her lovely blue eyes studying me with a look of faint recognition. Then she smiled as it dawned on her.

"You're Allen Williams. I remember you. We dated once."

"It was twice. We went out to eat, then another time we saw a movie," I blurted.

Feeling a little flushed, I looked around to see if anyone else overheard. The room packed full of clerks typing away while others filed, opening and closing in syncopation none seemed to notice business taking place at Amy's desk.

Recounting why she was there, she answered my question.

"I had to come back to help my Mom with the kids. My Dad died in December, and I needed to get a job, so… here I am. Her expression was wistful, but her voice betrayed some bitterness. I thought how tough it would be being drug back to the old neighborhood when her dream had only just begun.

She broke in, "So now you're working here, too. I guess we have something in common, huh?"

I thought, *"If you only knew right then that I didn't want you to go away again."*

"I'm supposed to get this application signed by the steward."

She smiled, there was an awkward pause as she looked me over.

"I can take those for you. I'll put them on his desk right away."

I wanted to say much more, but it was clearly not the time or place. Instead, I settled for a polite "thank you" and turned to leave. Then, I stopped, forcing myself to do something out of character. Turning back, I overcame my initial shyness.

"Amy, I don't know if you're seeing anyone since you've been back, but I was wondering, could I give you a call sometime?"

She didn't hesitate.

"Sure, do you still have my number?" I was so thrilled I almost blurted, *"of course, I keep it in my top draw with other important things."* Recovering quickly, I told her I was sure I could find it somewhere. She wasn't taking any chances. Jotting it down on a scrap of paper, she handed it to me.

"I'll talk to you soon, Allen, goodbye."

I left the office feeling certain I should have said more. The whole way back to my station I reminded myself just how damned lucky it seemed lightning just struck twice in the same place. It was as though someone had pinned a bright light on my heart that glowed all the way back to the line.

Vinny sensed I wasn't all there after I arrived.

Seeing that certain look in my eye he warned, "You better get your mind off those front office gals or you're gonna be missing a finger."

I assured him.

"There's just one I'm interested in seeing."

The rest of the day seemed to breeze by and soon I found myself jostling for a position on the crowded bus. When I plunked down in my seat, Vic followed suit.

"So, I guess you're looking forward to the field trip tomorrow, huh?"

Truthfully, with Amy occupying my thoughts I had temporarily forgotten about Mr. Ryan's class field trip. Every year, he takes his class on a bus tour of Philadelphia's historic landmarks. June the third was the day many of us had been waiting for, especially me.

"That's right," I said with enthusiasm. "We're going tomorrow."

Usually, high school students wouldn't care to wake up to spend an entire Saturday with their history teacher in downtown Philadelphia. Yet, this was the event of the year for most of us. Mr. Ryan did this once a year and it was special. It would be the last time we would spend any time out of the classroom with him before graduation. On the other hand, Vic saw it as free lunch and fun with the class on the town. Unfortunately, his sense of history extended as far as the batting averages of the Phillies starting lineup.

When the big day arrived, the tour began on time with twenty-four students piling aboard our yellow bus at seven thirty that morning. As we pulled out of the school parking lot, Mr. Ryan took his place standing at the front of the bus. As we passed through the streets of the historic district in downtown Philadelphia, he acted as guide talking about points of interest.

The bus driver made his way north on Sixth Street skirting Washington Square on our left. Our first stop was Independence Square on Sixth and Walnut Street Park rangers there were distributing maps and giving talks as Mr. Ryan passed out tickets to Independence Hall. Next, we proceeded to the National Constitution Center on Sixth and Arch Street. We learned this was the only museum dedicated solely to the U.S. Constitution.

While the exhibitions were entertaining for most, Vic found it all too "straight up and square" as he put it. He chose trying to make time with one of the re-enactors dressed in character until she brushed him off warning that John Hancock, aka her husband, was standing nearby. After that rousing brush with history, Vic pretty much kept to himself.

Across Market Street most of us rediscovered the Liberty Bell. A sight most of us had seen on some sort of outing with our parents before. The difference was Mr. Ryan knew enough to enthrall us all with lively accounts of the Bell's history. He could make anything from the past come alive. That was his gift.

He recounted how the Liberty Bell wasn't always the revered icon it came to be. He cited Colonial Philadelphians often grumbled about its insistent ringing at inopportune moments. He went on to say later in the 19th century, plans to scrap it as an antiquated hunk of metal were considered more than once. His insight often held us together as a group waiting for the next story to unfold. Truly, he had a way with words which made me dream about what I might achieve someday myself. My only regret was that Amy could not be along to share the day with me.

As we passed through the West Wing of Independence Hall, we stood in hushed reverence in front of the exhibit of the original documents critical to the founding of the United States. There was the Declaration of Independence, annotated drafts of the Constitution, and the Articles of Confederation all laid out before us next to the silver inkstands used to sign them.

Seeing it all there before me gave me cause to consider what courage it took for our founding fathers to put it all on the line to see this great experiment in nation building come to fruition. I saw these men involved were drawn closer together not only by that which they believed in, but by that which they were willing to sacrifice. At the time, I could not possibly know the extent of this bond until I discovered something more of it myself.

The remainder of our tour centered on topics of diversity, conflict, resolution, faith, and freedom, and then all too soon it was ending. We slowly boarded our bus sharing a few final moments listening to Mr. Ryan wrap up the tour with some commentary on what our part in America's future might be. He encouraged us all to provide input on what the tour meant to us. Like any well-meaning teacher, he then passed out his last assignment aimed at stimulating our thinking on that very subject. Vic was not amused.

"Great, just when you think it's all over, you get hit with one more paper to write."

I replied with tongue in cheek. "It could be worse."

"Yeah, and how's that, Allen?"

"He could have made you pay for your lunch."

He quipped, "There you see they were right, there's no such thing as a free lunch."

I consoled, "Look on the bright side, by this time next week you'll be a high school graduate." Vic held up his assignment page slapping it for emphasis.

"Yeah, I'm a high school grad all right, ready to take on the world."

Personally, I was thinking more about the night ahead with Amy. I called her and landed a date for that night.

Vic just slumped in his seat looking a bit dejected. As for Amy and me, it was to be dinner. I purposely picked a neutral ground where she and I might talk about the past. I had a lot of things I wanted to ask her. Knowing she, too, had lost her Dad I already knew we held that pain in common so I decided to avoid the subject. What I really wanted to know was what her plans were for the future. I was already hoping they would include me.

As soon as the bus let Vic and me off, I wanted to head straight for home. Vic had other plans. When he noticed I was going in that direction, he tried persuading me to come with him.

"Come on, Allen, let's head over to Norm's. Business should be picking up right about now."

I knew what kind of business he had in mind and I wasn't interested in risking the money I set aside for my date. After collecting my pay, I made a point of making a ten-dollar bill prisoner in my wallet just for that night. Nothing could make me gamble that away.

Vic offered, "I feel lucky tonight. I just might let you in on some of the action if you join me."

"No thanks, Vic. I feel lucky enough as it is. I'll see you tomorrow." As I parted he chided.

"She's got you under her thumb already, buddy. You haven't even had your first date."

I just waved him off walking away without comment. Tonight, I certainly had better things to do than risk my money in some pick up pool game. I arrived home just in time to see my sister, Ginny, leaving.

"Where are you headed, all dressed up like that?"

"Oh, I'm just going over to the Knights of Columbus Hall. I'm meeting some friends at the dance tonight." I tried sounding authoritative representing myself as head of the household.

"Try not to be too late sis; you know how mean these streets can get after dark." She brushed me off with her own parting shot.

"See that you're not late yourself, *little* brother." The word little came across with surly emphasis. I shook my head as I mounted the stoop to our building mumbling,

"I don't know what this generation is coming to, no respect at all."

Taking the stairs two at a time, I was feeling good about everything in general. When I slipped in the door, Mom was glad to see me home safely.

"Hello, son, welcome home. How was your field trip?"

"Excellent, Mom", I called out disappearing down the hall.

"I've got to hurry now and get ready for my date. I'll tell you all about it when I get home tonight."

Grandma grumbled, "It seems all this family is interested in doing is getting back out the door."

Once in my room, I picked out my white button down shirt from the closet laying it on the bed next to my blue jeans. It felt good to be in the shower after touring old Philadelphia. Using my Mom's shampoo, I made sure my hair was squeaky clean. I found some shaving cream under the counter that my Dad used applying it liberally. Finding the tiny blond hairs on my face was no easy task, but I managed to shave without incident. Complimenting myself on my skill, I reached for after shave. Fortunately, I had a bottle of Old Spice saved for just such an occasion. One last inspection in the mirror and I was ready to get dressed.

After combing my hair straight back, I was ready to pull on my boots. The heels on my black steel capped boots gave me an extra two inches of height adding greatly to my self-confidence. Confirming my best look of the evening in my bedroom mirror, I was ready to take on the town.

As I said goodbye to Mother and Grandma, Mom leaned over and whispered in my ear.

"Do you need any money, dear?"

"No thanks, Mom, I've got it covered. Don't wait up. I'll probably be late."

She gave me that pleading look as only mothers can.

"Don't make it too late, son."

I reassured her on my way out.

"It won't be much after twelve, Mom, O.K.?"

She allowed her voice to trail off saying, "Goodbye, dear."

I thought, *"Leave it to a mother to make you feel guilty just as you go out the door."*

Nothing could change my mood now. I was out and on the street. It was a starry Saturday night and I had a date with a beautiful girl. What more could I ask for? I took the streetcar up Front Street to Race Street then walked the rest of the way to Amy's house.

When I arrived, her Mom greeted me at the door. She was dressed in a shift with an apron. She was wearing her hair up in a rather unflattering bun. It appeared she had been doing house work. The living room was tidy and smelled of Pine Sol. Their flat was not much different than ours on Arch Street. The only difference was they had an extra bedroom off the back. I assumed Amy slept there since the door was shut now. The other doors were slightly open, and I could see her little brother playing on the floor in the front room. He looked to be all of ten years old and was amusing himself with an electric train.

I wished I could go in his room and talk to him. Anything would be better than waiting in the living room under the scrutiny of her two younger sisters and mother. Then the questions began.

Her mother asked," Didn't you date Amy before she went off to college?"

I unconsciously scratched my knee peering over her shoulder at Amy's closed door.

"Yes Ma'am, we went out to dinner and to the movies."

"That's nice, what movie did you see?"

I immediately I felt my face flush as my mind raced.

"What will she think of me if I tell her the title of the movie was, 'Some Like It Hot?'"

I stared over her shoulder again at Amy's door. Then realizing I was running out of time I blurted.

"Some Like It Hot; I mean we saw the movie, *'Some Like It Hot'.*"

Both of her sisters giggled in unison. I just looked down at the floor waiting for the other shoe to drop. It seemed an eternity before I heard her soft voice speak again.

"Oh, that was the one with Tony Curtis and Jack Lemmon. How was it?"

I knew this woman was just making small talk for Amy's sake, but it was getting hot in the room and all I could think of was when would that back-room door open. Finally, I managed to answer carefully so as not to set off the girls who were now ready to pounce on my slightest impropriety.

"It was a comedy. I thought it was funny."

As soon as the words left my lips, I couldn't help but wonder what a fine impression I must be making on her. She must have thought I was a craven idiot who wanted to take her daughter to a nasty movie. Then she inquired politely.

"Where will you be going tonight?"

Finally, I thought, a question I can sink my teeth into.

"China Town, I'm taking Amy out to eat in Chinatown. We're going to Hu Ming's. We should be back by nine if we catch the trolley back on time," I volunteered. The sisters seemed bored with my answer and decided to run off somewhere to play.

"That sounds nice. Amy and I like Chinese food." Then, I went too far. "Would you like us to bring you some?"

Her polite response stopped short of telling me what I just said was out of place.

"Oh, heavens no, I've already eaten. Thanks anyway. I'll just go and see if Amy's ready now." Now I was left alone to stare at the cat. Thankfully I knew *it* wasn't about to ask me any questions.

When Amy did appear at the door she wore a pink cotton top with a robin's egg blue skirt. Her long black hair cascaded over her shoulders. It framed her creamy white complexion leaving sparkling blue eyes peering out like gems from beneath her long bangs. To me, she was the vision of loveliness. She made me feel as if I was getting away with something just by taking her out.

She said, "I'm sorry I kept you waiting so long." She made some excuse. Her lips were moving. I did not hear. I was too caught up in the moment. I couldn't take my eyes off her. As I stood, I felt weak in the knees. Then it dawned on me. I should be complimenting her instead of just staring.

"You look lovely tonight, not like you did at work. I mean you looked nice at work and all, but now you look so different." I was just beginning to find this compliment business hard work when she rescued me.

"They make us dress that way at work. They say we can't wear anything too flashy. Are you ready to go?"

"Sure, there's no hurry though. We don't have reservations or anything like that." I held the door for her as I turned to say goodbye to Mrs. Martin. She had the last word.

"Have a good time kids and don't be too late." Outside the door, my heart began to resume its normal rhythm.

"Your Mom is nice. Does she work, too?"

"Yes, my Mom is a secretary for the Philadelphia Transit Company."

I thought, *"I bet she makes them keep the buses running on time."*

Amy asked, "How do you like working for the Cross Brothers?" I was silent for a long moment trying to truly describe just what it was like for me. I felt the need to be completely truthful with her from the start. I knew, even then, that I did not want even the slightest thing to ever come between us. She waited patiently for my answer as I started in slowly.

"Don't get me wrong. I like the money and everything. It really helps the family right now, but it's not what I want for the future. My dad worked there fifteen years and all it ever got him was a heart attack." I watched her initial look of surprise turn to one of sympathy.

"That must have been tough for you and your family. What is it you really want to do, Allen?"

When she spoke my name, I felt as if she were genuinely interested in my future. The tone of her voice was completely sincere. I wanted to hold her hands in mine and tell her all about my dreams of becoming a history teacher and how Mr. Ryan was going to do all in his power to help me. Then reality sunk in, I wasn't going to do anything of the kind unless that 'Millionaire' came to my door. I don't know why I felt the way I did, but I thought I could tell her anything right then and there. We stood on the curb waiting for the trolley to Chinatown and I told her what was really on my mind. It felt good, too, because no one at home wanted to discourage me with the truth about my future. When I finished telling her of my hopes and aspirations, I looked in her eyes for her take on all of it. She was looking up at me with a smile.

"That's a wonderful thing to want to do, a noble thing. I bet you would be a great teacher, too. You already seem to have a way with words. I bet you like to read a lot, don't you?"

I was bursting with joy to hear her say those things to me.

"Yes, I love to read, and you?"

"I read all the time. I don't waste my time with those silly romance novels though like most of the girls I know. I like more serious reading like poetry and biographies of important people. In fact, I'm reading a book now about Alexander Hamilton. Did you know he's one of the few persons whose face appears on our currency that wasn't a President of the United States?"

Her interest in history intrigued me. She made me forget all about my being trapped in a dead-end job, at least for the time being.

"Yes, I did know that. Do you know who the others are?" She pursed her lips and thought for a moment. Then she snapped her fingers when the answer came to her.

"I know, it's Benjamin Franklin on the hundred-dollar bill. You don't see many of those around, I'll bet."

"Not hardly," I replied. "But, I can go you one better than that. The other person was the financier and Secretary of the Treasury, Salmon P. Chase," I stated with pride. "He appeared on the ten-thousand-dollar bill issued from 1928 to 1946."

"Wow," she exclaimed! Just imagine having all that money in one place. Then she laughed out loud. It was such a pretty laugh, too.

Then she said, "Where would you get change for a bill like that?"

I replied, "Not from *my* pocket, I can assure you of that."

By the time the trolley rolled up, we were both laughing. We laughed and talked all the way to Chinatown. The night breeze was filled with the scent of various eateries along the way making us both think about the meal ahead. When we entered Hu Ming's the hostess found us a nice booth in the back and lit a candle on the table for us.

Amy asked, "Have you eaten here before?"

"No, but I heard about it from a friend. He said the food here was authentic Mandarin Chinese."

She asked innocently, "Does that mean it's good?"

I answered authoritatively, "That means it's prepared milder than most."

She replied, "I didn't know you knew about Chinese food."

"I don't really; I just know some things about China, in general."

"Like what for instance?"

"Well, let me see. I know they were the first civilization to record their history in writing. Also, they have experienced twenty-eight dynasties in their time."

"My, you certainly are full of surprises, aren't you?"

I wasn't quite sure how to answer her remark so I was just as glad to see the waiter hovering over us.

"Are you ready to order now?" I asked.

"We'd like a few more minutes, if you don't mind? I really haven't had time to look at the menu yet."

The waiter asked what we would like to drink and I waited for her to order. When she asked for a Coke, I decided to have the same. When the waiter left, I made my suggestion.

"I like the Orange Chicken and Broccoli; you might want to try that."

"I thought you said you've never eaten here before?"

"That's true, I haven't. I just know I like that particular dish, that's all."

"O.K., I guess I'll try that. Whenever my family gets Chinese, we just get carry out. I've never really been to a Chinese restaurant before."

I ventured, "It's all pretty much the same. I don't think you'll be disappointed with the orange chicken." When the waiter came back we placed two orders for the chicken and talked about work for a while.

Amy asked, "Do you think your friend, Vic, will be joining the union soon?"

"Yes, I'm sure his dad will convince him of that. His dad has been a foreman there for a long time."

She asked, "Do you know Steve Agresta? He joined the union last month."

"No, I don't know him. What shift does he work?"

"He's on first shift. He said he was hired last year. He was in my graduating class. We went out a couple of times. I just thought you might have met him."

"Not much chance of that. I don't have time to talk to the guys on first shift. They're always hurrying for the door."

She replied, "It's just as well. He's a regular hot head."

"What do you mean?"

"Oh, like I said, we went out a couple of times. Anyway, we were in Tony's Pizza Parlor and he put on this big show about my being his girl when some friends came over to talk to me. He acted like a real jealous jerk just because they were talking to me. I told him to buzz off after that. I don't like those possessive types."

I agreed, "I don't think I would like that either, if the shoe were on the other foot."

Suddenly, she changed the subject as if it were time to move on.

"The other day I did meet the most colorful character." Then suddenly she caught herself in mid-sentence with a laugh.

"I mean he's a Black man. He works on the cleanup crew for the company. Anyway, his name is Barnabus Kurt Jenkins. He came to my desk to return his union membership papers. He's sixty years old and claimed he's never been in a union before and wasn't about to start now. I told him it wasn't necessary for him to explain his position it was just part of the union's annual membership drive. Then, he said something curious."

"What was that?" I asked. She looked up and to the left as if she were trying to recall his exact words. A look of recognition crossed her face as she went on.

He said, "They's always been after me to join up after I told them what I seen beneath this place."

"I asked him what he meant, but he just started walking off mumbling something about the tunnels and all those poor souls down there. I wanted to ask him more, but he was gone before I could ask. What do you suppose he meant by those poor souls down there, Allen?"

"I have no idea. It sounds to me like he's some kind of crazy old coot."

Our orders arrived just then and we busied ourselves with our napkins and dinner. The subject of Barnabus Jenkins soon took a backseat to other dinner banter. The rest of the evening went well as we learned more about each other. From my point of view, there was nothing I didn't like about this delightful girl. She was only nineteen, but her body was in full flower. She was witty, understanding, and pretty. My greatest problem was revealing too quickly just how head over heels I was about her. I saw her lips moving again and shook myself back from my reverie long enough to understand what she was saying.

"So, you'll be graduating next week? What then?"

"More of the same, I'm afraid. I did fill out all the applications Mr. Ryan had for me, but I don't see much change on the horizon." Then she did something unexpected.

Amy reached across the table and held my hand in hers.

"Don't feel too down. Remember there's more than one pulling for you right now."

Immediately, I thought, *"Who is she referring to my family or her?"* Right then I wished it were her.

She asked, "I'd like to come to your graduation. Is that alright?"

"Sure, of course you can. I should have thought to ask. I guess I just wasn't thinking." The waiter arrived again wanting to know about our preference for dessert. I left it up to her, but she declined saying she was finished. How nice I thought, *"Finished, she could have said she was too full, but she chose to say finished instead, how refined."* It didn't hurt my wallet any either. I asked for the check and paid with little to spare. After a quick calculation, I was shocked to discover I didn't have enough for the return trolley fair. My mind leapt into emergency mode as I planned a course of action.

"It's such a nice night, would you like to walk back home?"

"Sure, I guess that would be all right. I hope we won't be in too late, though."

"I think we can make it," I replied. "We'll just walk a little faster. It will be good exercise." I hoped I wasn't coming over too cheap. At any rate, she was gracious enough to never let on as we walked along, window shopping on the way.

Closer to home, we passed by Norm's Pool Hall. I shot a glance through the yellowed pane glass window noticing Vic holding court with three others I did not recognize. I shrugged my shoulders murmuring, "Hustling again."

"What was that?" asked Amy.

"Oh, I just saw my friend Vic in there playing pool."

"Would you like to stop and talk to him? It's alright with me if you do."

"No, that's all right. He's busy now; I'll probably talk to him later. Besides, I wouldn't want to get you home late on our first date."

"Third date," she corrected.

"Oh, yeah, that's right, thanks for remembering." She reached down taking up my hand giving me a wink and a smile.

"Don't mention it," she said.

We reached her front door at half past nine and she invited me in for a while. I thought about sitting in the living room with her mother and the kids again and asked if she would mind just sitting outside on the steps for a while.

"O.K., but Mom doesn't want me to stay out in the hallway too long."

I offered, "We can just talk for a little while, O.K.?" We sat there making small talk while I schemed how to get a kiss that night. Finally, I got up the courage to put my arm around her shoulder. Soon, she rested her head on my shoulder. I was anxious to make my move before she said we were outside too long.

"You know, I want to see you again soon. Is that alright with you?" I asked.

Her voice softened as she considered my eyes with sincerity.

"Yes, of course, that would be very nice. You know you're not like some of the boys I dated in college." Selfishly, I really didn't want her to talk about dating anyone but me, yet I was curious to know why she found me different.

"What makes you say that?" I asked. She ran her fingers playfully along the top of my hand stimulating my skin.

"Well, it's just that you seem more quiet and thoughtful. I don't know. I guess you seem more serious than some others I've dated. You'd think the opposite would be true, wouldn't you? I mean since they were older than you."

Then she went on talking about others again when all I wanted was to talk about me.

"Some say I'm more mature than most, if that's what you're getting at."

"Yes, I think that's it. You know what you want in life even if it's a struggle to get there." After saying that, she suddenly got up giving me the signal our time was up for the evening. As I rose with her, she surprised me with a kiss on my cheek. Not exactly where I wanted it, but it would have to do.

"I really enjoyed having dinner with you tonight, Allen. Just remember what I said. I'm pulling for you, too."

After I heard that, I just couldn't help myself. I reached behind her neck drawing her close to me kissing her full on the lips. She held her lips tight with surprise at first then she relented returning a soft, glorious kiss. Naturally, I was elated until I caught sight of her mother propped against the door frame.

She spoke with a hint of sarcasm in her voice.

"Well, good evening, Allen. Would you care to come in for a visit?"

I stammered releasing my hold on Amy's neck.

"Uh, no ma'am, Mrs. Martin. I was just leaving."

"I see," she said. "Well, I understand. After all, it is a bit late."

Amy was chagrined but managed to say good night as I retreated down the stairs.

As I left Amy's stairs, I felt as though I were ready to fly. Her mom was no obstacle to me. I recognized she was there for her protection. At least, she didn't try to stop me from seeing her. I was too overwhelmed by Amy to care anyway, even if she did. A few steps further down the street I felt like I wanted to celebrate. All I could think of was joining Vic at Norm's Place.

By the time I arrived, he had his three marks at bay. Yet, once again, he was doing the very thing I hated most about him. There he was winning a gob of money while goading the losers, taunting them to new heights of humiliation. I could only look on in frustration as he played out his role.

The inevitable occurred shortly after he finished taking money from the first of his latest marks. The tall dude dressed in the black leather jacket paid his respects to Vic in a surly manner.

"I'll catch up with you later, Mister Big Time Pool Player."

Vic pretended he wasn't in the least bit affected by the taunt from the tough guy who was at least a head taller.

With an air of sarcasm, Vic replied, "That's right and it will take a lot of catching up just to get even with me." As he turned away sliding his cue stick into its rack, I could hear one of the loser's buddies mutter.

"Let's take him now; this skinny guy got nothin."

Fortunately, the tall loser showed more control pointing at the door, indicating he was ready to leave. When the last one stepped outside, I gave Vic a piece of my mind.

"You're always doin' the same damn thing, Vic. It's like you want to end up with your ass in a sling. Do you have a death wish? Or maybe you're beer blind? Did you really get a good look at that bruiser you were messing with? Hell, it's one thing taking their money, but why do you have to give 'em the finger while you're at it?"

"I dunno, Allen. It just seems like I gotta give them something to think about, that's all. It's like I can't get enough out of just winning. It makes me feel like I'm better than them when I do it, O.K.?"

"No, it's not O.K. Winning should be enough, Vic. It's not like you got the body to back up your remarks, you know." Vic pushed his jet-black hair from his forehead as he lifted his beer in a mock toast swinging his short, skinny arm in the air. With a sly grin, he gave me that air of false confidence he was so good at releasing.

"That's why you're here, pal." I walked to the rack and selected a cue stick. Then I poked it into his chest.

"One of these days, buddy boy, I'm not gonna be there for you. Then, it's gonna be like Jackie Gleason says, "POW, straight to the moon Alice!" Vic shook his head and snickered.

"Hey, you do that pretty well. You sound just like him." I just shook my head in dismay as I rounded the table racking up the balls. "Come on champ, let's play another round. I feel lucky tonight."

We played for another hour off and on. Sometimes I would sit out a game or two while Vic won us enough money to keep us in beer and pay for our games. It wasn't such a bad arrangement if I could just keep Vic from shooting off his mouth at the losers.

By midnight, Norm was ready to throw us all out because of the 'Blue Laws'. Funny thing, he didn't mind selling us beer, but he sure wasn't about to get shut down for serving alcohol on Sunday. So, we hit the street ready to get home when Vic had another of his brain storms.

Let's go down by the water front. We could play on that table at Kelsey's. I wasn't much in favor of the idea. Yet, I guess the beer must have affected my better judgment because we went anyway. The fact that it was the last place my father drank the night he died kept eating at me even before I got there.

As we approached, I could see pools of light spilling from the dirty, yellowed window panes onto the grimy, broken sidewalk in front of the seamy establishment. The faded neon sign flickered, *Kelsey's*. Even with a few beers in me, I thought, *"What a dump."* Inside my thoughts were confirmed. Kelsey's looked like a saloon pictured on the screen of one those old movie houses where the projectionist never cleaned the lenses. The only thing that shined in the place was the streak stained mirror behind the bar. The chairs and tables all shared that same lack luster look of wear and tear splintered and frayed with time. The floor even had a sticky feel to it, like in those old movie houses.

The patrons didn't seem to share any sense of liveliness. Like fabric covered lumps, they just existed on the furniture murmuring in a steady drone. The tinkle of glass carried from behind the bar where Kelsey himself finished stacking another pyramid of freshly toweled glasses. Under the dull glow of a green overhead lamp, I could make out the sole pool table. Its old green felt had a sheen worn through to the slate in spots. No one was playing at the time, so we approached the table. It was so old, it didn't even have a coin box attached. I reckoned we had to pay Kelsey in person if we wanted to play.

I said, "Vic, why don't you go up and pay for our games. I don't want to deal with the man."

"Sure, no big deal, Allen. I'll be right back." I watched his back as he approached the bar. Just then, a shaft of light from a street lamp penetrated the dim light in the bar. Some people entered the front door, but I couldn't make out their faces. There were three of them and they headed straight for the table where I stood. I narrowed my focus on the one in front. His black leather jacket soon made it obvious these were the same three Vic was hustling at Norm's Place. I looked past them to see why Vic was taking so long at the bar. He was headed back toward me with a beer bottle in each hand. Just then the big guy in the jacket recognized me.

"Are you playin' on this table," he asked?

"Yeah, I'm just waiting on my partner." He turned to see Vic coming.

"Well, if it ain't the Lone Ranger." Vic didn't look too pleased to see him.

He countered, "Sorry, fellas, this table is already taken."

"What's the matter Mister Big Time Pool Player, are you afraid I might get even?"

Vic replied with characteristic sarcasm.

"Sorry, I don't have that much time. I gotta work tomorrow."

"Oh yeah, what's that supposed to mean? Are you saying I can't beat you?"

Vic just handed me a beer then cocked his head squinting up at the big guy.

"Yeah, I guess you could take me after all. Let's see, now that would be about the time one of those guys on Mount Rushmore stood up and took a leak." With that, the thug instantly reached out grabbing Vic by the collar causing his beer to drop smashing on the floor. As he raised his clenched fist to punch out Vic, a loud voice boomed across the room.

Kelsey shouted, "Take it outside or I call the cops!"

He backed up his order slapping a blackjack, with a resounding thud, on the bar. Obviously, he had a lot of practice doing that very thing. The big guy in the black leather jacket hesitated for a moment weighing his options, then, reluctantly released his grip on Vic.

"Come on fellas, we'll take care of this asshole later." The guy in the black jacket led the way storming out of the bar. The rest of the customers resumed their activities seemingly unfazed by the interruption in their routine.

I said, "Well, you nearly did it again this time, didn't you?" Vic just shrugged his shoulders saying, "Well, what are you gonna do? Let's just finish our game in peace, then we'll get going o.k.?"

"That's fine with me. This place gives me the creeps."

What I did not know was all those hours spent in the gym studying martial arts with Coach Johnson were about to pay off. As we pressed into the night outside Kelsey's, the air was misty.

Vic said, "It must have rained while we were playing."

"Yeah, I guess so, the street's still wet." As we walked up the street past an alley, the darkness of the street seemed to close in on us. I felt a certain pressure, almost like someone leaning on my back. The feeling grew until gradually it dawned on me. We were being followed. Just as I reached out to alert Vic of impending danger, I heard a voice from behind. Then I felt a hard shove on my right shoulder.

"Outta the way. This ain't your fight." It was the guy in the black jacket speaking with his two friends standing behind him. I spun on my heel to see them grabbing at Vic pulling his arms behind his back.

I shouted, "I can make it mine. It's up to you." The next thing I knew, I was being pushed backward by this guy until I lost my balance. I landed against a bunch of trash cans. By the time I could get back on my feet, two of them were holding Vic by the arms while the first guy pounded his face. I heard Vic yelling in his bravado voice.

"If anyone else wants in, I'm here, I ain't budging! Stay out of this, Allen. It's mine!"

After that, everything started flowing automatically. I felt myself leveling out shooting a roundhouse kick to the temple of the guy pounding Vic. I connected instantly causing him to grasp his head in agony. Quickly recovering my balance, I stood ready to take on the others. Apparently, they had enough after seeing their buddy bent over bleeding from his ear. They dropped Vic running back up the alley they came from. So, I turned and kicked the first one in the ass sending him into the trash cans where I lay before. Now Vic was on his feet lifting his head back pinching his bloody nose, his other hand resting on my shoulder.

He snorted, "Let's call it a night, Tonto."

Fortunately, for Vic, he would have all day Sunday to recuperate before returning to the line with me on Monday. Our high school graduation ceremony was set to take place the following Friday. Beyond that, another chapter in our lives was about to begin.

Chapter 3

Whenever your foreman asks you to do something, it is customary you take the request seriously. That is the point I was just trying to make with Vic after he absolutely refused to help me in the chemical storeroom where I was asked to volunteer my services.

"I'm not going down there," Vic insisted. My father told me about that storage room. It's in the oldest part of the building. There's hardly any ventilation down there. Dad told me a guy almost died down there once from the fumes of some cleaning agent spill. Before he could get far enough away, the fumes overwhelmed him."

I stared at Vic in disbelief. "Are you serious? 'Cause if this is another one of your bullshit stories to get out of work, I'm gonna overwhelm you myself."

"No, it's true. I swear it," he protested. You can ask my dad if you want to." With that, I decided this time he was probably telling the truth. That didn't change my situation.

"Well like it or not, I gotta go down there and see what needs to be done. Can't you at least go with me while I find out what they want done? It's supposed to be done right away on day shift. That means we could have a couple of nights off this week."

Vic's dark, bushy eyebrows rose a bit. Finally, I convinced him to come down there with me just to see what the job was. When we reached the south end of 'the house', I spotted Karl Grafton sitting on a wooden crate next to a bulletin board. The board was plastered with notes pinned to the cork board to entice fellow employees to take up their offers. There was a note with a photo advertising a '57 Chevy for sale, low mileage, clean interior, A.C., never been raced 327 cu.in., hanging above his head. Its owner was asking for best offer. He was ready to take us down to have a look. When Karl stood up, he revealed numerous offers for free kittens, cheap puppies, and rooms for rent. Grinding out his cigarette butt on the concrete floor, he waved.

"Now that you're here gents, I got something to show you." We innocently followed his lead as he walked under an aging brick archway to a set of concrete steps leading down at a sharp angle. He flipped a light switch as he went down illuminating a brick lined room twenty feet below. I would guess the room was nearly one hundred by fifty feet in dimension. The overhead lamps were twentieth century but the entire room was at least a hundred years old. The brick work of the interior looked like those reconstructed buildings at historical sites on the surface. At one end of the rectangular room, it appeared as if half the floor was taken up with pale blue colored fifty-five gallon drums with large labels marking them as caustic chemicals. The remainder of the room was empty with a large metal overhead door at the far end. This obviously was a much later addition to the crumbling brick enclosure. I imagined the metal door adjoined a receiving dock outside for chemicals arriving by truck. Beside the door were two stacks of heavy oak pallets nearly reaching the twelve-foot ceiling. The atmosphere in the room was dank like that of a musty old basement. The air was infused with a strong scent of chemicals.

Karl reached the bottom step on the narrow stairway. He was gesturing toward the end of the room filled with drums containing concentrated disinfectant. He was giving us the lowdown on what this room was about as he walked.

"This is our chemical storage room. This, gents, is where we keep our stock of cleaning agents and disinfectants and so on. Management has decided we need to palletize all this stuff because some of the drums are starting to corrode."

I glanced over at Vic for his reaction. I could see his eyes widen a bit.

I could almost see the wheels turning. He was probably wondering how he got himself so far into this right about now.

Karl continued, "I'm sending Jenkins down here to work with you. He's one of our forklift operators. What we want to do here is get all these drums on this end of the room on to those pallets by the door."

I couldn't help but marvel at how Karl could take a back-breaking task and render it down to its most fundamental level. I caught a glimpse of Vic in the corner of my eye shifting his feet nervously. I'm sure he felt trapped by now. His agreeing to come with me into this dank dungeon implicated him by default. Now he was in the awkward position of having to refuse Karl. Naturally, when Karl saw Vic and me, knowing we were friends, he assumed I picked Vic as my helper. What I neglected to tell Vic earlier was Karl said I could choose whoever I wanted to work with me. Naturally I thought, *"Who would I rather share this job with than my old friend, Vic?"*

By the time, Karl got around to asking if we had any questions, Vic was really fuming. After Karl left us there to wait on Jenkins, he started in on me.

"Allen Williams, you frickin' sly son of a bitch."

"Hey, watch it now. You're talking about my mother."

He continued, "You asked me to come along knowing he was down here waiting for us all along. You just had to get me in on your little filthy detail, didn't you?"

I smirked, "Well, I must admit the thought did cross my mind." Vic slugged my arm in protest. Of course, he wasn't threatening he knew better than to try that with me.

"Come on," I said cajoling him. "It could be worse. At least, we'll get a break from the line. I bet we can stretch this job out at least two days. What do ya' say?"

"What *can* I say?" he protested. "Wait 'til my dad finds out about this."

"We just won't tell him, that's all. By the time we start in, he'll already be punching off his shift anyway."

Vic shook his fist in my face.

"I'm gonna get you for this, Allen, you just wait." Just then we both heard a voice from behind us on the stairs.

"Here," he admonished, "you two boys are supposed to be workin', not fightin'".

We turned to see a gray haired black man in his sixties at the top of the stairs. He was very heavy set wearing a thin growth of gray beard. His arms were heavily tattooed with something long and indistinguishable faded with age. He leaned heavily on the handrail furrowing his brow sizing us up.

I looked up with a smile, "You must be Jenkins, the fork lift operator." He replied in a gruff voice.

"That's what they say I do in between any other piddlin' things they want done."

He started down the stairs slowly with a decided limp. The closer he got, the easier it was to see this man was ripe for retirement. I wondered why he was even working now. As he drew nearer, I could see his dim bloodshot eyes watering in the half light. Clearly, they had seen better days. From the looks of his rumpled clothes, he probably lived alone with nobody to care for him. Even his fly was left open.

"Hello Jenkins, my name is Allen. This is Vic. We'll be working with you today. By the way, your zipper is down." Barnabus didn't bother to look. He waved his hand idly through the air.

"That don't make no never mind. What's down there's just a waterspout anyhow. I'm Barnabus Kurt Jenkins, at your service."

He made the slightest bow causing Vic and I to chuckle at the good-humored Negro before us. Then it occurred to me. I'd heard that name before. It was from Amy. I remembered her mentioning the old coot who talked about tunnels beneath 'the house', and all those poor souls down there.

Now the old man aroused my curiosity.

"You must have been working here a long time, Barnabus; I bet you've seen a whole lot come and go."

He lowered his head in thought, then raised it slowly with a sense of pride in his voice.

"That's true boy. I seen a whole lot roll before my eyes and heard a lot, too. My pappy worked here before me. That's how I come by this job in the furst place. He told me lots of stories about the beginnings of this here place that was told to him by his grandpappy."

He must have detected my sense of history peaking with some sort of internal radar because his eyes grew more animated as he walked toward me and Vic.

"I seen things folks don't *even* wanna talk about. Like I said, I heard things, too."

"Like what for instance?" Barnabus took a deep breath letting out a ragged sigh. He eased down on a nearby crate allowing his heavy hands to rest on his knees. He seemed reluctant to speak at first, as if he were tired of talking. Then his eyes took on that glimmer again as they shifted upward in recollection.

"It was my grandpappy who tole me about what his pappy knew of this here place 'bout a century ago. Back then, there weren't no part of this slaughter house right here. No sir, it was all houses lined up along old Front Street. They was the homes of workin' folks from the slaughter house back then. Some of the homes were special though. Some had white bricks goin' all around the bottom of their chimneys. Do you know what that means?" he asked.

I replied, "No, I can't say I do, Barnabus. How about you, Vic, do you?"

"Nah, but I'm sure he does though. It's his story. Let him tell it."

Vic folded his arms looking at Barnabus skeptically. Barnabus ignored his air of skepticism lowering his voice and continuing.

"That was a sign. The white bricks meant they were part of the Underground Railroad. It meant those houses were safe for runaways, at least for a while anyway. Those houses had folks livin' in em' that didn't believe in slavery. They were willing to risk being in trouble with the law for helpin' slaves hide out and get on to freedom.

"Now underneath those houses some of em' had tunnels that led from one house to the other. Others had trap doors, hidden stairs, and fake fireplaces and what not to help them folks hide for a while. Anyway, Grandpappy told me there was a whole mess of tunnels that led away mostly headin' north toward freedom." Barnabus shifted uneasily on top the crate as he came to a part of his story that was difficult for him to relate.

"Grandpappy said his father's best friend went down in them tunnels and found somethin' that turned his hair white as snow. His father was about the same age as that young man, but when that man come out his hair had done gone completely white. He was plenty scared, too. It took about two days before they could drag it out of him what he seen down there. He told them he found a tunnel alright, then another and another and before he knew it his coal lamp went plumb out of oil. It was then he knew he was lost as hell." He looked up at the two boys assuring they were following his every word.

His eyes narrowed as he continued, "That's what he said. He was lost as hell would have it. He was scared, too, that he might die right down there in that mess of tunnels and wouldn't nobody ever find him. So, he said his prayers and commenced walkin' on until he came to a wide spot in the tunnel. There he could smell the air was foul with somethin' rotten-like. That's when he stumbled on what done turned his hair white. At first, he felt another body in the cramped tunnel with him, but it didn't move. He felt around some more and come up with an old lantern lying next to it. When he struck his last match to light it up there was twelve folks all huddled together ain't none of them was movin'. The light from his lantern shook all over the faces of those poor folks in that tunnel. He could see they didn't look like no skeletons. They was mummies with all their clothes on, too. Some wore scarves and hats on their heads, others were small children in their mammies' arms. There they was all shriveled up old mummies with their belongings lyin' right beside em'."

Now Vic's face grew taut with anticipation.

"What did he do next?", he asked.

Barnabus took another labored breath, then went on.

"Well, Grandpappy said he looked around and found another coal oil lamp lying on its side under the arm of one of the mummies. He held his breath and slid it out from under. Thanks be to God, there was some oil left in the bottom of it. He poured that in his own lamp and went on searching for a way out." Allen stood back shaking his head in disbelief.

"So, obviously, he did get out telling his tale to your Grandfather's father."

"Yes sir, his prayers was answered, praise the Lord."

Vic broke in, "But what about the mummies, I mean the twelve people. Did they ever go back and take them out?"

Barnabus looked down sorrowfully at the wooden crate between his legs, shaking his head slowly from side to side.

"Nope, ain't anybody ever gone down in them tunnels again. Some started sayin' they was haunted. I don't know if I believe all that. But I damn sure ain't goin' down there myself. Anyhow, all them houses in a row were taken down after my grandpappy died. Cross Brothers' got bigger and they just built right on over that property. There is a place, though, underneath this very floor that I seen when they was pourin' concrete. It's an entrance to an old root cellar they covered over. Some say that's where the tunnels begin."

"That's some tale there, Barnabus. You wouldn't be exaggerating just a bit to entertain us, now would you?" Allen queried. A bit of ire stirred in Barnabus' eyes.

"No sir", he replied emphatically.

"My grandpappy ain't ever lied to me in his whole life, and *I* ain't lying now."

"All right, don't get all worked up about it. I was just asking."

Barnabus struggled to shift his heavy frame off the crate where he was sitting.

"I think it's time we was all gettin' to work before they take a stick to all of us."

"Yeah, I guess you're right, Barnabus. Vic and I will tip back a drum while you slide a pallet under. Then, we'll spin it around on top.

Vic complained, "Don't we have some kind of a strap to wrap around the drum so the lift can just pick them up and set them on the pallets?"

Barnabus replied, "I think they's afraid some of these old corroded drums might bust out if we try that."

Vic shook his head in disgust.

"It's always the hard way with these people. I swear if I see so much as a trickle come out of these drums I'm out of here, and I ain't lookin' back."

I said, "Don't worry we'll all be careful, won't we, Barnabus?"

"Yes sir, that's for damn sure."

Vic and I put on protective rubber gloves and started tilting back the drums while Barnabus eased under with a pallet. Once we had one on, we rocked the drum around making room for more. Then, we placed a two by four on the edge of the pallet as a ramp and repeated the process until we had four drums up on the pallet. Then we strapped them all together. Next, Barnabus would slide his forks under the pallet and take it to the other side of the room. We went on this way all morning. By lunch break, we had succeeded in moving nearly half of the drums. It was slow going and sometimes the lift truck's tires would lose traction as the concrete floor under the drums was of poor quality, crusty, crumbling, and easy to break away.

I said to Barnabus, "This must be the original concrete used to cover up the old row of houses all those years ago."

Barnabus wiped his brow with the back of his sleeve.

"I reckon it is, at that, Allen. Let's go up and get us some lunch. All this work makes a body hungry."

Vic rolled his eyes speaking in a low voice.

"His fat ass hasn't left that fork lift all morning and he calls that work?"

After lunch, I made a detour by the front office on my way back to the storeroom. Amy was sitting at her desk. I took the chance to stop by the glass window to the office and wave. She looked up seeing me and motioned for me to wait there. Soon she was up from her desk and headed out the door to meet me.

"Won't you get in trouble if you're away from your desk?" I warned.

"Not if I'm going to the restroom," she said.

"Well, are you?"

"No, silly, I'm here to see you."

"I can't stay long. I'm doing a work detail in the chemical storeroom today."

"That doesn't sound so good. Let's walk down the hall so they can't see us talking here. What are you doing in the storeroom?"

"Vic and I are working with a fork lift operator. We're moving some storage containers and putting them on pallets. As a matter of fact, the fork lift driver is that old guy you told me about. You know the one who says there are tunnels under 'the house'."

"Oh, yes, Barnabus Jenkins," she recalled.

"Yeah, he sure had a tale to tell about those tunnels. You wouldn't believe it."

"I don't know," Amy remarked. "Why don't you try me?"

"I don't have time now, but I can tell you after work if you want to meet me. Since I'm doing this detail, I should get off by three."

"Sure, Allen, why don't you meet me at the malt shop?"

"O.K., I should be able to get there by four, if that's good for you?"

"Sure, that'll be just fine. I'll see you then, Allen. I'd better get back to my desk now."

She walked down the hall a little, then turned looking both ways before blowing me a kiss. I smiled pretending to catch it. We both knew we were growing closer every day. Things were moving fast and I was glad.

When I returned to the store room, Karl was there waiting for me. He was standing next to the metal garage doors. Seeing I was alone, he waved me over.

"It looks like you're making pretty good headway on this job. I'd like to get you and Vic back on the line as soon as possible, so I'm gonna send down another man to help. That way you should be able to finish all this today."

I thought, *"so much for stretching out the job."*

I smiled, "That's fine by me, Mr. Grafton, the more the merrier." Something about working for him with merriment didn't set well with Karl. He parted with a frown as he headed for the stairs. Looking back, he called over his shoulder from the landing.

"I'll send Steve Agresta down to help you. He's a steady worker. Just be sure you guys get this detail wrapped up today. I need you all back on the line tomorrow."

"Yes Sir, Mr. Grafton. I'll tell the others."

Steve Agresta, I repeated, *"Where have I heard that name before?* Just then, it did not come to me. Just as I tried jogging my memory Vic appeared at the top of the stairs yelling down at me.

"Aren't you finished in here yet, Williams. I thought I told you to get this job finished while I was out to lunch." Leaning over the railing he continued lecturing me pretending he were the foreman.

"Just get your smartass down here. It just so happens I talked to Grafton and he actually does want this job finished today before we leave."

"What? I thought you said we could make this job last another day?"

"Well, that was then and this is now. The boss man decided to put on an extra man so we can finish up today. He says he needs us all back on the line as soon as possible."

"Where's Jenkins?"

"I don't know. It's not my day to watch him. Now get down here." Vic started sauntering down the stairs.

"Where's this other guy who's supposed to help?"

"Grafton said he was sending along some guy named Steve Agresta."

Vic lamented, "Oh great. Now we get to work with that jerk."

I said, "Where do you know him from?"

"He graduated last year. I used to shoot pool with him. He still owes me for some games, too. What a Welch."

Steve appeared at the top of the stairs. He was a sturdy looking guy with a huge mass of jet black hair. His movements on the stairs were quick as he descended. His dark brown eyes darted about taking in the scene below him, never staring at either one of us for more than two seconds. I could tell he was the kind of guy who was quick on the uptake even before he spoke. When he did speak, he was standing one foot in front of Vic's face.

"If you had been playing fair that night, maybe you would have gotten your money sooner, wise ass."

Anyone could see Steve was a small dynamo who could back down Vic in a heartbeat. Even though he stood only five foot five, he had that sort of compact muscular frame most guys would envy. Vic back peddled.

"Yeah, well, that's what you think. I always play fair, don't I Allen?"

I just waved my hand through the air at him.

"Don't get me involved in your petty jam. I'm just here to get a job done. Which reminds me, where is that Jenkins anyway?" Trying to be funny he replied.

"Do you mean Barnass Jenkins? Vic never noticed how deftly I had changed the subject for him. Just then, I heard Jenkins shuffling down the steps shifting his excess weight from hip to hip as he negotiated the steep concrete staircase.

"Are you boys lookin' for me or somthin'?"

I answered, sarcastically, "You could say that Barnabus. Grafton thinks it would be nice if you drove the forklift and helped us finish the job today."

"Well, a man's gotta eat, don't he? Then I gotta take my dump, and wash my hands, and walk clear down here, too. Just how fast you think a man can go?"

Realizing it was futile to say anymore, I just waved him on.

"Let's just get started, alright?"

Steve stopped razzing Vic long enough to address me.

"Who died and made you the boss?"

"Well, I figure since Mr. Grafton said I could pick anyone I wanted for the job, I guess that puts me in charge."

I did not like Steve's attitude from the start. Now, he was starting to just plain annoy me.

"Look, I really don't care who's boss. Trust me, on this job it doesn't pay any extra. All I wanna do is get this detail over with before we leave today."

Steve seemed to back off a bit.

He asked, "Just what exactly are we supposed to be doing anyway?"

Now it was my turn to be simplistic. I explained the task the same way Karl did with one addition.

"The real trick is to get these drums palletized without bustin' them open."

Vic added, "You don't wanna know what happens if they do."

Steve defended his intelligence.

"I can read. I got a pretty good idea what happens if we bust open a drum of this stuff."

"Well then," I said, "Let's get started."

Barnabus already had the propane powered forklift running and ready for the next pallet. After about an hour of loading drums and strapping them into place, Steve had a suggestion.

"Say, Allen, why don't you let *me* do the strapping for a while and *you* rock those barrels onto the pallet. I could use a break."

I thought to myself, "*This guy is a regular smart ass. It's no wonder Amy didn't like him.*" Yet not wanting to appear unfair, I relented.

"Sure, O.K. you strap for a while, and then we'll let Vic take over. That way everybody gets a break."

After Steve's first pallet was strapped, I was ready to pat myself on the back for being fair when suddenly it happened. Barnabus was starting to back the lift away while simultaneously raising the load. Suddenly, the strap gave way with a loud snap. Now all four of the three hundred and thirty pound drums came crashing down on the floor! Weakened by corrosion, one of the drums ruptured crumpling under its own weight causing the full contents to spew out in a cascade of caustic chemical on the concrete. None of us waited to see what might happen next. By the time Barnabus had waddled up the last stair step, eye searing fumes had pervaded the entire storeroom.

At least no one was injured in the mishap. The only casualty was Karl's timetable. It would now take two more days before 'the house' safety officer pronounced the room safe for our return. When we did, we found a curious thing had occurred. The leaking drum was completely empty without a trace of chemical anywhere. At first, Barnabus assumed the liquid evaporated, but I knew better. Fifty-five gallons of chemicals don't disappear without a trace.

On closer inspection, I discovered where most of it went. The caustic chemical completed the job on the cheap concrete. Eating through the crack the drum made in the floor, it leaked down into a hole hidden somewhere beneath the floor. The others just stood around looking down at the floor dumbfounded. After a moment of reflection, I looked up at Barnabus.

"Do you suppose there might be one of those tunnels down there?"

Barnabus immediately took a step back at the mere thought of it.

"If they is, I don't want no part of it, you hear?"

Now my curiosity peaked.

"Vic, grab me that pry bar over there in the corner. I want to try something."

When Vic delivered, I poked the end of the bar between the cracks in the concrete floor applying pressure. Some of the edge crumbled away at first. Then, I pushed the bar further into the crack. As I started prying on the edge, a piece of concrete about a foot square popped right up from the floor.

I said, "See if you can move that piece away, Vic, so we can get a closer look."

Vic complied. As he did so, a level of wood appeared underneath the concrete. It looked roughhewn and checked with age. It was plain to see it wasn't part of the slaughter house floor plan. Barnabus took another step back. His eyes grew wider as he did.

"I done told you, I don't want no part of this. I'm going on my break now and when I gets back this hole best be covered up. You understand, boys?"

I was kneeling on one knee trying to get a closer look as Steve looked over my shoulder.

Steve said, "Go on, take your break old man, if you're scared."

Barnabus headed straight for the stairs. When he reached the top, still panting from his effort, he called down to us.

"You 'member what I said, now. You got to cover up that hole." Vic waved his arm in the air acknowledging his admonition while peering down into the hole.

Steve asked, "What do you suppose it is, Allen?"

"Well, you see those grooves running along the length of the wood at intervals?"

"Yeah", he replied.

"To me, it looks like unfinished lumber like part of an old barn door."

Vic added, "Or, a cellar door."

"Yeah, if what old Barnabus said is true. This could be a root cellar door from one of those row houses they built over," I said.

Steve suggested we dig out some more concrete around the wood under the floor. I looked up at the arched entrance at the top of the stairs. It seemed we were all alone. Slipping both hands under the edge of the concrete around the hole, I leaned back pulling hard with all my strength. Suddenly, the chunk I was prying on gave way causing me to fall flat on my butt. I sat there for a moment catching my breath, while Vic wisely took up the pry bar starting to enlarge the hole. In a matter of minutes, he revealed a complete door with latch and hinges underneath the storeroom floor.

I remarked, "This *is* a cellar door built some time ago, I'd say."

Steve speculated with an air of mystique.

"I wonder what's down there."

Vic quipped, "Probably a few quarts of Granny's preserves."

"Whatever it is that's down there, I know for sure that's where the chemical went", I said.

Steve agreed, "Yeah, if we did try to open this thing, we'd have to be careful of the fumes."

"Although, I speculated, it had already had a couple of days to evaporate. Maybe the chemical soaked into the ground below."

Vic commented, "That makes sense to me. Why don't we just open the door and let it air out a while?"

I laughed sardonically.

"Do you suppose the safety officer and our foreman would mind if we left a big hole in the store room floor for a couple of days?"

Steve chimed in, "Yeah and what are we supposed to do with these chunks of concrete?"

Vic replied, "Well, first we need to decide if all this is worth it. I mean, what if we do only find a few preserve jars down there. Is that worth risking our jobs for?" Each of us looked at each other weighing the prospects of the unknown looming before us.

Steve suggested, "Why don't we leave the concrete around the hole? We'll open the door to let it air out only we'll place some drums all around so it can't be seen. I'll bet nobody else wants to come down here for a while after that spill anyway."

I remarked, "You know, you're probably right. Even if they did find the hole, we could just tell them we were trying to find out where the chemical went."

Vic added, "Yeah, like for safety concerns and all."

It didn't take long for curiosity to overtake our sense of job preservation. Besides, we all figured the worst that could happen is we would have to cover the hole up and get back to work. So, for the next half hour before lunch, we completed our clever disguise by rolling fifty-five gallon drums around concealing the hole. Then, I volunteered to open the wooden door.

At first, the rust encrusted latch would not budge. So, Vic provided the muscle of a sledge hammer knocking off the latch. Once the latch broke away, I pulled up on the doors creaking hinges as I cautiously pried it back. Everybody sensed the remnant fumes of chemicals rising from the dark hole. At that point, we stood back immediately deciding it was time for lunch.

During lunch, we conspired on how to convince Barnabus to let us operate the forklift while he served as guard at the storeroom entrance. When we returned, we completed palletizing the remaining drums leaving a small island of drums hiding the door in the floor. Barnabus decided he was just as happy with a few jelly donuts we invested in, while taking up his post pretending to read the bulletin board. If he didn't have to enter the storeroom, we had our look out posted.

Before leaving for the day, we all checked out our hidden entrance. We all agreed the scent of the chemicals in the hole wasn't nearly as strong as when we first opened it. I suggested we could check out the hole as early as tomorrow morning.

Vic responded to my suggestion with one of his own.

"Why don't Steve and I just keep an eye out for you while you go down in the hole now?"

With some trepidation, I agreed saying, "O.K. Of course, you know whatever I find is mine."

Vic's eyes narrowed. I could just see him calculating the odds of me coming out with something worthwhile. Steve suggested we flip for it to see who went in first. Vic decided he didn't like the odds.

He ventured, "Oh, go ahead. You go first. You'll only come back with cobwebs anyhow."

At that, Steve said he'd flip me for it, so I agreed.

Steve asked, "Who's got a flashlight?" At this point our plan met an impasse.

So, it was settled. The following day, we planned to meet during first break in the storeroom. That evening, as I jostled homeward on the bus, I couldn't help imagining what I might find. Maybe there would be something of interest, something long hidden in the dark recesses of the hole underneath 'the slaughter house'.

Then it occurred to me, *"What if I come across some of those rats I've seen in the dark corners of 'the house'?"* These weren't just any rats, they were Norwegian Wharf Rats the size of house cats. They were born carriers of pestilence and disease. One bite could give you rabies, if they were so afflicted. Maybe I was being a bit too adventurous. Then, I felt a pang of pride goading me to consider going through with my foray into the cellar. I told myself, *"After all, it's just one little room under the floor. I'll just keep the light trained on every place I step; besides all those chemicals probably drove anything alive away by now. There's no sense making the guys think I'm chicken."* By the time I reached my stop, I convinced myself all would be well.

That night, I went to my room and found my history text. Mr. Ryan told me I could keep mine when the rest of the students turned theirs in at the end of the year. He told me I could keep it all summer if I liked, and return it when I was ready. I recalled Barnabus' story about the people in the tunnel. It reminded me of something I read about. It was the Underground Railroad in our U.S. History course. I decided to look it up again.

There I found the narrative about the history of *The Fugitive Slave Act*. It soon became clear the act itself stacked the cards in favor of so-called 'slave-catchers'. Unfortunately, it was a clear-cut victory for the cause of slavery. The *Fugitive Slave Act* did more than strengthen the hand of slave-catchers; it offered a strong temptation to kidnap free Blacks. The law denied alleged fugitives a jury trial and provided for special commissioners to get a $10 fee whenever they delivered an alleged slave. In fact, Federal Marshals could even require citizens to help enforce the act.

I learned, within a month of its enactment, claims of protest were filed in New York, Philadelphia, and other major cities. It seemed any Black who walked the streets of Philadelphia in those times was fair game for slave-catchers. Fortunately, many were rescued through the efforts of those operating the Underground Railroad.

Maybe it was the anticipation of exploration that set me thinking. Or, perhaps, the reading about slavery caused me to dream that night.

Either way, I found myself dreaming Amy and I were trapped in the dark cramped recesses of a tunnel struggling to find our way out. She was unnerved and, naturally, I tried to comfort her. I sought to reassure her. I knew the way out, yet we just kept going in circles until I awoke with a deep sense of dread and foreboding within me. The dream left me feeling uneasy all that morning.

As I got dressed, I couldn't seem to shake that feeling of uneasiness the dream left behind. Over breakfast, I explained to my mother that I was going back on second shift. I told her I'd be leaving early because I wanted to take Amy to lunch.

As I reached the bus stop, a light rain began. I hopped on board with my flashlight rattling in my lunch pail. The streets held the sheen of freshly falling rain reflecting the taller buildings we passed along the route. I opened my window a crack allowing the fresh air to tousle my hair. It felt good like cool fingers running across my scalp releasing me from the remnants of my dream.

When the bus brakes squealed and hissed to a stop, I checked my watch. It was 11 a.m.; already I was anxious to meet Amy. Even though we had dated less than two weeks, I felt I wanted to be with her as much as possible. I know she felt the same which is why she asked me to take her to lunch.

When I arrived outside the office window, I could see she was looking for me. As soon as I appeared, she grabbed her purse leaning over to tell the girl at the desk next to her she was leaving for lunch. Seeing her smile was just the thing for me. It lit me up like a new penny banishing the last thought of the dream the night before. As soon as she stepped out of the office, she took up my hand in hers.

"Where should we go to lunch, kind sir?" I smiled at her little endearment.

"I thought we could go to that Philly cheese steak place next to the news stand on the corner. That way, we'll have more time together over lunch."

"That sounds great, but could we split one. I can't eat a whole one of those sandwiches by myself."

I assured her we would, all the while wondering if she was really trying to save me money or just being lady like. Either way it didn't matter. We were off spending time together. As we strolled along, I was bursting to tell her what I had been up to lately.

I mentioned casually, "You'll never guess what happened yesterday."

"What Allen?"

"While I was on the work detail in the storage room, you remember the job I told you about?"

"Yes".

"There was an accident. I quickly headed off the look of concern that suddenly appeared in her eyes with a smile. It's all right no one was hurt. We just dropped some barrels of chemicals off a pallet. Anyway, we noticed some chemicals seeping into a crack in the floor made by the barrel. We left the room in a hurry because of the toxic fumes. When we returned, we wondered where the liquid went, so we pried up the concrete around the crack. Beneath the old concrete, we found some boards covering what looked like an old root cellar. Isn't that weird?"

She said, "I think that's fascinating. What's in it, the cellar I mean?"

"I don't know yet. I was planning on finding out during our first break today."

"Couldn't that be dangerous?"

Acting out of my need for exploration I answered.

"Oh, I don't know, I sort of like exploring new places, don't you? Besides, Steve and Vic will be there with me."

"I wonder if either of them really wants to have a look."

"Actually, Steve said he'd flip me for the chance."

"That sounds just like him." Her remark made me recall she didn't like him much ever since their first date. I reassured her it would be me going in for a look see first.

"It's my flashlight, so I think he'll see things my way, if you know what I mean. That old black guy, Barnabus, seems to think the cellar might be part of the homes that got bulldozed over when the Cross Brothers expanded 'the house' over the old Front Street property."

Amy cautioned, "If you do go in there, be very careful. You never know what you might find underground. Those old homes were built before the Civil War, you know. It could be dangerous."

"I can take care of myself, Amy, don't worry." She gave me a sideways glance finding my wide grin dispelling any further doubts she had for the moment.

With a raised eyebrow for emphasis she urged, "Promise me you'll tell me if you find anything interesting, O.K.?"

"Sure, I'd be glad to share with you. Right now, let's try a Philly cheese steak. Here we are." I stepped in line to place our order temporarily putting aside any thoughts about what might take place later that day.

Chapter 4

The rest of our lunch date seemed to race by until our time together was ending. I spoke to her about things I dreamed of and just as easily she shared with me. We both found it easy to talk with each other not allowing a moment of stillness to come between us. We had so much to say about what mattered most to us. When our time together did end, I felt as if a cloud was forming over my heart. I couldn't help thinking of that Buddy Holly tune, *"It's Raining in My Heart"*. That's exactly how I felt when I knew we had to part. Love sick? Yes, I was, but the beauty of it was she was, too. Like two butterflies caught in a whirlwind, we felt our hearts inexorably spinning, entwined together. So much so, that it became more difficult to disengage each time we met.

As I walked her back, I promised I would see her that night after work. By now, her mother was accustomed to our late-night rendezvous out in the hallway. She even relented, allowing us time together inside on the couch. That is, provided she was within earshot.

The following day when I returned to the storage room, I found Steve and Vic standing near the hole in the floor. They were engaged in an animated discussion. As I approached, I could tell they were arguing again. Each of them suddenly grew quiet when they saw me. I shook my head looking at both.

"What is it this time, fellas? Did someone forget to say please and thank you?" I chided.

Vic started in first.

"Steve, here, thinks he's going in first."

I turned to Steve looking for an explanation.

"Is that so? I thought you said you would flip me for it."

Steve blustered, "I got here first, so I should go. You're more interested in seeing that girl of yours than taking chances anyway."

"You can leave her out of this right now. Besides, I don't see you holding any flashlight. It's gonna be tough seeing anything in that hole without one, won't it ole' buddy?"

I didn't wait for an answer. Instead, flipping open my lunch box I produced a large dry cell flashlight. Switching it on, I played the light around over the hole in the concrete floor.

"Either I go in first, or you go in the dark. What's it gonna be, Stevie boy?" Steve looked down at his feet realizing he was not going first after all. Taking a step back he assessed the situation.

"Well, if you're going in you better get a move on. We should put a pallet down in the hole for a ladder."

"Good idea," I conceded. Vic slid a pallet off the stack nearby dragging it to the edge of the hole. Tipping it up on its end, he held on with both hands allowing it to slide into the hole. The little room beneath was not deep. The pallet rested on the earth below with its top edge leaning against the concrete surrounding the hole.

"O.K.," I said. "Here goes nothin'." I positioned my feet between the spaces on the boards of the pallet, then stepped down.

The air felt cool inside the little room. As I shined my light around, it revealed old crumbling brick walls covered with mildew. The whole room was rectangular about ten by six feet wide. The floor was earthen and I could make out some old board shelves lined up against the wall in front of me. I was completely in now, hunching over looking up at what was left of the crumbling cement ceiling.

The little room smelled dank and musty laced with chemicals and cobwebs. As I worked my way along the back wall, I saw the end of the room in front of me. I angled the light down in front of me crisscrossing the floor hoping I would not discover a rat or some other creepy crawler in the room with me. So far, I felt relieved nothing else was sharing the cramped space with me. It was a root cellar alright. I saw several glass canning jars lining the shelves. Although most root cellars I'd seen had jars with something preserved in them. These jars were quite empty except for cobwebs.

As I played my light to the very end of the room, I could see what looked like a squat doorway. It was a little wooden door about a yard square.

Steve asked, "Well, what's it look like down there?" I glanced over my shoulder seeing his face protruding into the hole behind me.

"It's a brick lined room." I announced. "I think it used to be a root cellar. I can see some shelves with jars on them."

"Anything in 'em?" he asked.

"Nope, they're all empty. There's a small door at the other end, though. I'm going towards it now."

The room was little more than five feet high. I had to hunch down to make my way. When I reached the little door, I could see its hinges and latch were completely rusted over. I could tell this door hadn't been opened in ages. There was no lock on the hasp, so I pried at the door, yet it wouldn't budge. On closer inspection, I discovered the door was made to swing outward away from me. So, I sat down placing one foot against the dry wood giving it a hard shove. It still didn't budge. I tried both feet kicking harder this time. Suddenly, the door burst open allowing a rush of foul air to fill my nostrils. Holding the light up, I stabbed the beam of my flashlight way into the pitch black before me.

What I saw surprised me. The beam of light revealed a tunnel about the same dimensions as the door. It was an earthen tunnel leading straight away from the root cellar for about twenty feet. As near as I could make out with the light, there was another door just like the first at the end of the tunnel. I sat there pondering; staring down the musty tunnel. I could hear Vic's voice from behind me.

"What is it, Allen? What do you see?"

"Right now, I can only see a dirt tunnel. It leads away from this brick room. I'm not sure if I want to go in, though. I'm afraid it might cave in on me."

"What's inside the tunnel?"

"Nothing, Vic, it's just a tunnel with another door like this one at the other end. I think I'm going to come out now."

I could hear Steve chattering to Vic above.

"He's probably too scared to go any further. I told you I should have gone in first." Not wanting Steve to get the best of me, I determined to return to the tunnel when the time was right. By the time I reached the opening in the floor, it was already past our break time. I knew we all had to get back on the line quick before we were missed."

For the rest of the day, my thoughts kept returning to that tunnel. I wondered what was behind that second door. Moreover, I was curious about the purpose of the tunnel.

I thought. *"Could this be part of the tunnels Barnabus told us about? If so, there could be something of historical interest down there. I wonder what Mr. Ryan would say if I told him about it."*

It didn't take long for me to ask that question in person. I found myself drawn toward Mr. Ryan's apartment that day. It was late afternoon when he returned from his year-end routine at school. I greeted him on his stoop.

"Hello, Mr. Ryan, I suppose you're wondering why I'm standing out here?"

He graciously replied, "Well, the thought crossed my mind. What is it? Is there something troubling you? You know I haven't had any word on your scholarship to University of Pennsylvania yet. Though, I doubt you'll be disappointed."

"No, sir, it's nothing like that. I just wanted to talk. That is, I just wanted to ask you a few questions about history."

"In that case, maybe I can be of some assistance. Come on inside where we can talk."

We climbed the stairs together to his apartment. He lived alone with his old cat, Marcie, and his dog, Marshall. Marcie was a tortoise shell cat who remained aloof on the window sill as I sat down at the kitchen table. Marshall on the other hand busied himself nuzzling my hand unpretentiously seeking attention. He was an unabashed Bassett hound who normally sought attention from all.

Mr. Ryan assured, "Just scratch his ears a bit, then he'll leave you alone." As I gave Marshall his due, I told Mr. Ryan what was on my mind.

"I was wondering, do you think it's possible people used tunnels in Philadelphia to hide slaves? You know like the Underground Railroad."

Mr. Ryan answered thoughtfully.

"Why, yes, as a matter of fact they did. However, the term Underground Railroad is somewhat of a misnomer. It wasn't a real railroad, and it wasn't exactly underground. The term refers to a system of safe houses along various routes used by runaway slaves to reach Free states and Canada. Because it was against the law to aid and abet runaways, the whole system operated clandestinely, hence the name underground. As for actual tunnels used in Philadelphia, yes there's a long history of tunnels underneath Philadelphia for a variety of reasons."

"Are you suggesting people tunneled underneath Philadelphia even before the Underground Railroad?"

"Oh yes, several wealthy colonists used tunnels to hide their valuables underground. They feared the approaching British troops would ransack their homes and take everything they had. They would have, too, if it weren't for some enterprising colonists. Then, too, there were those who stored weapons and gunpowder underground during the occupation of Philadelphia. You know, General Howe captured the city on September the 26th 1777. Of course, you recall from your studies, Philadelphia was then America's capitol city. It was a dark time in our nation's history. The entire Congress was forced to evacuate to York, Pennsylvania while General Howe remained in Philadelphia with 15,000 troops throughout the entire winter."

Mr. Ryan looked across the table at me.

"What makes you suddenly interested in that part of Philadelphia's history?"

"Oh, I was just doing some reading about it after someone at work mentioned the Underground Railroad."

My mentor mused for a moment, then seemed to recall something.

"I have a book somewhere in my study that deals with several recent archeological projects funded by the government. I'll loan it to you if I can just lay my hands on it."

I had an interest, but I didn't want to pursue it now. I didn't want to let on to Mr. Ryan that I was crawling into holes at work. At the time,

I figured if I did he might recommend I leave that sort of thing to the archeologists.

"Thanks, Mr. Ryan, if you can find it. Right now, I'd better be going."

"I tell you what, if you're in a hurry, I can just send it to you when I do find it."

"That's great, Mr. Ryan. I guess I should be going now. I'll check back with you later."

I exited the apartment with a cheerful goodbye hoping he wasn't wondering about what I was up to. After all, he was my mentor. I knew he meant well. Although, right then, all I could think about were other possibilities. Perhaps I might discover something substantial I could share with Amy. It seemed crazy at first, but the idea kept running through my mind. After all, important people did once hide valuable things underground. I wondered, *"Could there still be some of those things there just for the taking?"*

Though it was improbable, somehow, I couldn't dismiss the notion… I was ready. I was a teenager in need. It all seemed plausible that colonial riches awaited me. If I just pushed further, it may not be a pipe dream. After all, Mr. Ryan had already validated the idea that someone could make the find of a lifetime. I dared dream, *"What if I could find some family heirloom secreted away by a wealthy colonist."* While standing at the crossroads of discovery, I decided not to let some archeologist pass me by. Whether my friends came or not, I was going through that next door.

As I walked along Arch Street, I decided to see if Vic was over at Norm's Place. It was a warm spring evening and the walk gave me time to think. I reasoned, *"maybe I'm jumping the gun thinking I can take on the job of exploring that tunnel myself. It would be smarter if I took along at least one guy just in case something went wrong."*

When I reached the front window of Norm's, I could see Vic inside. He was talking to someone else whose back was turned. I wasn't sure, but the guy's silhouette looked familiar. As he turned back to take his shot at the pool table, I could see his face. It was Steve Agresta. Immediately, I felt suspicious wondering what those two could be talking about.

I entered the door and Vic spotted me right away. He waved me over so I started in their direction. Steve lit up a cigarette and blew smoke in my general direction.

"Well, if it ain't our man, Allen, back from the underworld." I wasn't at all pleased with Steve's off handed smart ass remark. The way I saw it, the less people who knew what we found the better. Now Steve was wise cracking about our foray in the storeroom in a room full of people. I waited until I was close enough to grab his neck and pulled him close whispering in his ear.

"You might wanna keep a little quiet about our business, don't you think, punk?" I balled my fist giving him a quick punch in the stomach as I held him there. Fortunately, for him, I pulled my punch enough to let him think I was joking. However, when he caught the stern look on my face, he knew better. He stepped backward snatching a comb out his back pocket wielding it as if it were a knife. Then he whisked it through the air winking as he pulled the comb back through his greasy black hair.

He smirked," No sweat, Allen, I get the picture."

I ignored him for the moment turning to Vic.

"So, what are you up to tonight?"

"Just playin' pool like always, what's up with you?" Vic appeared a little skittish. It made me wonder even more what they had been talking about before I showed.

I said, "Not too much. I was just talking to Mr. Ryan."

"Oh yeah, is that so? What's he got to say for himself?" Vic seemed pleased to change the subject. I decided to let the rest ride. Whatever these two had been talking about couldn't come close to the news I had. By now, I decided to take them in on the deal with me. Cutting in, Vic was O.K. As for Steve, he'd probably squeal on us if I didn't. Stepping toward the pool cue rack, I summoned them both to a nearby table. I could see their curiosity was aroused.

"Sit down you two. I got something to tell you." Lowering my voice, I said, "It's about that tunnel back in the store room. Mr. Ryan just finished telling me that back in the Revolutionary War there were all kinds of tunnels underneath old Philly."

Vic broke in, "You told him about the tunnel?"

"Keep your shirt on. I just told him a guy at work told me some story about the Underground Railroad and that I was curious about it. Well, he told me about that and more. He told me colonists used to hide their valuables in tunnels so the British wouldn't get to them. He also said they hid weapons and gunpowder in tunnels, too, for the same reason."

Steve didn't fail in making the connection. At least, I can say that much for him. Like I said before, he was quick on the uptake.

"Are you thinkin' there might still be somethin' valuable down there in that tunnel?" I could see his eyes gleaming with imagination.

Vic soon shared his captivation. I could see it wasn't going to take much to convince them we should have a crack at the possibilities. I began with my plan.

"Since our good Jewish employers, the Cross Brothers close 'the house' on the Sabbath, I suggest we go on a Saturday. That way, we'll have Saturday, Sunday, and half a day on Monday before we're missed. One of us must get in the storeroom before we leave Friday night and pull the pins on the overhead delivery door. That way, we can let ourselves in at first light on Saturday and lock the door behind us. We'll need flashlights and spare batteries, plus I think we should bring at least one lantern, just in case."

Vic added, "I've got one of those miner's helmets with the light in front. It was my brother's when he used to work in the coal mines."

"O.K., bring it along", I said.

Steve asked, "What about shovels? I've got an entrenching tool my dad kept from the war."

"What about food?"

I hesitated, thinking, *"How long are we planning to be down there?"*

I said, "You know we each need to sit down and think up a list before we meet again. We should decide then on how long we plan to keep looking. I think it's important we decide when we're going to stop searching before we go into the tunnel. Let's think this thing over carefully before we go. I don't want anybody going off halfcocked."

Vic agreed, "He's right. It's only Tuesday. We still have plenty of time to plan this. I say we sleep on it and meet back here after work tomorrow night, O.K.?"

"It sounds good to me," I said. Steve nodded in agreement.

After finishing breakfast Wednesday, I told my mother I was going over to Norm's after work to meet Vic.

She warned, "Don't let him get you mixed up in any trouble. You're always sticking up for him and that just leads to more trouble. Let him take care of his own business."

Grandma advised, "You really should listen to your mother. That boy needs to stand up for himself."

"Don't worry about me," I said. "I'm not staying long. I just want to talk to him on my way over to Amy's."

I went into the hall to make a call to Amy. The phone rang twice before Amy's mother picked up.

"Hello".

"Hi, Mrs. Martin. Is Amy there?" There was a pause as she muffled the receiver with her hand calling Amy to the phone. Then her voice returned.

"She'll be here in a minute. She's getting ready for work."

"Don't worry, I won't keep her long, Mrs. Martin."

"Well, alright. Here she is now."

Amy answered breathlessly.

"What is it Allen? I'm almost late for work."

"Well, that's a fine way to say good morning to the man in your life."

"Oh, I'm sorry, Allen, but I really do need to get going. What is it?"

"I just wanted to say I'm coming over tonight to see you."

Her voice sounded hesitant.

"Allen, you know Mom doesn't want you coming over so late."

"It's just for a little while. I won't even come in; we can talk in the hall."

"Why don't we go to lunch together instead? Then we can talk, if we like."

"I wasn't thinking of talking much."

"Please, Allen, don't be difficult." I sensed the stress in her voice and settled for a lunch date.

"Alright, baby, whatever you say. I'll meet you at Ronnie's Malt Shop around twelve-thirty, O.K.?"

"That's fine, now goodbye." I heard a click and said goodbye to the phone in my hand. I thought, *"So much for my love life."* At least, I had other things that could keep me busy.

Glancing at the clock in the hallway, I was reminded it was time to run some errands before lunch. Stepping out the door, I hurried downstairs to catch the eight o'clock bus. When the bus arrived, I stepped aboard going over my mental checklist. My first stop would be the Army Navy Surplus

Store. There, I hoped to find an oil burning lamp, a backpack, fifty feet of rope and an Army entrenching tool. Next, I also planned to go to the local grocery store to pick up a box of kitchen matches and extra batteries. Then, it was on to Barnabus' rented room. I was counting on him to allow me to stow my gear at his place until Saturday morning. Hopefully, my partners would come up with the rest of the supplies needed. As it was, I would be putting a strain on my budget. I hoped it wasn't all misspent on an errant hunch. After all, our little expedition might end up a dead end, for all I knew.

The bus ride to Barnabus' room was interesting to say the least. One old gentleman sitting behind me leaned forward offering his unsolicited two cents.

"You'll probably need better boots than those up in the mountains."

I thought, *at least,* the other passengers only stared.

When the bus pulled up at the corner of Richmond and Front Street, I was at the back door ready to exit with my gear. The old gentleman called after me.

"Have a happy outing, son."

Fortunately, I didn't attract too much attention the last few blocks to Barnabus'. I could tell this was one of those neighborhoods where folks kept to themselves. Across the street, a row of aging unpainted tenements lined a long stretch of broken sidewalk. The buildings seemed devoid of inhabitants most of whom had long since gone to work.

My side of the street was different. There were individual bungalows with narrow drive ways separating them into different parcels. One could see these homes were once fashionable, in a charming sort of way, in the thirties. They were probably the project of a developer with a dream of how communities should look. Now they were lifeless, faded, sagging shadows of their former selves. Several were punctuated with broken windows and unkempt lawns.

The house where Barnabus rented a room was the home of Miss Mildred Schuck. She was a widow in her eighties holding out against time's thief and the rest home. She had a crippled right leg which limited her mobility. It was a cruel reminder of an automobile accident when she wore a younger woman's clothes. Now she subsisted on Social Security and the rent from Barnabus leaving little for the pleasantries in life.

She was alone except for Barnabus, though, she seldom spoke with him. He had an entrance to his room in back and came and went by the driveway. Usually, he met with her once a month when rent was due. Otherwise, he left her alone to her infrequent visits from relatives. Today she was sitting in her usual place in the living room with her leg propped up on a foot stool watching television. I decided not to cause her to come to the front door choosing instead to go directly to Barnabus' back door.

I knocked and waited for him. Soon the door opened a crack as he got a look at his visitor.

"Hey, Allen. Well, I see you're gonna go through with it. You may as well bring that stuff in then."

Barnabus had been expecting me since I told him of our planned adventure. At first, he told me we were all crazy kids and would have nothing to do with our fool plan. So, I explained what Mr. Ryan told me about wealthy colonists hiding their valuables. After I offered him a small share of the loot, he changed his tune leaving me with a warning about what happens to folks who put their noses into other folks' business. So, warned, I managed to persuade him to take a small part in our little venture.

I stepped through the door reminding him all he had to do was keep our stuff until we came for it early Saturday.

"Don't forget now, I'll be here before dawn about five o'clock."

He replied, "And don't you forget if you get caught, cause I won't know who you is".

"Don't worry, Barney. We're just gonna have a look at what's already there. If we don't find anything we can use, we'll come right back before we're missed."

"Well, your momma's gonna miss you if you done get lost in that damned place like them other poor folks did, and don't call me Barney. You talk like we is friends and all that. Me, I'm just an ole' fool who's doin' you a favor. If I happen to make some money at it, that's just fine and dandy with me."

"Whatever you say Barnabus, I'll see you bright and early Saturday morning."

I headed for the bus stop feeling confident our plans were coming together. What I didn't know, was someone else I knew was making plans, as well.

My dad used to joke about women, in general. He would say there are three forms of communication of which the third is fastest. There's telegraph, telephone, and tell a woman.

At the very moment I was boarding the bus, Amy was sitting in the malt shop waiting to join me for lunch. Connie Warren stopped by her booth to have a conversation with Amy.

Connie said, "You're Amy Martin, aren't you?"

"Yes, I am."

"I'm Connie Warren. You were a senior last year at school. When I was a cheerleader, you were on the girls' track team."

Amy recalled, "Oh, I thought you looked familiar. Well, it's nice to meet you, Connie. Would you like to sit down?"

"Sure, are you waiting for Allen?"

Amy seemed surprised that she even knew Allen.

"Why, yes, as a matter of fact I am."

Connie slid into the booth across from Amy.

"Allen and Vic are friends, and I'm his girlfriend. So, I guess that kinda makes us friends, too." Amy just smiled at her logic.

She replied, "So, you're Vic Rubio's girl?"

"Yeah, that's me; we've been goin' together six months now."

"Yes, well, I've heard a lot about Vic. Maybe we can double date sometime."

"Yeah, that would be great." Connie leaned over the table making sure no one else was listening. Then she whispered coyly. "Vic told me all about how he and Allen and Steve are goin' down in that tunnel they found under the storeroom at 'the house'".

Amy's blue eyes widened a bit at the sudden revelation.

"Oh, really," Amy said coolly. "When did Vic say they were going to do that?"

Connie raised her hand continuing to whisper with a touch of drama in her voice.

"Vic says they're going just before dawn on Saturday. They're going in through the overhead door of the store room. They've got rope, shovels, and lanterns. Isn't it exciting? I wish Vic would bring me along. I'd love to go exploring with him."

Amy warned, "That sounds a little dangerous, if you asked me. Aren't you afraid someone might get hurt? What if the guard sees them? They could get in big trouble; maybe lose their jobs."

Connie brushed off her concern. They've got it all planned. Don't worry. It's not like they're breakin' in or anything."

"Oh, and how's that?" asked Amy.

Connie leaned over taking her in confidence once more.

"They're going to leave the lock pins out of the overhead door just before they leave Friday night."

Amy admonished, "Connie, it's the same thing. They would be entering the premises without permission, don't you get it?" One look in Connie's innocent, blinking, brown eyes told Amy the point was lost on her. She could see this plan would require a bit more sophistication to say the least. Meanwhile, Connie did pick up on Amy's look of concern.

"Look," she observed, "it's not like they're going on safari. They just wanna look around to see where some door they found at the end of a tunnel leads to. It's no big deal." Amy made up her mind Connie's perspective on the plan was dim at best. As she saw it, the plan needed something more.

Chapter 5

I was unaware of the reception I was about to receive at Ronnie's Malt Shop. Had I known, I would have kept right on walking. From the door, I immediately spotted Amy's hair resting against the back of her booth, although I couldn't see who she was with until I rounded the corner. Somewhat taken aback, I smiled awkwardly.

"I'm sorry, am I interrupting anything?"

Amy cocked her head replying coyly.

"Why, no, Allen, do sit right down. I've been expecting you."

I sensed something about her tone didn't sound quite right. I quickly dismissed any misgivings assuming she was just being polite in front of her company. Sliding into the seat next to Amy, I cordially greeted Connie.

"It's nice to see you here, Connie. Will you be joining us for lunch?"

Amy inserted, "I think it would be best if she stayed awhile. At least until I can clear some things up. That is if you don't mind. *"There it is again,* I thought. *There's something in her voice. It sounds almost sarcastic."*

Now, Amy paused looking me in the eye, before continuing.

"Just what exactly do you have planned for this weekend, Allen?" Now I knew for certain she was clearly fighting back a rising anger. *"But what is the cause of this,"* I wondered. Suddenly my mind's eye quickly processed an image of the words from my dad's joke leaving his lips. Suddenly, I discovered I was mouthing the same words, *tell a woman.* In an instant, I realized Vic must have told Connie about our plans to explore the tunnel. With all the innocence I could muster, I now faced Amy.

"I don't suppose Connie has told you any more about the root cellar and the tunnel? I was going to tell you all about it over lunch."

Amy replied stiffly, "Not a wise course, Allen Williams. You knew about it, and you weren't going to tell me. What about your promise to tell me what you found in the root cellar, remember that? Were you just going to run off with the boys leaving me to wonder where you went for the weekend?"

I sought to answer her question cautiously seeking to avoid any further damage.

"You see, Amy, I really didn't think you would want to know about this. That way, you wouldn't have to lie to your mom."

Amy narrowed her eyes waiting impatiently to hear the rest of my story.

I explained, "We all figured that we might need more time to find out how far the tunnel went. So… we decided to tell our parents we were all going to Ocean City to the beach. That way, they wouldn't miss us if we had to stay out an extra night. You see if you knew about that, you might have to lie to your mom if she asked where I was."

Completely exasperated Amy asked, "Now really, Allen, do you expect me to believe that?"

Connie quickly came to my defense. "Vic did tell me they might use that story, Amy, really."

I urged, "It's true. Please listen to what she's saying."

"Oh, all right, but don't you see one lie is as good as the next."

Now that observation of Amy's really left me perplexed.

"What are you getting at?"

"Well, it's like when two girls wanna stay out all night. They each tell their mothers they're staying over at the other girl's house." Then an impish grin began to widen across her face. "That way, we can join you in your little expedition."

I was shocked. Until now, I'd never dreamed Amy would be interested in such a venture, much less that she would lie to get a chance at going. I recovered long enough to express shock and dismay.

"Why, Amy Martin, I never thought you would do such a thing."

In response, Amy found she could not contain the tom boy inside her any longer.

"Oh, I don't know," she said, "I think it might be fun."

Now Connie was giggling like a schoolgirl.

"I wanna go, too. I think it would be a great adventure."

I looked down at the table realizing I'd been had.

"You're both serious about this, aren't you?"

Amy nodded, "Yes. I think we can handle it and maybe keep you guys out of trouble, too. Lord knows you guys need some looking after." Connie giggled again.

Amy asserted, "Anyway, we could be helpful. We could keep a look out for you when you go in through the garage door."

I narrowed my eyebrows looking directly at Connie.

"So, you know about that, too." Upon reflection, I spoke aloud. "Dad was right."

Amy asked, "What?"

"Oh, never mind. It's not important now. Just what else do you propose to do to help us?"

Amy replied, "I can find out what the guards scheduled rounds are from inside the office."

Sitting back looking smug she observed.

"So, you see, we can be quite helpful." Before I could counter she asked, "Did you think to include string on your list of things you'll need?"

I was shaking my head again.

"What the heck would we need string for?"

Still smug she answered, "You might find more than one tunnel. You'll need to mark a trail or else you might get us all lost down there. You see, I bet you didn't think of that, now did you?"

Not to be out done Connie chimed in, "We can also use lipstick to mark our way. You see there, all you need is a woman's touch."

I was beginning to feel a headache coming on. I hoped that it was just my hunger.

"Look, we haven't got all day. Let's order something to eat, then we can discuss this further."

Amy sat back in the booth folding her arms across her chest.

"There's really nothing more to discuss. We're going and that's that."

Connie nodded in agreement.

With an exasperated sigh, I announced, "Well, we still should eat, so let's just do that one thing first, O.K., girls?"

We ordered and soon the waiter slid three platters of burgers, fries and shakes across the Formica topped table.

"Will there be anything else?" he asked.

I answered, "No, I think that will be enough, thank you."

As I reached for the ketchup, Amy raised her milk shake glass while making another suggestion in the form of a question.

"What about food? What are you bringing?"

At this point, I couldn't resist a comeback.

"I thought since you two were coming you'd oversee that."

Amy half sneered replying, "Alright, we can do that, can't we Connie?"

"Sure," she replied, "I can make peanut butter and jelly sandwiches." Then she stopped to think. "I'm not so sure I could sneak milk out of the house without Mom noticing though."

Amy and I both laughed relieving whatever tension there was between us. We knew we were too much in love to let any matter stand between us for long. Soon, we were all enjoying lunch making subdued conversation about our unusual clandestine plans for the weekend.

By the time Thursday night rolled around, our shift ended in turmoil. Vinny was standing between Vic and me on the line when he made a mistake. It would cost him his right thumb. As the line moved along in its non-stop grinding pace, Vinny wielded his knife in such a way as to strike a bone sending his blade glancing off nearly severing the thumb that was helping grip the bloody round shank he was holding. He yelped in pain instinctively jumping back from the line clenching his gloved hand. He started shouting.

"I've cut it, I've cut it, goddamn it! Now I've done it." He continued cursing and blaming himself. Maddened with pain, he clutched the injured hand pressing it between his legs.

I got to him first.

I had to shout over the noise of the line which kept grinding by.

"Keep it held up, Vinny! You've got to elevate it!" I watched nervously as Vic automatically headed for the first aid kit hanging on the wall near our station. As he ran, he shouted to the foreman ahead.

"Shut it down, shut the line down! We got a man injured here!"

The foreman went into action immediately. Lurching forward, he hit the large red button on the gray control panel. As his fist slammed down on the emergency stop button, the line suddenly fell silent. Only the whirring drone of the large overhead ventilation fans could be heard punctuated by Vinny's groans.

By the time the foreman reached us, I had Vinny's rubber glove off holding his arm up with the thumb hanging by a tendon. A steady spurting stream of blood was gushing over me, where the appendage had been. Vic threw the first aid box down on the bloody conveyor belt snatching it open awaiting the foreman's instructions. Fortunately, he was well trained for such an emergency. At first, he yelled," Call the infirmary, tell the nurses to get an ambulance here quick!" Then he took control of Vinny's arm from me. Looking over at Vic, he hurriedly called out orders.

"Hand me the tourniquet hose, Vic. Allen, you steady his arm this way." The foreman demonstrated showing me how to hold the arm level on the conveyor while pressing on Vinny's arteries at the bend in his elbow. Next, the foreman took the thumb, wrapping it together with the remaining strand of tendon. By now, Vinny was slipping into shock. In an even toned voice, he asked the foreman.

"Can you save it for me? Maybe the doc can put it back on."

The foreman assured, "Don't worry, Vinny, we'll take good care of everything. Just try and relax while I wrap you up."

After applying the tourniquet as tightly as possible, he began wrapping gauze around the thumb in a figure eight until it was the size of an apple. A tinge of red stubbornly seeped through the outer layer, but at least the spurting was under control.

Now he instructed, "Vic, you take him under his arm. Allen, you get on the other side. I'll keep his arm up while we walk to the infirmary." The four of us moved along the walkway cautiously trying not to jostle Vinny's arm. As soon as the foreman saw the nurse, he advised her.

"We might as well just keep him bandaged up until the ambulance gets here. If we try anything else, he'll just start bleeding again."

Vinny was sitting on a chair in the nurse's office looking quite pale.

The foreman told the nurse about the small member hanging by a tendon wrapped in gauze.

"We managed to keep it all together in case they can reattach it", he said.

Vinny moaned, "I think I'm going to be sick."

The words just parted his lips when he jerked his head forward spewing all over my pants and shoes. I just stood there bravely raising my eyebrows at the nurse. She got busy cleaning up the mess, then told Vic and me we could go.

"I'll take it from here boys. Thanks for your help."

So, that was it. The excitement was over, and it was time to go home all at once. *At least this day is over,* I thought. Turning to Vic I expressed my feelings.

"I don't think I wanna go home right now. This whole thing has got me pretty shook up. Do you wanna go over to Norm's for a while?"

"Sure, I'm with you pal. Say do you think they can really put his thumb back on?"

I shook my head looking doubtful. "I don't think so. That would almost be a miracle."

"Yeah, I guess you're right."

Looking glum we were both inclined to change the subject as we walked out of 'the house'.

I asked, "How are you coming with your list?"

"Oh, pretty good so far. I found some ham and cheese to make sandwiches with."

"Good maybe you can get us some candy bars for energy, too."

"Yeah, I can do that alright, also I got a flashlight. I just have to get new batteries for it."

"See if you can bring some gum, too. I'm bringing a hunting knife and my dad's old canteen", I said.

Vic summed up, "I guess if the girls do their part we should be ready to take on that tunnel for at least a day."

"That's about what I figured, too, Vic. Any longer and I think the girls will get spooked. I still can't believe Amy wants to do this with us. Somehow, I never pictured her as the type who would like crawling around underground."

"Well, I know my Connie wouldn't do it unless Amy was. She just doesn't want to be left out."

Vic and I walked together into the night air. The warm breeze felt especially welcome compared to the chilly blood infused stench of 'the house' we left behind. Realistically, I knew we never could really leave it all behind. We were a part of it now. Vic and I were becoming like our fathers. It was depressing for me to think I had not managed to change a single thing. I decided to keep those thoughts to myself for now though remaining silent as I walked beside him until we reached Norm's. I found myself wishing our upcoming adventure that weekend would somehow change everything for us.

The night at Norm's ended with me narrowly avoiding a fight. I chose discretion as the better part of valor. In other words, Vic managed to piss off more guys than I could possibly handle. Firming up my powers of persuasion, I convinced Vic it was time to leave. Placing my hand on his shoulder I squeezed down hard enough to distract him, momentarily, from the ape in his face holding a cue stick over his head.

"Come along, Vic," I said. Tell the nice man you're sorry. Tell him you didn't mean what you said about the circus being in town. Tell him it was all a big mistake and that you're ready to go now. Go on tell him that, Vic. Before I bust you one myself!"

Vic shrugged his shoulders trying to wiggle free of my vice grip. It was no good. I had him by thirty pounds and four inches. My upper body was in much better shape than his and he felt it. He remorsefully spoke to the guy holding the stick. As he did, he held his guard just in case the guy changed his mind.

"Hey, man, I'm sorry. I had you mixed up with some other guy that was in here last week."

The stony eyed would-be-assailant seemed unmoved by his apology. Before he could take a step closer, I made my play. Enforcing my grip, I spun Vic around to face the door. As I did so, I was careful to look backward over my shoulder at his opponent.

I offered, "There, you see, he didn't mean you. He just made a mistake that's all, and now he's leaving. See?"

I tightened my grip to the bruising point, as I placed my other hand on his other arm. Giving it a slight twist, he began moving ahead of me towards the door. The bruiser behind us hurled one last epithet at Vic as we passed through the door together. This caused me to speed up the exit process as Vic vainly tried spinning around to address the big man's taunt. The four guys with him had already lost interest when they saw we were leaving, so he backed off allowing us to depart unscathed.

I remarked sarcastically, "I can't begin to tell you what a thrill it's been to be out with you and the losers tonight. Maybe next time you can tell me more about this death wish of yours. For now, I'll just have to be satisfied with parting company until tomorrow, my friend. Oh, and don't bother thanking me for saving your ass *again,* I just think of it as my lot in life. Goodnight."

I left him standing on the corner across from Norm's. It was late, and I was more than tired. I could only hope he would have the sense God gave a rabbit and stay the hell out of Norm's for the rest of the night. As for me, I felt he finally taught me how to say I just don't care. In the morning, things had to get better, at least that is what I hoped. Friday was the last day of the week and the beginning of a new adventure for us all. One more day on the line would bring us all closer to the day we eagerly anticipated.

There was just one more detail I had to take care of before the big day arrived. Friday morning I awoke early. I planned to take the trolley over to a pawn shop off Dock Street. The night before it stormed, leaving a fresh washed look to the streets between my family's flat on Arch and the pawn shop. Unfortunately, no amount of rain could remove the grimy look of the aging shops huddled there together holding each other up along the Delaware River. I knew what I wanted and didn't want to linger. It was a part of town I'd rather not spend time in. Soon, I spotted the shop I remembered from a long time ago. As I entered the aging little shop, a bell on the door announced me.

A sense of closeness suddenly came over me. The merchandise stacked inside challenged the shop's capacity to the point where I felt leery of something falling on me. It was clear more people pawned than purchased in this place. The burden of items spoke volumes of the shop's history.

I was there for one thing only. I visited the shop once before with my father. He took me there one Saturday to pawn a gold watch he won in a poker game. He did not notice I also saw him pass a few of his WWII medals across the counter for good measure. I made my way to the glass case where I spotted a compass sharing space with numerous watches, rings, and medals. As luck would have it the compass I remembered was still there. It was a military compass. The dealer allowed me to look it over. The reason it caught my eye was the face of it could be lit up. I knew, even then, if I were ever lost this was the compass I would want in my hand.

I paid the owner ten dollars and pocketed my prize. On the ride home, I took it out watching the needle flicker at each turn and faithfully return to true north. Now I felt confident. I was ready to begin our foray into the darkness. If everyone else did their part, we should be prepared to spend two days underground, if need be.

That night, a normal shift passed and workers left for home. All that remained now was to clean up, collect my pay, and head for the door. Vic and Steve waited at the door for me.

Steve said, "Here's grandma now. What do you *do* in that locker room anyway?"

I shot back, "Some would say it's personal hygiene. Obviously, you're unfamiliar with it."

Vic interceded, "Knock it off, Steve. If Allen wants to smell better than you, that's his business." Steve settled for shoving Vic in reply.

"Let's get going. We got an early day ahead of us. You girls are gonna need your beauty sleep."

With that, I trotted towards the bus stop.

Vic caught up to ask, "Speaking of girls, where are we going to meet up with them tomorrow?"

"That's a good question," I replied. "I'll have to call Amy when I get home and settle on a spot."

Steve spoke out, "I don't see why we have to get those girls involved in this. If we do find anything worthwhile, they're just gonna want a piece of the action."

I said, "Forget it, Steve. It's already settled. Like I said before, Amy knows the night watchmen's schedule. She and Connie are gonna be our look outs so we don't get spotted going in the door. That reminds me, Steve. Did you pull *both* pins on the overhead door?"

Steve complained, "What, now you think I'm an idiot, or somethin'? Of course, I pulled both pins."

"Alright," I said, "Don't go flyin' off the handle. I just wanna make sure everything goes smooth, that's all."

"Yeah, well, when somebody gives Steve Agresta a job to do, it gets done right. You get it?"

Vic assured, "Alright, Steve, we get it. No problem, O.K.? Allen, we'll meet you in front of Ronnie's at five-thirty sharp. Oh, and one more thing. If I were you, I'd get a sack to carry your stuff. Otherwise, you might look a little suspicious carrying a bunch of rope and a shovel down the street."

Mocking Steve I replied, "What, now, you think I'm an idiot, or somethin'?"

Steve replied, 'Oh yeah, Allen, you're real funny, and a regular laugh riot, you are."

Just then the bus appeared rounding the corner. The driver mashed the brakes bringing the bus to a squealing halt, while simultaneously swinging open its door. We all piled in filling the bus with other meat cutters for the ride home.

The late shift bus rocked in and out of lanes making good time through the lighter evening traffic. We sat huddled in the back in the darkness reviewing our plans.

I asked Vic, "Did you remember to tell your mom where we would be staying in Ocean City?"

"Yeah, and I remembered to tell her the room we're renting doesn't have a phone, too."

"Was she O.K. with that?"

"Sure, I just told her we wanted it that way 'cause we'd be on the beach mostly and besides we were planning on relaxing, not taking calls from home."

Steve added, "My mom said she doesn't care if I'm out of her hair for the weekend."

"I just smiled knowingly."

The next item to check on was appropriate clothing.

I said, "Be sure you bring a warm jacket and good shoes, preferably boots. The rest is up to you, but it wouldn't be a bad idea if you brought along a knife. One last thing, guys. Be damned sure you take your swimsuit and a change of clothes." Steve gave me a screwy look until I reminded him.

"It's for appearances, Steve. Remember where we're supposed to be going."

He just nodded standing up to catch his stop. His parting words came with a determined look on his face.

"Remember, Ronnie's at 5:30 sharp. Be there, or be square."

Vic laughed, "Yeah, pleasant dreams, sweetheart." The brakes of the bus squealed again. Then Steve disappeared through the swinging door out onto the street.

Vic leaned over speaking with a wry smile.

"Do you think that guy will remember his pants?"

"Oh, he'll be alright," I said, "It's just his first time away from home, that's all."

Next, Vic and I jumped off the bus headed for home. I told him Amy's plan was to go with Connie in the morning. They would pretend they had an early day of shopping planned. I assured him they would be across the street from 'the house' waiting by 5:30 a.m. As we reached the stairs to Vic's place, he mounted the front steps briskly.

At the top of the stairs, he turned and waved.

I quipped, "I'll see you in the morning, champ."

He rejoined, "Not if I see you first."

A torrent of thoughts coursed through my mind. What would we say if we were caught? Would I be able to see Amy again after deceiving her mother so? I felt I could never forgive myself if that happened. This was all my idea. I would be to blame. How could I explain it to my family that I lost my job over some crazy treasure hunt? Somehow, lying there in bed, it didn't add up the way it all did before. The real misgivings were only just beginning when I heard a light knock on my door. It was my mother. She called to me softly through the door.

"May I come in?"

"Uh, sure, Mom, you can come in. It's alright."

She was dressed for bed. I guessed she probably heard me come in and just wanted to say goodnight. As she entered, I sat up turning on my night light.

"What is it, Mom? Is everything O.K.?"

"Yes dear, I just wanted to say goodnight to you and wish you a good time and say I'm happy for you. I'm glad you can spend some time away with your friends from work and celebrate your graduation. You deserve some time off for fun. You've earned it. Your father never seemed to make time to get away. I wish now that he had. It would have been better for him in the long run.

Now, I felt more apprehensive than ever. I also felt like a heel for perpetrating the hoax I was about to pull off. I felt I couldn't say more to her now. Not wishing to further the lie, I simply nodded. She patted me on the shoulder speaking with assurance.

"I know you'll have a good time, because it's something you really want to do."

"Thanks, Mom, don't worry about breakfast. We're getting an early start."

"Alright son, I'll see you in a couple of days then." She started to leave the room then turned at the door. Her voice changed to one of concern.

"Please don't let Vic draw you into any trouble over there in Ocean City. Some of those people over there play rough, you know."

I lied through my teeth.

"Don't worry, Mom. I'll see that he stays out of trouble, you'll see."

"Good night, dear."

The door closed slowly and I was uncomfortably alone again with my thoughts. Getting to sleep was a forced effort that required all my concentration. Sleep did eventually overtake me in the wee hours. It was a deep and dreamless sleep that ended all too soon. The sound of my alarm clock jangled me awake at 4.00 a.m. I arose quickly and went into my well-rehearsed routine. A shower, shave, towel dried hair, and I was ready for coffee. I crept down the hall past the girls' room wrapped in my towel entering the kitchen to make some.

When I returned to my room everything was hung up ready to go. The night before, I chose a two-pocket long sleeve blue denim Sears work shirt to put on over my gray tee shirt. Staying with a profile of dark clothing, I pulled on my blue jeans and black steel capped boots. I finished with a gray cloth cap my father left me, which I thought gave me a jaunty look. Then, I finished a bowl of Cheerios with my coffee and made for the door.

In the darkness, the street appeared devoid of any traffic. It seemed the only thing working that time of day was the faded green bus that heaved over to my stop with an escape of air from its brakes. The streets were still damp from an evening's shower. Every street light along our route sent its reflection beaming back from the glistening road surface as we passed by in a spray. The clock on the bus said a quarter until five. I fingered my compass nervously in my jacket pocket hoping Barnabus would be up.

Leaving the bus with a hop, I hurried up the broken sidewalk to his room. The paper boy was out bicycling toward me tossing papers on various lawns. He passed by giving me a look of scrutiny. I gathered he wasn't used to seeing strangers walking with an empty bag over their shoulder in the neighborhood. I must admit it must have seemed suspicious to him. No one else seemed to be moving in the neighborhood. Those who did own cars had them huddled close to the curb on the tenement side of the street.

When I reached Barnabus' place, I was encouraged to see a light flooding onto the driveway at the back of the small house. As I reached up to tap on the back door, it opened suddenly in front of me. I jerked back in surprise seeing Barnabus filling the doorway.

"Jeez, you scared me."

"I was waitin' on you. You're a little late."

"Well, I'm glad you're up," I said, catching my breath.

"Come on in and get your stuff, so's I can get back to sleep."

I entered with my dad's old Army duffel bag in hand. All my things were piled up in a corner on the small wooden floored porch attached to his room.

"I sure appreciate you doin' this for me, Barnabus."

"Well, if you asked me, I think you're plum crazy wantin' to go crawling around in the dirt in a place like that. It just ain't natural."

"Oh, it'll be alright, Barney. We won't be there long. Should I give the ghosts a message from your grandpappy while I'm down there?"

Barnabus screwed up his face in disgust.

"Oh, *hell* no, and don't call me Barney. I done told you that once already. Now, you best get a move on before your friends leave without you." Then, I heard him remark under his breath sarcastically as he closed the door behind me, "Now wouldn't that be a shame."

By the time, I reached the end of the driveway his porch light was out. I had to hurry now. When the bus left me near 'the house' its clock said 5:30 a.m.. I rushed up the block catching a glimpse of Amy peeking out from behind a big trash receptacle. As I came into view from the other side, I found everyone huddled there waiting. I saw the tension in Vic's face as I hugged Amy.

"Is everything alright?" I asked.

Steve sounded a bit rattled.

"We thought you weren't gonna show. We just missed being seen by the guard."

Amy assured, "Oh, don't mind Steve. That old guard couldn't see us if he looked right at us."

I couldn't help thinking Amy looked cute in blue jeans and high-topped sneakers. She wore a long sleeved plaid shirt and a Phillies ball cap I had given her. I thought, *So much for the subdued look.* Connie was another story. Sporting a red bandana on her head, she wore a Penn State sweatshirt and a pair of Vic's black rubber boots and jeans. At least the guys were dressed appropriately. They wore jackets with their jeans and hiking boots. Steve did look a bit comical wearing a miner's helmet in our present surroundings. I took stock of our equipment. Then I told the others I would head for the door first. Rounding the trash container, I crouch walked across the alley. At the door, I looked back seeing the others huddled watching in anticipation.

Slowly, I grasped the door handle pulling steadily upward. I'd forgotten how much it creaked on its rollers. The sound was enough to alert anyone within earshot. I held my breath for a moment waiting to see what happened next. No one seemed the wiser, so I slipped under the door dragging the bag of equipment in behind me. Once inside, I stayed close to the door. Now the moment of truth came. I was about to turn on my flashlight when I reasoned if anyone had noticed the pins missing from the door, this would be the spot to lie in wait for the perpetrator. I took a deep breath turning my light on playing it all around the room making sure I was the only one there. Then, I put my hand under the door and waved the rest on. Soon, we were all huddled just inside the door. I slid the door down slowly shutting out the first crack of dawn. I cupped the flashlight so it only emitted a diffused light.

"Well boys and girls, this is it," I said. "Now we need to get over to the barrels. Follow me close, Amy. Vic, you and Connie come over next with Steve."

Amy and I crept along cautiously until we reached the circle of barrels. Now, I had to wait for Vic. When he came up beside me, I whispered.

"Hold your light on this barrel. Steve, help me roll it back." Steve and I grasped the top rim of the barrel tilting it up, then we rocked it back and forth walking it back enough so they could slip through to the cellar entrance. Then Steve and I rolled the barrel back in place. Once we were all assembled around the hole, I told the others I would go in first. Steve silently protested putting his arm in front of me.

I spoke in a low stern voice.

"It's not the time, Steve. You know I've already been in here. It makes sense I go first."

His eyes flickered in the half light. I could see he was thinking it over. Then, slowly he withdrew his arm taking a step back. I shined my light in the hole inspecting it for any changes or critters that might have entered since I was there last. When I determined all was clear, I helped Vic lower a pallet in for our ladder.

I took a few minutes to get my entrenching tool and knife attached to my dad's old Army belt. The belt had utility value with its several metal hooks protruding from eyelets placed around it. Next, I handed the rope to Steve.

I suggested, "It's probably best we keep the rope behind us in case someone gets in trouble."

Steve placed the rope over his head and shoulder realizing I was asking him to go last.

"Amy, you can follow me, then Vic and Connie, O.K.?"

Amy nodded apprehensively. I could tell by the nervous look on her face she was wondering what she had let herself in for. I stepped onto the pallet and started down. As I went, I reassured her with a wink and a smile. She smiled back bravely watching me disappear into the hole.

Once I was all the way in, I turned and went into the tunnel making room for the others to come in. When Steve got situated in the small cellar, he lifted out the pallet placing it over the hole. It was a thin disguise, but we hoped it might discourage discovery of our passage if someone came into the storage room.

Now it was up to me to crawl twenty feet to the next door and break it open. When I reached the little door, I sat down placing my boots on it.

Then, I began kicking it with all my might. I slammed my heels into the door right in the middle where I thought it might be weakest. After several tries, I trained my flashlight on the door.

"I can see a crack, Amy. I think I can bust this thing out in a while."

She warned, "Be careful, Allen."

Then she said something else that I could not hear above the pounding I was giving the door. Suddenly, a board in the middle cracked, then broke through, leaving a small hole in the center of the door. Taking my entrenching tool, I pushed it through then used it to pry at the rest of the boards. Soon, they were cracking. I could now reach in and work the boards back and forth with my hands until the whole door was out. By now, I was dripping with sweat. With hindsight, I could not believe we had not brought gloves. I turned back to Amy speaking breathlessly.

"It sure would have been easier if the hinges had worked."

I moved on through the opening cautiously. Once inside the new tunnel, I found I could move in a crouched position. The floor was earthen as was everything around me. With the beam of my flashlight stabbing into the pitch darkness ahead, I led the others straight in about thirty feet.

The next thing I saw were two tunnels branching off at ninety degree angles from ours. The tunnel I was in ended abruptly leaving me with a decision. Should I go left, or right? I stabbed my beam into each tunnel. I could discern no difference between the two. At this point, I consulted my compass. I knew the better part of old Philadelphia was to the east, so I chose to turn right to maintain an easterly course as much as possible.

Just then Amy reached forward tugging on my pant leg. It gave me such a shock; I nearly hit my head on the top of the tunnel.

Trying to regain my composure, I quickly asked, "What are you trying to do, Amy?" As I waited for my pulse to return to normal, she said, "I just wanted to get your attention."

"Well, don't do it that way again, O.K.? You startled me."

"I'm sorry, but why did you go right instead of left. I mean, what's the difference?"

"I'm trying to head east as much as I can. I figure that's where the old part of the city is."

"Oh, O.K. I guess that's as good a reason as any."

Close behind Connie whispered, "What are you two talking about?"

Amy answered, "I just wanted to know why Allen turned to the right, that's all. Why are you whispering, Connie?"

"I don't know. I thought we were supposed to stay quiet."

"Not now, Connie, that was before when we were in the storage room."

Vic asked, "What are you two jabbering about?"

Connie shot back in full voice.

"We're not jabbering. I was finding out what she and Allen were talking about."

Steve chimed in, "Hey, what are you guys talking about up there. Did Allen find anything?"

Amy stopped walking long enough to tell Connie to pass it on to the others they were going to the right. Connie told the others.

Now Steve asked, "Why are we going right instead of left?" Connie passed his question up to Amy. Amy decided the nonsense had gone far enough.

Turning to Connie she blurted, "Because Allen has the compass."

As I continued walking, I noticed the air was growing cooler. I imagined the building over top of us had provided insulation. Now, we must have left 'the house' behind. The tunnel bent to the right for a few yards then straightened again. Just as quickly, the tunnel widened about four feet. The top of the tunnel remained the same height. It was interesting sightseeing darkness dissolve before me as I stabbed my beam of light forward. The other beams from four flashlights behind me danced along the walls intermittently. It was then I wondered what it would be like for another person inside watching our approach. I quickly dispelled the notion realizing no one else would be waiting here in the dark if they could help it.

Moving on a few yards, my flashlight revealed something curious on the floor of the tunnel. As I drew near, I saw it was an old oil burning lantern lying on its side. I stopped to examine it more closely. Amy moved up looking over my shoulder.

"That looks pretty old, Allen. Do you think it was left here by that man Barnabus spoke of?"

"If it was, that person must not have had any use for it. Look there's still oil in it. Now why would a person leave their lamp behind in a spot like this?"

By now, Vic, Connie, and Steve huddled together looking on.

Steve ventured, "Maybe he had another lantern."

"Could be", I said. "But, why not bring this one along just in case it was needed."

Vic tried scaring the girls with his overactive imagination.

He exclaimed, "Maybe this is where he saw the ghosts. As they chased him down, he threw his lamp back at them! Ghosts hate fire, you know."

He held his flashlight up under his chin giving himself a ghoulish appearance. Then he leaned forward into Connie's face grinning.

"That's enough," I said. "Amy, hand me a match."

I held the lamp up sliding off the glass chimney. Scratching a blue tipped match on the box, Amy held it and I lit the lamp. Adjusting the wick upward, I allowed the lantern to gain a brighter flame.

"Well, this will certainly come in handy if our batteries go down."

Amy worried, "Don't even think about that, Allen."

"It still makes me wonder why anyone would leave a perfectly good lamp behind."

Vic chided, "Let's just solve that little mystery later, O.K.? We're wasting time and batteries standing here."

Steve agreed, "Yeah, let's get this show on the road, Allen."

"I guess you're right. We better move on now."

I held out the lamp returning to our search of the tunnel. The next twenty feet looked the same to me until I saw something unbelievable emerge from the shadows. At first, I thought I was looking at mannequins like the kind you dress up in a store. As I drew nearer, the jumble of mannequins lying over each other on the floor of the tunnel became bodies. Their clothing lay stretched over leathery skin which could only be described as mummified. It was, at once, a horrible incredible sight to see. I could not accept it as real at first. My mind raced to make sense of it all. As I stood there frozen contemplating, Amy arrived at my side.

The scream she let out instantly convinced me that what I was seeing was real. Instinctively, I spun around trying to force her to turn away. She stood in the tunnel hyperventilating as Connie rushed up. Of course, she screamed, too. Then, Vic grabbed her leading her away from the gruesome scene.

Steve shouted, "What is it? What's happened?"

He pushed his way forward to where I stood comforting Amy and saw for himself.

"What the hell? What is…this? Holy shi…!"

I interrupted, "Steve, don't talk about what you're seeing, not in front of the girls."

Out of reflex he continued, "What's going on here? Who…What the hell is this…?"

Then suddenly, he fell silent trying to fathom what it was he was seeing on the floor before him.

Somehow, I felt drawn in myself wanting to examine the macabre scene more closely. Revolting as it was, I couldn't resist satisfying my curiosity. Here were twelve mummified bodies. Some apparently poised in a final embrace. Others lay propped against the wall showing no signs of a struggle. Their tattered clothing was clearly that of slaves from the nineteenth century.

Vic tried holding Connie back, but her knee jerk reaction was to free herself from his shoulder long enough to see what he was hiding from her. When she saw them all there, she got hysterical, screaming and pounding Vic's chest.

"Oh, my God, Vic!" she cried. "What is it? It's so horrible? Are those people?"

Vic responded by pulling her away against her will. It only made matters worse. Now she was crying and gasping for air as she worked herself into a frenzy. Amy broke free of my arms stepping up to slap her hard on her right cheek. Her desperate attempt at bringing her to her senses had little effect. Vic finally had to wrestle her to the ground holding her there whispering in her ear as he struggled to help her regain control.

"Connie it's going to be alright. It'll be alright. I'm with you, baby. I won't let anything happen to you. We're not in any danger here. Just listen to me, won't you please."

I could see it would take a while to get her settled down. In the meantime, Steve came up beside me staring wide eyed at the horrific scene.

In a hoarse whisper, he asked, "What do you suppose happened here?"

"I'm not exactly sure, Steve, but I have a hunch. I think they must have been runaway slaves. That lamp we found some ways back must have been dropped by someone else. You can see these people here had no lamps with them."

"Why would they all stay and choose to die here together? Why didn't they try to escape?" Steve queried.

"I don't know for sure. I'm guessing they were lost. It's possible they were double crossed. Maybe the guy who was supposed to help them took their money and left them in the dark with a promise to return when it was safe to go ahead."

"You mean some slave catcher might have left them here to die?"

"It sure looks that way. Some of these folks must have been related. Look at the way they're clinging to each other. See the one clutching the child's body."

Steve recoiled at the thought of it.

"Their skin is all shriveled."

"Yeah, the constant temperature and lack of humidity has preserved them like mummies."

"Damn, how could anybody be so cruel? He just left them here in the pitch dark with them not knowing the way out?"

"It certainly looks that way," I said. "I wonder how long they waited before they realized no one was coming for them."

Steve took another step back. I could see him shivering. I turned looking him straight in the eye.

"Maybe we should go back. You know, the way Connie's carrying on and all. I think she needs to be out of here fast before she cracks up completely."

Steve hesitated. I could tell he was working things out in his head.

Then he spoke with deliberation.

"You know as well as I do if we get caught coming out of that storeroom it's breaking and entering for us all. We don't know where that guard will be now, do we? We could all end up coming out right in front of him." I replied, "Well, at least, we didn't really break when we entered." He frowned, "You know, it's still the same, Allen. We'd all lose our jobs."

"Well, what do you suggest?"

Steve reasoned, "I figure we owe it to ourselves to try the other passage that went to the left. Maybe we'll find something in that direction. Who knows, we've got to try making all this worthwhile, don't we? Besides, if we're coming out anyway, what have we got to lose?"

"I don't know, Steve, that still doesn't take care of Connie."

Steve smiled knowing his next suggestion would benefit him alone if he did find something.

"I guess you're right. You guys can stay here and comfort Connie. I'll go ahead with my miner's helmet and investigate the left passage. By the time I get a look see, she should be ready to come out with you guys anyway. I'll just meet you at the intersection, O.K.?"

I was reluctant to agree, but reconsidered thinking, "*What harm could it do? It isn't worth fighting over.*"

Steve had already decided waiting for us at the intersection was a good idea and went forging ahead. So, I explained to the rest we were planning to call it quits and return as soon as Connie felt like walking. Amy was kneeling beside Connie taking turns with Vic speaking softly to her. It seemed to be working. She was slowly coming around. I figured it would only be a little longer before we could all return. Yet, ten minutes passed before Vic and Amy had Connie up on her feet slowly walking her back. I led the way as usual. I was truly disappointed thinking of the opportunities I might be sacrificing behind me.

Just as we passed the curving section in the tunnel, we heard sounds of constant pounding. It was Steve's entrenching tool striking against something hard. I figured he must have found something worthwhile. Just then a terrific roaring sound rushed through the tunnel like a great wind blowing past us. It sounded as if the tunnel was coming down around our ears. Suddenly, we were engulfed in a billowing cloud of dust. We could hear rocks falling directly in front of us. The worst of my fears suddenly materialized. In an instant, I realized somewhere ahead the roof *had* just caved!

I tried rushing forward, but the dust cloud was so thick light would not penetrate it. Every instinct told me to freeze and wait it out. Just as suddenly, the tunnel went silent again. The only reminder of catastrophe was the dust slowly settling on our clothes. I was first to move again suspecting the worst. Sending a beam of light stabbing through the haze, I followed cautiously. The others remained close behind.

Working my way through the dust and debris, I called out to Steve.

"Steve, are you O.K.? Can you hear me, Steve? What happened?" When I reached the point where the tunnels once intersected, the floor ahead was littered with a jumble of rock. Beyond that, the entire passage was completely blocked with freshly fallen rock and earth. The shattering realization came like the force of increasing gravity buckling my knees under its weight. The way back ceased to exist. I fell to my knees unable to bear up under the heartbreaking reality. Steve was forever gone, along with our hopes of returning the way we came. The others came upon me there in the depths of my despair. They didn't need a compass to tell them the way out was gone forever.

I turned to Amy with tears streaming down my dust caked face.

"Steve's in there somewhere, Amy. Dear God, what can we do?"

Vic lurched forward clawing at the solid impasse of earth and rock.

"We've got to dig him out! Come on everybody let's dig! We have to free him before he suffocates!"

Amy just stood by my side not saying a word. Caressing my hair, she allowed me to cry out my torment. She, too, realized the futility of digging through tons of earth and rock on the chance of retrieving a lifeless body crushed under its terrific weight. Vic was losing control. Wrenching my entrenching tool from my pack, he proceeded to hack furiously at the wall before him. Occasionally, he would cease his frantic digging and remove a large rock casting it aside with super human effort.

Connie stood directly behind Vic with trembling hands held to her mouth. She stared wide eyed, witnessing the hopeless task before her. Her entire body quivered as she slipped into a state of catatonic shock. There was really nothing else any of us could do. Each of us struggled in our own way trying to work through the horrific tragedy.

Suddenly Vic's feeling of hopelessness turned to rage. He threw down the shovel shouting at us.

"Well, are you all just going to watch me fight for his life? What's the matter with you people? Don't you have any feelings? He's in there. He needs our help! For Christ's sake, why won't somebody do something?"

Next, he flung himself against the mound that blocked the tunnel from top to bottom. Bursting into tears, he beat his fists against the mound crying repeatedly.

"Why can't somebody do something? Somebody help him! Get him out, get him out!"

Amy left my side going to him. Kneeling beside Vic she sought to assuage his pain. Speaking softly, assuredly, she placed her arms around his slight frame pulling him closer rocking him like a small child. I'd never seen such inner strength as Amy displayed just then. I stopped sobbing when I saw how she was handling the horror with courage. It reminded me of something I'd read once.

"It's how we handle adversity that makes us who we are."

I got to my feet and went to Connie. I wanted to offer her the same solace. Somehow, I felt I could steadily work my way through my own pain by comforting her. Eventually, we all got through it, at least to the point where we could talk about it. Sitting there on the floor of the tunnel, we must have spent a half hour just dealing with each other's emotions.

"Where do we go from here?" I wondered. Then it dawned on me in a cruel heartbeat. *"What else can we do but go ahead?"* After all, it was the only way out.

Amy must have read my mind. She rose speaking with deliberation in her voice pointing her light into the blackness of the open tunnel.

"This is the way out. We might as well set our minds to that and get going."

Without saying another word, she turned walking toward the darkness with her light pointing the way. We followed on numbly with the split-second suddenness of Steve's crushing disappearance indelibly etched in our minds. Clearly, his loss delivered a simultaneous shock to our collective consciousness. Moreover, for Amy the event forged a sense of resolve in her that I had not seen before. As for Connie, she had to go on with the aid of Vic's encouraging words of comfort. For the next hour, Amy led us through a dank, muddy, pitch black, claustrophobic riddle of hidden passages. Well into the tunnel now, her progress began slowing as she encountered an ever-narrowing passage. Soon, another series of twists and turns led her to an abrupt halt.

I called out, "What's the matter, Amy?"

She answered, "It's getting very narrow ahead. Do you want to have a look see?"

"I'm coming up now," I called.

When I reached her, I could see the problem immediately. She was lying in front of a passage that had suddenly narrowed to nearly two feet square. The walls were considerably damper, too. Amy's clothing was smeared from head to toe with a loam colored grime from the walls she had been bumping into. Her face was smeared in places where she wiped her face. All in all, she looked strained and spent, almost at the end of her rope.

I made it clear to her. "I'm going through this opening to see what we're up against. Tie your string line to my boot once I'm in. I don't wanna get lost in there."

"O.K. Allen, but promise me you won't take any unnecessary chances."

I chuckled at the thought.

"Considering this is the only passage we've seen since we left the cave in, I consider this trip extremely necessary."

"You know what I mean, Allen. Do be careful."

I crawled in further holding my flashlight in front of me. After sliding through the opening, I stopped long enough for Amy to tie a string to my boot. Then, I proceeded alone noticing the consistency of the walls inside were a moist blend of clay and rock. The passage itself took a decided turn downward to the point where I could propel myself forward with little effort. I was nearly sliding down the slippery surface now as the passage continued to narrow. This thought was very worrisome when I considered what might happen if I met face to face with a wharf rat in such a narrow passage.

Pushing that thought from my mind, I followed as the passage took another turn. I couldn't tell what direction I was sliding in trying not to think about a rat until another thought crossed my mind. *"How will I ever get back up this passage? I can't even turn around."*

Just then, yet another turn delivered me into a larger portion of passage. I breathed easier now. In the next four feet, it widened further still, until I found myself in a spot wide enough to turn around. It was such a relief. I had to force myself not to turn back. The only thing that changed my mind was I could see ahead dimly. I could just make out a sort of chamber ahead. I crawled another ten feet noticing the walls were composed of wet limestone.

As I continued my exploration, the entire tunnel opened into a room with a ceiling vaulting upward at least twenty feet. I was playing my light along its walls seeing an interior made from natural limestone formations. There were small stalactites coming from the ceiling and stalagmites pushing up from the floor. I was amazed at my discovery. Sliding out of the cramped tunnel, I could stand upright inside the small cavern. I was giddy with excitement. Here, all around me, was the largest portion of the underground I had witnessed since we entered.

The ceiling was dome-like with walls curving down about ten feet all around me. It was beautiful with minerals sparkling all along the walls. The surface of the limestone was slick with moisture and the floor was hard packed sand. I panned my light slowly to the right hoping I would not discover I was sharing this magnificent space. Then, I saw an opening in the chamber wall. It was above the floor level about five feet in height. Before I could explore any further, I heard Amy's muffled voice calling out to me.

"Allen, are you alright? The string's not moving, why are you stopping?"

I returned to the narrow crawl space entrance yelling upward.

"I'm O.K. here. I found a chamber. It's big. It looks like there might be a way out. You can come ahead now. It's narrow, but you can make it."

Amy shouted, "O.K., we're coming through."

While Amy made her way toward me, I considered the other opening with my light. It seemed to go on a lot further, at least as far as my beam could expose. Then, I directed my light back to the narrow entrance to help Amy find her way. Soon I saw her grimy face appear in the narrow passage.

"Welcome to my chamber, please come in," I beckoned.

Amy exclaimed, "Wow, this really *is* big! How do you suppose it got this way?"

Just then Connie's face appeared at the entrance. She appeared haggard and weary. Although, I could see her spirits lift visibly when she saw the open chamber. She did not speak as she entered, but offered a thin smile as she looked all around herself.

Next, Vic marveled, "This is different. Is there a way out?"

I replied, "I think so. I found an opening over here that goes in some ways. I suggest we stop awhile and rest."

Amy agreed, "That's a good idea, Allen. We haven't had anything to eat or drink since we came down here. We should take this opportunity to eat something before we go on."

Vic said, "I could stand to eat a sandwich. Would you like one, Connie?"

Connie nodded her approval, then proceeded to sit on a nearby outcropping. Amy came over to her and kept her busy helping to retrieve sandwiches and juice from their back packs. In the meantime, I checked my compass finding the passage leading out of the chamber headed roughly southward. I tried to imagine where the Delaware River was in relation to our position. I figured it must be southeast of us. Upon reflection, I realized it didn't matter much now since we only had one option. I did know we must go where the cavern leads until we found an alternative.

Vic came up with a sandwich in hand.

"So, where do you think we are, Columbus?"

I could see some of the old Vic survived the crises.

"Near as I can tell, we must be northwest of the river. I'm estimating we have come about two miles since we left 'the house'."

"Is that all, man? It feels like we've come two hundred."

"Well, it can seem that way. Everything down here kind of gets you turned around, if you know what I mean?"

"You can say that again. I'd need a seeing eye dog to find my own ass in a place like this."

Amy asked again about what made the chamber so large.

"I've had a chance to think about that. I figure with the sand on the floor and the dome shape above this must have been a basin for an underground river."

Vic marveled as he looked around him.

"No kidding. Then if that's true, that passage out of here was probably filled with water at one time, right?"

"That's the way it looks to me," I answered.

Connie asked, "Can the water come back?"

She began to look worried.

I said, "No, Connie, that had to be hundreds of years ago. It took a lot of time and water to carve out this piece of work. It was probably a river on the surface that was dammed up a long time ago. That's why there's no water here now."

Whether I was right or wrong, right then it did not matter. I told myself whatever it takes to keep Connie calm is more important now.

Amy reasoned, "So, if we can follow where this river used to be, we might be able to get to the surface and out of here, right?"

I cautioned, "Now, I didn't say that, but it's still the best and only chance we have right now."

Vic chimed in, "Now, you're talking. No big decisions just straight up and out of here."

"Well, let's just see how far it takes us anyway. I'll keep the lead for a while and Vic you bring up the rear, O.K.?"

"No problem, Tonto. Wanna sandwich?"

"I don't mind if I do, partner."

We all stayed in the chamber for the better part of an hour. Each of us was reluctant to leave its relative security behind in exchange for the unknown, even if it might mean escape. For the time being, we had to remain content to be together.

Chapter 7

Finally, I found enough courage to give voice to that which was on everyone's mind.

"We can't get out by sitting here. It's time we get moving again."

No one spoke a word. We all just rose starting to move in the only direction, left. I assumed the lead with Amy behind me. Then, as usual, Vic followed Connie. I let myself think her condition was improving. I wanted to believe the worst was over for her. She did seem to keep up well enough, although she was never as chatty as before.

After several twists and turns amongst the wet rocks, I came upon a sight I wished I could shield Connie from seeing. I froze in my tracks turning quickly to Amy speaking in a whisper.

"Rats."

"What's that, Allen? What did you just say?"

I pressed my finger to my lips repeating emphatically.

"There are rats ahead."

Now, Amy froze. In the dim light, I could just make out her frozen expression of total repugnance. By the time she regained composure, Connie was right behind her. Before I could say another word, Connie bumped right into her. As she did, she inadvertently caught a glimpse of movement under my light just over Amy's shoulder. I wanted to switch off my light, but feared if I did I'd lose track of where the rodents were. Then, Connie's high pitched scream echoed in the tunnel conveying her complete sense of horror. At least a dozen sets of gleaming red eyes came into focus reflecting the light of my beam as the rats teemed over each other. Fighting the distraction of Connie's repeated screams, I wondered how many more rats were behind these.

Quickly, I grabbed Amy by the shoulders spinning her around for a hasty retreat.

"Get back, Amy!"

Using her to push back the others, I shouted.

"Get back all of you! MOVE," I demanded!

They did not need convincing. Soon, all of us were running down the slick sided tunnel jostling each other as we went. Then, just as suddenly, we all stopped instinctively assessing we were clear of immediate danger. Vic reached out clasping his hand tightly over Connie's mouth pleading with her to get control. Catching my breath, I tried speaking to everyone.

"Alright, now let's all… try to keep cool. We might have expected this. After all, this is their turf. Let's just try to stay calm and think this through."

Amy protested, "How can we go forward with those things up there? They carry all sorts of diseases. What if one of us were bitten?"

Connie reacted to Amy's words struggling even harder in Vic's arms. Vic glared at Amy, assuring her she was not helping matters. My mind raced trying to think of a way to drive off rats. Then it occurred to me.

"Amy, how many sandwiches do you have left?"

She shot me an incredulous look.

"Allen, how can you think of food at a time like this?"

No sooner had the question left her lips she realized what I was after. She answered, "I think I have three left in my pack. I'll look."

When she pulled three out of the bag, I told her to save one for us. I took two and let the others in on my plan. By now, Connie was ready to listen. She was willing to go along with anything that might get rid of the rats. Only after she promised, Vic slowly released her from his hold.

"Vic, I want you to cut a length of rope a little longer than the width of the cavern. I'm going to toss these sandwiches over to the rats. Then, when they get busy with them, I'm sure they won't bother us while we slip by. Now, once we get further along, we'll determine if there are more of them where we're headed. If not, then I think we should set fire to the rope to keep them from following us."

Vic thought about my plan momentarily.

"Rats are smart you know. What if they just jump over the rope?"

I must confess my plan ended there.

Amy said, "Wait a minute. We could weave the rope along the floor making it wider so they can't jump the fire without landing in it. That should hold them off."

Vic observed, "Well, it could work for a while, but then what?"

I suggested, "We could use our string to affix our knives to our entrenching tools. That way we'd have a two-ended weapon."

Vic grinned, "Sure, I'm pretty good with a stick in my hand. At least, we could take a stab at those rats, if we had to."

"O.K. then, I guess that's it. Let's see if we can get this rope to burn."

Amy held out her arm preventing me from moving on our plan.

"Wait a minute. I've got a plastic raincoat folded up in my backpack. That should really keep the rope burning."

"Great, Amy, that ought to do it. Stay close to me. I'll throw the sandwiches to the other side of the tunnel, then we'll make our move."

We gathered together on the right of the passage with me in the lead. Amy shadowed me and Vic shielded Connie walking in front of her as she stuck close to the wall. Of course, the rats stood on their haunches, noses up sniffing for any weakness in the interlopers passing by. Fortunately, we could slip past without incident when they began fighting over the sandwiches. Then suddenly, I saw what I thought was their leader starting to follow. Quickly, I partially unwrapped the wax paper ham and cheese sandwich tossing it as far back along the tunnel as I could.

Amy grinned, "Look at them go for it. I wish they were poisoned."

Vic quipped, "Yeah, why didn't we bring poison on this picnic?"

"Let's just get busy lighting this rain coat," I said. "Hold it up so I can get my lighter under it. Don't go too far girls. We still gotta check out the passage ahead."

Amy assured, "Don't worry, we're standing right here near the fire."

Vic held the rain coat up until I had it burning well. The flames were starting to melt the plastic as I waved it around to accelerate the process. As the flame started licking up toward my hands, I gave Vic the nod.

"Coil the rope on the ground and step back."

As soon as he put it in place, I draped the length of the coat over the rope as best I could without getting burned. The flame grew higher as the coat was consumed.

"That should do it, Vic. Now, let's see what's ahead."

Turning my light into the blackness ahead, I proceeded cautiously with Vic by my side. Our light beams probed ahead side to side penetrating the blackness. After a few more paces, I turned staring at the burning rope forming a gooey puddle of hot plastic. I smiled observing no rat was willing to brave our little barrier so far.

Vic warned, "You know, it's just a matter of time before we see those rats again."

"I don't know. You might be right, but I think they're here because of the moisture. A rat must drink, too, you know. Speaking of which, what have we got left to drink girls?"

Amy answered, "We already drank most of the apple juice."

Connie chimed in, "I've got a bottle of milk."

"Let's have it, Connie. All this rat business is making me thirsty."

I popped the cap on the quart bottle and drank my fill. Feeling refreshed by the fortifying liquid, I wiped my mouth on my sleeve passing the bottle to Vic. He, too, held back his head swilling the soothing milk. Both Connie and Amy took turns finishing off the bottle. As a final jab, I threw the bottle toward the rats shattering it on the wall making them scurry away from the glass.

Pointing ahead, I said, "Let's move, cave people."

As we made our way along the cavern, my sense of bravado soon faded. The walls remained moist, mostly made up of limestone with occasional stalactites and stalagmites. Fortunately, there was still enough height in our cavern to permit upright walking. For that, we were all very grateful wherever our pathway was taking us. I decided to stop and consult my compass once more. Holding up my hand to signal a stop, I knelt lighting up the face of my compass.

"It looks like we're turning steadily toward the east now." The look of concern on my face was not lost on Amy.

"Shouldn't we be trying to head west toward the city? The way we are going now might wind us up in the Delaware River."

"Or worse, Amy," I replied.

"What do you mean?"

"I'm afraid we might be going further down. It's possible we might encounter flooding as we get nearer to the river."

I heard Connie's hoarse voice croaking over my shoulder.

"Did you say flooding? Is this cave going to flood?" she shrieked.

As I turned to reassure her, she started reacting to her fears with anger. Starting to pace, she entered a rant throwing her arms about her head for emphasis.

"That's just great. First, we find dead bodies! Then, we lose our friend in a cave in! Then, we must fight off stinking rats, and now you think we might get flooded out? What the hell's wrong with you people? Why did you ever think of leading us down into this hell hole in the first place? Oh, that's right, let me think. Wasn't it you who wanted to find some Revolutionary War antiques? Have I got that right, Allen? Isn't that about the size of it?" putting her face in mine as she yelled. "Isn't that about the size of it, mister boy scout explorer type?"

I recoiled from her milk breath as Vic grabbed her arm wrestling her away. This was a whole new Connie I was seeing. She no longer was the timid, frightened, half hysterical girl cowering at every shadow. She was now taking a decided turn for the worse. All her pent-up fears were now spewing out at me.

At first, I felt somewhat responsible. It was my idea in the first place. Then righteous indignation overtook me.

"I distinctly recall telling Vic I didn't want you girls having any part of this scheme. Was it not I who tried to stop Amy from coming along? Yet, I was voted down at every turn. That's the way I remember it. How do you remember it, Connie?"

I stood up hanging my compass on my belt turning slowly toward Connie ready to give her a real piece of my mind, when suddenly the sight of something else changed everything.

Right behind Connie's head, the leader of the rat pack we thought we left behind was clinging to the wall. I was amazed at his agility. I had no idea rats could climb vertical walls. Yet, there he was scaling the side of the cavern followed by his friends. I knew then that was how they got around that fire.

There was no time to warn Connie. She was too close. The others must have thought I'd lost my mind after seeing what I did next. Ripping my entrenching tool off my pack, I swung the shovel between Connie and the wall. Missing her head by inches, I slammed into the lead rat's body sending its blood spurting all over Connie's face. Recoiling in horror at the sight of my shovel swinging toward her, she screamed bloody murder. Before she realized what I did for her, she started shouting.

"Are you trying to kill me, you bastard? Vic stop him. He's trying to kill me!"

Vic saw it all. From his perspective, he could see I was protecting her. He took his shovel and started for the wall. Connie shouted encouragement.

"That's right, get him Vic! He's gone nuts; he'll kill us all, if you don't!"

Amy jumped forward pulling Connie backward shouting in her face.

"You've got it dead wrong, Connie. Allen's after the rats. They're right behind you!"

"Don't give me that. I know what I saw. He's trying to kill me," shouted Connie.

Amy just spun her around shouting, "Look, whadda ya see?"

Just then, Vic was slamming one of the dark brown ten inch rats to the floor. I was busy using the knife end of my tool making sure my rats were dead. I could see we were holding the rest of the pack at bay for the moment. Twisting around sharply, I shouted to Amy.

"Run, we'll be right behind you!"

As the girls ran, I stabbed a few more rats as Vic swung wildly at others. Win or lose, I'm sure they sensed a meal either way. Finally, I saw a chance to make a break.

"Run for it, Vic, I think we got enough to keep the rest busy for a while."

"I'm with you, pal."

As the rats busied themselves devouring their fallen comrades, we rushed forward following the girls. Running down the corridor, I felt Vic and I had won that round. At least, we were leaving the rats behind. Yet, as we rounded a curve, we each witnessed a startling event. Both girls' lights suddenly disappeared before our eyes. The earth just swallowed the girls up. Coming to a sudden halt, we each found ourselves hovering breathlessly over the precipice of a huge hole in the floor of the cavern. A hole about six feet around took the place of where the girls were. They were just gone in an instant. Nothing remained but a choking hole filled with dust.

As the dust slowly cleared, I stabbed my light into the darkness below. Vic's light soon joined mine as we frantically searched the pile of debris twenty feet down. I traced the beam of my flashlight across what looked like someone's leg jutting out from the rocks below. Focusing intently, I could just make out Amy's high topped tennis shoe.

"Shine your light next to mine, Vic. I think it's Amy."

His light pierced the darkness joining mine. We were elated to see Amy's shoe and part of her leg sticking out of the rubble.

I cried, "It is her! I think I saw her leg move."

Now, I could see her arm emerge from beneath the pile of rock.

"She's alive, Vic. We've got to get her out of there."

"Where's Connie? I can't see her anywhere, Allen. Get your rope ready. I'm going down to look for her."

"O.K., but be careful of the edges. We don't want to send anymore rock down on them."

Pulling off my pack, I took out the fifty-foot coil of rope. Leaning back against the wall of the cavern bracing myself, I handed the other end of the rope to Vic. He passed it around his chest under each arm, then knotted it securely in front. Then, he backed away toward the opening behind him. Planting his feet on the edge, he allowed one foot to find a hold against the side of the hole. I leaned back against the tension as he lowered himself down the rock wall. In a few moments, he was inside standing near Amy. His voice sounded hollow as he spoke from the bottom of the hole.

"I can see Connie. She seems to be alright. Hey, there's water coming in here. The cave in must have broken something lose. I've got a small stream of water coming out of the wall about two feet up."

Vic found Connie sitting upright with her back to the wall. She had somehow managed to pull herself out from under the rubble. He spoke calmly to her as she sat there shivering in shock.

"It's alright now, Connie. I'm gonna get you out of here. Just stay calm. First, I have to dig Amy out."

Amy must have heard Vic's voice near her as she started trying to free herself from the rocks. Soon, Vic was bending over her lifting rocks off her body casting them aside frantically.

"This hole's starting to fill up. I gotta get you girls outta here quick. Can you stand up, Connie?"

"Yes, I think so, but my ankle's twisted bad, Vic."

"You'll just have to do it, Connie. I must help Amy right now. Get over here to the rope and I'll tie you to it in a minute."

Amy was moving on her own now that Vic had lightened the load of rock pressing on her. She could feel the cool water soaking into her clothes as it seeped up underneath her. Vic could see why she couldn't help herself now. Her left arm lay back underneath her at a crazy angle. Clearly, it was broken. With her good arm, she continued extricating herself with Vic's help. Vic leaned over close to her face. He could see her grimacing through mud caked lips. He spoke slowly with a deliberate tone.

"I'm going to have to move you, Amy. It's going to hurt, but I have to get you out before the water gets any higher."

By now, the small stream had widened, sending a steady stream of water filling the bottom of the hole. Vic told Amy to take a deep breath. Then he placed his arms under hers, lifting as gently as he could. Amy gritted her teeth as she could then let out a scream that resonated in Vic's ear.

"I've got to get you against the wall, Amy. I need you to stand for me."

Amy bravely cradled her broken arm and with Vic's help struggled to stand up. Breathing heavily, she made her way to Connie leaning against her. Now Vic moved to Connie's side placing the rope around her. She looked at Vic with her mud streaked face showing obvious strain.

"Take Amy first, she's hurt worse than me."

Vic looked at Connie. His eyes told her to go, but he relented to her logic feeding the rope carefully under Amy's arms first. He knew the pain would be much worse when Allen started pulling her up. He reached back pulling a handkerchief from his pocket. Folding it twice, he told her to open her mouth.

"Here, bite down on this. It will help some."

I looked on helplessly from the edge of the hole as she did so. Vic finished knotting her harness then shouted up to me.

"She's ready to come up. Just take it easy. Her arm is broken."

I started pulling with all my strength. It was very difficult at first with Amy's dead weight. Eventually, Amy could get her feet against the rock, then, push herself away as I pulled up. Her arm was broken just below the elbow across the radius and ulna. For the most part, it was completely useless. The pain was so severe, I'm sure she felt near to passing out. By the time I got her to the edge of the hole, she slid into my arms sinking mercifully into oblivion.

In the meantime, the bottom of the hole filled to Connie's knees. Hurriedly, I untied the rope from Amy and threw it down to Vic. Soon, he was sending her on her way.

"Try using your feet along the wall to help Allen pull you up. Now go."

Once again, I braced myself for the long pull up out of the hole. As I did, I caught a glimpse of the rats coming for Amy. One was already sniffing at her bleeding arm. Others were on the way. With my hands on the rope with Connie below, I had little choice but to continue pulling. When Connie finally did crawl over the edge, I felt my arm muscles starting to tighten up. Drenched in sweat, I could feel my strength ebbing away. It was then I saw Connie acting selflessly, literally grabbing the rats on Amy's body and tossing them aside like they were dirty laundry. Reaching down deep within me, I summoned the last of my strength. I knew I must concentrate on Vic now and leave Connie to her gruesome work. Vic was in chest deep water now, and it kept rising under him. Another glance at Amy, Connie, and the rats gave me the renewal of strength I needed to pull Vic up out of the hole.

Vic summed up their dilemma in one breathless sentence.

"It's all downhill from here, isn't it?"

I said, "That's what worries me. If we go forward, the water could catch up to us. If we go back, we got rats and no way out."

Vic looked at the two girls now propped up against the cavern wall. Each of them was muddy, wet, and shivering with pain.

Vic asked, "How are we going to get along with these two?"

I truly felt despair sinking in at that moment. Everything I tried so far had turned to crap. Out of sheer desperation, I made my final assessment of the situation.

"We must go forward. I see no other way. What do you think?"

"I guess you're right for now. Only *I* wanna vote on what we do next."

"I promise you, Vic, I'll get us out of here some way."

Inevitably, I ended up placing Amy over my back in a fireman's carry while Vic helped Connie limp forward. With Connie and Vic holding the flashlights, we made our way into the blackness ahead. I was grateful the roof of the cavern was high enough for me to carry Amy this way. I just prayed it would stay that way until we could put some distance between the rats and the rising water.

Fate must have smiled on us all when ahead we beheld our lights reflecting off a divide in the tunnel. Ahead of us there was, what I considered, a blessed choice.

"Vic, we can either take the new path or stick with this one. The way I see it, the one off to the right seems headed more west. I believe that's the one we want. Don't you think so?"

Vic said, grinning "Is this where I get to vote?"

I smiled "It sure is, ole' buddy. Now's the time, Vic."

"I say we take it. It may be a little narrower, but it sure isn't going downhill."

Connie chimed in, "What about me? Don't I get a say?"

Vic pushed her hair back from her eyes kissing her on the cheek.

"Sure, you do, baby. You've earned a say in this. Just don't take too long making up your mind."

Connie smiled bravely. "I guess you guys think I've been a real pain in the ass so far."

"Oh, I wouldn't say that. What you did back there for Amy took real courage."

Connie replied, "She would have done the same for me, you know. I apologize for flying off the handle back there, Allen."

I grunted under Amy's weight.

"Apology accepted. Now would you care to tell us what your vote is?"

Connie appeared contemplative, then replied, "I say we go to the right."

"Good, now for Amy's sake, you won't mind if I allow her to abstain, now do you?"

Trying to sound intelligent, Connie replied, "All things considered, I don't mind at all."

"Then, to the right we go." I said.

After moving sluggishly through the new tunnel for about two hundred yards, it began to narrow. Soon it was about three feet in width, and I was inadvertently bumping Amy's feet into the walls. After a few hundred yards of that treatment, Amy came to. I was so exhausted we decided to call a halt.

"I need to rest and look at my compass."

Vic offered, "Do you want me to carry her for a while?"

"Not just yet, but I do need a break. Speaking of which, we must try and set Amy's arm. We can't just leave it that way."

Vic replied, "I understand, but what are we going to set it with?"

I stopped and lay Amy down gently. She was breathing heavily. I wished I had something for her pain. She lay on the ground looking glassy eyed as I inspected her arm closely with my flashlight.

"I'll have to use my entrenching tool to splint her arm. That leaves us with just one, but it's all I have that will do the job. Get me that spool of string and your handkerchief. I'll have to make do with what we've got."

I knelt forward speaking softly to Amy.

"Amy, honey, we must put a splint on your arm before we go any further. Do you think you're ready to handle it now?"

She just nodded, accepting the situation resolutely. I leaned closer whispering in her ear.

"Oh, Amy, I wish it was me instead of you. I must make you hurt to help you get better. Please understand I wouldn't do anything to cause you pain if I could help it. Please forgive me. You're so strong. I really admire your grit. I must do this now, honey."

She took her good arm and placed it around my neck and ran her fingers through my hair for a moment. Then, she sighed heavily and whispered.

"It's alright. I know you love me and don't want to hurt me. I love you, now, just as much. Go ahead and do it."

She closed her eyes preparing for what was to come. Feeling awkward, I turned to Connie.

"Connie, I'm going to have to ask for your bra."

"Amy has to have something elastic wrapped around her splint to stabilize it. If I can't immobilize the break, she'll only be in more agony when it shifts. Do you understand?"

Vic gave me a dumbfounded look, then turned to Connie.

"It'll be all right, honey. Do it for Amy's sake."

Connie nodded affirmatively in silence. She then turned walking into the darkness for a moment returning with her bra in hand. She stretched out her arm handing it to me.

"Here, is there anything else I can do for her?"

"Just hold her hand while I take care of the rest."

Vic stepped forward handing his comb to me.

"Here let her bite down on this. It might help."

Now the rest was up to me. Slowly, I pulled back the sleeve on Amy's arm. I knew I was hurting her even then, but I had to force myself to keep going. I laid out a small towel I had in my pack on her thigh. Taking the arm up as gently as possible, I pulled steadily at the wrist and forearm until the bones were as straight as I could make them. By now, Amy's head was shaking back and forth in a rigid shiver. Beads of sweat formed on her brow dripping down each side of her face. She bit the comb nearly in half. I kept wishing she would pass out as I cursed the filthy conditions I had to work in. By the time Vic started wrapping the towel tightly around the break site, she did finally succumb drifting into unconsciousness.

Awash in a sense of relief, I deftly started binding her arm to the shovel handle with the bra. Then, I laid the handkerchief over that and proceeded wrapping the string tightly around the entire splint. The last thing I did was secure the split alongside her knee to hold the arm in place. Looking down at my handy work, Vic nodded his approval.

"I think you did a hell of a job, Doc."

As I rose, I felt light headed. I didn't realize how much I had been sweating. Connie had been wiping the sweat from my face with her scarf until it was soaked. I must admit the whole job did look sturdy. The handle of the tool formed a point to tie in around her hand and knee and the shovel portion formed a shield outside of her upper arm.

Connie smiled, "You were wonderful, Allen. You did a great job."

I did not think I could feel such a sense of pride in the crude work I had done, yet I really did at that moment. Glancing at my watch, I noted it was 4 a.m. It startled me to think we had been underground so long.

"Do you guys know we've been down here for over twenty hours? It's no wonder we're exhausted. We need to get some rest. I suggest we stop right here and try to sleep. I know Amy needs the rest. I'm sure all of us could stand some."

I could see Vic was ready.

"Why don't we leave Amy undisturbed and Connie and I can prop up against the wall here at her feet. That way you can sleep near her head in case she wakes up, Allen."

"It sounds good to me," I said.

Connie worried, "What if the rats come?"

Vic assured, "I've still got my entrenching tool with my knife attached. If anything crawls on me, I'll know it before you do. Just stay near Amy's side."

"You know I've been thinking. Rats are nocturnal; they live in burrows and come out when humans are normally asleep. It won't be much longer before they will be sleeping wherever they are."

Vic mumbled, "Yeah, that sounds about right."

It was the last I heard from either of them until I awoke seven hours later. We all succumbed to the sleep we had been deprived of until around eleven a.m. I awoke with a start not quite knowing why all was dark around me. Then reality slowly crept back along with my consciousness. *"Yes, we all were in a cavern somewhere beneath Philly."*

My first instinct was to see to Amy. Turning my flashlight on, I ran the beam of light up and down her splinted arm. Everything seemed well. Thankfully, the skin was not broken with the break and she managed to sleep throughout our time there. I knew if we could manage to keep the arm immobile, the swelling should go down with little risk of infection. That was a consoling thought as I knew there was nothing in our first aid kit that could really do much good if the arm were infected.

My thoughts turned toward our chances of survival in the underground maze. *"How much longer would our food and drink hold out?"* I decided to wake the others and take an inventory of just what we did have amongst us for the duration of our interment. Reaching over Amy, I jostled Vic awake.

"Vic, wake up. It's time we got going again."

He was slow to awaken. I could see from the expression on his face, he, too, struggled with his reemergence into the strange surroundings. When he was alert, he woke Connie. She immediately wanted to relieve herself and limped further into the darkness for privacy. It occurred to me Amy would need assistance in doing the same. I waited until Connie returned before waking Amy. I discreetly suggested Connie help Amy with her needs and they both limped away. Connie supported her on the way back. I could see a faint smile on Amy's face. Just that alone was enough to keep me going. I couldn't help but admire her. She never complained. She just took things head on.

Once we were together again, I suggested we take stock of our supplies. Everyone opened their backpacks fishing around for what was left. To our surprise, Connie produced a one pound can of Maxwell House coffee from her pack. Then, she laid out two flattened Baby Ruth bars, a large comb, and two peanut butter and jelly sandwiches. Vic looked on in amazement.

"Well, you're just full of surprises, aren't you? Where's your coffee pot, doll?"

Before she could respond, I quickly interceded knowing this was no time for sarcasm.

"Don't worry, Connie, we'll make use of that coffee, you'll see."

Connie sat stone faced arms folded across her chest glaring at Vic. In the meantime, I counted the rest of our loot. In all, there were two six packs of Eveready batteries, one ham and cheese sandwich, two packs of Charms candy, two boxes of Chiclets gum, one carton of Mott's Apple Juice, and two cans of fruit cake out of a C-ration box. There was also a p-38 G.I. can opener that came from the same box.

"Well that's it. This is what we must live on for I don't know how long. I do know this; we're going to have to start rationing this stuff if we want it to last. I say we divide it in two packs. One goes with me and the other with Vic."

Connie asked, "How come it goes with you guys?"

Vic antagonized, "Because, Connie, us guys are gonna need it to throw at the rats."

Connie's eyes narrowed as she cocked her head addressing Vic.

"Look buster, all I did was ask a question. Why you gotta always take everything out on me?"

Amy spoke out, "That's fine. You two just fight it out, as if we don't have enough to deal with already."

Connie shot back.

"Well, it's true. I just wanted to know why the guys carry the stuff, that's all."

Now it was my turn.

"Look, Connie, it just makes sense. We can carry the weight so you don't have to. Besides, what if something happened to one of us? I just think it would be best not to put all our stuff in one bag."

Connie conceded, "O.K., I guess that's kind of a good idea."

Vic interjected, "That's right, sweetheart. So, that's why we thought of it."

I decided it was a good time to suggest we have something to eat rather than gnaw at each other.

"What do you say we all settle down and have something to eat? Then, we'll all feel better. We can discuss what our next move will be, o.k.?"

Everyone seemed ready to call a truce, so I sat down and divided a Charms pack among us. Then, we all shared the apple juice knowing it was the last liquid we would be having unless we encountered water again. I told everyone I thought it best we kept track of the time. That way, we would know when to stop each day and sleep while the rats were inactive. Vic agreed we should take turns on watch with the girls sleeping in the middle. Our plan was set. We had some nourishment so all that remained was to keep us falling forward, as it were. Amy persevered despite her hardship, and we continued up the tunnel which remained three to four feet wide.

Close to noon Amy stopped, saying her arm was throbbing so much she felt like she needed a rest. I checked it over for signs of swelling. It didn't look all that bad. At least, it still was not seem infected. I recommended she wear a sling to keep her arm more elevated. She agreed, so I fashioned one out of my tee shirt which seemed to do the job. After several readings of my compass, I determined we were now heading in a southwesterly direction. This was a distinct improvement over our last course. I figured the branch we took off the main tunnel earlier must have been a tributary at one point in time. Not knowing its source, we would just have to be content with traveling in a good general direction for the time being.

Chapter 8

We traveled southwest for several hours without seeing as much as a rat. Amy walked directly behind me with Vic and Connie bringing up the rear. Connie was walking more slowly now because of her sprained ankle. She was slowing our pace more than I wished. Just then, Amy started speaking to me as we walked. If I guessed correctly, she was trying to keep her mind off the constant throbbing in her arm.

"Do you think we'll have enough to see us out of here, Allen?"

"Sure, I do. I have faith in all of us to see this thing through."

"I mean food, Allen. Do you think we'll have enough to last until we find a way out?"

"I think we have what it takes either way, Amy."

Just then it occurred to me. I might be able to inspire the others with a story of survival I read about in *Life Magazine.*

"You know I saw in *Life Magazine* the Air Force investigated a bomber that crashed in the desert back in WWII. The plane wasn't found for sixteen years. It was lost in the Sahara Desert after its crew bailed out. When the investigators pieced it all together, they found the missing crew. They had all tried walking back to base, but were way too far into the desert to make it. Anyway, they learned the crew of nine had only half canteen of water and a ham and cheese sandwich among them. With that little bit of food and water, they lasted a week according to the diaries they kept. In that time, they marched one hundred and forty miles across the scorching Sahara. Just imagine, temperatures there go from 130 degrees in the day to near freezing at night. Yet, they made it that far. Just think of it."

Vic retorted, "Is that supposed to make us all feel better about ourselves, hearing about nine dead guys in the desert?"

"Of course not, but don't you see, we have it a heck of a lot easier than they did. Sure, they died, but look how far they got under those conditions. We're not freezing or sweating right now, are we? The temperature is steady down here. I mean I'm not sayin' we're livin' the life of Riley here, but we sure got it better than they did."

Amy chimed in, "We have a lot more food than they did, too."

Vic sneered, "Yeah, I could sure go for a big bite of that coffee right about now."

"Oh, think about it, Vic," I said. "They made it a hundred and forty *miles*. How big do you think Philadelphia *is*?"

Vic replied, "I don't know for sure, but this part is too big for me. Maybe I should take the next trolley that comes along. What do you think, Connie? Do you wanna take the trolley with me?"

"I just wanna take a break, Vic. My ankle is killing me."

Although, my efforts to boost morale seemed not good at the time, a rest did seem good. So, I suggested we stop for a while. Once we got settled in, I sat with my back to the wall staring blankly out in front of me. I do not know why, but I flicked on my flashlight scanning the opposite wall. Immediately, I could see there was something different about the texture of the wall. It was dry and crumbling along a straight line about four feet up. Curiously, the surface of the wall was indented in the form of a long rectangle. Amy noted my curiosity as I flashed my light all around the perimeter of the area in question.

"What is it, Allen? What do you see?"

Suddenly she gasped, spinning around to see what I was looking at.

"Is it the rats?" she cried.

Now Connie cringed closer clinging to Vic as he snapped on his light to see.

"Whata ya got there, Allen?"

I answered pensively.

"I don't know quite yet. I need to get a closer look."

Realizing it was not the threat of rats, Amy resumed her position of repose.

"Thank goodness," she sighed. "I thought it was those filthy, stinking rats again."

"No, Amy, I said as I examined the wall. "This is something quite different, and I'm certain it does not bite."

I brought my light to focus point blank on the part of the wall I was interested in.

"Vic, shine your light over here, too. I think we got something."

As I looked at the crumbling spot on the wall, I gingerly rubbed my hand over its surface. Immediately the wall fell away where I brushed against it. I rubbed harder finding the surface was giving way in large pieces now. Slowly and deliberately I pulled away at the pieces of wall until I forced an opening about a foot square. To my surprise behind the wall there was a smooth layer of solid wood. At least, the surface seemed solid, but I could also tell it was dry rotted. It was man-made. There was a layer of wood behind the wall of the tunnel we were in. It seemed to be running parallel behind the wall.

"What is it, Allen? What do you see?"

"It's a board. It's a wooden surface behind the wall."

"Vic hand me your entrenching tool. Stand back Amy. I don't know what might happen when I give this board a whack."

Connie cried out, "Don't make it cave in on us, Allen!"

"Calm down! I'm not going to hit it that hard."

I took the point of the shovel and poked at the center of the board. Nothing happened at first. After using a little more force, a large crack in the board appeared. Then, with a few more stabs, I managed to break a hole through the board. After enlarging the hole with my tool, I slid my flashlight in peering into the void. What I saw was so unexpected I almost jumped.

There inside was a length of pipe attached to wood running along the opposite side. It was about two inches in diameter covered in rust and bolted to the side of the wall. I determined the pipe was running through a box like structure which was probably five feet square. Clearly, it was large enough for a man to stoop and walk through. I turned to Vic.

"Come here and look. Tell me what you think you see."

Vic complied coming closer. Using his light, he peered inside. He remained silent for a moment then pulled his head back slowly.

"What I see is some rusty pipe running through an underground box."

"That's exactly what I saw. Do you know what I think that is?"

"No, but I'm sure you're about to tell me."

"I think it's an old gas line. From the looks of it, I'd say it was probably put in around the turn of the century or earlier. Unless I've missed my guess, we've uncovered an old gas line. The box around it is supposed to keep it dry.

Vic asked, "Why is the box so big?"

"That's probably because they needed to make it large enough for a man to access the line if repairs were necessary."

"Do you think the line still has gas in it?"

"Oh no, I doubt that very much. This line is so old it was probably used for lighting street lamps."

Suddenly, I realized what I had stumbled on to. Vic could see my eyes widen in the beam of his flashlight.

"Vic, if this *is* a street light gas line, then, do you know what we've found?"

Before he could answer I blurted out.

"We're near a street!"

Amy opened her eyes in surprise.

"What did you say? Did I hear street?"

I knelt giving her a hug being careful not to squeeze her broken arm.

"Yes, my dear, you heard right. There's probably a street above. I know they don't use gas light anymore, but it means we have a straight path to follow into the old part of the city. I'm going to open this wall up until I can crawl inside. I wanna see how far this thing goes. It's got to go where they had a source of gas once. That means buildings, plumbing, and possibly a way out. Do you see what this means?"

Vic said, "I'm sure you're gonna want to vote on this right?"

I didn't stop to answer. I was too busy chipping away at the rest of the boards.

Connie asked, "What happens if we get in that box thing and it caves in on us?"

Vic had to concede. For once, she did have a point.

"Yeah, Allen, what if it falls in on us? You know that wood is pretty rotten."

I stopped banging away at the boards long enough to catch my breath addressing his concern.

"Look, Vic, this structure has been around for a long time. It's well built. I'm sure it can handle a few people crawling through it. This thing was built for people to crawl in and maintain it."

Amy spoke out, "I don't know, Allen, it does look pretty rotten."

"Not you, too. I thought at least you would see the logic here. This boarded passage could lead us to a bigger building. You know, this could be our best chance at getting out. The tunnel we're in now has no chance of meeting up with man-made structures. It wouldn't even exist if it weren't for some creek that was dammed up long ago. The tunnel we're in now is just a remnant of an underground watershed. The best it can do is lead back to more water, eventually."

Vic countered, "Then why did you choose to take it in the first place?"

"I didn't, by myself. We voted on it, remember? I just figured it was the best shot we had. Now that we have this way to go, we don't have to meander along wherever the tunnel leads us. This is a sure thing. It's going in a straight line. It's man-made, so it should lead us to other things man-made. Or, maybe it didn't dawn on you by now, that we might need a man-made way outta this mess."

"Vic retorted, "Yeah, well, I ain't so sure about all that. I say we vote on this right now."

Connie echoed, "Yeah, let's vote on it, Allen."

I shot a glance at Amy to see if she picked up on my logic. I already knew how the vote would go with Vic and Connie. Amy seemed to be mulling things over before she made up her mind.

"I say we give it a try. It just might lead us into the old part of town."

Vic groused, "Yeah, good mites are on chickens. I'm gonna need more convincing."

"Alright," I said. "I say you guys take your break right here while I go in and check this thing out. If it looks like it will hold up, I'll come back and get you."

Vic appeared to be lost in confusion at my suggestion. He was not being asked to take any risk, yet he still knew he did not like the idea. While he considered my proposal, I went on with my work opening a hole big enough to crawl through. When I finished, I laid down the small shovel.

"Well, what's it gonna be? Do you want me to do some exploring for you?"

Vic conceded, "Go ahead, take your walk. I'll stay here and take care of the girls."

Amy reached up tugging at my sleeve.

"Do be careful, Allen. We can't afford to lose you. You've gotten us this far. We're counting on you."

Vic retorted, "Say, what does that make me, chopped liver?"

I just stepped into the hole leaving them behind in the tunnel.

"I'll be back for some of that chopped liver, Vic."

Vic shot back, "Yeah, you're too funny pal, you're killing me here."

Once I entered the box-like structure, it was obvious I would have to hunch down to make any forward progress. I followed the pipeline along for at least two hundred yards until I encountered a maintenance access way. It was like a small manhole with a ladder leading upwards, I presumed to street level. Taking my time, I gingerly stepped on the old wooden steps making my way up. It was not long before I reached a disappointing conclusion. From the looks of things, this passage was sealed a long time ago presumably since the old coal fired gas line was shut down.

The cover over the passage was akin to a modern manhole cover that was welded shut. Although, I tried poking and prying at it with my small shovel, it was to no avail. It was securely sealed and for good reason. This gas line was replaced around the turn of the century when safer sources of gas production became part of Philadelphia's technology. It was immediately depressing to know the way out was sealed. Yet, I still had faith in the line leading us due west. At least, it was a means of traveling under the streets of Philly with assurance of our direction. I still held out hope it might lead us to a pumping station where we might break free from our dark underworld. Deciding to turn back, I planned on arguing for taking the path westward under the city. When I got near the others, I could hear them debating about whether to continue in the tunnel or try the gas line. I emerged with a determined look.

"I could hear you talking down the line. It's weird how far sound travels down there. I think you all should hear me out on this."

"We have been meandering along down here without a glimpse of a way out for over thirty hours now. This line leading due west is our best shot at finding a way. You know how I feel about it. The chance of finding a pumping station or some housing where this line ends is greater than just crawling up out of the ground somewhere."

Vic observed, "I know, you think something man-made will lead us out. What about it, Connie, are you ready to give something else a try?"

Connie demurred leaving it up to Vic.

Amy added, "Well, that's it then. We'll move on down the line."

I hesitated to slow their momentum since it was my idea in the first place, yet I felt it best to tell them first about the sealed manhole.

"Guys there are some things you should know before we go."

Now both Vic and Connie were staring at me with arms folded.

Vic urged, "Alright, out with it Allen. What's the catch?"

I explained, "I went down the line about two hundred yards and found a maintenance entry way. It's sort of like a manhole with a ladder leading up."

Immediately, I could see looks of jubilation start to appear. I hated to crush their hopes, so I quickly followed up.

"The manhole was welded shut. It probably was done some time ago judging from the rust on the cover."

Clinging to some silver lining, Vic refused reality.

"Maybe the rust will make the welds weaker. Did you try breaking out?"

"Yes, Vic, I gave it my best shot."

"It might just take the two of us. That might make all the difference."

It's worth a try Vic. It's just I don't want you to get your hopes up."

"Let's go then, we can't move mountains by talking."

"That's the spirit, Vic. We'll give it our best shot."

We made our way down the line stooping sometimes groping our way along. We found the air in the passage very stale and tainted with the smell of coal tar. Naturally, the coal gasification left a residue in the aging, rusty line that seeped a residual scent even after years of disuse.

Now Amy expressed another concern about our new course of action.

"Allen, what if we find a pumping station, or something like you said, and it, too, is sealed. Are we going to have to double back all the way to where we started?"

I tried to sound reassuring.

"I gave that some thought myself."

"If it comes to that, maybe we can find some way of breaking out of this box near one of those maintenance stations in another direction. There might be a different way to gain access to the upper level. As for now, I think we should give this a try since it takes less energy."

Vic broke in, "That reminds me. Shouldn't we be taking a little lunch break about now?"

"Yeah, I guess so." I replied. "It must be a short one though."

Vic forced a chuckle, "Yeah, it will be sort of a box lunch."

Amy quipped, "Very puny, Vic."

I asked Amy, "Is that even a word?"

"Oh, I don't know, Allen. I think we're all getting a little light headed down here, don't you?"

I answered in a more serious vein.

"Speaking of light, my flashlight is starting to dim out. How is yours holding up?"

"Mine seems to be o.k. I've tried keeping it turned off as much as possible," said Amy.

Vic volunteered, "Mine seems a little dimmer, too. What about yours, Connie?

"I don't know. It's in my backpack."

Vic waited patiently for her to take it out and check.

"It seems to be O.K.," she reported.

I suggested, "Vic, I think it's best we change our batteries out for new ones before we lose light all together.

"Yeah, you're right, Allen. Let's stop for a while."

Vic and I were carrying the new packs of batteries between us and changed them out before sharing a meager evening meal with the girls.

This time our dinner consisted of two Charms candies each and the last portion of the ham and cheese sandwich. Because we had little liquid, I recommended we all chew one Chiclets for dessert.

Vic remarked, "That was delightful. Now, could you pass the Jell-O, please? There's always room for Jell-O."

I chided, "There's no sense in making things worse, Vic. It's five-thirty. Let's keep our cool and start walking."

As we moved on stooping in single file, I couldn't push the gnawing thought from my mind.

"We've been gone almost thirty hours now. We can't last much more than three days without water. What then?"

I started to talk about anything just to get my mind off the brutal reality we faced ahead.

"You know, I noticed the numbers on these maintenance stations are getting smaller as we go. I think that means we could come to the end of this line before too much longer."

For the first time, I got sarcasm from Amy.

"Oh really, that's funny. I seem to recall the last station number was #113. Now, let me see if I can do the math right."

Pausing for a minute she made the calculations in her head.

"That would mean at our current rate of about one mile an hour, with each station two hundred yards apart, we should zip right up to old #1 in, oh, say roughly a mere thirteen hours. That is, if we never stop walking, our backs hold up under the strain, and, of course, it goes without saying, we don't eat, drink, or sleep."

To praise her, I congratulated her on the math computation.

"Gee, that's pretty good math work considering you did all that in your head."

She replied snidely, "In case you've forgotten, I was an accounting clerk for the Cross Brothers' Slaughter House. I'm sure you remember that little place we left behind for a treasure hunt in the stinking bowels of the city."

I replied to her remarks good naturedly.

"Do I detect a whiff of mutiny amongst the crew?"

"So, sorry, Captain," she replied testily. "I'll try to keep it down to a mild uproar back here."

At that, I stopped abruptly turning to face her. Searching her eyes, I sought for some clue as to what was causing her contentiousness. Her eyes met mine with an intense willful stare. Her pupils were dilated, even for the dim light of the box we were in.

With sympathy, I asked, "Are you alright, honey?"

She retorted boldly, "No, I'm not alright. My arm hurts like hell, my back hurts, I'm hungry, were lost, and there's nothing you can do about it."

"I'm so sorry, honey. Let's stop and rest. I want to look at that arm."

"O.K., if you must. I suppose so. But, there's nothing you can do for me unless you knock me over the head and put me out of my misery."

I cajoled, "Just humor me a minute. Let me have a look."

She soon relented and sat down with her back against the wooden wall while I gently probed her arm under the split. She winced through clenched teeth as soon as I touched where the break occurred.

"It looks like the swelling has increased. We should stop awhile and let you rest."

Amy moaned, "At this rate, we'll never get out of here. Maybe you should go ahead without me?"

I scolded, "Don't you ever say anything like that again! Do you hear me?"

"You're a strong woman, and you'll make it out just like the rest of us, and that's final."

Hearing me speak sternly, Connie came to her side to comfort her friend.

"I know it hurts, baby. I sure wish there was something I could do for your pain."

Suddenly, Connie's mouth dropped open as a shocked look of surprise flushed over her face.

"Oh, my God, I completely forgot!" she said. Connie raised her hands to her face. "I have a bottle of aspirin in a pouch inside my pack."

I heard myself shouting as I nearly lost control.

"You what... you have aspirin, and you didn't bother to tell us!

"Well, I'm sorry. I forgot until just now."

Still incredulous, I tried lowering my voice, but it just was not working.

"We took everything out and counted what we had. How could you miss that?"

Now Connie was getting flustered.

"It was in a side pocket of my pack. I didn't see it. So, I forgot."

She began to whimper holding her head in her hands repeating how sorry she was to Amy. I just stepped up to her tugging on her pack strap demanding the aspirin.

"Alright, let's have it right now, Connie."

Vic countered, "Leave her alone, damn it! She said she was sorry. I'll help her get her pack off. You just leave her be."

By then, I had my anger under control at least enough to start feeling good for Amy. I knew the aspirin would not only help with the pain, but would also reduce the swelling. Amy just sat looking dumbfounded at Connie's recent revelation as Vic produced the vital bottle.

Connie knelt beside Amy speaking softly.

She asked soothingly, "How many do you want to take, hon?"

Amy looked at the bottle thoughtfully.

She answered, "I'll start with six, please."

I flinched at such a large dose. Then reasoned, I was not the one with a broken arm.

Amy wondered, "How am I going to take these? I don't have anything to wash them down with."

I said, "You'll just have to chew them up, honey."

She shrugged her shoulders resigned to tossing them into her mouth.

Just then, I reached out quickly stopping her.

"Wait, I've got an idea! Do you remember when you were a kid your mom would give you Asper gum for sore throats? Well, that's what you're going to get now. That is, if the others vote to let you have their share of the gum."

I looked up expectantly at Vic and Connie.

Vic generously said, "Sure, no problem. Right, Connie?"

She quickly nodded her approval as I gave Amy four Chiclets, the entire contents of our first box. Feeling happy for Amy, I chuckled.

"I suggest you start with the gum first."

It was late Monday evening and my mother looked worried. She sat alone in the kitchen looking up at her black and white *Felix the Cat* clock watching its eyes shift to and fro above its shifting tail moving in sync with the sweep hand. The cat clock was a gift from Dad. He'd won it in a raffle at a local bar. She truly hated it from the start, but after he died she could not bring herself to take it down. Now, it hung there with its goofy, leering smile mocking her with its eyes and tail through the long, lonely hours.

Usually, when Allen told his mother he would be home at a certain time, he was true to his word. Tonight was an exception. She mulled over the words she remembered him saying searching for a discrepancy in what she understood him to say. She recalled Allen telling her that Vic Rubio and Steve Agresta from 'the house' were going with him to Ocean City for the weekend to celebrate graduation. It was now ten until twelve Monday night, and Allen still wasn't there.

Allen's mom thought, *"If he did manage to make it to work, he probably didn't get enough sleep to make it through the day."*

Grandmother entered the kitchen interrupting her thoughts.

"Where in heaven's name could that boy be?" she asked.

She watched Betty look up with worry lines creasing her face.

"I just don't understand it, Mother; he's never pulled this before. You don't suppose he had to work late, do you?"

Grandma replied, "I think he would have called by now, don't you? He probably made it in late because he was making the most of his fun with the boys. You know how that can be."

"Yes, I'm afraid I do. He's such a responsible boy, though. You know he's never given us any trouble before. Oh, little things, I know, but he was just a boy then. He's nearly a man now graduated and all with a man's job. I must admit, I do worry about him losing that job. I know that sounds selfish of me, but with Bill gone we just can't afford to lose his help right now."

Grandma patted her hand upon her shoulder trying to console her.

"Why don't you let me make you a warm glass of milk? Then, maybe you can come to bed soon. How does that sound?"

Betty reluctantly agreed.

"Oh, alright then, Mother. I suppose so. If he's not home first thing tomorrow, though, I'm calling the other boys' homes, and if that doesn't help, I'm calling the police."

Grandma did not answer. She only put her hand to her mouth in dismay.

Morning came. Before Mom could make her call the phone rang. It was Amy's mother. Already the plan the girls made about staying at each other's homes for the weekend was unraveling.

"Mrs. Williams, this is Donna Martin, Amy's mother."

Mom could tell how anxious her voice sounded fearing the worst.

"Please call me Betty."

Donna went on, "Yes, well, Betty, I'm calling about Amy. Have you seen her lately?"

"Why, no, I haven't. Has she been gone long? I mean I have been wondering about my own son. He's not come home from work."

"I see," Donna said, sounding more distraught than ever.

"So, you haven't seen your boy or my girl at all?"

"That's right, Donna."

Betty pressed the phone closer to her ear empathizing with a sense of concern only a mother could feel.

"My boy, Allen, went with his friends Vic and Steve to Ocean City for the weekend.

They left very early Saturday morning. They were all supposed to be at work on Monday by 3 p.m. I haven't seen Allen since he left. I'm so worried."

Donna was gripping the phone now as her mind raced ahead sorting out the possibilities.

"My daughter told me she was going to spend the weekend with her friend, Connie Warren. Yet, when I called there her mother got upset because Connie told her she was staying with Amy."

Still sensitive to Donna's feelings, Mom could not help but confide in her that she and Connie's mother had been bamboozled.

Donna also confided, "I can't believe I didn't check with Connie's mother before Amy left. I just felt like I could trust Amy. She's been through a lot lately after losing her father and having to come home from college. I just wanted her to have a little fun for a while. God knows she deserves it. She's been working so hard to help the family. Now, I feel like such a fool."

Betty could hear Donna starting to cry on the phone. She waited a decent interval allowing her to pull herself together. Then, Mom spoke cautiously.

"Do you suppose she wanted to be with Allen in Ocean City?"

Donna immediately switched from self-effacing sorrow to a mother defending her young.

She spoke emphatically barely containing her emotion on the phone.

"My Amy is not that kind of girl."

Betty backed off quickly realizing how Donna could take affront at such a statement.

"Please, please, Donna, don't be angry with me. I can see how you might take what I said the wrong way. I was only suggesting that both girls might have used their excuse to get away. They could have gotten their own place."

Donna was silent for a moment, until it sunk in.

Sounding apologetic she replied, "I see, so you think the girls cooked up their scheme to get a place at the beach in Ocean City. I must confess; that is a possibility. After all, that way, they could split expenses. Now that

I think about it, no reputable business would rent a room to three boys and two girls...would they?"

"Of course not, Donna. Now honestly, don't you feel just a little bit better about knowing where they might be?"

"Yes, I suppose so, but where are they now? Amy had to report for work this morning. All of them had to work yesterday, didn't they?"

Betty assured, "Yes, of course. So, don't be too concerned just yet. I say we wait a little while longer before we take any action."

"Oh, you can rest assured I'm going to take some action. When that girl gets home, there's going to be a few changes in her lifestyle."

"I know what you mean, Donna. Just stay in touch if you have any developments, alright?"

"Certainly, Betty. It was nice to have you to talk to, thank you. I'm sorry we had to meet on the phone, especially under these circumstances. We must get together sometime. I think we'll find we have a lot in common."

"Yes, we must, Donna. Goodbye."

Mom put the phone down slowly still struggling to quell her feelings of trepidation. Despite her own advice to Donna, she was finding it hard to deal with her son's disappearance. Another two hours dragged on before she decided to call 'the house'. The receptionist took her call.

"Cross Brothers', how can I help you?"

"This is Mrs. Williams. My son Allen works second shift on the line there. I was wondering, could you see if he came to work yesterday. I'm trying to get in touch with him."

"Yes, Mrs. Williams, I can have someone check his time card to see if he punched in yesterday. What is your phone number? I'll call you back after we check."

"Oh, thank you so much. I would appreciate that."

Betty left her number with the secretary, then went into the kitchen to wait. A few minutes later the phone rang.

"Mrs. Williams, this is the receptionist at Cross Brothers'. Your son did not clock in for work on Monday."

The worry lines crept back.

"Oh, I see. Well, thank you very much. Goodbye."

Betty put down the phone. She felt numb as she placed her head in her hands to think. Then it occurred to her, she could call the motel where Allen told her he would be staying.

She wondered, *"What was the name of that motel? He said it was near the beach. Oh yes, the Loggerhead Motel, that's it."*

She picked up the phone hurriedly dialing the operator.

"Yes, operator, I would like to speak to information please in Ocean City, New Jersey. Yes, I'll hold."

Now that she had something to go on, she began feeling a little better. She noted the number the operator gave her and asked her to connect her to the motel.

A man answered, "Loggerhead Motel."

"Yes, are you the manager?"

"Yes, what can I do for you?"

"You don't know me, but my name is Williams. My son, Allen, and his friends stayed the weekend at your motel. Could you check your register and tell me when they checked out?"

"Well, Mrs. Williams, as you say, I don't know you. Normally, I keep my records confidential. I have to respect my customers' privacy, you know."

"But, I'm the boy's mother. I need to know where he is, you see. He hasn't come home, and he's overdue."

"Well, I usually don't give out that information unless it's the police asking."

"I understand, but this is sort of an emergency. Couldn't you just tell me if he was there at all?"

The manger sensed her frustration and reluctantly opened his register.

"Oh, alright, what was his name again?"

"It's Allen Williams. That's spelled A-l-l-e-n- W-i-l-l-i-a-m-s."

"Yes, I'm checking now, Mrs. Williams. No, I don't show any Williams signed in on my register."

Betty's heart sank.

"Are you sure? It would have been for Saturday and Sunday could you look again, please, just to be sure?"

"Look madam, I'm looking right at the book open here in front of me. If there was a mister Allen Williams registered on those days, I'd know it. I was here all weekend."

"Oh, that just can't be. Wait, could you check and see if the room was signed for by one of his friends. Their names are Vic Rubio and Steve Agresta."

There was a short pause on the line. She sensed his patience was wearing thin."

"Please, sir, it's my only hope."

"Alright, I'm checking."

Mom's heart raced in the silence.

"Nope, I'm sorry. I've got nothing under those two names either. Maybe they stayed at another motel instead. There's lots of competition here, you know."

"No, no that's where he told me he would be. Did you have any vacancies over the weekend?"

"Yes, I did as a matter of fact."

The manager could hear her distraught voice trail off as she thanked him and said goodbye. Just as she put the phone down, the bell jangled in her hand. She grabbed the receiver quickly placing it to her ear.

"Hello?"

"Yes, Betty, it's Donna. I just learned from the receptionist at Cross Brothers' that Amy never reported for work Monday."

Mom spoke sadly, "Yes, I figured you might find that out. My Allen never punched in Monday evening."

Donna blurted, "Well, I'm calling the police. Listen, could you call Connie's mother. I tried talking to her on the phone. She's nearly hysterical."

"Alright, but promise me, Donna, you'll call and let me know everything the police say."

"Don't worry, I will. We'll get to the bottom of this, you'll see."

Donna put the phone in its cradle and sat back closing her eyes. She was not sure which pain was worse her headache or the dull gnawing sensation in the pit of her stomach telling her something was very wrong. She went to her girls' bedroom to look in on them. They were sitting on the floor completely absorbed in a board game. She quietly closed their door. Moving down the hallway, she reached her son's room. He was playing with his electric train set again. She also closed his door, then went back to the phone. Taking a deep breath, she sat down, picked it up, and started to dial.

Sergeant Kilpatrick answered on the second ring in a gruff voice, "Police Desk, Sergeant Kilpatrick here."

Donna was surprised she was speaking with a policeman so soon.

She stammered, "Ah… this is Donna Martin, I'd like to report some missing persons."

"Hold on please, I'll transfer you to one of our detectives."

A man in his mid-twenties reached across his coffee cup answering the phone.

"Detective Dodge here, how can I help?"

"Yes, Detective Dodge, I'm Mrs. Donna Martin and I want to report some missing persons."

"Excuse me did you say persons?"

"Yes. I'm calling on behalf of my acquaintance and myself. You see my daughter and her son are missing. There are three others missing as well. That would be two teenage boys and a girl."

His previous look of concern slowly started slipping from his face as he picked up a pencil drumming it idly on his desk.

"Now, let me get this straight. You want to report your daughter's disappearance, as well as your friend's son's disappearance, and three others?"

"Yes, I have all their names if you're ready to take them down."

Donna held the phone with both hands nervously fidgeting with the long cord.

"Ah Mam' …"

"Mrs. Martin," she interrupted.

"Mrs. Martin, how long have these people been missing?"

"Let me see now."

Donna glanced at the clock in the hallway.

"They've been gone about thirty-six hours now."

Detective Bill Dodge slumped in his chair running his hand back over his buzz cut, brown hair looking slightly annoyed.

"Mrs. Martin, we generally prefer waiting at least two days before we take reports on missing persons. Of course, if you have reason to suspect foul play, we can make an exception."

Donna felt a chill racing down her spine. For the first time in her life, she was hearing her daughter being referred to as a missing person.

She stammered, "I ... I really don't know where they were going to the beach together. Wait, I'm sorry that's not right. The three boys said they were suspect. You see, they all said they going to the beach together to celebrate their graduation. My daughter and her friend said they were going to spend the weekend together, yet they didn't because they each told us that's what the other was doing."

Bill started smiling slightly as he began seeing the girls' subterfuge take shape in his mind.

"Yes, Mrs. Martin, I think I understand. Let me suggest, these people are all teenagers and friends, right? Unless I missed my guess, they're all from the same high school, too. Am I right?"

Donna was getting more flustered as she detected his drift.

"Yes, yes, they're all teens, but that doesn't mean they're not missing."

Bill sat up straight in his chair putting his pencil to paper.

"I tell you what, Mrs. Martin, I'll take down your information here, but take my word for it. I think you'll find your daughter and the others will show up as soon as they have had their fun. In my experience, graduation makes a lot of teenagers turn up missing, but it usually doesn't last for long."

Donna retorted indignantly, "Is that the best you can do? Do you expect me to just sit around doing nothing but wish my daughter will come home?"

Bill could tell by her tone she was not about to give up that easily.

"Calm down, Mrs. Martin. Just give me the details and I'll see what I can do."

Donna provided all the routine information she could about the group of missing teenagers. Bill dutifully took down all the answers to his questions on a notepad, then told her he would call the minute he had something. Although she felt somewhat relieved, she suspected the detective was not yet taking the matter seriously.

Feeling hopeless, she sat in the hallway near the phone in case it rang. She began to dwell on all the things that might have happened to her daughter. Suddenly, she felt a strong urge to share her pain with someone who understood. She quickly found the scrap of paper with Betty's number and started dialing. Betty picked up on the first ring. Her desperate voice sounded strained on the phone.

"Hello, William's residence."

"Hello, Betty. It's me, Donna."

Betty's sense of despair suddenly lifted with an air of hope.

"Oh, Donna, I'm so glad it's you. What did you hear from the police?"

Not wishing to alarm her, she attempted sounding unaffected by the detective's apparent apathy.

"I spoke to a Detective Dodge. I gave him all the information I could about our kids and the others. He asked me about their ages, where they worked, and went to school. He asked me when they were last seen. Since the girls probably joined the boys later, I tried to explain about my daughter's little scheme."

Donna hesitated for an instant. Then, she decided to share her inner most feelings.

"I'm afraid I didn't do too good a job convincing him the kids are missing."

Mom asked anxiously, "What do you mean?"

Donna struggled, "Well, I think he believes the kids are playing a prank. He suggested we just wait a while longer to see what happens."

The line fell silent.

Donna offered, "I have his number. You can call him yourself, if you want. Maybe if we both hounded him a little, we might get more action."

The strain in Mom's voice returned.

"I don't think it would help very much. They probably will need more convincing. That can only come with time."

Mom's calm and wise assessment of the situation surprised even her.

Donna suggested, "We should call Vic's and Steve's parents. They must be worried sick."

Mom replied, "I don't know Steve's parents, but I would imagine Vic's mother isn't too concerned. She doesn't exactly keep a close eye on that boy."

"I'll call Steve's parents, if you want to call Vic's." Donna offered.

"Yes, I suppose I should. It's the decent thing to do. Maybe one of them has heard something."

Donna found herself wanting to stay on the phone a little longer not wishing to lose a friend to commiserate with. She confided in Betty.

"Please stay in touch. I need to talk to someone who cares, or I'll just go nuts."

"I understand, dear. I'll be here anytime you want to call, and if I hear something first I'll call you right away."

Donna smiled, "Thank you, Betty. That means a lot to me right now. Goodbye."

Another twenty-four hours passed since Vic's and Steve's parents were contacted by Donna and Betty. At that stage, the parents were successful in convincing the police the matter should be investigated. Consequently, Detective James Ditty was assigned to work the case with Detective Dodge. The two had never worked together before since Detective Dodge was only recently promoted to the detective force. Between them, the two had all of four years' experience as detectives. They began working as partners on the case by interviewing each parent of the missing persons.

It's often said in police work; an initial hunch is hard to shake when a detective sets out to learn the facts. With Detective Bill Dodge, this was no exception. He relentlessly clung to the idea that these were kids perpetrating a hoax. Like a dog with a new bone, he steadfastly examined the facts looking in that direction. On the other hand, his partner's lack of experience led him down too many blind alleys. During the interview with Vic's mother, Detective Ditty discovered Vic garnered a few enemies in the local pool halls. Why he would expand that notion to include others in the group totally escaped his partner, as James pursued this line of questioning.

"Now, Mrs. Rubio, were there other pool halls besides Norm's that Vic frequented?"

"Yes, he went to several, but that is where he went the most."

"What are the names of the other halls?"

Mrs. Rubio was a small woman of Italian descent. She expressed herself best with her hands and dark eyes. Her dress was less than stylish, leaving her with a less than desirable house-wife look about her. Nothing to get excited over, she was a sturdy five-foot woman with jet black hair and ample bosom. She knit her eyebrows concentrating on her every answer to Ditty. Looking up to address him at his six-foot level, she replied.

"He mentioned playing at Kelsey's Bar and Bob's Pool Emporium."

Ditty looked down scribbling on his note pad, frowning as he processed mental images of these so-called establishments.

Ditty completed his initial interviews with all the parents asking all the usual questions about places the missing kids frequented, people they knew well, where they spent their free time, etc. Unfortunately, no clear pattern emerged for Ditty or Dodge. They decided their next move was to interview people they worked with hoping to get a lead from those who saw them together last.

One of the next people they interviewed was Karl Grafton, which, in turn, led them to the name of a fellow worker.

Karl confidently answered Detective Dodge's question.

"The last time I saw those boys together was Thursday night on second shift. I remember clearly 'because that's the week we lost our safety record."

Dodge asked, "How did you lose your safety record?"

"One of my men got careless on the cutting line. He cut off his right thumb."

Dodge winced at the thought. Karl went on sounding genuinely disappointed.

"Yeah, we had eighty-two days going without a single accident before that. I could almost taste that ninety-day bonus ham."

Noting there was little remorse for the injured worker, Dodge continued.

"Did you notice anything unusual about the boys' work habits prior to last Thursday? Did you see them talking together, perhaps planning something?"

"Well, they were all together earlier in the week. I had them straightening out some barrels in our storage room."

"Were they all doing the same job?"

"Yeah, I had them working with one of our forklift operators moving fifty-five gallon drums."

"So, they weren't working alone, there was someone else with them?"

"Yeah, like I said, they were with Barnabus, one of my fork lift drivers."

Dodge inquired, "I wonder if we could we speak with him?"

Karl answered, "Sure… uh, wait a minute, I just remembered, he hasn't been in lately. I think he's been out sick these past two days."

Ditty asked, "What do you mean you think he's out sick? Didn't he call in sick?"

"Well, no. You see, Barnabus doesn't have a phone. Whenever he doesn't come in, we just kinda figure he's been sick, you know."

"Do you have his address," asked Dodge?

"You can check up front with the personnel office. I'm sure they have a record of it." Dodge flipped his note pad shut signaling his partner with a tilt of his head toward the front of 'the house'. "Thank you, Mr. Grafton. You've been most helpful."

Chapter 10

The hope of interviewing Barnabus Kurt Jenkins slipped away like a rope of sand when the two detectives arrived at Mildred Shuck's front door. The old woman appeared more than a little distraught when she shared the state of her renter's condition.

"I think he's dead."

Even for such inexperienced detectives, the odor wafting from the back room of her home was unmistakable. Resisting his initial desire to head for the car and call it in, Detective Dodge asked Mildred if they could enter.

"Certainly, gentlemen, it's too warm to be standing out there. Do come in."

Detective Ditty asked, "Is his room back that way?"

Dodge thought grimly, *"Just follow your nose, partner."*

A few steps closer and both men produced their handkerchiefs covering their noses as they approached the back of the house. There was only one door between the back room and the rest of the house. Dodge found the door locked.

Dodge asked, "Excuse me, Mrs. Schuck, do you have a key to this door?"

"Oh, heavens no, I'm afraid I misplaced that some time ago. He always locks the door with a deadbolt from the inside, anyway."

Ditty inquired, "Do we have your permission to force the door open?"

Mildred was quivering now at the thought of what was on the other side.

"I suppose you must do what you have to do. Yes, go ahead and open it if you can."

Detective Dodge had done this kind of job before. Stepping back to gain momentum, he forced his upper shoulder into the door with all his two hundred pounds behind it. The old wooden door easily burst backward on its hinges, bouncing off the wall behind it. Unfortunately, the momentum of Dodge's efforts brought him quickly over the threshold into the small room with Barnabus. Despite the horrendous smell filling the room to the gasping point, the detectives could not discern when the man had died.

I could not know that only moments after I collected my gear early that Saturday morning, Barnabus succumbed to a massive coronary. It was now Wednesday morning in the unventilated room.

Detective Ditty tried entering the small room after his partner. Overcome by the sudden strength of the stench, he spun on his heel reentering the house gagging.

He blurted, "He's dead, alright."

Not even four years of service with the Philadelphia Police Department had prepared Dodge for the ghastly scene before him.

Barnabus, all three hundred and twenty pounds of him, was sitting bolt upright in a rocking chair with arms outstretched as if he were waiting to embrace Dodge when he entered. In the heat of the room, over time, edema had set in allowing the body to bloat. This, in turn, caused the arms to swell lifting them into the grotesque position they were in now. Dodge could see his skin was stretched almost to the bursting point. This accounted for the nearly transparent tattoos covering most of his lower left arm.

Ditty mustered enough courage to re-enter the room joining his partner. His watering eyes were inadvertently drawn to the man's face. Here skin was stretched to make his head approximately the size of two footballs. His eyes and ears oozed fluid. A blackened tongue the size of a cucumber protruded unrepentantly at the two repulsed detectives. Barnabus apparently was preparing to undress. One shoe was on, the other off. Dodge speculated he was probably reaching to untie the other shoe when the heart attack struck.

Ditty pleaded, "Let's get the hell out of here and call this in. This isn't our department."

Dodge's voice was muffled under his handkerchief.

"Just one more minute, I need to get a closer look."

The very thought of doing just that made Ditty retch into his handkerchief. He tasted salt forming in the back of his throat, a sure-fire precursor to an upcoming upheaval. Pushing off his partner's shoulder, Ditty rushed from the room making the front door just in time to project his breakfast out over the front porch rail. Meanwhile, Dodge stepped closer to the rocking chair. He reached down picking up a small piece of paper crumpled on the floor.

At first, he thought, *"Is that a suicide note? Naw, this has got to be natural causes. Either way, that'll be one for the boys in the lab."*

He reached down picking up the piece of paper dropping it into his coat pocket. Then, he beat a hasty retreat for the door and fresh air. As he stepped out the door, he could see Ditty was more than ready to leave.

Dodge called back over his shoulder to Mrs. Schuck.

"We'll be going now. Our work is finished here. An ambulance will arrive soon for the body. We're sorry for you being inconvenienced."

Dodge turned to walk toward the car when he heard Mildred call from behind.

"What about my door?"

Dodge turned back once more fishing a card from his top pocket. Returning to the front steps, he handed her the department's card.

"Just send the repair bill to this address. I'm sure they'll take care of it. Goodbye."

Mildred stood on the front porch waving until they were out of sight, then limped over to the neighbor's house. Her tale of woe would keep them busy until the ambulance arrived.

Most people would think Barnabus' story ended there. Sadly, it did not. When the ambulance attendants arrived, they discovered the body would not pass through the back door as they had hoped. Instead, they were faced with the gruesome task of breaking the body's arms to get it out on a gurney. The act alone would make anyone cringe at the very thought of it. Yet, that was the least of their problems. They had to concern themselves with popping the already bloated body allowing the stinking gaseous fluids to escape. They decided a mound of sheets placed over the break points would spare them being inundated. As predicted, the body's taut skin did tear open when each attendant applied pressure effectively breaking each arm. By now, the stench was horrendous.

Police who responded to the scene witnessed the strange and horrific sight, as three attendants eventually managed to get the sitting, hulking, dripping body up on the gurney. The police stood back giving them a wide berth as they rolled the mound of former humanity known as Barnabus Kurt Jenkins to the ambulance.

Once the body was loaded, a heated discussion arose amongst the attendants. Apparently, one of them must suffer the added indignity of riding in the back to the morgue. The on-looking police watched as they drew lots determining who would be so unfortunate. By all that is holy, this should have been the final scene, but fate would not allow.

The ride to the hospital was long, hot, and nearly unbearable for the young man riding in the back. His dilemma was particularly enhanced by his erstwhile partners' teasing. They had offered him a tuna sandwich through the open window from the front seat. When they finally arrived at the rear entrance of the hospital where the morgue was located, they had to share the ride down on the cramped freight elevator with the body. It was there in the morgue that they were informed the body would not fit into the aging hospital's vaults. Instead, of ridding themselves of their putrid, repulsive, burden, they learned they must return in the elevator to the ambulance for yet another ride across town to the county hospital with their revolting companion. A new debate ensued over who would ride in the back with their charge. Their relief was intense when they finally reached their destination.

However, one final indignity awaited them. The medical examiner told them they must wait for a doctor to officially pronounce the body dead. Once again, the attendants found themselves unable to separate themselves from their loathsome passenger. Waiting anxiously as far away as they dared, they chain smoked to mask the horrible odor permeating the hallway. Hearing footsteps coming from around the intersection of their hallway, the attendants eagerly awaited their emancipation from the dripping, stinking, hulk lurking under soaking sheets.

When the doctor finally rounded the corner holding a clipboard, he set eyes on the mounded gurney just as the stench struck his nostrils. Spinning on his heel, he held up his clipboard checking the prescribed box on the form. Without missing a beat, he called out loudly.

"He's dead," as he disappeared back around the corner.

For Detectives Ditty and Dodge, their association with Barnabus soon passed on to a different sort of lead. Holding the scrap of paper found in Barnabus' room, Dodge read the print appearing on it.

Ditty asked, "What have you got there, Bill?"

Bill replied, "It's a receipt from a surplus store, Jim. It's that one over on Ninth Street. I found it on the floor in Barnabus Jenkins' room."

Ditty placed his hand over his stomach rolling his eyes.

"Please don't remind me."

Dodge leaned forward in his chair holding the receipt up to the light on his desk. "There's a list of things on this receipt that don't make sense."

"What do you mean exactly?"

Dodge studied the list reading off the items that appeared on the crumpled receipt.

"There's two entrenching tools, fifty feet of rope, two Army backpacks, and an oil lamp. What would Barnabus be doing with all this stuff?

Ditty ventured, "It sounds like he was getting ready to go camping or something."

Dodge chuckled, "Yeah, now does that sound like the Barnabus we met up with?"

Ditty rubbed his chin thoughtfully.

"No, it doesn't add up, does it?"

Dodge stood up, pulling his coat off the back of his chair.

You know what, I think we ought to have another little chat with Mr. Grafton over at the slaughterhouse."

Ditty asked, "Do you think he'd know what Barnabus was doing with all that stuff?"

Dodge answered, "Maybe, or maybe we can learn why none of the stuff on this receipt was found in the old man's room."

Karl Grafton answered the phone from the second shift line. It was

Thursday afternoon. His voice conveyed a sense of annoyance. The day was not going well. Shorthanded since the disappearance of Steve, Vic, and Allen, one more interruption certainly did not help.

"This is Grafton here, what now?"

"Karl, this is Cindy in the front office. The detectives are back. They want to speak to you."

Karl screwed up his face.

"Can't it wait until break time?"

"I'm sorry, boss's orders. We are to cooperate fully with the investigation."

Heaving a sigh, he replied, "I'm on my way."

Karl clanged down the line phone on its receiver, then walked over to his assistant. Cupping his hand beside his mouth, he half shouted in the man's ear over the din of the constant clattering steel conveyors.

"Take over here, Fred. I have to go up to the office."

Fred nodded his assent stepping back from the line. Karl made his way toward the front of 'the house' passing several busy work stations. He came upon a large blood spill forming on the floor behind a few busy cutters. He quickly vented his frustration on them shouting to no one.

"Somebody get this mess cleaned up before you bust your ass and spend a week off without pay."

Moving up the line, he considered stopping off at the locker room to clean up before meeting with the detectives. Then, he abruptly changed his mind.

"Let them see a little blood. It's not like they're not used to it."

Karl could see Ditty and Dodge ahead seated in the break room through the large pane window. They appeared stone faced, as usual, staring blankly out that same window as he approached. He couldn't help wondering why they wanted to speak with him again. He couldn't comprehend how anything he had to say would help them find his missing workers. Looking down at his bloody rubber apron, he decided to remove it before entering the room. Hanging it on the coat rack outside, he stepped into the stale, sweat smelling, oblong room.

"Good afternoon, gentlemen. Did you want to speak to me?"

Dodge gestured toward an empty, cracked, vinyl chair between them.

"Yes, Mr. Grafton, please have a seat."

"You can call me, Karl. Only the paperboy calls me Mr. Grafton."

Dodge greeted his small attempt at levity with a wan smile. Thinking he had heard just about everything except that one.

Ditty chimed in, "We just wanted to ask you a few more questions about the people who work under you."

"Sure, anything I can do to help. Have you got anymore leads on the missing kids?"

Dodge decided to play his cards close to his chest.

"We think we might, but we just want to be sure on a few more details first."

Ditty reached in his coat pocket producing his pen. Pulling the writing pad closer on the table, he looked up at Karl.

"How well would you say you know Barnabus Jenkins?"

Karl looked thoughtful for a moment, then answered cautiously.

"Well, if you're asking if we were friends, I'd have to say no. I knew him for over ten years, but we weren't buddy buddy, if you know what I mean? I mean he traveled in a different circle, you know."

Dodge decided to throw in a little shake-up question to see what fell out.

"Are you referring to the fact that he was colored and you're white?"

Karl hesitated, considering his answer carefully. He was on relatively new ground with this race relations business. Not wanting to appear bigoted, he struggled with the proper use of words to describe the unseen wall that stood between Negroes and whites. To him, it was a mere fact of life in his generation.

"No, it's nothing like that or anything. I just didn't socialize with him."

Dodge let him off the hook with a thoughtful, "I see."

Ditty was seated on Karl's right and came right back.

"You just spoke of Barnabus in the past tense three times. How did you know he was dead?"

The question was clearly intended to get some knee jerk reaction such as shock or remorse. Karl sized things up quickly. He could see right now he was the anvil and Ditty and Dodge were the twin hammers. In truth, Karl did hear about the death of Barnabus, even though it was not in the papers yet. News travels swiftly in a close-knit community of working people. As the saying goes, people talk, word gets around, you hear things.

Karl stammered struggling to answer the question.

"I…I didn't know, I mean I heard…"

Dodge was the good cop now saying, "That's O.K. Karl. We know you didn't do it. Tell me something, though. We found a receipt in his room. It was for a purchase made at the Army Navy Surplus Store on Ninth Street. Do you know the place?"

Karl responded, "Sure, I know of it."

Dodge continued, "The receipt was for a couple of shovels, fifty feet of rope, an oil burning lamp, and two Army back packs. Do you have any idea what Barnabus might want to do with those things?"

Karl shook his head slowly from side to side, truly perplexed.

"I really have no idea."

Ditty shot back, "Would you say that it was unusual for him to buy such gear?"

"Why, yes, I guess I would."

Ditty pressed, "Well, then maybe you would find it even more unusual that none of those things were found in his room. What do you suppose happened to them between last Thursday and yesterday?"

Karl answered truthfully, "I have no idea."

Dodge decided to shift gears.

"You were one of the last persons to see the missing kids and Barnabus together, weren't you?"

"Yes, that was Thursday afternoon last week."

Dodge added, "The missing kids all worked the second shift on Friday according to their timesheets. How come they worked the first shift the previous day with Barnabus?"

"I already told you. I assigned the kids to help Barnabus in the store room earlier that week and they finished on Thursday."

By now, everyone could make the connection between the boys and Barnabus and the work completed on Thursday. The work detail was the only thread holding all of them together. Now Diddy gave his partner an imperceptible nod, signaling they were through with Karl. It was a signal they should regroup before proceeding further.

Dodge slowly pushed back his chair from the long table.

"Well, once again, Karl, you've been most cooperative. I think that just about does it for now unless you have any questions."

Karl appeared thoughtful, then, asked, "Is there anything I can do to help you guys, cause if there is, just say the word?"

Dodge replied, "No, I think that's it for now. Just don't plan on taking any vacations real soon. We may need to talk again before this thing is resolved."

Karl appeared apprehensive at Dodge's last remark as he rose from his chair.

Ditty looked down at his notepad as Karl walked away.

"Well, partner, where did this get us?"

"I know one thing for sure. He's telling the truth, and he has no apparent ulterior motive."

Ditty shifted his eyes looking at Dodge.

"You don't suppose Barnabus had anything to do with those kids disappearing, do you?"

"Well, it doesn't look so good from the list of things he purchased, does it?"

"Yeah, but what could his motive possibly be?"

That's what bothers me. I can't see it either. I say we go back and interview some of the kids' parents again. Maybe something will slip through the cracks that make sense."

Dodge suggested, "Why don't we try the girls' parents. Maybe we'll hear something different from that angle."

"O.K., I'm with you, but let's stop and get some decent coffee first. This break room stuff is the worst. It tastes like burnt cardboard."

Dodge offered, "Maybe it's the ambiance."

The two detectives made their way out of the huge slaughter house where the sights and sounds of the city streets seemed a distinct improvement.

Dodge stopped to take in a deep breath.

"Ah, there's nothing like fresh Philly air to clear out a snoot full of slaughter house."

The two detectives got in their car and drove to a nearby donut shop. They sat at the counter stirring their coffees.

Ditty asked, "Which parent do you want to start with?"

Dodge replied, "I thought we might talk to Mrs. Warren. She was so hysterical last time. It was all I could do just to get her name down."

Ditty recalled, "Yeah, that Doc was awful protective of his patient."

"Maybe she's had time enough to settle down now," Dodge ventured.

A half hour later they arrived in front of Mrs. Warren's apartment.

Dodge suggested, "Maybe it would be best if I approached her alone. I don't want her to feel like we're ganging up on her."

"Sure, go ahead, I'll just go over my notes here. Let me know if you need any help."

Dodge knocked on the door and to his surprise her husband appeared. He was a slight man nearly five foot six with a thin frame. He wore glasses that were perched low on the bridge of his nose now. He seemed slightly annoyed, as if he had been taken away from something more important than the man at the door.

Peering over his glasses at the detective standing on his front porch he asked, "Can I help you, sir?"

Dodge held up his badge for inspection.

"I'm Detective Dodge, from Missing Persons."

Robert Warren examined his badge thoroughly without saying a word

"I was wondering if I might talk to your wife about the case."

Robert appeared to take offense at the request.

"Don't you think she's been through enough already? Why don't you ask me the questions and let her rest? The doctors had her sedated these past few days."

Dodge sympathized, "I'm sorry to hear that, Mr. Warren. I just wanted to ask some follow up questions, routine you know. It will keep until later."

Robert appeared edgy. "Well, there's no tellin' when she's gonna be ready to talk to anybody. She's a nervous wreck. I don't feel much better, but if it would help any, I'll try and answer your questions."

"Well, if you really don't mind, that is, if it's not too inconvenient."

Robert opened the door wider looking beyond Dodge at the detective's car.

"What about your partner, does he want to come in, too?"

"No, that's alright, he's fine. I'll only be a minute."

Robert stepped back allowing Dodge to enter the living room. Once inside, he could see the place was unkempt. One could say, it lacked the touch of a woman. Newspapers were strewn about the room draped over furniture. The dining room table in the three-bedroom apartment held stacks of dirty dishes. Robert must have caught Dodge's eyes scanning the house.

"Sorry about the looks of things. We're a little behind on our housekeeping lately."

Dodge replied, "That's alright. I can understand how things get overlooked in times of family crises."

Using that as a segway, Dodge continued.

"That's partly why I'm here. I'd like to go over the report you gave us that day when your wife was indisposed. I just want to be certain we're not overlooking anything that might help us find your daughter."

Robert pointed to the only chair free of newspaper.

"Please sit down, Detective, right there, and I'll try and answer all your questions."

"Thank you, Mr. Warren. May I call you Robert?"

Robert accepted his attempt at making him feel at ease

"Certainly, Detective, that would be fine."

Robert lifted a newspaper off the couch opposite Dodge taking a seat.

"Now, then, what is it you'd like to know?"

Dodge began, "Robert, when was it you and your wife first noticed your daughter was missing?"

"Well, at first, we didn't really know she was missing. We just felt she was late in coming home. It was my wife, Doris. She got worried and called Amy's mother. That's when she learned Connie never even went to Amy's for the weekend. She's come home late before, but she's never pulled anything like this. Her mother has been beside herself."

Robert leaned forward confiding in Dodge.

"She's always been a bit high strung. So, you might imagine this sort of thing really put her over the top."

Dodge nodded, while listening intently.

Robert went on. "Well, the next thing you know, we're hearing about Allen and the other boys going off to Ocean City and how they were late in coming back. Naturally, you know how parents worry about their children. We started putting two and two together, and you see we thought the worst. At least, Doris did at first. It took a little more convincing for me to believe my daughter would run off and do such a thing. She's always been a good girl. Did I tell you she won a letter in cheerleading?"

Dodge smiled, knowingly, allowing the father to take pride in his daughter's accomplishments. In the back of his mind, he was formulating his next question whilst reminding himself of the rule of interview, *"Let the person talk, it's not about you."*

Robert prattled on, not giving up anything of substance until Dodge found an opening.

He asked, "What did you think of her relationship with Victor Rubio, Robert?"

Now a scowl appeared on Robert's face. Dodge could see he clearly struck a nerve.

Robert unloaded, "That gamblin' pool player has cost Doris and I a lot of sleep."

Dodge urged, "What exactly did he do?"

Robert fumed, "Despite her mother's and my wishes, Connie kept seeing that boy. I told her he was no good for her, but she was like a moth drawn to the flame. Connie has always had a sense of adventure about her, and I think she found that in him. Anyway, they would stay out late beyond curfew. Once, I caught her with beer on her breath. I just knew she was hanging out in those pool halls with him. I was just ready to put my foot down when I heard she wanted to spend the weekend with a girlfriend for a change. So, I was all for it."

Robert stopped for a moment reflecting on what he'd just said.

Dodge had been there before. He could see the look of guilt coming over the father's face.

Robert pounded his fist down on the couch harmlessly.

"How could I have been so stupid? Why couldn't I see through their little scheme? Even my wife was taken in."

Dodge replied, "Trust is a two-way street."

He wanted to say if you had told your daughter you trusted her she might be here today. Instead, he bit his tongue deciding to end yet another fruitless interview. The streak of false leads and bad information stymied the detectives thwarting their every effort to learn the whereabouts of five Philadelphia teenagers. It was as if the earth had swallowed them up.

Chapter 11

Something was happening to us as we struggled to free ourselves from the bowels of Philly. I wasn't sure why, but we were all suffering the same symptoms. We had continued our course along the gas line for days now. Each junction brought a new manhole offering, a possible way out. Yet each one only discouraged us more than the last when we discovered it, too, was welded shut. Our last hope was reaching a pumping station as a means of escape from the box we were in.

Food was low. One candy bar, some Chiclets; our backs were aching constantly from walking in the stooped position. Worse, each of us experienced symptoms of a burning sensation around the eyes combined with an inexplicable feeling of lightheadedness. Of course, we blamed the latter symptom of starvation. Yet, as hours wore on, it seemed something else was attacking our systems. Finding it difficult to understand, I only knew we all felt the same way.

After Amy worked through the aspirin, I had only a half canteen of water. It did not take a doctor to tell us what to expect in a few days if we did not find water. I tried pushing those bad thoughts from my mind, but the torment of scratchy, burning eyes only made it worse. Several times, I heard the others moaning. All of us were hurting bad and dreamed of flushing our stinging eyes with cool fresh water. It was a maddening feeling to endure. I thought of Amy and how it must be doubly painful for her. Connie stopped whimpering some time ago. Now, she wept openly. I would have asked Vic to shut her up, but thought perhaps the flow of tears might rinse her swollen eyes. I was about to place some spittle on my sleeve to rub my own burning eyes once more, when Amy pounded her fist on my back. I listened as her dry, raspy voice whispered hoarsely.

"Stop, please, no more. I need rest."

I turned, embracing her, offering the only solace I had left to give. We stood still embracing in a hug for a long moment.

I whispered, "Alright, Amy, we'll stop."

We sat huddled together immediately turning off our flashlights. This was our routine now to save batteries. Every time we stopped, it was lights out. As we sat in the pitch blackness, I could hear Vic's voice droning listlessly.

"When will we ever get out of this place? What's happening to all of us? My eyes are burning up. What is it?"

"*What indeed*" I thought to myself. I didn't bother to answer. I ran out of answers some time ago. Lowering my head, I remained silent forcing myself to concentrate. My mind drifted back to chemistry class when we learned about irritants. I was certain our eyes were being irritated. I just could not imagine the source. Think it through, I reasoned logically asking myself, "*What is different about our surroundings. Why weren't our eyes irritated earlier? Why now?*"

I started processing what I knew about our surroundings in my mind. "*We're in a coal gasification maintenance shaft; the coal was burned producing coal gas which was also burned after being sent through the pipe. What happens when things are burned?*"

A light suddenly came on in my head. I spoke out loud to no one.

"There's always a residue."

Amy just moaned, then Vic responded above Connie's crying.

"What in hell are you mumbling about?"

I explained slowly.

"When coal is burned, there is always a residue left behind. What would that be? Now let me see. Coal tar, yes, that's it, the residue is coal tar. Coal tar is caustic, its dark brown and greasy like creosote. Yeah, like creosote. It's also an irritant. After all those years, these gas lines must be lined with coal tar. We've been traveling through here for days rubbing up against those rusty pipes. A lot of those pipes were rusted through and broken."

Vic interrupted, "Amy, check on Allen. I think *he's* starting to hallucinate now."

I answered Vic, "The gas lines are what are causing our eyes to burn. It's also causing us to feel light headed."

Vic scoffed, "You sound light headed."

"No, don't you see? We've been brushing up against the pipes and probably wiping that stuff all over our clothes and into our eyes. That's what it is, dammit. We've poisoned ourselves with coal tar, and whatever other chemical remnants are in these pipes."

Vic asked, "Suppose you're right, what are we gonna do about it?"

"Well, one thing I know for sure, we've gotta steer clear of those damned pipes."

Unfortunately, my thoughts of a remedy left me even more depressed. We needed water, and lots of it, to flush away the irritants in our eyes. What we would do about what was already in our systems, I hadn't a clue.

I said, "Obviously, we need to get out of here and soon. If I'm right, we've already ingested some of these chemicals and that's what's making us feel light headed. If we don't get out, and soon, we could lose consciousness."

Upon hearing that, Amy reached down deep within her finding the courage to get up. She stood forcing the words from her parched throat.

"Let's get going. We're not done for yet."

Connie took inspiration from Amy's encouragement rising to meet the challenge.

She sounded off, "If we make it, you're gonna get one helluva a bill from my beauty parlor, Vic."

Her meager attempt at humor was uplifting considering how she had been handling things thus far. Clearly, a common bond was forming amongst us. Our suffering took us to a place where we all felt the same way about each other, if they can make it, I can make it. It was just then I caught a glimpse of our chance to really make it out. It was a bit off from our calculations, but there, nonetheless.

Playing my light beam up ahead and down I demonstrated we had reached the pumping station, at last. No one could be more relieved than my Amy. She summoned up a raspy cheer.

"We're there, Mister Underground Navigator. We finally made it!"

There, before us, was a brick lined room large enough to stand up in about ten by ten feet square. We huddled inside gratefully stretching out our backs to full height for the first time in days. I examined the walls all around me. The pumping apparatus was bolted to the middle of the floor taking up nearly half the space of the room. It looked pretty much as I had imagined. It was a rusted-out pump with two major ports on either end. The simple design had an intake pipe on one end that allowed coal gas to be pumped in. At the other end was a larger exhaust tube nearly eight inches in diameter. This, in turn, was stepped down in sizes through a series of pressure valves to the final gas release point at the half inch pipe we had been following. One large pressure relief wheel was rusted shut on the side of the boiler, which likely served as an emergency relief valve in case pressure rose to unsafe levels. It was a crude design right out of the late 19th century.

There was a ladder leading up to another sealed manhole. By now, it was a depressingly familiar site. I continued my inspection with the help of Vic's light as backup. Suddenly, I saw something on the floor that made my heart leap. I could scarcely believe my burning eyes. There on the floor was a manhole sized port with one blessed major difference from all the rest. The manhole on the floor was only bolted shut.

My hand was still shaking as I called Vic closer to witness what my jittery light was revealing. He peered over my shoulder gasping. Like a breath of fresh air, a few precious words escaped his gaping mouth.

"Allen, it's not welded."

I almost laughed out loud with joy.

"That's right, my boy, it's only bolted."

His next reply sounded less enthusiastic.

"Yes, it's only bolted."

The realization sunk in simultaneously as Vic gave voice to our dilemma.

"Where the hell are we going to get a wrench that big?"

Neither of us had a clue where the manhole led, yet here we were already speculating on how we could remove the obstacle. Our desperation had sunk to a pathetic level. We were ready to do anything to free ourselves from the depths of our despair and death by poisoning. It took a level-headed person like Amy to snap us out of it.

She reasoned, "Look, someone had to bolt that thing on, right?"

Totally absorbed in self-defeat, I could only nod numbly.

"Well then, it stands to reason they might need to take it off again."

I just stood there staring at the floor wondering what the hell she was talking about.

Amy persisted jogging my senses back to life.

"Let's just look around here for that damn wrench."

She led the way snatching the flashlight from my hand. Walking along the brick wall she searched closely moving around the pumping station. Then, I heard a tapping noise on wood coming from the other side.

"Here," she shouted, "Look, here's a tool box inside the wall right here."

She continued thumping on the door until Vic came around to her side.

"Holy crap, she's right! It must be a tool box. It's got a lock on it."

Anxiously, I felt along the wall until I saw everybody huddled around what looked like a toolbox built in flush with the wall. I allowed myself to think it truly could be, after all. Feeling the excitement build, I took my entrenching tool out. I affixed my knife to its handle with multiple wraps of string. When I thought it would hold, I took the knife blade and slowly slid it under the hasp. Then, I grasped the other end of my shovel and pried outward using the brick border for leverage.

Looking up at the others expectantly, I said, "Here goes nothing."

Exerting as much force as I dared on the rusty hasp, suddenly to my surprise, I heard the sharp sound of breaking steel. Much to my disappointment, I stared down seeing the point of my knife lying on the floor.

Vic cried, "You should have slid it further in. Here let me try."

I felt my pride bruising as I relinquished my grip on the shovel.

Vic wielded the remainder of the blade shoving it in as far as it would go. When he applied pressure, I could see everyone's eyes widen with expectation. This time the knife sadly folded over on the shovel handle. I reached forward grabbing the shovel from his hands. This time, I told everyone to stand back. Raising the shovel blade end in the air above the lock and hasp, I came down hard with a swift stroke breaking the hasp off with the lock still attached.

Vic quipped, "There, you see, after I softened it up for you, now it comes off."

I didn't bother answering. I was so happy just getting the damned thing off. Vic shone his light into the box. There inside stood a wrench in the corner. It seemed our luck was turning. I spied an oil can in the back of the tool box, too. Soon, Vic and I had the wrench out and the bolts sufficiently lubricated. I allowed Vic the joy of giving the first bolt all he had. His face reddened with the effort, but eventually he broke the hold on the rusty bolt and began turning it slowly. We each took turns until we removed the last of twelve bolts. The task proved exacting for us both.

I sat back breathlessly on the floor allowing the heavy wrench to land on the floor with a clang.

Vic caught his breath saying, "All we need now is a lift truck to get this thing up."

Looking around myself, I spotted my trusty entrenching tool. Still catching my breath, I spoke haltingly.

"What we need is your shovel on the bottom laying cross ways with mine on top. I'll wedge my shovel blade in the crack of the manhole lid, and we'll both push down on the other end. Amy, if we do get it up, I want you to shove my boot in under the lid."

Connie crouched down starting to tug on my boot. I could see the zeal in her eyes. She was hell bent on getting out, whatever it took. Pulling it off, she handed it to Amy. In the meantime, Vic and I readied ourselves for the big lift. Straining at the end of the shovel handle, I thought I could hear the wooden handle starting to split.

Vic cried, "I think it moved, Allen. Keep up the pressure."

I felt my palms taking on the imprint of the shovel handle as I kept pushing down.

Vic cheered me on. "Keep going, Allen, you're moving it. I see it coming up."

With one last effort, I strained leaning into the handle. Suddenly, I could feel the handle going to the floor. It was working; the lid was coming up a few precious inches.

I shouted, "Now, Amy, shove in the boot!"

Amy was sitting near the edge of the lid waiting. She shoved the boot into the open space yanking her hand back as I released my grip on the handle. The weight of the lid smashed down on the heel of the boot leaving a gap wide enough for our fingers to grasp the edge. Heaving a sigh of relief, I fell back on the floor catching my breath.

Happily, I looked around myself while lying on my back. Connie held a flashlight over me.

Laughing for the first time in days, I shouted, "We did it guys. We really did it."

Connie allowed her light to flash upward momentarily. As I lay on my back, the light passed over some white letters stenciled on the brick surrounding the welded manhole above. It read Second and Market Street.

I was so startled at that bit of information, I blurted out to the others still laying on my back.

"Hey guys, I know exactly where we are."

Vic quipped, "Yeah, me, too. We're in a hole in the ground. Now, why don't you get up off your ass?"

"Shut up, Vic! Shine your light up there above the manhole."

As he did, everyone got quiet. For the first time in days, we all knew exactly where we were.

Vic shook his head in awe.

"Well, whatta ya know about that?"

That one piece of information instantly sent a ray of hope in our direction.

I remarked, "That puts us right downtown. We're bound to find a way out from here."

Amy spoke cautiously, "However, we must first go down before we can go out. I suggest we start working on moving that lid, the sooner the better."

We put our backs into it, lifting the heavy lid with our fingers just enough to slide it aside. After rescuing my boot, I was prepared to join in yet another attempt at freeing ourselves.

I took the lead as we started our descent on the rusty handles of the ladder. I wanted Amy just above me on the ladder. That way, I could support her weight as much as possible. It was slow going for her with only one arm to hold on with. Connie came next with Vic right behind.

I could sense immediately we were entering completely different surroundings. The atmosphere inside was cool and damp. I was certain my mind was playing tricks on me as I climbed down further. I thought I heard running water. The ladder extended down about thirty feet. Three quarters of the way down I stopped. Straining, to hear what I thought was the sound of running water again. My hopes soared, *"Could it be our prayers have been answered?"*

Stopping for a moment, I played my light down the ladder. At the bottom, I could see we were entering a manmade structure. I was elated to see we were entering what looked like an abandoned storm drain. There was a narrow stream of water about six inches deep running in it. I could not help thinking that trickle of water was a precious God sent source of relief for our swollen eyes.

Being the first down, I steadied Amy as she stretched out her foot seeking the ground. Once she had her footing, I helped Connie down. Soon, we all stood in our new surroundings sending our flashlight beams all around in hasty exploration. The first thing we could think of was tending to our eyes.

I warned, "Be careful, that water could be contaminated."

Vic shrugged, "If it's wet, that's all I care about."

I cautioned, "You had better soak your handkerchief in it first before you wipe your eyes. You don't know what you might be rubbing on your face."

Vic took my advice stooping down by the small stream of water running through the storm drain. I could see the drain was built to contain thousands of gallons coursing through after a storm. The ceiling was arched six feet above us. The construction of the tunnel was made entirely of brick. Clearly, it was built some time ago. I guessed it must have been in operation in pre-Revolutionary War days. I already knew from the intersection above us, we were in the heart of old Philadelphia. Now, the trick was to head in the right direction. The storm drain tunnel only ran north and south, so the choice was simple. The center of the city was southwest of us, so I recommended we head south.

"Listen guys, I think we should head this way," gesturing southward.

"The greater part of Philly lies in that direction. I think our chances of getting out would be greater if we headed that way."

Amy replied, "I'm with you, Allen, you haven't steered us wrong yet."

Vic answered, "I guess it's alright with me, too. What about you Connie?"

Connie looked up from the small stream of water where she was dipping her bandana to wipe her eyes.

"Sure, I'll go along with that. Anything that gets us out of here sounds good to me."

I cautioned, "I can't guarantee anything, but I think our chances are definitely better this way."

We all stayed near the stream taking our time bathing our sore eyes. The water was not potable, but it wasn't filthy either. Its soothing effect was a wonderful tonic for us all. It seemed our lot was improving. Despite the fact we had little food or drink left, our spirits were boosted by our escape from the effects of the toxins we were enduring.

I took stock of what we did have. We now had in our possession one oil burning lantern, a box of kitchen matches, three flashlights, fifty feet of rope, two entrenching tools, three back packs, a broken tipped knife, a quarter of a canteen of water and one flattened Baby Ruth.

"I vote we split up the Baby Ruth before we move on. We could all use the energy."

I got no argument from the others. So, we sat with our backs against the brick wall dividing up our last bit of food. The taste was wonderful. I had eaten that last portion of Baby Ruth many times in my imagination. Now, the reality of it left no room for comparison with my wildest dreams. No one said a word as we sat there silently, reverently relishing our delectable repast.

Eventually, we agreed to press onward. As we stood up to depart, Connie's flashlight dimmed out for the last time. With two flashlights left, we decided to light up the lantern. Moving on, we made our way southward through the tunnel with Vic and I leading the way with our flashlights. Connie held the lamp, bringing up the rear. Checking my watch as we set out, I noted it was 7:00 p.m. It would soon be dark on the streets above.

As we trudged along, I thought my tired eyes were playing tricks on me. In the small stream ahead, I began seeing small objects plopping into the small stream ahead of me. Whatever they were, they weren't heavy;

they barely made a splash. The increasing rate at which they feel alarmed me though. Vic saw them too.

"Hey, what the hell is that, Allen? What's that dropping into the water?"

I quickly diverted my beam of light upward looking for the source. What I saw made my hair stand up on the back of my head. I froze in my tracks staring upward in disbelief. Vic gasped as he played his light over the ceiling.

He shouted, "Holy crap, there's thousands of 'em."

Amy looked up screaming uncontrollably. Connie chimed in as her lamp light revealed the rippling waves of albino roaches teeming along the ceiling scurrying frantically upside down in our direction. Their helter skelter melee caused many of them to fall from the ceiling as they madly scurried over each other. Suddenly, coming out of nowhere, they now seemed to be everywhere. We scrambled to the edge of the tunnel avoiding the path of swarming white roaches that had never seen the light of day.

Connie swatted herself constantly wherever she could see them landing on her.

"Get them off me! Vic, get them off me!" she pleaded.

Amy, too, was flailing her good arm above her head trying to fend off the milky white insects from landing in her hair.

Vic tried sheltering Connie as best he could, but she was difficult to keep up with. Everywhere I stepped, I heard the crunch of insects squashing beneath my boots. My psyche told me my life was not threatened, but experience told me it was far too repulsive to deal with. I felt the urge to run, but where could I go? Instead, we finally just huddled together trying to cover ourselves with our own clothing. The scene continued making me wonder why there was such a mad mass migration of bugs. The answer came in a fluttering noise directly above our heads. I became instantly aware as the noise grew in intensity all around us.

I yelled instinctively to the others.

"Bats, keep your heads down!"

In a matter of seconds, we were surrounded. We were trapped in a whirlwind of bats. They enveloped us, locked in a feeding frenzy. They were preying on the albino cockroaches. Intermittently bouncing off our bodies, they scooped up their prey in their mouths. We became inanimate objects standing between them and their meal. Being so tightly huddled together, the girls alternately screamed in our ears. Vic and I had to shout to be heard.

"If we can get out our shovels, we can wave them off," I shouted.

"To hell with shovels, I'm not getting bit by some flying rat."

"I guess we'll have to ride it out then."

Just then, a bat struck Connie in the back of the head starting another round of screaming from both girls.

I shouted, "I don't think I can take much more of this. I'm going for my shovel."

I stood quickly swinging my arms like fury above my head. The bats continued swirling between us and the ceiling continuing to devour their prey.

Not as many as before, I thought to myself. I took a chance during the lull pulling off my pack letting it fall to the ground. Squatting down, I removed the entrenching tool in the dim light of Connie's fallen lamp. Just then, another heavy swarm of bats entered the air space over our heads. I used my shovel taking a wide swipe at them. The rest slowly began to scatter as I continued waving my shovel around in the air.

Then, I stood up to see the swarm of bats leaving the way they had entered. The roaches were almost completely gone. I'd never witnessed such a phenomenon of nature in my life. I could not help wondering if this same dramatic feast played itself out each night.

At that moment, I realized we had something to be thankful for. Despite their terrorizing us, the bats had shown us a way out. Holding my flashlight up, I examined a smaller side drain about shoulder height. It was a place where the last of the bats flew. In the early evening darkness, the bats were flying out to forage in the night skies of Philly. I had watched the last of them disappearing into the smaller drain pipe.

"You can get up now. The bats have gone."

Amy asked timidly, "Where did they all go?"

I trained my light on the pipe leading away from the storm drain.

"They flew through there on their way outside to forage."

Connie asked, "Where did all the bugs go?"

I replied, "The bats ate most of them for us. Did you know a bat can consume twice its weight in insects in a single night?"

Vic winced, "Uh, not exactly a fun fact to know, Allen."

I shrugged, "Anyway, they can, and that's what they'll be doing all night."

"Good riddance," mumbled Connie.

"Well, now that we're safe for the time being, I propose we start making our way out of here once and for all."

Amy stood up trying to wipe off the dirt.

"It couldn't be a moment too soon, Mr. Williams. You sound pretty confident."

"Well, I am. You see, it's like I've been saying, the bats go out each night to forage. All we have to do is follow which way they went, and we should be out of here in no time."

Amy started shaking her head nervously.

"Oh, I don't know, Allen. I don't like the idea of crawling through a small drain pipe even if it does get me out of here. I seem to remember the last time we did something like that, we all got sick. We're still not over the effects of that. Besides, what if we get stuck in there? Who's gonna come rescue us?"

Vic stepped forward.

"I say we vote on it. We could just keep going the way we were, you know. Maybe that will lead us out, too."

I insisted, "I'm telling you, I saw the bats exit through the drain pipe. We can go that way, too."

From the looks on their faces, I could see I was not convincing them of my logic. At that point, I saw no harm in taking another track. With hindsight, I do regret shamelessly using psychology on Connie, but, then again, I must say the end did justify the means.

"I can't believe you would put these girls in harm's way again, Vic. Do you really mean you would go in the same direction where all the bugs came from before?"

Vic gave me that 'deer caught in the headlights' look. Before he could muster a response, Connie gave him a simpering look. I knew only too well I could count on Connie's fear of bugs and bats to gain her vote. Amy just glared at me, knowing full well what I was up to. She knew I was desperate to make my point. Yet, I was convinced it was best for us all. I just knew it was the right way to go. The vote to take the smaller drain pipe soon carried three to Amy's one dissenting vote.

Amy went along, resigning herself to my wicked ways. Feeling a twinge of guilt, I volunteered to go first. The pipe was thirty-six inches in diameter. It was possible for me to crawl in with my backpack on, so I started down the pipe on my hands and knees. Upon entering, I found the brick lined pipe held only about one inch of water. Gray sediment lined the bottom with moss growing in it. I went forward about ten yards holding my flashlight out straining to see ahead, hoping I would soon see a place where the bats went out. Ten feet in nothing seemed to change. There was just a long line of brick pipe that lay ahead as far as my light could pierce the darkness.

Turning my head backward, I called out for Amy to come along next. I could tell there was some delay at the other end before she finally allowed Vic to hoist her up into the slimy pipe. Once in, I could hear her expressing displeasure at crawling on her hands and knees in the muddy moss covered pipe.

"Yuck, this is nasty. How long do we have to stay in here?"

"Until the maid comes to clean it up, Amy. Now come on, let's get going," I replied sarcastically.

"I don't know why I let you talk me into such things," she said.

"Now, let me think, Amy, maybe it was your sense of romantic adventure back at the malt shop that helped me influence you. You know the romantic underworld where only the adventurous dare go."

No reply came from behind save the sound of Connie complaining to Vic as he lifted her into the drain. As we all moved down the pipe, we saw only a few roaches scurrying along the walls beside us. The girls learned not to react so strongly at the sight of them by now. Fortunately, they only appeared occasionally. It was nothing close to the albino mass of sewer dwellers we dealt with before.

Now my flashlight revealed a new challenge just before us, though. What I saw truly made my heart sink. The size of the pipe reduced to twenty-four inches. Immediately, I was forced to remove my backpack to proceed. Worse, we would all have to crawl on our bellies in the slime, which, by now, I deduced was mainly bat droppings. Naturally, I decided to keep that bit of information to myself. I determined some time back that was why the moss grew so well in the pipe. The only advantage I could possibly derive from this development was that the moss allowed us to slide through the narrowed pipe with ease. I hesitated at the juncture trying to decide if Vic was possibly right. Perhaps a return to the larger pipe was best.

Amy asked suspiciously, "What's going on, Allen? Why are you stopping?"

It was only a matter of time before she discovered my dilemma, so I called back to her.

"It seems we have a little problem here."

Amy answered hesitantly.

"Yesss…what is it, Allen?"

"The pipe has gotten smaller."

Apprehensively she asked, "How small is it, Allen?"

"Well, it's twenty-four inches now."

A long pause ensued, then Amy asked.

"Well, then, what do you want to do, Allen?"

I shined my light down the pipe once more straining my eyes to make out what was ahead. It was no use. I could only see as far as the beam of light allowed. From my perspective, all I could see was straight slimy pipe ahead.

"Allen?"

"Yes, I'm thinking, Amy. Tell Vic what I'm up against. Let me know what he thinks."

Amy passed the word, and Vic sent his reply.

Amy conveyed, "He says we should go back to the bigger drain pipe."

"Wait a minute," I said. "Let me go on ahead a little further just to see if I can find where the bats are getting out of here."

Amy pleaded, "Look, Allen, we're all wet, hungry, and tired. We don't want to be here anymore. Can't we just go? Come with us. Let's turn back."

Something inside me kept saying, "Find out." I just had to know if there was a way out. I knew none of us had much time left. If we turned back now, more precious time would be wasted. I also reasoned, if we returned to the larger drain, the whole cycle of terrifying events would more than likely be played out the following night. I wasn't sure either of the girls could take that. On the other hand, my friends had every right to seek a way out of their own choosing. I was the undecided one. Who was I to disagree?

Before I gave Amy my answer, I reached down in my grimy jacket pocket pulling out my compass. I held the smudged glass up to my flashlight reading the needle.

I thought, *"I'm headed east. So far, we've come south since the big drain from the intersection of Second and Market Street. What could be east of this point?"*

It was hard to imagine without reference to landmarks above. In fact, I was finding it difficult to think clearly anyway. The lack of food and water combined with all the stress and coal tar was taking its toll on my ability to focus.

I forced myself to concentrate. *"I'm basically headed toward the river. There was more activity there than in South Philly when this tunnel was built. My chances are better this way."*

I called out to Amy.

"I'm going to try this direction by myself a while longer. Just trust me. I won't be long."

"Allen, I'm not leaving without you. I'll wait here for you. What do you want me to tell the others?"

"Tell them if they wanna go, take a damn vote on it."

With that, I removed my pack and slid into the slimy pipe holding my light out in front. After about twenty yards of crawling, I came across a small overflow pipe leading straight up out of the pipe I was in. The size of the pipe was a mere eight inches in diameter. I rolled over on my back looking up through the pipe. For the first time, in what seemed like an eternity, I could see stars.

For the first time since we went underground in Philadelphia, I was gazing at the night sky. It was beautiful. I just laid there for at least a minute taking it in. Like a prisoner longingly viewing a world he could not tread, I languished. My mind drifted as I marveled at the tiny bat's ability to come and go through this conduit connecting them to the outside world above. The thought was particularly disparaging knowing I could not join them. My last hope and reason for being in that stinking pipe had been snuffed out. I could hear Amy calling me. She seemed so far away. My dream of escaping was the only thing that seemed more removed. A wave of remorse rippled over my body as I trembled in the wet darkness thinking what the end would be like for us. She was calling to me again. It was time for me to slide backward out of my stinking pipe dream.

I do not know why I did what I did next. Yet, instead of backing out, I slid forward for just one more look. When I did, I was surprised to see my light did not stab into the darkness as far as it normally did. A sense of dread came over me. I suspected my flashlight was losing power. It did not surprise me since Connie's light gave out earlier. I thought perhaps the moisture was shorting out the batteries. I just hated the thought of having to slide backward out of the tunnel in total darkness.

I held the flashlight up near my face giving it a few taps. Then, I projected my light forward again. It was the same. I could barely see five feet down the pipe. I slid forward a little further just out of curiosity. This time, I saw the familiar bricks used to line the pipe, but they were lying in a heap in front on me. What I saw was a jumble of bricks jutting out of a pile of dirt. It struck me like a bolt from the blue. The drain ahead had collapsed. Immediately, I shouted back to Amy.

"The drain is collapsed!"

Amy shouted, "Are you alright? Can you get free?"

"No, I don't mean it collapsed on me. I mean the pipe ahead of me has collapsed."

Amy heaved a sigh of relief then shouted back.

"Allen, don't do that to me again. You really scared me, you know."

I could hear her scolding, but the words weren't clear. I was busy crawling forward to investigate. After seeing the overflow pipe, I realized we must be close to the surface. That could only mean the cave in ahead must connect with the surface in some way. If we could remove the bricks and dirt, there was an outside chance we could make it to the surface. At any rate, I felt it was worth a try.

"I'm coming back out, Amy."

"Good, it's about time you did."

I soon found sliding backward in a small pipe is nigh on to trying to put a sausage back in its casing. With some effort and expenditure of energy, which I would rather have conserved, I finally reached Amy. She looked me over pronouncing me the filthiest guy she had ever seen. Then, she threw her arms around me hugging me tight as we knelt in the larger drain pipe. I could not wait to tell her my thoughts about the possibilities of the caved drain.

I explained excitedly, "Amy, that cave-in is close to the surface. I know it is because that pipe the bats went through was no more than ten feet below ground level."

I could see Amy was receiving my news half-heartedly.

I tried convincing her of the importance of my discovery.

"We could remove those bricks and dirt. We could dig our way out of here. Don't you see what this means?"

Amy bit her lower lip trying to prevent her lack of confidence from showing. She hesitated for a moment then spoke slowly.

"Allen, we've tried a few of your ideas, but it seems clear to me this isn't the way to go."

"How can you say that? Haven't you been listening to what I've been saying?"

"Yes, I have, Allen. To me, it just sounds like a lot of dirty work and effort which could be better spent exploring that big drain out there."

I started to argue, "But, you can see the sky through the pipe." She held up her hand interrupting my attempt.

"Allen, look at me. What do you see? Do I look like a person who can participate in some excavation? Because, I gotta tell you right now, I don't think I have the energy to dig my own grave. Connie and Vic are worn out, too. Look at yourself. Let's face it, Allen, we're just not up to it."

I protested, "You don't understand."

"No, you don't understand. I said we're done. This was the last straw. No more crawling in small spaces. If I have to die in this underground shit hole, I prefer to do it walking upright."

I could see the fire in her eyes, perhaps the only energy she possessed. It was unlike any emotion I ever witnessed in her. I still felt I had to find a way to make her see it, but, at the time, she was too worn down. She was ready to give up, and it affected her ability to see any hope in my plan. I knew she needed rest and the best I could do now would be to let her sleep. I decided to go along with her for the time being, in hopes that by morning she would see things differently. I glanced at my watch.

"Wow, did you know it's after midnight? I understand what you're telling me, Amy. Right now, I think we should get some rest before we try to decide anything. Let's just join the others."

Amy agreed, "Now, you're making more sense."

After we made our way through the larger pipe, we gathered at the entrance.

I spoke to all of them.

"I'm sure we can all agree that those bats are going to come streaming back in here before dawn. So, I suggest we get down out of here and spend the night in the storm drain away from this pipe."

Judging from their nods, I assumed they were in favor of my suggestion.

Vic said, "We can move down the storm drain some ways and sleep up close to the wall."

"Right." I said, "Then, tomorrow we can discuss our options."

Connie whined, "I'm hungry, Vic."

"I know you are, baby. We all are. When I get you out of this mess, I'll buy you the biggest hamburgers in town fixed all the way with chocolate milk shakes on the side."

Amy interrupted, "Vic, I know you mean well, but I don't think it's such a good idea talking about food right now."

"Oh yeah, I guess you're right, Amy."

Vic put his jacket around Connie's shoulders and walked her away.

"At least, I'll keep you warm until then, Connie. Come on, let's find a soft spot for the night."

The two of them went off. Amy and I trailed behind. I put my arm around her shoulder whispering in her ear.

"I'm proud of you. You're holding up extremely well, all things considered."

Amy turned to me.

"Yes, and when we get out of here, I expect lots of rewards, too."

"You shall have it, my lady. Oh, but don't forget I must also present my bill for medical services, you know. I guess that should pretty much even things up, don't you think?"

Amy playfully bopped me on the head with her good arm. Then, she rested her head on my shoulder as we walked to a spot where we could rest. We made no provision for guard duty. I suppose it was foolish, but exhaustion eats away at better judgment. Fortunately, we all passed the night without incident. When we awoke, it was near 10:00 a.m. I took my flashlight and played it over the ceiling confirming our little black friends were back. The entire ceiling was lined, row upon row, with clinging, sleeping bats.

Connie looked up and started shivering at once.

"I'm just not gonna look up anymore, Amy. I'm just gonna pretend they're not even there."

Amy shrugged, "You might as well. They're sleeping now anyway. They don't even know you're here."

"I'm all for keeping it that way, too", she said.

As for me, I decided the subject of excavating the caved-in pipe had waited long enough. Though I knew it would take a lot of convincing, I was ready to give it my best shot. Choosing my words carefully, I started in cautiously.

"You know it sure was weird being able to see the stars through that pipe last night. It made me feel as if I could climb right out of here. Do you all know how far it was to the surface from where I was?"

Before anyone could answer I quickly followed up.

"I'd say I couldn't have been more than ten feet from the outside."

Amy chimed in, "Let me guess. That means you want us to dig ten feet up and just pop right out in downtown Philly, right?"

I defended, "No, but it could be closer than that if you hear me out."

Vic took the bait asking, "What do you mean, Allen?"

"Just this, Vic. That pipe to the outside was probably in an alleyway between buildings. That means there's a building over that cave-in. I'd bet money on it. Think about it for a moment. The building must have a basement. That means we don't have to dig ten feet. We only must dig as far as the basement. Don't you see?"

I could see Vic was starting to get it. I moved closer to his side strengthening my point.

"With you and me shoveling in shifts, we could move away that dirt inside a day. I'm sure you'll agree, we're pressed for time. Right now, we need to find the fastest way out. I don't think any of us can guarantee this big storm drain is going to lead us out. Either way we take a chance. Why not take the closest way out?"

Amy replied, "How would you get the dirt and bricks out. The drain pipe is too small to turn around inside."

When I heard her question, I was secretly elated. I knew I had her to the point where she was considering it. I moved swiftly to complete my argument.

"With one entrenching tool, one digs while the other loads bricks and dirt in the back packs. Then, we pass them down the pipe to Amy."

Amy conceded, "I suppose that could work. Of course, Connie that means you and me must be in the pipe passing along the bricks and dirt."

She looked down at the ground.

"I guess so, but if it gets us out of here sooner, then I'm ready to give it a try."

"Well, then," I said smiling. "Let's do give it a try."

We were all parched and hungry with just enough energy to make it another day. I did not say so, but I felt this was the last time we could make such an attempt. Our energy was sapped to the point that it felt burdensome just to shift our own weight around. Moving a pile of dirt and brick would call for our utmost effort, perhaps more than we could endure.

Once again, it was my idea. I volunteered to go first.

"I'll go in and you can transfer the diggings to Connie, if that's O.K. with you, Vic. That way, Amy won't have to push the debris very far."

Amy spoke up for herself.

"I can do my part. I'll take turns with Connie."

Connie surprised Amy with her answer.

"You might wanna think that over some more, Amy. I don't think you want both of us crawling back and forth over what we've already pulled out."

Vic raised his eyebrows giving her a look of genuine respect for her astute observation. I, too, was taken aback at her keen observation.

I urged, "We best get a move on. We've got about eight hours before the bats will be using our pipe for a breeze way."

We had our work cut out for us in the narrow pipe. Every shovel full of dirt and brick had to be slid along the pipe out to Amy. She, in turn, would dump it into the larger pipe. In this way, we would still have space to abandon the small pipe if necessary. The work went slowly. Whenever exhaustion overtook any of us, we would all stop to rest.

At first, Vic and I took turns up front shoveling. Eventually, we each needed a rest from that job, as well. It would take us several minutes to switch positions since all of us would have to back out then reorganize. To say the least, it was a painstaking process.

By two o'clock, we had removed almost a third of the mass before us. I remember reaching up above me to remove a brick lodged in the dirt when another came down with a thud on my forehead. I was nearly knocked unconscious and a mandatory break ensued. While I was resting, Vic asked me what I thought we would find once we cleared the tunnel. Lying on my back with eyes closed to keep out the dirt, I answered.

"I'm thinking this brick pipe must have collapsed at this point because the earth above it was weakened somehow."

"Do you really think there's a basement up there?"

"Well, if there isn't, I expect it's something like it."

"Do you mean you think it's man made?"

"Yes, of course. That's what I would expect at this level. Besides, I'm through with caverns, pipelines, and drains. I'm ready for some fresh air."

Vic laughed, "Me, too, brother. I'm ready for some real food right now. I hope they left something good to eat up there."

"Just try not to think about that right now, Vic."

"Yeah, yeah, I know, don't talk food. I get it."

Connie called up to me, "Allen, do you want to change places? I can dig for a while."

"No, that's O.K., Connie. I just need to rest a bit longer. I can start again as soon as my ears stop ringing."

Vic asked, "Does it hurt badly?"

"Naw, I can shake it off. I'll be O.K."

After five minutes, I forced myself to start digging again. I managed to keep it up for another half hour before asking Vic to relieve me. When he got into position, I shifted each shovel load backward just as he had done for me. The process continued for another hour. Suddenly, Vic shouted back to me.

"I've got dirt sliding down on me. It's not much, but it's coming from above for sure. I must have broken through to something."

Vic started poking upward with his shovel. Each time he struck upward more dirt would flow into the hole. He would stop intermittently to load a pack then send it along before resuming his poking. Finally, a small hole appeared over him in the dim dust-filtered light. Just then, he noticed his flashlight lying near his head was growing ever dimmer.

"Allen, there's a small hole above me, but my batteries are going."

In another second, Vic's end of the pipe fell into darkness. He felt the grip of fear that closes in around you when you can't see your hand in front of your face. I heard a tremor in his voice.

"It's plenty dark up here, Allen. Have you got a light?"

I recognized his sense of false bravery coming through.

"I'll pass mine up right away. I'm warning you though; remember, we both changed out our batteries at the same time. So, don't expect this one to last very long either. O.K., buddy?"

Sounding brave he answered, "Gotcha."

I passed my light up to him and asked Connie to bring her lamp up near me.

She protested, "What about Amy? She'll be in the dark."

I assured, "It won't be for long. Vic has found an opening above him. Tell her that and say it won't be for long."

Connie moved the lamp forward with a trembling hand. I noticed she stayed closer to me after I handed my flashlight over to Vic.

Vic said, "I've got the light on the hole now. If I can just widen it up some, I'll try standing up in it."

I wasted my breath with a cautionary, "Be careful, Vic."

Straining to see ahead, I could just make out the end of Vic's shovel stabbing into the earth above. Each time he did so, another shovel full of earth fell through the widening hole. I could hear him choke as the dry earth from above formed heavy dust in his small breathing space.

Clearing his throat, he croaked, "Just a few more licks and I think I'll have it clear."

It was then I heard an ominous sound. It was like the sound of someone dropping a heavy load of laundry on a wet floor. Vic's light suddenly extinguished.

I yelled in fear, "Vic, are you alright?"

There was no sound coming from his direction. I realized the worst. The ground had caved in on him.

Instantly, I turned to Connie.

"Give me your lantern quick!"

I lifted the lamp in the narrow space up just high enough to confirm my fears. The upper part of Vic's torso was covered in dirt. Part of me said, *"It should have been me lying there. I should have relieved him long ago."* My instincts propelled me forward placing the lamp where I thought his face would be. Immediately, I started clawing at the dirt pulling it from his face. Connie looked on helplessly. She could only watch while I fought frantically to free his face from the cloak of dirt smothering him.

Soon, I began feeling his features as I swept away the dirt from around his mouth. Connie was hysterically screaming at me to save him. Amy's mind was in turmoil. Lying there in total darkness, she could only hear Connie's screams. She could not understand what was happening. As I continued to work on Vic's face, I heard him make a sound. It was a muffled groan of sorts. The first thing I could think of was elevating his head and trying to clear his mouth. The space in the pipe would not allow much elevation. I reached for his shovel and propped it under his neck and head. Then, I went back to clearing his airway. He moaned again; then rose on one elbow. He was trying to get on his side.

He began retching, trying to expel the rest of the dirt clogged in his mouth.

"Aaahh aug, augh," between gags he said, "Wow, that's nasty."

I grinned from ear to ear looking over my patient.

"That's the best sound I've heard you make all day, partner."

"What happened?"

"Well, from the looks of things, you were trying to take a shortcut out of here. You wouldn't run off and leave your friends behind, now would you?"

"Naw, I guess I'll stick around and see how it all turns out."

Wiping the dirt from his face, he looked up with a grimy grin pointing at the hole above him.

"Look what I made."

"You did good, Vic. Really good."

Connie stopped crying long enough to call out to him.

"Are you alright, baby? I thought you were gone, for sure."

"Hell, no! It'll take a lot more than dirt to bury me."

Amy cried out in the darkness behind us.

"What's going on? What happened? Is he hurt?"

I shouted, "Its O.K., Amy. Everything's alright now. We just experienced a little landslide."

Vic quipped, "What do you mean *we*, Kemosabe?"

"We're going to send you the lamp so you can make your way up here, Amy. We have a hole open above the pipe that we'll want to explore. Vic, you deserve to take the lead when you feel up to it."

Vic shook the dirt off his shirt. Then, looked up at the new passage his friends could take.

"Thanks partner just give me a little time to catch my breath."

No beam of light showed around the hole's edges, but it was a way out of our present predicament. It not only offered room to stand, but a new path that could lead us out of the hell hole we had worked our way into. I knew with only one oil lamp between us, it was our last chance to find daylight.

When Vic was ready, he led the way. Handing him the lantern, I hoisted him up to the edge of the hole above. With a bit of struggle, he managed his way to the top edge leaving us behind in total darkness. It was an eerie feeling. For the first time, we were huddled together looking up at the only light we possessed. Vic lowered his arm and pulled Connie up with my help from below. Amy and I struggled out next. Once we were all standing together, Vic raised the lamp high so we could see what we had gotten ourselves into. There was a collective gasp, we found ourselves standing in the middle of a dirt floor in a room. Crude in construction by any standard, it was nonetheless a room built with human hands.

Vic looked on in wonderment expressing our sentiments best.

"Where the hell are we?"

All I could say in reply was, "Let's look around."

We appeared to be in a box like room with a stone ceiling. It was constructed of roughhewn boards. There were no windows or doors. Apparently, it was a room built over and forgotten. It was approximately eight by eight feet. In one corner, there was a box with a hinged lid. It was about four feet by three. Of course, my first thought was to look inside.

"Hold your lamp closer, Vic. I'll see if I can get this thing open."

Vic complied and I tugged on the lid. It did not give way easily, so I took out my broken knife and slid it under the lid. I pried away at several points until the lid finally gave way. Lifting the lid made the rusty hinges creak adding dramatic effect to its opening. Once the lid was fully raised, we all took a step closer to view the contents of the box. My heart leapt with joy when my eyes beheld an old whale oil lamp in one corner. It must have been used in pre-Revolutionary War times. I reached down and pulled it out to examine it closely. There was still oil in the lamp and the wick was intact. I was even able to turn the knob to adjust the wick length.

I held it up with a smile, "This lamp looks like it will still work."

Amy passed me a kitchen match. I struck it on the low stone ceiling. Removing the chimney on the lamp, I held the match to the wick. It started burning right away. Then, I held it high above my head.

Proudly I stated, "My friends, we now have twice the light. Let's see what else this box has to offer."

Vic had already grasped what looked like a wicker basket. When he raised it up, he felt weight to it. He soon discovered it was a gallon crock wrapped in wicker with a wicker handle and cork stopper. Of course, his curiosity did not end there.

"Let's see what's in this jug", he said.

He started twisting on the old cork right away. After a few starts, he put the jug between his legs and really twisted on it. Suddenly, it pulled loose with a dull pop. Immediately, he had the bottle up to his nose sniffing its contents. Everyone looked on expectantly as he paused identifying the scent in the bottle. His eyes grew wide with delight that comes from discovering something long lost, then found.

Vic announced with glee, "It's brandy."

A small cheer arose from our midst. What a find, indeed, for such a thirsty party. Vic lifted the bottle toward his mouth preparing to take a long tug on the bottle. I raised my hand stopping him in mid-motion cautioning him.

"Vic, you better take it easy on that. You don't know what's happened to that stuff over time. Think what it can do to you on an empty stomach, too. Besides you're no good to us drunk."

"Don't worry, Allen, I just want to take a little taste. You know, just enough to sip off the poison for the rest of you."

Sarcastically, I said, "Oh well, by all means, then. Thank you for your selfless service, old man."

Amy just laughed, "Oh, go ahead. Let him have a sip. How much trouble can he get into down here? After all, he deserves a little something to wash down that dirt."

I relented, "Alright, go ahead, Vic. Just be sure you don't overdo."

Connie rushed to Vic's side to relieve her thirst, as well.

"Let me have some, too, honey."

I warned, "Don't make yourself sick."

Amy chided, "Gee, Allen. Come off it. You sound like my grandmother."

"I just don't want us to lose control. We're not out of this thing yet, you know. Besides, we could use some of that brandy as disinfectant for your arm you know."

"Why, Allen, you are ever so thoughtful. Then she laughed saying, "But first, let's have a blast for our insides."

I could see an all-consuming thirst was at work here. Otherwise, I might have thought I was in the company of craven alcoholics. It was then we discovered another item in our box of dreams. A full ten-pound sack of corn. I speculated it was some prized strain of seed corn set aside for future planting. In its current form, it was not exactly food, but could provide a ready substitute for those in a state of hunger. The last item in the box was a paraffin sealed crock of flour. It was this last item that held the most hope for sustenance.

Vic was overwhelmed.

"I can't believe it, Allen. We've got something to eat and drink."

I cautioned, "Let's just be sure it's gonna be alright for us."

Vic took another swig of the brandy shouting, "We'll be eatin' flow cakes tonight."

"What are you talking about?" I asked.

"Didn't you learn nothin' in history class? Remember, Mr. Ryan tellin' us about starving Johnny Rebs sticking their bayonets over the fire with mixed up gobs of flour and water on them? They called them flow cakes. It was their only meal in the field when they ran out of regular provisions."

"Yeah, I guess you're right. It seems to me I did hear something about that."

"Well, let's get busy," Vic urged. We've got flour and we've got brandy. We can mix up a mess of flow cakes."

I could already detect Vic's changing attitude as he took another hit on the brandy jug.

"Whoa, whoa there," I cried, "Let's just be sure we know what we're doin' first."

"What's there to know? You just take a little flour, then stir it up with brandy, and you hold it over the fire. Here you can use my knife."

Amy could see he was getting overanxious. Even though we were all hungry, and it sounded good, we all saw he was moving a bit too fast.

"Let's just be careful. We only have a small amount of flour in this jar. I just want to be sure we use it wisely."

Before I knew it, Vic swept his hand over mine snatching the jar into his possession. Holding it high over his head, he swaggered back and forth. Clearly, he had more interest in *his* next meal than our best interests. As I lunged forward to retrieve the jar, he held it up too quickly. Some of the contents spilled on the ground. His act of wasteful defiance suddenly caused something inside me to snap. I just went crazy in a heartbeat. I was all over him pounding him with the last of my strength. Nothing the girls could do would stop me. Falling backward under my flailing blows, he lost possession of the prized jar sending it crashing to the floor.

I heard myself shouting, "Damn you, Vic. You're going to wreck us all."

I guess there was too much pent up inside, years of disappointment in my father's drinking, the times Vic lost his cool when drinking, and the surrounding frustrations of our entrapment. It all came bursting forth in a fit of rage.

I felt a shovel pounding my back before I came to my senses. Vic's head was between my knees as I rained down blows on his head and shoulders. Finally, Connie's beating on my back with a shovel got my attention. I stopped hitting and watched Vic's bloody face writhing as he gasped for breath from between bloodied lips. My mind filled with revulsion at what I saw. Now, a wave of shame washed over me as I struggled to regain control. It was as if I were somewhere else in that claustrophobic room looking back from a dark corner. I truly wished I were tucked in that corner instead of feeling the way I did. Slowly, I rose to my feet panting and feeling remorse for my actions. I turned away actually putting myself in that very corner where I belonged. Right then, I felt I did not deserve to be near my companions. What I had done set me apart and I felt broken inside.

Amy tried consoling me. She could see the self-loathing on my face. She knew me well enough to know my actions were not like the person in my heart of hearts.

"She looked up at Connie, still holding the shovel perched on her shoulder like a baseball bat."

Catching her breath, Amy murmured in my ear.

"Be still now, Allen. It will be alright soon enough. She cautioned Connie in a low voice, "Put it down, Connie. He's stopped now and so should you."

Connie stared at me defiantly slowly lowering the shovel. I stood still next to Amy with her arm around me repeating, "I'm very sorry, Vic, I'm so, so sorry."

Amy advised, "We all just need to cool it a while. Let's just keep to ourselves for now."

Connie took off her bandanna starting to wipe the wounds on Vic's face. Taking a corner of the cloth, she gingerly dipped it in the remnants of the turned over brandy bottle to swab Vic's cuts. I stared ahead blankly wanting to say something strong like a leader might, but my mind refused to convey any thought to my lips. In my heart, I was not feeling like a leader anymore.

An uneasy silence passed between us before Amy took charge.

"We all need to eat. Let's get that corn and make the best of it. We can use Allen's knife to break some of it up on the shovel blade. It may be dry, but it's something to chew on. Come on, let's get started."

We all went to work feeling grateful to be doing something together for the common good. With a lot of pounding, we managed to render a coarse form of cornmeal to chew on. Although it was dry, it did bring saliva to our mouths not unlike desperate souls who learned to place pebbles in their mouths when crossing the desert. With a little something in our stomach, the tense situation eased a bit.

The pain from the shovel blows to my back was no worse than the cuts and bruises I left with Vic. We each began getting over it, putting the more important task of escape before us.

I began feeling along the roughhewn walls looking for any sign of a weak spot in our box-like room. I figured it must have been an old root cellar that got built over in a hasty phase of reconstruction. Consequently, it must have been sealed up under the stone flooring above us. At least that meant one ray of hope existed. We were nearer an existing surface structure than we had been previously. In any event, it was clear the course that remained was to leave the cellar. I decided to make my plan known to the rest.

"I say we need to get through one of these wooden walls. What do you think Vic?"

He nodded, "Yeah, which way do you wanna go?"

I replied, "I can't see anything that looks likely. Why don't you take the shovel and start at one corner, and I'll use the butt of my knife? We can tap all around to see if anything sounds likely."

"O.K. by me," he said.

Each of us went around the room starting in opposite corners tapping along listening for any sign of hollowness or weakness in the wall. As I came along the short side of our rectangular room, a distinct hollow sound came about mid-way in the wall.

"Listen right here," I said.

I ran my knife butt back over the area tapping slowly as everyone cupped their hands over their ears listening intently. As my knife knocked along, the sound changed from a firm thud to a lighter sound.

Amy stopped me.

"There it is. I heard it right there."

Connie urged, "Do it again."

This time, as I thumped my knife butt along the board both Connie and Vic stopped me.

In unison, they cried, "Stop… there, that's it."

I stood back sheathing my knife.

"I think we've found our spot. Let's give it a try."

Vic brought over the shovel and engaged the spot stabbing into the rough timber. After several attempts, he was winded and handed the shovel to me.

The going was slow, but by taking turns we managed to chip away at the spot making a hole about six inches square. We were not through the wood completely, but it was a start. Eventually, even Connie took a whack at it making the chips fly some more. Finally, I pushed the blade through making a small slit. A half an hour later, we had a small hole chopped out. Our excitement began building as we steadily realized there was at least a space of sorts between the wall and the other side. Now, it only remained to make the hole wider. As soon as it was large enough, I held our lantern up to the hole. As I peered in, I saw shapes in a room larger than the one we were in. It was difficult to get the light to shine through the hole to the room. Tipping the lamp at a steep angle, I made out one of the shapes to be a long table against a wall. I could also see several wooden casks on the floor in front of the table.

"There's stuff in there," I whispered excitedly.

Vic asked anxiously, "What kind of stuff is that?"

"Well, there's a table, some chairs, and some wooden casks on the floor."

"Let me look."

Soon, Vic was on his knees holding the lamp at an angle with his eye close to the wall.

"Hey, I think I see some old rifles stacked up in there."

I was so excited I was shaking.

"Maybe it's some of that Revolutionary War stuff we've been searching for."

Amy scoffed, under her breath, "That'll be the day."

I pretended not to hear her as I took up the shovel again.

"Come on, guys, let's keep chipping away here. We might have found more than just a way out."

Vic joined in, "Yeah, this could make it all worthwhile, girls."

Connie looked at Amy returning a similar look of sympathy. They did not have to say it would take a whole hell of a lot to make it all worthwhile in their minds. Meanwhile, I turned my attention to making the hole larger, striking the timber with more determined blows. In another fifteen minutes, our journey beneath Philly would take another interesting twist.

Chapter 13

The room we saw ahead revealed several things at once. The floor was covered with fitted boards laid down intentionally for that purpose. The walls were roughhewn wood like we had just hacked through. Once we had a hole large enough to access the room, I went in first. Finding the room thick with cobwebs, I had to constantly swing my lamp before me as I pushed into the pitch-black room. There was no sign of ventilation, but there was a crude arched wooden door to my left on one end of the rectangular shaped room. I guessed the room to be about twenty feet long by ten feet wide.

The contents of the room fascinated me at once. As I held up my lantern, I could make out a long bench along the opposite wall. Apparently, it was a work bench. I could see several old tools hanging from hooks on the wall above it. It was obvious the tools were of the Revolutionary War era. There was an assortment of chisels, hammers, awls, and screwdrivers in neat rows above the bench. I held my light up to the hole in the wall beckoning the others through. Vic entered first holding his lantern out making his way.

He remarked, "This looks like a storage room. Wow, look at this over here, Allen."

Vic was standing near a corner of the room to his left where a stack of

Revolutionary War muskets stood together like lonely sentinels. Rusting with age, they were covered in cobwebs. It was an eerie sight, knowing someone left them there at the ready, if ever the call came. Under the bench on the floor, there was a row of gunpowder casks. I could be sure by the markings on the lids, still legible after all these years. A tingle went up my spine as I realized this was part of what we came for, after all.

Now Amy and Connie cautiously entered the room reaching out carefully brushing away cobwebs hanging in their path.

Amy ventured, "This place has sure seen better days. Is this some kind of storeroom, Allen?"

"You bet it is," I replied enthusiastically. Somehow, I didn't feel the constant gnawing of hunger that dogged me for so many days. Instead, I was caught up in the moment of discovery.

"Look here on the bench. There are wooden boxes. Come here, Vic. Help me open one up. Maybe there's something we can use."

Vic slid his knife blade under the lid of one box. It was about a foot square and three inches deep. Prying up the lid, he revealed a layer of sawdust. As he brushed it aside, it revealed a dozen neat rows of round lead shot balls.

"Well, that's no surprise," I said. "We've found a magazine with ammunition."

Amy returned my observation with a blank stare.

I explained, "You know, an ammunition storage room."

"Sure," she replied. "Why didn't you say so in the first place?"

Connie was quiet as she hesitated to say what she had found on the end of the bench on a bottom shelf. It was another wicker basket like the one we found with brandy in it. Vic watched as she slowly slid the jug back onto the shelf.

"What did you find there, Connie?"

She shifted her eyes back and forth trying to think of something to say. She just wasn't that quick at lying though. Vic was soon standing over her asking again.

"What is it, baby?"

All she could think of was turning to face him blocking his view. Her little maneuver was not enough to dissuade Vic. He smiled broadly. Then, he stooped reaching around behind her, laying his hands on the prize.

Recognizing its feel and weight, he knew exactly what it was. Gripping the handle, he raised his prize for all to see. Then curiously, he handed it over to Allen.

"Here, Allen, I think you know how to handle this better than I do."

I graciously received the jug placing it on the bench.

"I think we had better look for a way outta here first before we do any celebrating."

Amy echoed, "Amen."

Vic and I both approached the door with our lanterns. While Vic held his light up, I tried working the rusted door handle. It would not budge, so I took out my shovel and began beating on the door latch. After several strikes, it fell off leaving just a hole where it was installed. I found this action really brought me no closer to opening the door. Standing back, I studied the situation. It occurred to me I might have had more success removing the hinges.

Going back to the work bench, I selected a couple of screwdrivers that might do the job. After several halting attempts, I asked Vic to grab the brandy jug on the shelf.

"You're not giving up that easily, are you?"

"No, Vic. I think the brandy might work to lubricate the screws a bit."

He quipped, "Yeah, I find it an excellent lubricant myself."

Amy just rolled her eyes as she looked on.

Connie whined, "How long is this going to take?"

I replied, "That depends on my strength and the stubbornness of these rusted hinges. Don't worry. If I can't do it, I'll give Vic a try, right Vic."

"Yeah, why don't you girls get busy and crack some more corn for us. After this job, we're gonna need it."

The girls soon got busy grinding up the rest of the corn while Vic and I took turns at the hinges. Each screw fought us all the way making it a slow tedious process. Finally, we managed to remove one of the three hinges. The others came just as hard. I stopped at one point, suggesting we all have a little corn and brandy just to fortify us. Amy appeared doubtful at first, but soon relented after the rest of us all took a swig. Fortunately, Vic kept himself under control. Before long, we were all feeling light headed and giddy. Under the effects of brandy without much corn to soak it up, with we all sat around laughing.

It took some strong-willed effort for me to get up and start working again. The new-found energy from the potent brandy seemed to make a difference though. Eventually, the last hinge fell to the dusty floor. I stood up straight making an announcement.

"We now have a door before us with no hinges."

As I stuck my shovel blade between the door jamb and the door, I began prying backward as I stated too loudly.

"As we all know, a door without hinges cannot stand alone."

As those words left my lips, the door broke loose propelling me backward as I fell on my butt.

Everybody had a good laugh as I sat there smiling with the door on top of me. The room ahead awaited our exploration. It was late Saturday night, over a week since we left. Our clothes were torn and besmirched with every kind of grit, grime, and slime imaginable. We were weary from hunger and thirst parched. As I look back on it all, I cannot fully account for our actions. With hindsight, I must admit our judgment was clearly clouded by the brandy. Instead of moving ahead as curiosity might impel us, we chose to sit together passing the wicker jug in celebration of dismantling the door.

Amy just seemed to naturally plop down on the floor next to me. She helped me slide the door off my legs, then passed me the jug. Somehow, in the moment, it seemed the thing to do. So, I partook.

"Wow, that's strong stuff," I exclaimed! Lowering the jug, I looked over at Vic and Connie sitting on the ground next to me. I slurred, "Want some of this?"

I held the jug out toward Vic. As he reached for it, I jerked it back taunting him.

"Now you see, you missed it. You gotta be faster than that, old buddy. Come on, try again, my friend."

He seemed game lowering his gaze staring me down. I reached forward once more holding out the prize. He lurched for it, and, once again, I deprived him of his goal. Now, he bore a more determined look turning toward Connie.

"Watch this, Connie. He thinks he can fool me again, but I'm too fast for him."

Naturally, I taunted him again with the jug. Only this time, he faked a grab for it with one hand falling toward me with the other hand open for the jug. Instead of grasping it, however, he fell on his face beside me. As he struggled to sit upright, I took pity on him.

"Oh, you poor boy…you missed your brandy. Here have some of mine."

This time, I held it steady for him. Yet, he still had some trouble grasping it. Finally, he got a grip on the handle and helped himself to a masterful tug on the bottle.

"Aaahh… that's what I call brandy. Connie, where's the corn? Pass the corn, please."

She giggled, "It's all gone. We'll have to grind some more."

"Well, then, get busy and grind."

She gave him her best glassy-eyed look and broke out laughing.

"You're not getting any more corn until you give me that jug. You hear me?"

Vic looked down where the jug rested in his lap smiling like an opossum.

"You mean this jug, Connie?"

"Yep, that's the one."

Vic graciously passed the jug over to Connie. She held it by the handle and wiped her dirty sleeve across her mouth, then tipped it back to her lips. Taking a long swig, she set the jug on the floor looking around her, then belched.

"Where's the corn, Amy?"

"It's right over there on the bench, Connie. Can you see it?

Connie turned her head looking whimsically at the bench where the last of the corn lay in the cloth bag. To her, it might as well have been a hundred miles away. She seemed unable to retrieve it.

Connie pleaded, "Could you get the corn please, Amy?"

Amy replied coyly, "If you pass me the jug, I will."

Connie leaned over too far with the jug falling on Amy. Then she struggled to rise on one elbow. Making another stretch, she connected with Amy's out stretched arm. Amy helped herself to another large swig. Then, she did manage to stagger over to the bench. She had to hold on there for what seemed an eternity before she could muster enough equilibrium to make the trip back with the corn.

Sadly, the passing of the jug continued. We drank until good sense was a nagging memory. Eventually, we ended in such a state that we found it more convenient to crack corn with our teeth while passing the jug. This went on until all of us had our fill, each dropping out of the circle one by one. We did not rise until Sunday morning with our heads throbbing and our bellies grumbling. None of us was pleasant to be around.

Ordinarily, when someone awakes with a hangover, they want to be alone. It's not an anti-social thing. It's more of a recovery process. The afflicted usually want to deal with the malady by themselves. When I raised my head for the first time, all I could think of was finding relief from the overwhelming thirst in me. My mouth felt as if it were coated in sandpaper. Even my breathing was affected by the dried-out membranes in my throat. At first, I tried speaking to Amy, but to no avail. The sounds emanating from my mouth were useless guttural croaking noises. Knowing I must find relief, I pulled myself up on my knees. The lamp next to Amy's head was burning low.

At first, I made it to the lamp on my hands and knees. Turning the wick upward, it illuminated the room where we had slept. Of course, nothing had changed. We were still lying at the threshold of a room that might hold promise of escape. Realizing that, I struggled pulling myself to my feet only to stumble across that threshold. I recognized one thing different about the next room immediately. It lifted my spirits a bit.

The ceiling was no longer a low overhead barrier of stone. Instead, I saw thick wooden beams above me that supported planks of flooring. The room was also semi-furnished. There was a round table with four chairs. Also, a large cherry desk with ornate glass knobs on its small drawers stood against the wall near the table. The drawers were arranged in rows on either side of a large middle drawer with double knobs on it. Clearly, the furniture dated to Revolutionary War times. While I found it all intriguing, my biological drive sent me in search of something else.

I felt I must have liquid soon or I would surely die. Looking all about the room with my lantern held high, I investigated its contents further. To my far right at the end of the room, there was a tall wooden shelf standing almost as high as the ceiling. By far, my most important discovery so far was a row of crockery jars on the shelf that appeared to be sealed. I had seen the result of my grandmother's canning efforts and these jars appeared to be the genuine article. My heart leapt at the very thought of it.

As I approached the shelf, closer inspection revealed it was better than I expected. There before me, were several crocks labeled as various fruit preserves. Strips of cloth were labeled pears, peaches, and apples. In addition, there were some smaller crocks labeled blackberry and gooseberry jam. My hand was shaking as I closed in on them. I was beside myself with delightful anticipation. I reached for the crock labeled pears grasping it, then, greedily looking over my shoulder. I felt no compunction to feel sorry for the others. At that moment, my survival instincts completely took over. Quickly, I unsnapped my knife from its sheath. I removed the metal lid holder from the crock, then pressed my broken bladed knife tip into service. Cautiously, so carefully, so as not to crack the lip, I pushed the blade under the edge of the lid. Unbelievably, I heard a slight hiss as I released pressure on the crock of preserves put up at least one-hundred and eighty-five years ago. Gingerly, I removed the lid pressed in paraffin. Driven by incredible thirst, I tripped up the crock drinking the juices letting the pears bounce against my tongue. It was pure delight. I stood there draining every single drop that would fall from the mouth of the crock. Then, I started in on the pears. My own voracity surprised me. I was slurping the last pear down preparing to lick my lips when I heard a sound behind me. Jerking my head around like an animal caught in the act, I saw the outline of Amy's body standing in the dim lit room.

Amy's voice cracked, "Find something you like, Allen?"

Immediately, I froze cloaked in guilt. It was such a heavy burden to bear. I felt I could not speak at first. Then, I turned slowly putting down the empty crock on the shelf. The first words from my mouth sounded child-like, as you might expect someone would sound when caught in the act of doing something terribly wrong.

"Guess what, Amy? I found some preserves."

"I see that. Would there be enough for us all if I hadn't come along?"

"Oh, no! It's nothing like that, Amy. There's enough for us all here."

Amy's voice was croaky, like an old witch from a fairy tale.

"I wonder if you even gave the rest of us a thought."

"Amy, it's not like that. You should know better."

I felt so ashamed. Even my voice sounded better than hers with the golden nectar of pears still coating my throat.

I gestured, "Here, come and get some. I'll help you open it with my knife."

A glint immediately formed in her eye. I could see her licking her cracked lips as she thought of herself. It was only a fleeting moment though. She straightened her back. Then she turned to get Vic and Connie. I felt so low she could have used my butt as a doorstop. Amy didn't say another word about the incident. She just awoke the others and showed them what was waiting for them. Lost in the reverie of eating such a feast, none of them questioned me about my discovery. It was enough that I alone knew. The thought of my behavior gnawed at me for some time thereafter.

In the meantime, Vic and Connie downed a quart crock of preserved fruit each, then busied themselves exploring the contents of the room. Vic soon found more muskets standing a lonely vigil in a corner. It followed he would also find more gunpowder and musket balls tucked behind a stairway that led to the ceiling. More importantly, he discovered there was a trap door at the top of the stairs. After several exhaustive attempts, Vic and I gave up on trying to open it the conventional way. There was simply too much weight on the other side. We could not be sure whether it was nailed shut or floored over. For all we knew, it might be both.

I soon turned my attention elsewhere. What intrigued me most was the large desk against the wall. It was a fine piece of work, itself. Nicely finished, it looked as if it could have belonged to a wealthy merchant or someone of importance during the Revolutionary War era. I wondered why such a fine piece was tucked away in an old musty cellar.

Vic and I each set upon getting past the locked drawers of the big desk. My first attempt ended in another piece of my knife blade breaking off as I pried on the top drawers to the left. Vic fared much better managing to break the first lock on the right side. When he slowly pulled open the drawer, we were all there peering over his shoulder. What he revealed made us gasp. Inside were three large silver goblets lying side by side.

I remarked breathlessly, "Those look like they're made of pure silver."

Vic smiled broadly, "They do have that tarnished look, don't they?"

Amy and Connie were anxious to see them up close. Amy pushed against me to get nearer.

"Let me see. I want to hold one."

Connie exclaimed, "Me, too. I want to see one up close, Vic."

Vic dutifully pulled them all from the drawer handing them over for our inspection. As soon as Amy had a goblet in her hand, she hefted it for its weight.

"It sure feels heavy enough to be silver." Then she turned it over.

"Look here on the bottom." She showed us the bottom of the goblet bearing a die stamp with the word "REVERE" in quotes.

She spoke slowly, almost reverently, as the revelation sunk in.

"Oh, my gosh…these are genuine Revere Ware goblets. Look at the stamp on the bottom."

Holding it in the light for all to see, we acknowledged the stamp on each of the goblets looked genuine, though none of us was acquainted with real Revere Ware.

"My grandmother showed me a plate once that had this same marking. She told me there were lots of copies made during the same period, but only Paul Revere possessed a die that left the letters raised up like these. These goblets could be worth a lot of money, Vic."

Vic retrieved each goblet from the girls and me, quickly stuffing them in his backpack.

"I'll keep that in mind, Amy, if we ever get out of here."

I decided to speak before things went any further.

"Look, before we go on with this treasure hunt, I suggest we divide the contents of this desk equally."

Vic stood back folding his arms across his chest looking on expectantly.

"Oh, yeah, well what do you have in mind exactly?"

"Just this, you found those on the right side. I say you can have the contents of the right side of this desk, and I will take the left. Does that sound fair enough?"

Vic started nodding warily in agreement. Then he said, "Hey, wait a minute. What about the middle drawer? Who gets what's in the middle drawer?"

"We can flip for it, O.K.?"

Amy protested, "Sure, you'll just flip for it. What about us girls?

Don't we have any stake in this treasure hunt, or are we just along for the exercise?"

I could see that fiery look rising in her eyes again. I knew she was serious as a heart attack.

I looked each of them in the eye asking, "Well, what do you think is fair?"

Now, Amy started to change her tone to one of reason.

"I think we should split whatever is found by you guys on either side. That should be fair enough. What do you think, Connie?"

Everybody could see by the blank look on Connie's face she had not given the matter much thought either way up to that moment. Now, she seemed deep in thought. In her own time, she came up with her notion of an equitable settlement.

"I think it's fair to share with the guys, after all, they're breakin' into the desk and all."

I could not help chuckling at her simplistic solution.

"Well, then, that settles it," I said. Let's get started on the rest of these drawers."

Vic began pulling other items out of his long open drawer, while I bent my efforts toward getting the top drawer open on my side. I noticed, as I pried away, he was pulling other items out of his drawer. At first, he produced a small magnifying glass with a lens about three inches across. It had a pearl handle with ornate filigreed silver trim. He held up his prize speaking without looking away from the drawer.

"This should bring a few bucks down at the old pawn shop."

In shock, I responded to his offhanded comment.

"Vic, I hope you're joking. You wouldn't get a fraction of what that's worth in a pawn shop. In fact, I doubt they'd even know what period of time it came from. Please tell me you're not thinking of pawning it."

"Well, what would you do with it, Mr. Historian?"

I continued struggling with the first lock on my drawer thinking the thick blade of my broken knife was not helping.

"I would, at least, take it to a fine jeweler and have it appraised before I did anything else. Also, for your information," I said testily, "a museum might pay a good bit more for it, too. You know they do pay well for historical artifacts."

Vic continued rummaging.

"Right, I'll think about that, too."

Finally, my persistence paid off as my rusty drawer lock gave way with a snap. Hearing that, I quickly slid open my long drawer. Inside I found a flat rectangular box made of dark, polished mahogany. At once, I recognized there must be something valuable inside. Mahogany was hard to come by in the colonies. It had to be shipped in from the Caribbean. It was usually reserved for gun cases or silverware collections, and other such valuables.

On the face of the box, there was something that appeared to be a family crest made of silver. It depicted two knights' helmets facing each other with two lances crossed beneath and some Latin inscription underneath which I could not read. On the lid of the box there was a small silver handle. I spent my time prying at the small lock on the face of the box. Though, I did not wish to damage the crest, it was impossible to gain leverage at any other point. Taking the risk of denting the small crest, I laid my blade across it and pried. Suddenly, the little lid popped up. There, before me, shiny as the day they were minted, five rows of twelve silver coins standing on their edges in green felt slots fitted into the box. I recognized immediately it was a coin collection.

"Wow, look at these," I enthused. Picking one out for closer examination, I blurted, "These are solid silver." Taking a few more out of their slots, I noticed something else.

"Hey, they all have the same date, April 10 1771."

I admit, I don't know much about old coins, but I knew one thing for sure. They were all minted in the same place. The face of the coins featured a portrait labeled Carolus III with the Latin words "DEI GRATIA" and "HISPAN.ET.IND.REX. Amy stepped forward and translated. The words mean, "By the grace of God, then it says King of Spain and the Indies".

Connie asked in amazement, "How do you know that?"

Amy replied, "I studied Latin in high school."

She continued looking on as I flipped the coin over. The reverse side of the coin displayed a crowned shield of Castile and Leon with three crosses in the center and a pomegranate. At either side of the coat of arms, stood the Pillars of Hercules with a motto beneath on ribbons which read "PLUS VLTRA". Amy leaned over again translating.

"That means more beyond."

Vic let out a low whistle, "Man those coins must be worth a lot, Allen."

Amy added, "I'll say, look there's the Mexico City mint mark. The denomination of these coins is eight Reals. That's like eight Spanish dollars apiece. Because of their age and mint condition, they would be worth a small fortune to a collector."

Amy turned back looking at me. I could see the pride in her eyes as she spoke.

"You've really got yourself a find there, Allen."

"You mean we," I corrected.

Inspired, I went on searching in the long drawer. Next, I found several long-feathered quill pens and a bottle of India ink. Then, I spotted something white lying on the bottom of the drawer. I reached in and picked up a letter opener carved from a single piece of ivory. It was beautiful with little elephants carved out of its entire length. As the curved blade tapered toward the sharp point, the elephant carvings grew smaller. They were all attached with one elephant holding the other's tail like an act in a circus parade. It truly was an unusual, ornate piece painstakingly carved with patient, skilled hands.

Meanwhile, Vic had turned his attention back to his drawer. Toward the back, he pulled out several embroidered handkerchiefs which he unceremoniously tossed on the floor behind him.

Amy chided, "Vic, these are all historic articles of interest. You should treat them with more care."

"Yeah, well, what I care more about is some silver or gold maybe. You can have those other knic knacks if you want 'em."

I half way apologized for his actions.

"You'll have to excuse Vic, Amy; his sense of history goes back about as far as last Saturday."

Amy sighed watching him continue his foraging.

The second drawer Vic pried open was empty. Amy just laughed as he balked staring open mouthed at the empty drawer.

"There, you see, it serves you right for being so greedy."

I went back to working on the lock of my second drawer, which eventually gave way revealing a wooden case that nearly took up the entire drawer. As I gingerly removed it, I could tell it was a gun case. It was made of finished black walnut. The hinges were brass as was the lock on the front of the case.

Amy suggested, "Before you go breaking into *that* box, I suggest you look in the drawer for a key. Maybe you can save something in one piece for a change."

I gave her a sideways glance concealing my frustration. I thought, *"Here I am doing all the work and she's giving me suggestions on how to preserve museum pieces "*. Of course, I knew she was right. It just bothered me a bit that I did not think of looking for a key myself. As it turned out, there was one right under a metal clip on the bottom of the gun case. I removed it carefully inserting it into the lock and turned until it clicked.

"It's open," I cried excitedly.

Vic stopped his rummaging watching me open the lid. Sure enough, it was a beautiful pistol inside in excellent condition. It was as if it were placed there the day before. Not a bit of rust appeared on its brass barrel. It was a wooden handled pistol about thirteen inches in length with inlaid decorative silver on its handle. I started to reach in to pick it up.

Amy placed her hand upon my arm.

"Better use this, Allen", she offered. Stretching her hand out, she held one of the discarded handkerchiefs.

"Yeah, I guess you're right. I wouldn't want to spoil the finish."

Amy smiled as I reached in with the handkerchief picking up the pistol. I guessed it weighed about a pound and a half. The wooden handle and stock were made of a polished, dark wood. As I held it up to a lantern for inspection, I could see under the barrel there were letters stamped which read, 'Hawkins', London 1748.

I held it up toward Amy.

"Look, this must be the manufacturer's mark. It says it was made in 1748, Vic."

He had already started working on the third drawer on his side.

Without looking up, he remarked, "That's a keeper."

Soon his sharp blade broke his last drawer open. As he slid out the long drawer, he hissed with disappointment.

"Shoot, there are only candles and glass candle holders in here."

Amy replied, "That's great, now we can have more light."

Vic shook his head as she and Connie busied themselves setting up the candles lighting them one by one. The room took on almost a cheery glow, if it were not for the fact we were still trapped underground. Reverently returning the pistol to its case, I began work on my third drawer. It seemed I was getting the knack of lock breaking. My knife busted the third lock in record time. However, much to my disappointment the drawer was completely empty. I stood looking downward at the empty drawer looking forlorn.

Vic wasted no time.

"Well, Kemosabe, it's time to flip for the middle drawer."

"Yeah, I guess you're right."

He quickly reached in his dirt covered jeans pocket producing a quarter.

"Here goes." he said. "You call it."

"Heads," I cried feeling as if things were moving a bit too swiftly.

He allowed the coin to hit the ground calling out.

"Heads, it is, Allen."

I could hear disappointment in his voice as the candlelight flickered over the coin.

"Maybe this drawer will be empty, too," I said trying to soothe any hard feelings.

Vic just bit his lip taking it like a good sport. Then, he began to goad.

"Well, come on, now let's see you get it open, lucky boy."

I paused for a moment with my knife blade slid between the crack of the drawer and lock bar. I thought to myself, *"Top drawers are reserved for important things, aren't they?"* Then, I gave my blade a quick twist and heard the lock bar break like the others. Slowly, I slid back the double wide top drawer of the desk. The first thing that caught my eye was a scroll of parchment rolled up just like the replicas of documents like the Declaration of Independence sold at tourist shops all over Independence Park. Judging from the artifacts already found in the desk, I knew all too well this was the real thing.

My hand was trembling as I reached for the rolled-up parchment. It was sealed with red wax from one of the very candles we were now burning throughout the room. The flickering light cast shadows that danced on the walls of our sealed room. My friends' faces looked tense and drawn as they watched me ease the scroll from the drawer. I now looked at Amy with an inquisitive expression.

"Should I break the seal, Amy?"

Vic interjected, "Of course, you should. All of this stuff is ours for the taking. Isn't this what we came for? You know finders keepers, Allen."

Connie sided up close to Vic. She said nothing, but her closeness spoke volumes.

Amy had to agree with Vic.

"He is right, you know. Everything here is our find. We can do what we like with it, I suppose."

I knew she was as sensitive as I about the property of others. Though, I am sure she considered that along with other factors. By now, she would have every right to justify in her mind the rights of ownership of such articles from the past. I reached the same conclusion simultaneously.

Taking my knife, I held it next to the edge of the seal and carefully sliced across the glob of hardened wax. As expected, the wax crumbled away under the pressure of my blade and the pent-up scroll sprung partially open. I had to lay it on the desktop to flatten it out entirely while holding the bottom curl down with the other hand. Before me lay a written document penned long ago. According to the date found in the upper right hand corner, it was written on May 15th 1775.

Amy's eyes widened as she observed the date.

"Oh my," she exclaimed in awe. "That sure puts a date to this place we've found here, doesn't it?"

No one else said a word. I stared at the script of the 18th century document before me for what seemed a full minute before I began reading.

By the will of our hearts we do set forth this pact between ourselves. We do pledge our lives, our fortunes, and our sacred honor to each other in the common cause of freedom. As we are bound in the common brotherhood of man as free and accepted masons, we do solemnly swear to uphold and defend the rights and properties of our brethren in our cause of rebellion against tyranny under the monarchy of King George III.

To this end, we will sacrifice all to assure the freedom of one should their liberty be threatened by any who might dissuade us from our common purpose. May blessings of heaven rest upon us, and all regular masons. May brotherly love and compassion abide with us and may every moral and social virtue cement us in this pledge.

Benjamin Franklin   John Hancock   George Washington

I held the document with shaking hands as I read it through a second time. Placing it reverently on top of the desk, I took a step back looking around myself at the others in wonderment.

"Do you know what this is?" Even if they did, they chose not to answer. Instead, they continued staring at the document in wide-eyed disbelief.

I almost shouted, "This is nothing less than a sacred pledge of unity between three of our greatest founding fathers over a year before the signing of the Declaration of Independence! They all signed this document together. It shows they were all freemasons, as well."

I glanced around myself at my friends, their mouths agape. I couldn't help expressing elation at my find.

"Do you have any idea what this might be worth?"

I could see I had Vic's full attention now. Before, I believe he had a notion something important lay before him, but it didn't sink in until I mentioned it's possible worth. Amy, on the other hand, flung her good arm about my neck. Understanding the full import of such a find, she hugged me hard.

"Oh, Allen, you're going to be famous for discovering such a rare document."

Connie was all aglow, but I was not convinced she knew exactly why.

Chapter 14

For all of us, that day's discoveries changed everything. Thus, I remember thinking, *"If only we could escape from our dark world, all our sacrifice would be worthwhile."* That night, as we shared more of the preserves in crockery jars, we counted ourselves lucky. Then, using our packs as pillows, we laid down to rest for the night. We knew by morning we must renew our efforts at breaking free of our underworld.

The days of struggle that came before wore on us all. That Sunday night, it seemed we slept the sleep of the dead. I was the first to awake to a strange sound. It entered my brain slowly as if it were a distant memory. I shook my head at first, trying to clear any physical interference with my hearing of it. Then, I heard it again. It was a steady scraping sound. In the entire week spent underneath Philly, I never heard such a noise. Glancing at my watch, I noted it was 9:10 in the morning. I reached over jostling Amy awake.

"Amy, wake up. Come on, Amy, get up now."

She opened her eyes slowly, reluctantly accepting her surroundings.

"What is it, Allen?"

"It's time to get up, Amy. I want you to wake up and listen."

She jerked her arm suddenly with a start.

"Is it the rats? Are they in here?"

I assured, "No, it's not that. I hear another noise. I'm not sure what it is, listen."

Amy strained to hear what I detected. She sat up allowing her ears every chance to tune into it. I watched her face as her eyes widened. Before she reacted to what she perceived, she remained still, listening momentarily. Then she turned toward me.

"It's a scraping sound up above us."

"Yes, that's what I hear, too."

I spoke across the room in a low voice, though I don't recall why.

"Vic, get up. Can you hear that?"

Vic rolled over on his side with his back toward me.

"Go away, Allen, I'm trying to sleep."

"No, Vic. You've got to get up and hear this."

Vic rolled back over giving me an annoyed look.

"What is it now, Allen?"

"Amy and I hear scratching noises coming from above."

By now, Connie was stirring next to Vic.

"What is it? What's going on, you guys?"

I repeated, "Amy and I are hearing sounds coming from the ceiling."

Vic said, "Quiet, let me listen a minute."

Vic was sitting upright now looking upward listening for something, anything.

"I don't hear anything," he said.

He was right. The sound was gone now.

I insisted, "I know I heard something before. Amy heard it too. It was a scraping sound, wasn't it, Amy?"

Just then the sound returned. I could tell from Vic's reaction he was hearing it too.

"What is that? It sounds like a tool scraping on something hard."

I agreed, "Yes, it's something scraping on the level above us."

I was more than ready to speculate. Enthusiastically, I cried out.

"It's someone scraping. Humans are making that sound. Someone's trying to rescue us!"

Amy wondered, "How would they know we're down here?"

I retorted, "I don't know. What does it matter? We've got to make some noise right away to let them know we're here."

Vic grabbed his shovel and climbed the stairs. He began beating the blade of the shovel on the trapdoor above. I brought my knife along. Standing beside him, I banged the butt of my knife on the wooden door alongside him. We continued making all the racket we could until our arms grew tired.

Vic lowered his shovel looking at me with sweat dripping from his brow.

"Do you think they heard us?"

"I dunno. Let's rest a bit and try again."

On the floor above, a team of six restoration workers continued their task of removing the old flooring from the site of the Old City Tavern. They were contracted to gut the dilapidated pre-Revolutionary period building to make way for restorations being made for the Philadelphia Historical Society. The site of the old tavern was to be listed as a Registered National Historical Landmark. It was slated to be part of the tour of historic landmarks in old Philadelphia known as the 'City Tavern'.

I said, "O.K., Vic, that's long enough. Let's give it another try."

The girls stood together looking upward praying we would be heard. On and on, we banged away on the trap door hoping to be heard. Directly above us, one of the workers was using a long-handled scraper. He was busy scraping off one of the many layers of linoleum left behind in a tavern that had seen many renovations before. He took a brief respite from his scraping leaning on his tool. Now, he could discern the odd thumping sound emanating from beneath the floor. Both shocked and surprised, he stood still listening. He looked over his shoulder at his foreman across the room. He was reluctant to tell him what he heard for fear of ridicule. He was afraid his fellow workers and his boss would make fun of him for hearing things under the floor in the old tavern. He could just imagine their teasing. *"What's the matter Billy, are you hearing ghosts under the floor?"*

He shrugged his shoulders and went back to his scraping. Then, he stopped abruptly. The sound was there again. This time, he made up his mind to say something, come what may.

"Hey, boss, come over here a minute."

"What is it, Billy? I'm busy."

"Come here, anyway. You gotta hear this; it's coming from under the floor."

The foreman put down what he was doing and came toward the worker with an inquisitive look on his face.

"Now, just what have you got here, Billy?"

Billy urged, "Just listen, boss."

Taking up a position next to his worker, the foreman stood still giving a listen. He did not have to wait long before he heard Vic and Allen desperately thumping on the door below.

"Something's bumping on the floor."

"That's what I've been hearing, boss. It sounds like someone's down there."

Billy's boss looked puzzled.

"That's crazy, who could be under the floor in this tavern. We're the only ones who have a key. How could anyone get down there?"

Billy held his finger up to his lips.

"Shh, listen, there it is again."

Both men listened as Vic and Allen continued pounding on the trap door.

Billy and his boss were joined by other curious workers above the point where they all heard pounding on the floor beneath their feet.

Billy up ended his long handled scraping tool and pounded on the floor. Suddenly, the pounding beneath stopped.

The foreman remarked, "This is really weird, but I think someone's down there. Jerry, go to the truck and get your circular saw."

As soon as Billy stopped thumping the floor, the pounding under the floor resumed. When Jerry returned, his boss put his ear to the floor listening. When he thought he had zeroed in on the sound, he stepped back. Using his finger, he indicated an imaginary line.

"Cut a line along here, Jerry."

Jerry knelt and pulled the trigger on the high-speed saw. As he pressed the blade into the linoleum floor, his saw produced a high-pitched whine slowly traversing a line across the flooring. Vic and I nearly fell down the stairs when we heard the saw cutting across the floor. Small particles of sawdust filtered down from the trap door as we watched in awe. The girls squealed with delight. We had been found! It was unbelievable. All at once, a rush of elation coursed through my body. Vic was jumping up and down at the bottom of the stairs now. He looked upward with an expression of hope and delight.

I turned to the others yelling triumphantly.

"This is it, guys! We're being rescued just in time! I told you we'd make it, we just had to stick together, that's all."

Anything else I said was quickly drowned out by the sound of the saw as it completed its cuts across the floor. We all looked up anxiously as the last cuts were made. Then, I looked back at the dark room that gave up its fortune. Strangely, I felt as though I was about to leave a part of me behind. The whole experience of being trapped beneath Philly flashed before my eyes. It was a time of trial, but also an experience of self-discovery. I knew it was an experience of a lifetime and our lives had been changed forever because of it.

My thoughts were soon interrupted by a bright flash of light from above. For the first time in over a week, we were seeing daylight as the sawed portion of the trap door was pulled back. The look on the workers' faces was priceless when they gazed down at four filthy squint-eyed teenagers.

A voice boomed from the light.

"Hello, down there."

I blurted out, "Hello, we're right here. We've been trapped underground for a week."

I didn't know what else to say. Those were the first words tumbling out of my mouth. All of us stood looking up with our hands shielding our eyes from the harsh light. It would take a few moments before our eyes could adjust. Soon, a man's face appeared in the square they had sawed away. He wore a helmet and a blue denim work shirt with rolled up sleeves. He had blue eyes set in a square-jawed face. He extended his muscular arm speaking with a grin.

"My name is Charles Selway. I'm the foreman on this work crew. How in hell did you get down there, anyway?"

I clutched his rough hand shaking it gratefully.

I spoke gleefully, "I'm sure glad you found us, Charles."

As I ascended the wooden steps, I noticed for the first time my legs were a bit wobbly. Our discovery and rescue were all just a bit too much for me now. Before I even attempted answering Charles's question, I started telling him about the others.

"This is my girlfriend, Amy Martin, and my friend, Vic Rubio, and his girl, Connie Warren. We went on a little exploring trip that went all wrong. We started last week from the Cross Brothers' Slaughter House."

"Cross Brothers", Charles said in amazement. "That's clear across town. How did you ever get from there to here?"

I laughed and answered, "That, my friend, is a long story."

Once we were all standing in the old tavern, the work crew looked us over. We must have been a strange sight to see. There we were with filthy clothes and grimy faces. Vic and I sported a week's growth of beard. Amy, with her soiled arm in a sling, looked like some wild woman from a carnival freak show. Connie wavered weakly back and forth in her besmirched clothing feeling as though she were going to be sick. I hadn't realized just how much of a strain it had been on all of us until Connie fainted. One of the workmen caught her just before she hit the floor. The rest of us instinctively looked around for a chair. Then Charles suddenly snapped into action.

"Billy call for an ambulance. These people need to see a doctor."

Billy ran for a phone as the workmen helped us to a chair and offered us water. It felt so good to feel the cool liquid filling my mouth and soothing my throat. All of us drank heartily. So much so, Charles cautioned us not to overdo it at first.

Thankfully, there were no more questions about the how and why of our circumstance. There was time enough to rest and contemplate that it really was all over. My mind drifted ahead to what would become of our jobs. "*Would we be fired when they learned how we got into the storeroom in the first place? Or, would they regard us as heroes for surviving our ordeal? What of the artifacts?* So many questions raced through my mind."

Suddenly, I felt faint. Then I saw an arm reaching out for me. That was all I remember until I awoke in my hospital bed two days later. When I awoke, my mother and grandmother were there by my side waiting for me to open my eyes. I heard my mother speaking softly.

"Hello, sleepy head. You've been resting for some time now. How do you feel?"

I lifted my head to speak and felt the room starting to spin. Slowly, I lowered my head back to the pillow. My mouth felt dry as my eyes traced an I.V. tube in my arm to a bottle hanging on a pole near my bed.

All I could think of was, *"Where are the others?"*

We had been through so much together, by now, they felt like an extension of my being.

"Are the others all, right? Where is Amy?"

My mother smiled knowingly at my grandmother.

"I told you he'd be asking about the others. Don't worry, son. They're right here in the same hospital with you. They're all doing well. I guess you'll all be going home soon."

"Why did they take us here, Mom?"

"Honey, you were all dehydrated and suffering from severe stress. You just needed rest and nutrition, that's all. Of course, Amy had to have her arm reset."

I tried sitting up again when I heard about her, which started the room spinning again.

"Just lie still. I've seen her and she's awake and feeling better. I don't think you realize how much stress you were under."

My grandmother added, "You lost twenty pounds."

"Well, I feel O.K. now. I just feel a little light headed when I try to sit up."

"The doctor said you probably would. That, too, will pass. You know you're a very lucky boy. You are all very lucky for that matter…"

Mom's voice trailed off momentarily. Then, she took on a pained expression.

"What's the matter, Mom?"

"It's just that Mrs. Agresta has been around twice now while you were sleeping. She wants to know what happened to Steve. She's very upset and insists on talking to you as soon as you're able. She seems to think you might know where Steve is."

I felt a cold sensation creeping over my body. The stark reminder of his loss made the memory come flooding back. I would never see him again. It all happened so fast at the time. Shortly thereafter, other matters like our own safety crowded my mind. At least, I could block his memory out back then. Now, reality was slowly seeping in making me feel the terrible loss all over again. I wondered how I could possibly tell his mother. The pain of losing a son was something I had no compensation for. How could anyone compensate for a lost son? My mom sensed my pain and tried changing the subject.

"Mr. Ryan read about you and the others in the paper. He's been asking about you. He'd like to see you when you're able."

I thought about the artifacts we tucked away in our back packs. I decided I wanted to see him, too, and soon. I had questions I hoped he could answer.

Mom went on sounding more serious.

"There are a couple of police detectives that want to talk to you, too. I thought I'd better tell you now so you can think about what you want to tell them. When you and your friends went missing, I contacted the police and reported you missing. I didn't know what else to do."

Mom started to tear up.

"It's all right, Mom. I'm just sorry I deceived you in the first place. I know that had to make things harder for all of you. Maybe somehow I can make it up to you."

She just patted me on the hand saying, "Just get well and come home to us, Allen. That's all we want."

Many things crossed my mind, but foremost in my mind was how I could make it up to everyone. It was my idea in the first place and now I felt responsible. I knew I must do something to compensate for our irresponsible behavior. The way to do so was not exactly clear. Yet, I thought in the back of my mind, the artifacts might go a long way toward making things right. Obviously, nothing could make up for Steve's loss, but, at least, I would be able to explain to his mother that he chose to go with us. I could tell her those artifacts were a part of history he helped to preserve. That meant Steve's efforts were not in vain.

"Mom, I want you to do something for me."

"What is it dear?"

"Bring me my backpack. I have something to show you."

"Everything is in the cabinet. What is it you want?"

"Just bring me the backpack and I'll show you."

Mother took the filthy back pack from the cabinet near my bed. She brushed at it trying to get some of the dirt off.

"This thing is filthy and heavy, too. I'll have to wash it for you."

"Just look inside, Mom."

She laid the pack on the floor by the bed and pulled the flap open. There she found the wooden gun case and the rolled-up parchment.

"What are these things, Allen?"

"They're things I found underground near where we were rescued."

Mother slid the long gun case out of my pack as my grandmother looked on.

"Go on, open it", I urged.

She fumbled with the latch, then, I remembered.

"Oh, I'm sorry. There's a key in the right pocket of my jeans."

She returned to the cabinet and picked up my jeans.

"My word, everything is so filthy."

I chided, "Yes, Mom, I was crawling around underground for a week. Just look for a small key in the right front pocket."

Mom came up with the key and, with shaking hands, she inserted the key opening the box as my grandmother looked on.

"Oh my, Allen", she exclaimed.

Grandma commented, "Why it's an old Flintlock pistol. My grandfather used to have one of those."

"I found it in a desk in a room just beneath the tavern along with the scroll of parchment. Read it, Mom."

Mom complied, stretching the parchment out on the foot of my bed. As she and Grandmother read it, they both widened their eyes in surprise. Mom put her hand to her mouth as if she were bound to keep what she saw a secret. Grandma just shook her head slowly in disbelief."

Mom asked, "My word, can this be real?"

I replied with pride, "I sure think so, especially if you consider the other items found along with it. Vic found three solid silver goblets made by Paul Revere and a set of coins all dated 1774."

"Why, that's simply amazing, Allen! What will you do with these things?"

"Well first, I thought I would show them to Mr. Ryan. Maybe he can tell me what they might be worth. I'll try to convince Vic to do the same with his artifacts."

"That sounds like a start. I'll bet he would know something about them. If he doesn't, he might know someone who does."

Suddenly, a knock at the door interrupted our show and tell session. Mom quickly slid the artifacts back into the bag handing it to Grandma.

"Here, put this away while I answer the door."

Mom opened the door looking back making sure Grandma had my bag secreted away in the cabinet.

"Hello, Detective Dodge. I suppose you want to talk to my son."

"Yes, Detective Ditty and I would like to have a few words with him alone if you don't mind."

"I suppose not, just be sure you don't over tax the boy. He's still recovering from quite an ordeal, you know."

Detective Dodge just nodded perfunctorily as he entered the room. He waited until she and Grandma were gone before turning on me.

"Well, it appears you and your friends had yourselves quite an adventure. It's too bad it all had to end in tragedy. Tell me how the boy died."

Dodge's callous approach left me feeling reproachful. There was something about his manner I didn't like. Nevertheless, I knew I must recount the painful experience of Steve's death.

After explaining the circumstances surrounding Steve's death as best I could, Detective Ditty had something more to say.

"Well, I'm sure there will be other officers interested in hearing you recount your little story. He watched me for any reaction I might have. Then, he struck a match on the bed post and lit a cigarette. He puffed his first drag out toward me for emphasis.

"Just be sure you keep the facts straight for them."

I'd never met this man before, but already I liked him less and less. They both seemed cocky and unwilling to accept any answers as truthful. I thought, "*Maybe they figured they had a score to settle since we led them on a wild goose chase. Either way, I felt they would both be better employed as dog catchers.*"

Dodge intervened, "Tell me something, why were you kids down there in the first place?"

"We just thought it would be fun. You know, like an adventure of exploration, that's all."

I wasn't about to tell them we found something worthwhile down there. That is, at least not until I got confirmation of what our find was worth. I didn't lie; it *was* like an adventure for us all, at first. How could we know it would take a tragic turn? What I did not know at the time was that we made the newspapers with our escapade.

Ditty started in again.

"What made you think you could break into the slaughter house?"

I squirmed under my sheets a bit before confessing.

"Three of us work for Cross Brothers', so we figured they wouldn't mind us poking around outside on our own time."

Ditty pressed, "How did you get *inside* the building?"

This time I decided to lie for everyone's sake.

"We were just messing around in back by the loading dock and found the truck delivery door open."

Dodge spoke sarcastically, "So all five of you kids just happened to be hanging around the loading dock? Is that it? What time of day did you enter the building?"

"I think it was just around dawn on Saturday."

Dodge continued, "I suppose you didn't see a guard anywhere around either."

I knew *I* didn't, so I told him.

"No, I didn't see any guard."

I could see the look of frustration growing on his face.

Ditty finished his cigarette, rubbing it out on the floor as he glared at me.

"Well, I'll tell you something kid. If the Cross Brothers decide to press charges, you and your little buddies are going to be charged with trespassing, you got that? Also, the death of the Agresta boy is gonna' put a whole new spin on this case. That means you'll be getting another visit from the boys in homicide. Do you understand what I'm saying?"

I just shook my head affirmatively not knowing how else to respond.

Dodge got up from his chair giving me a parting shot.

"We deal with missing persons, but trespassing and homicide aren't our departments. We'll be sure to pass your case along. So, I wouldn't be taking any vacations over to Ocean City too soon, if you get my drift kid."

With that, they headed for the door leaving me alone to worry about the Cross Brothers.

They were not gone two minutes when Mom returned.

"Son, Mrs. Agresta is outside. She insists on talking to you now. I asked the doctor about it, and he says it's up to you."

I felt a little punch drunk, but decided to get it over with all at once.

"Tell her she can come in, Mom. I'll talk to her."

I propped myself up preparing to talk with Mrs. Agresta. I knew she was a widow with four other children to raise. Steve was her oldest. I knew how tough it would be to raise a family as a single parent. Now, I must somehow explain why one of her children never came home. I wished I were somewhere else right then, but I also felt I owed it to Steve to tell his mother how he died. So, I waited there alone in the room feeling a sense of dread descending on me like a cold bladed knife.

The knock came at the door.

I cleared my throat and said, "Come in, please."

There she was, standing in the doorway, her face sagging under the strain of the past week. Her reddened eyes bore witness to the bad news foisted upon her amidst the joy of our own rescue. I could not help thinking how that cruel twist of fate made her feel. While everyone else's family celebrated our rescue, she was learning of her son's sudden death. I did not know how she stood it. I was not there when they told her. I told the attendants in the ambulance about Steve. Now, she waited to hear it from me. What it was like for him, because I was with him last. Somehow, I would have to help her close the book on his life.

She came in slowly with a brave crooked smile. I could see her hands trembling as she drew near.

I managed to say, "Hello, Mrs. Agresta. We've never met before, but my heart goes out to you just the same. I'm so sorry about your son."

I kicked myself for not saying more, but my mind just froze up. I had never told anyone about their son's death before. My hands were sweating and my head began swimming again.

She must have noticed my condition and she took pity on me as she spoke.

"I know it was an accident, the way my son died. I just wanted you to tell me what my Steve was doing or what he said because you were the last to see him alive."

I heard myself saying, "Well, we were all together, at first. We had talked about turning back because Connie was pretty shaken up over something we saw down there."

I decided to skip the detail about the mummified bodies we found.

"When we discussed going back, there was another passage way we had not tried taking. Steve suggested he go back and use his miner's helmet to see if that passage would be worth looking into."

"Do you mean he didn't want to leave with the rest of you?"

I felt trapped. How could I tell her Steve cared had more about finding some sort of loot in that tunnel than about Connie? I knew it was selfish of him, but I wanted to spare Mrs. Agresta. I paused momentarily, preparing my lie.

"You see, Steve was hoping to find a quicker way out for us all."

She seemed relieved to be hearing my testimony. I could see she was more at ease.

Then, she suddenly burst into tears.

"I just knew my boy would do the right thing."

Taking up my hand, she held it tight.

"I know this must have been hard for you to talk about Steve, but I just had to know. You understand, don't you?"

I whispered, "Yes, of course, and I know he didn't suffer. It all happened so quickly."

Then, she released my hand and turned away without saying another word. When she was gone, I cried, too.

Later, Mom and Grandma came back into the room. I guess Mom could see I needed some good news. She told me the doctor said I could leave the hospital the next day.

"What about the others? Are they going home tomorrow, too?"

She replied, "I'm not sure, but I'll try and find out for you. We must go now to catch the bus home. I'll ask the nurse to find out and come tell you later, O.K.?"

"Thanks, Mom. It was good of you both to come see me."

"Oh, don't be silly. We've been in and out all along. We must go now, though. Your sister must be getting pretty tired of babysitting by now. Goodbye, son."

I guess there is a lot of truth in the expression, 'all's well that ends well'. As it turned out, the Cross Brothers' were happy to forget the trespassing charges. They preferred keeping the dangerous old store room and its leaking chemical barrels a secret anyway, until they could properly dispose of them. That way, we got to be heroes while they cooperated with the authorities in excavating the collapsed tunnel. After Steve's body was recovered, the Cross Brothers' had the tunnel entrance under the storage room permanently sealed.

In the days that followed, the artifacts recovered from beneath Philly created quite a stir in the historical community. After I first showed the artifacts to Mr. Ryan, he strongly recommended getting them together for a presentation to the Philadelphia Historical Society for authentication. I acted on his advice and contacted Vic. It took some convincing, but I managed to get him to agree to go with me.

Beforehand, he suspected the Historical Society would try to keep the artifacts claiming they were part of the state's property. I explained they were private artifacts found on private property and that we had a right to them according to Mr. Ryan. Placing his trust in Mr. Ryan, he decided to come with me.

I agreed to meet Vic at his house and brought along a small suitcase for all the artifacts. As I rounded the corner into Vic's neighborhood, I saw a couple of guys I knew. There was Benny from Norm's Pool Hall. He cleaned up around the place. He was hanging out with Joey, one of Vic's neighbors.

Benny called out, "Hey, what's with the suitcase? Are you leavin' town?"

I laughed, "Naw, I just got a few things I wanna show Vic."

Joey piped in, "Yeah, I bet I know what kind of things, too. We read all about you guys in the paper. So, why don't you show us what you've got there, Mister Treasure Hunter?"

It was against my better judgment, but I relented. Stopping by Vic's stoop, I placed the suitcase on the iron stair railing. Then, I opened it slightly giving them each a peek. I had the pistol box and the parchment rolled up inside.

Joey sneered, "So, what's that? It's just a wooden box and an old piece of paper."

I closed the lid smiling smugly, "It's what's inside that counts, my friend."

With that, they both stood back shaking their hands in the air.

Joey laughed, "Big deal, now he's an artsy fartsy collector."

With little time to waste, I mounted the stairs heading up to Vic's.

When I came in, he had his coin collection and goblets laid out on the couch under the watchful eye of his ten-year-old brother.

His little brother greeted me.

"Hey Allen, wanna look at some really old coins? It'll only cost you a nickel?"

Thanks, Tony, but I've already seen 'em. Where's Vic?"

"Oh, he's where he always is, in the bathroom combing his hair. Are you really taking all your stuff down town to be re-evaluated?"

"That's evaluated, squirt, and the answer is yes."

Vic entered the room. He was wearing a new white button down shirt and dark slacks. I wondered if this was the new look for Victor Rubio, explorer-at-large. He could see by the look on my face, I was ready to give him the business about his dress, so he headed me off.

"Mom said it would help me get a better appraisal if I was dressed up."

I just shrugged my shoulders questioning the accuracy of such an opinion.

It was a hot Friday morning, and I was anxious to get started. The State Historical Society would be open from ten-thirty to five. We had an appointment at eleven with Dr. Shapsmeir, the curator. Because the Historical Society was located on Locust Street in old downtown Philly, we had to make a couple of bus transfers.

I, myself, wore a pair of jeans and one of my best blue, banlon shirts, opting for loafers instead of tennis shoes. In my opinion, I was the well-dressed teenager ready to do business. Vic, on the other hand, spent most of the bus ride telling me I should start living up to a higher image of myself.

As he put it, "You know, after our discoveries celebrities will want to meet us. We'll be interviewed by the news; girls will ask for our autographs. Heck, we might even get on the Steve Allen Show."

After hearing his last remark, I tried suppressing a laugh with a cough.

I quipped, "You certainly look well-dressed enough for, ahem..., NBC."

Vic just called out the stop for our transfer, ignoring my sarcasm.

The last transfer deposited us on 12th Street just a block from Locust.

As we walked the last block, Vic pulled out his comb and started fussing with his hair.

I said, "Vic they're interested in what's in this suitcase. They're not going to interview you for a part in a movie."

Vic countered, "It never hurts to look your best, you know."

I just smiled shaking my head. It was his way or no way sometimes, I told myself. I should have known that by now after being his friend these many years.

We approached the steps of the old gray building that was also home to the Library Company of Philadelphia. It was now a research library, but was originally founded in 1731 by Benjamin Franklin. It was the first circulating library in America that documented U.S. History through the printed word.

The huge columns outside the entrance gave the venerated building a stately appearance. Once inside its doors, there was an atmosphere of quiet elegance and reverence for all American History that came before. The building itself was built in 1824, yet its architect managed to capture a certain Colonial feel in its interior.

We followed the velvet roped barriers cordoning off certain corridors from the public, until we reached the centrally located information booth. When I stated our business there, a woman quietly directed us to the main hallway behind her.

"You'll find Dr. Shapsmeir's office three doors down on the right."

Vic and I walked down the dark wood paneled hallway gazing in awe about us. There were life size statues of historical figures along the way, some of which we recognized as our founding fathers. Others were relegated to the obscurity of our intellect. Nevertheless, the entire scene with large paintings and murals was sufficiently impressive to leave us both in awe. I looked down at the worn handle of my mother's old suitcase and wondered fleetingly if our artifacts were worthy of the society's scrutiny.

Before I knocked on the massive oak door which bore the historian's name, I gave Vic the thumbs up sign.

"Now, it's our time to shine," I said to Vic.

I knocked on the heavy door, taking a deep breath, and then glanced at Vic. He did not seem the least bit nervous. I could not help thinking he knew something I was unaware of. Perhaps it was just his whole attitude about the artifacts we found. While I was overwhelmed with the significant pieces of history we found, Vic saw the objects as something to be sold out right to the highest bidder.

The large, heavy, wide, oak paneled door opened easily before us, and we were pleasantly greeted by Beverly Compton, Dr. Edward Shapsmeir's assistant. She was an attractive young woman, freshly out of college. I speculated she was serving a summer internship to pad her resume. Her long blonde hair accentuated the flow of her lovely curves. I must admit, she was not the bookish type I expected when she presented her hand in greeting.

"How do you do? I'm Beverly Compton. I believe you have an appointment with Dr. Shapsmeir this morning. Now, let me see, which of you is Mr. Allen Williams? No, don't tell me. Let me guess."

Correctly, she steered her hand toward mine. I was duly impressed and it showed.

"It's just a little game I like to play when I first meet someone. I hope you don't mind."

Vic stammered, "Lucky guess."

She went on, "You see, most people we meet here expect us to be stuffy, old, bookish persons. I guess it's just my way of trying to dispel that notion."

Next, her bright green eyes centered on Vic.

"Naturally, you must be Mr. Victor Rubio."

Vic's mouth was still slightly agape as he took her hand.

"Pleased to meet you Miss…"

"Please, just call me Beverly. I'm here to assist Dr. Shapsmeir."

Vic thought, *"Yes, you certainly are."*

I managed to pull my eyes away from Beverly long enough to observe Dr. Shapsmeir getting up slowly from his cluttered desk. At first glance, his appearance, unlike Beverly's, was pretty much what I expected. His steel rimmed glasses remained perched on his Roman nose where he'd left them after looking up from reading. He was tall. I guessed at least six feet, though he slouched a bit from age. He appeared to be in his mid-seventies, clearly on the committed side of retirement. With thinning silver hair, he remained natty looking in his tweed, vested suit. His eyes were piercing blue peering with an inquisitive look from beneath eye brows almost the size of moles. When he spoke, his voice lifted with a commanding tone clearly like that of a man who'd spent half his life lecturing.

"Do come in, gentlemen. I've read all about your adventure in the newspapers. It would seem you have something of interest to show me."

I would never have imagined reading *The Philadelphia Inquirer* and its competitors were a part of his daily routine. Feeling a bit embarrassed over our new-found notoriety, I proffered my hand. After shaking Vic's hand, as well, he gestured toward an empty table near his desk.

Beverly's soft voice provided a pleasant interruption.

"May I get you gentleman something to drink, perhaps coffee or tea?"

Dr. Shapsmeir spoke first, "I'd like a nice cup of tea, Beverly. Some of that Earl Gray would be nice. How about you two? What'll it be?"

Vic and I each asked for coffee and Beverly obliged gliding out through the heavy oak doorway.

"Now then, gentlemen, why don't you show me what you've brought? Don't be shy. Just place the case on the table here, and I'll examine the contents."

I lowered the worn suitcase slowly to the polished table being careful not to leave a scratch. I felt a little ashamed bringing such a lowly means of transport for our presentation. Though, I felt confident our artifacts were worthy of careful consideration. Mr. Ryan already told me he would love to have been a fly on the wall when we revealed the contents of the scuffed, black suitcase. He assured me the black and white photos in the newspaper did not do our collection justice. As it was, I had no choice but to hold my breath awaiting the expert's judgment. I raised the lid remaining silent, hoping that would have a dramatic effect. The old professor immediately bent over, placing his hands on the gun case. I told myself he must have recognized what the box held right away. Gingerly, he slipped his hands underneath the mahogany box.

Before moving a muscle, he looked up asking, "May I?"

Dumbly, we both shook our heads as if he could hear them rattle.

I insisted, "Oh, yes, by all means have a look."

Once he had removed the box, he set it gently upon the table. Then he stood back admiring its craftsmanship.

I hastened to offer, "There's a key attached to the bottom of the box."

His hands slid from the top of the box lightly caressing the lock.

"What a beautiful eighteenth century gun case. It's certainly in excellent condition."

I smiled proudly as he turned the box over slowly just as Beverly entered the room with a tray. She must have intentionally hurried in order not to miss a moment of the examination.

He found the brass key under the clip on the bottom of the box. Turning it carefully, the lock opened and he raised the lid. There he saw the 'Hawkins', 1754 musket pistol made in London. He pulled his handkerchief from his suit pocket removing the pistol from its case for closer inspection. Turning the pistol over, he confirmed what he already knew on sight. There on the bottom of the brass barrel the words 'Hawkins', London, 1754 were stamped clearly. He looked up at all of us speaking authoritatively without any reservation.

"This pistol belonged to George Washington. In his time, it was the only musket pistol he used. Our records indicate he purchased two that were shipped to him from England. He carried one throughout the entire Revolutionary War. It was his personal sidearm. Although the second appeared as being received on a manifest found at Mount Vernon, it was never located." Holding the pistol up to him he spoke in awestruck reverence. "That is, until now."

Naturally, the news left me flabbergasted. When I turned to get Vic's reaction, I could see anticipation welling in his eyes. Feeling a twinge of cynicism, I was sure I knew what he was thinking. He was already counting the dollars his collection of Revere Ware would bring.

Beverly leaned in close to get a better look at the pistol, inadvertently pressing her breast against my shoulder. It was then and there I determined resolutely not to embarrass myself in such distinguished company. Stepping aside, I decided it was best to present another of my finds. Quickly, I gestured toward the box containing the silver coin collection.

"If you like that pistol, wait until you see this."

Dr. Shapsmeir looked down at the box, then peered at me over his glasses.

"I trust all these objects you're about to show me came from the same room. Do I have that much clear?"

I hastened to assure, "Oh yes, we found them all in the same desk, as a matter of fact."

The professor replied with a curious humph. "Yes, we managed to recover that desk. It's in our restoration room right now." Vic turned to me with raised eyebrows. I returned his gesture with a scowl.

Holding the box in one hand, he examined the coat of arms appearing on the brass latch.

"This is interesting. It's the coat of arms of Castile and Leon. There's the motto, 'Plus Ultra' that would put this work at mid to late seventeenth century."

Hearing the news, I leaned back giving Vic a self-satisfied smile. Obviously, he could not wait for his turn at receiving noteworthy attention to *his* offerings.

Pressing the latch, Dr. Shapsmeir lifted the lid revealing the gleaming solid silver coins neatly lined in rows. His trained eye recognized them immediately.

"Why these are Pillar Dollars, Spanish Milled Dollars, commonly referred to in the times as 'Pieces of Eight'."

I interjected, "They're all dated the same, too."

The professor observed, "Yes, they're all dated April 10, 1771. These were all minted in Mexico City, destined to become a coin collection. You know the Pillar was granted legal tender status by the Second Continental Congress, prior to the Revolutionary War".

Vic asked, "Didn't our country have their own money back then?"

The professor replied, "Technically, yes, they did, but the Spanish Pillar was a far more stable and trusted form of currency at the time. What's more, these coins bear the motto 'Ultra Que Unum' meaning 'both are one'. It's the very precursor of our U.S. motto's 'Pluribus Unum'." Consequently, these became known as America's very first Silver Dollar. This is a fine collection; each coin was struck in .917 fine silver and exhibits nice detail."

"English speakers called them The Spanish Milled Dollar. The term 'milled' refers to the fact that the coin blanks were made on a milling machine to specifications of consistent weight and size. This technology made Spanish coins superior to other world coinage. Hence, they became the basis for the world monetary system. The coin, itself, is larger than our own silver dollar and stayed in U.S. circulation until 1857. Finally, they are highly valued simply because very few have survived in mint condition. All in all, I must say, so far you boys have hit the proverbial jackpot. Now, let me see what else we have here."

Vic had his three Revere Ware goblets which took little time to verify as authentic in Dr. Shapsmeir's eye. Then, there was the little silver and ivory magnifying glass and ivory letter opener. While Shapsmeir gave them his full attention, I knew I held the greatest prize to come. Reaching into the main pocket of the suitcase, I carefully removed the rolled parchment. Untying a ribbon placed on the document, I handed it over.

The good professor unrolled the parchment holding it back with one hand. I was watching his eyes for a reaction. As he scanned down, he saw the signatures at the bottom and took a deep breath. Adjusting in his seat, he sat forward pushing his glasses up on his nose. His mole like eyebrows arched considerably as he turned in his seat to face me. He looked at me for a moment in silence, then muttered in disbelief.

"It can't be. This appears to be authentic."

Gently rocking in his chair, he seemed to be talking to himself. It was as if he were trying to convince himself what he was seeing was real.

Then, he mumbled, "Of course, after all, they were all there. They met at the tavern regularly after the Second Continental Congress adjourned each day. But, no one ever recorded those meetings. They must have used the room below the tavern in secret after hours. Yes, that's it. That would explain everything."

Appearing introspective, his lips curled a little as if he were scheming something mischievous. I was beside myself wondering what he would say next when suddenly Beverly spoke.

"This does tie in with your theory doesn't it, Professor?"

He replied, "Why, yes, of course, it does."

I couldn't stand the suspense any longer.

Moving in closer I blurted out, "What is this theory you're talking about? Aren't these real signatures? Is it a fake? I mean it couldn't be… we found it with all the other stuff. Would someone please tell me what's going on?"

Beverly spoke for the Professor.

"Professor Shapsmeir has long believed that certain founding fathers who were masons held secret meetings to plan strategies for the Second Continental Congress. With this document, he'll have proof that at least three of them met at the tavern in secret."

The professor broke in, "You see, according to Masonic Rules, a quorum of three is required to conduct any official meeting. Of course, there were other masons at work, but this is proof positive that they met in secret at this critical juncture in the formation of our nation's government. As you can clearly see, the very words used in their pact foreshadow the preamble to *The Declaration of Independence*. That definitely points to a Masonic influence on the creation of that document, as well. With that, he placed both hands on the document in front of him and exclaimed, "Glory be, I knew it all along!"

Dr. Shapsmeir stood up from the desk presenting his hand to me.

"I would like to be the first to congratulate you on your significant contribution to our nation's history. With an afterthought, he turned shaking Vic's hand, as well.

"This has truly been a red-letter day for the Pennsylvania Historical Society. With a letter of assessment on the estimated value of your discovery, I trust our treasurer can make you a settlement to our mutual satisfaction."

Suddenly, for the first time since I entered the room, I felt things were moving too swiftly. Presently, I was feeling a strong sense of obligation to the others. We had agreed any value attached to our discovery in the top drawer would be shared equally. I knew I didn't have to remind Vic, but I did not expect an offer so soon. I thought it only right that I consult with Amy and Connie first.

"Dr. Shapsmeir, I want you to know that there are others involved. The four of us agreed to split any proceeds equally. So, if you could write your letter, I'd be happy to share that with the others so they can make a decision."

"Yes, of course, if that's your agreement, I understand. How soon do you think you can come to a decision?"

Vic piped in, "Oh, I'm sure we can make a decision real soon, Doctor. Can't we, Allen?"

"Well, yes, that is, I think so. Like I said, we must consult with the others."

Dr. Shapsmeir asked, "Do think it would be possible for you to leave your collection with me so I can better complete my assessment?"

I glanced at Vic, already shaking his head in approval.

I said, "Well, I guess that's it, then. When do you want us to come back for the letter?"

"I can have Beverley type it up for you by tomorrow morning, if that meets with your approval?"

Again, I got the nod from Vic.

"Yes, that should be just fine. Thank you for your valuable time."

"Nonsense, it is I who should be thanking you. Your find will make a superior contribution to the Society. Thank you both for coming. I'll let Beverly show you out. I look forward to seeing you tomorrow, at say ten o'clock?"

I replied, "That would be great, and thanks again, Professor."

As Beverly saw us off, Vic waited until we were out of earshot before providing me his unsolicited opinion.

"Man, I wouldn't throw her out of bed, unless the floor was softer."

Shaking my head, I replied, "It's a pity she's not around to share your observation."

"Is that right, Mister Smart Guy? Well, I noticed you didn't seem to mind so much when she got cozy with you."

"You don't know what you're talking about."

"Oh no, don't tell me I don't know she was puttin' a move on you."

"You're crazy. Besides, I'm taken."

Vic laughed skipping several steps ahead. Then, he walked backwards taunting me.

"Don't worry, Mister Smart Guy, I won't tell Amy."

"There's nothin' to tell, so mind your own business and watch where you're going."

Just as I spoke, Vic almost ran backwards into a lady carrying some packages. I enjoyed having the last laugh watching him bow and scrape as he apologized all over himself.

I sneered, "Come on, wonder boy, we've got a bus to catch."

The ride home seemed unending. I was bursting to get to Amy and tell her the whole story. I thought, *"How lucky can one guy get? I had the girl, I'd soon have the money, and the future was ours!"*

I couldn't help noticing how quiet Vic was on the ride home. I sensed he felt let down because he didn't have a bigger cut. Yet, just when I thought I had him figured he turned to me and confided something that surprised me.

"I'm going to break it off with Connie."

I was in shock.

"What did you just say?"

"You heard me. I'm gonna tell Connie it's quits with us. I've been thinking about it ever since we got rescued."

"But why, what's the matter? All of sudden we're coming into money and now she's not good enough for you?"

Vic's face grew red with anger. If we hadn't been jammed together so close on the bus, I think he would have taken a poke at me. Instead, he got hold of himself as he tried to explain.

"It's this way, Allen. Connie was alright for a few laughs if things didn't get too serious. Now that we are coming into money, like you say, I'll be able to do the things I always wanted. Well, at least, most of them. Anyway, it's hard to explain. I just don't see her as the kind of girl I could live with a long time. I was thinking, with the money, I could go into business for myself. Maybe open my own pool hall, who knows? Sure, with the money, I could afford to get married, you know that. But, she's just not the type for me."

"You're still not convincing me here, Vic. Tell me the real reason you wanna break up."

"Well, that's just it. I can't put my finger on it, exactly. It's just the way she is. You know the way she reacted to things when we were down there. It's hard to say this, but I'm afraid she just couldn't take it if we ever got in a real pinch."

I just stared at my friend struggling to understand what it was about Connie, and then it came to me.

"Are you saying she's too flighty? Is it like you're afraid she wouldn't make a good wife because she might crack up or somethin' when the chips were down? Is that what you're saying?"

I watched his face losing that contorted look of agony. It was being replaced with a steady calm as he sat back feeling grateful for a friend's understanding. Then, he cast his eyes downward nodding his head with the realization. I had nailed it. I could only sit in sympathetic silence for the rest of our ride together.

When the bus brakes squealed at our stop, Vic and I stepped out on the dirty sidewalk. Giving me a thoughtful look, he placed his hand on my shoulder swallowing hard.

"You know, Allen, I still want her to get her share of the money, just like we agreed"

I replied, "In all honesty, I wouldn't have it any other way."

Vic turned to leave. For a long moment, I just stood at the bus stop watching my friend's back trying to grasp how much our lives were changing. Then, instead of heading for home, I decided to pay Amy a visit. Suddenly, I found myself giving in to the temptation to tell Amy everything. If I was lucky, I might catch up with her before lunch break at 'the house'.

I found Amy at her desk working as diligently as a one-armed accounting clerk ever could. I tried catching her attention waving through the office window at her. When I caught her eye, she beamed waving back. She knew I was meeting the curator that morning at the Historical

Society. Consequently, she held off taking her lunch break hoping I'd come to see her.

In her conservative blue dress, she stood out in stark contrast to the Amy I came to know so well in the dark realm beneath Philly. She looked cute with her arm dressed up in a clean sling, though I am sure she would not appreciate my saying so. She was up in a heartbeat, closing the office door behind her. Running toward me, eyes bright, full of anticipation, she threw her good arm around my neck kissing me several times. Some of the office girls giggled, pretending not to notice us kissing in the hallway.

She asked excitedly, "Well, how did it go, honey? Be sure and tell me everything now."

"Hold on there, Miss Martin. There are people watching."

"Oh, let them look. I don't care if they do."

"Well, at least, let's go to lunch first, and then I'll tell you all about it."

Amy poked me in the side with her cast.

"You will not. You'll not wait another second, Mr. Williams. I've been waiting on pins all morning. The girls absolutely wouldn't leave me alone. Tell me right now on the way."

I teased, "On the way to where? You haven't told me where you want to eat yet."

"Oh, Allen, stop being so mean. Just start walking and talking. I'll think of something."

I tried tantalizing her with a tiny tidbit of my good fortune. Holding my head up at a jaunty angle, I took her by the arm mimicking a formal escort.

"Perhaps it should be a place of fine dining, my dear, some place befitting my lady's good taste in men."

Amy's face fairly well lit up.

"Oh, Allen, it's good news, isn't it?"

Holding her in suspense just one moment longer with a serious look on my face, I told her.

"My dear, I don't see how it could be much better."

Amy listened intently as I explained everything Dr. Shapsmeir said, making it clear that everything was pending upon his appraisal. I also reminded her of our agreement with Vic and Connie on the contents of the top drawer, just to be sure she understood. She was in such joy I hated to inform her of Vic's news about Connie. Yet, I felt I should share everything with her. As I told her, she reacted as expected becoming sullen and subdued right away. I knew she would take it hard. She and Connie had bonded while sharing the duress of our ordeal underground. Amy was not one to choose friends easily either. Once she became close to someone, she respected that relationship just as she did with me.

"Amy, try not to be too hard on Vic. I've known him longer and I know he never was much for settling down. He told me he'd rather go into business before he gets serious with a girl."

Amy sulked, "I guess you're right. I just thought they made a good couple."

I ventured, "They're not the same as you and me, Amy. I don't know what I'd do without you. Though, I don't know what you see in me."

Amy poked me harder this time.

"Stop it, Allen. There's a lot that makes me feel the way I do about you. You have certain qualities that make me want to do for you."

She smiled looking into my eyes.

"You're a born leader, Allen. That's only one thing that makes me care for you. That's just a part of it. You listen and you have a sense of caring for others. That makes you very special because you genuinely want to help others. I suppose that's what makes you want to teach."

Feeling humbled, I floundered trying to accept her compliment. When my brain didn't meet the mark, she stood in for me.

"It's all right, Allen. You're humble, too. Not like Vic, I'm sorry to say."

After that exchange, we found a nice Italian restaurant and shared a wonderful meal. It was one I felt I could afford for a change. Amy never made any disparaging remarks about Vic beyond what she shared with me that day. She was too good to harbor hate in her soul. That quality of forgiveness was the one I loved most in her.

When we returned to 'the house', I left Amy with a lingering kiss giving the girls in her office something to talk about. While I was there, I looked in on the main office secretary to find out when I should report back to work. She rifled through some papers on her desk and smiled handing me a copy of my new schedule. I was startled to see I was placed on first shift starting Monday. I wondered if they did the same for Vic. If they did, I could almost hear him now.

"There, ya see, all you have to do is go missing for a week in this place and these guys promote ya."

I chuckled to myself thinking, *"Even if they did promote us, I doubt we'd stay around much longer to enjoy it."* Then, I laughed out loud at the very thought of 'the house' having anything to do with joy. The secretary maintained her puzzled look as I pushed through the door wondering how many days I'd stay in that stinking place.

The bus ride home was stifling under the mid-June sun. What's worse, the guy sitting next to me had the window open with half his torso jammed into it. I surmised he could not know his sleeveless undershirt exuded sweaty armpit odor in my face. As I faced the isle seeking relief, he leaned back in.

He said, "It sure is a hot one."

I half nodded in agreement sheltering my nose with my hand.

He added, "You know it's not really the heat that gets you, though, it's the humidity."

I guess he felt compelled to share that news flash before hanging out the window again. Fortunately, he departed two stops later freeing me to seize the window for myself. I must have looked like a dog with its head hanging out the window, but at least the rest of the ride was breezy and uneventful. It did seem odd to be returning home at a time when I would normally be going to work. I surmised a lot of things would be different soon, especially for my family. The squeal of the brakes brought my daydreaming to an end. I stepped off, relieved to be leaving the stinking bus behind. Once again, I thought about the future. Riding the bus would be a thing of the past, if I played my cards right. Then, I hurried down the sidewalk for home.

Vaulting up the stairs to our apartment, I ran the three flights up breathless to tell Mom how everything went. When I threw back the door, I was happy to see her and Grandma at the kitchen table. They were snapping green beans into a large bowl on the table. From the looks of things, they were nearly finished. My younger sisters were sitting on the living room floor playing Monopoly. They seemed nearly done, as well. I could see at a glance Mary, the oldest, was asserting her dominance over Park Place and Boardwalk.

I called out, "Mom, I've got great news."

Mom wound up a big smile for me as I entered. Standing up, she wiped her hands on her apron and walked toward me with open arms.

"I bet you're going to tell me those things you found are worth a fortune."

Somewhat deflated I spoke haltingly, "Wa…What makes you say that, Mom?"

She explained excitedly, "Well, I just knew it, ever since that nice man from the Masonic Temple came around. He seemed so interested in meeting you. He called twice. The second time I told him you should be home anytime. That's when he asked to come and meet you. When he did, you weren't back yet. I told him you probably got delayed at the Historical Society. That's when he said he wanted to see you about the artifacts, too. That's why I figured you got a good offer because he wants to bid on them, as well."

"Mom, slow down. What are you talking about? What Masonic man did you meet? What's this all about?"

Grandma peered at Mom over the rims of her glasses.

"Now, Betty, don't get yourself so excited. Tell the boy what you know, but just take your time."

Mom managed to contain her joy long enough to make me understand.

"You see, Allen, this man, Harold Williamson, said he was the curator of the Masonic Temple's Museum and he wanted to see the artifacts. He said if they were genuine he would be most interested in bidding on them for the Museum's collection."

My head was spinning. It all seemed so incredible. I had not even seen the first appraisal and I already had someone else wanting to buy the artifacts. I told myself to stay calm; think it through. Wondering what I should do next, it came to me in a flash.

"Mom, did he leave you a card?"

"No, he didn't, but he left his phone number. He seemed very anxious to talk with you. He said you could reach him tomorrow at his office after eleven."

"Did he say where his office was?"

"Well, naturally, I assumed it would be at the Masonic Temple downtown. You know the medieval-style building just north of City Hall."

"Oh, yes, of course, you said he was a mason."

My mind was filling with a raging torrent of thoughts. Bells and whistles were pealing and screaming in my head. I was simply incredulous that all this was happening to me so fast. Suddenly, I felt faint. The room swooped around me as I saw myself falling head long for the Monopoly board on top of my screaming sisters. My mother stood frozen in shock. She had never seen me faint before. *I* had never fainted before. The next thing I felt was my grandmother pressing a cold washcloth to my forehead. I could barely hear her as she admonished my sisters.

"Get back girls. Give him air to breathe."

Mom had managed to come out of her state of shock. She was trying to move me clear of my landing spot on the game board. As she did, I could hear my little sister crying.

"Is he going to die, Mama?"

"No, dear, he's just fainted that's all. He'll be good as new in a minute or two, you'll see."

My other sister, Mary, stepped forward brushing off a red hotel stuck to my back. I could see my other sister smiling down at me. I could not tell if she was happy I was alright or pleased I interrupted the thrashing she was receiving at the hands of merciless Mary, the Monopoly queen. In any event, I managed to sit up and rejoin the family.

Mom fussed, "You scared us half to death, Allen. Don't try to stand up right away. Wait until the blood comes back to your head."

I just sat there on the floor for a while smiling sheepishly up at everyone.

"I guess I just had too much good news all at once, huh?"

Grandma remarked, "That's probably true, Allen, but you've got a tough decision to make. Which will it be that fella at the Historical Society or the mason who called?"

Mom said, "Leave him be for now. He's yet to hear from the Historical Society and hasn't even spoken to Mr. Williamson. Hearing that, I rose purposefully signaling to all the worst was over. Grandma reminded me I had to think things through before making my next move. More importantly, I felt obligated to talk things over with those who would be sharing my new-found wealth.

"Mom, I'm going to call Vic right now. We need to talk some things over."

Chapter 16

Everything started moving faster once I finished talking to Vic. He wanted all of us to meet at the malt shop.

Vic said, "I'll call Connie. You get Amy and meet us there at eight, O.K.?"

"I'll try, Vic. We didn't make plans to see each other tonight, though."

Vic was adamant, "Just get her over there. You know how important this is."

"Of course, I do, Vic. By the way, have you told Connie yet?"

Vic's response was immediate.

"No, and don't you tell her anything, either."

"I wouldn't tell her, but Amy might."

Vic appeared beside himself.

"Oh no, you mean you told Amy?"

"Of course, we tell each other everything."

"Yeah, well, that's just fine. If she hears it from Amy first, I'm doomed."

"What are you talking about, Vic?"

"Look Allen, you know how she is. If she hears the news from Amy, she'll go bonkers. Believe me, she'll absolutely positively flip."

"Listen, Amy can handle situations like that. I'm not afraid of this, are you?"

"It's not Amy, it's her. There's something I got to tell you, but you gotta promise you won't tell anybody, not even Amy."

"Well, I don't know about that. It depends on what it is, tell me. What's up Vic? You can trust me."

Vic explained hesitantly, "When Connie came back from the hospital, the doc ordered her to take sedatives. Connie's mom told me she hasn't been herself lately. She just hangs around the house looking out the window. She made me promise not to say anything. You know some people don't want that kind of news gettin' around."

"Did you go visit her, Vic?"

"Only once, but she was acting dopey and everything. She didn't really talk that much. She just kinda acted like… you know, like she didn't even know me. That's why I haven't told her yet. I didn't want her to flip out because of me."

"Oh, jeez, Vic. Now, what are we gonna do?"

Before I could say more, Vic came back, "Look, just let me call her mother and see how she's doin'. Maybe she's better. Anyway, if she *can* go to the malt shop, it might do her some good. After all, we'll be talkin' about good news for all of us, right? Maybe it will cheer her up knowin' she's comin' into a lot of money."

"I don't know, Vic. The whole thing sounds a little screwy, if you ask me. Besides, Amy might feel uncomfortable trying to hide the fact that she knows she's about to be dumped, especially under the circumstances, with Connie and all."

"I told you we're not supposed to say anything about that to anyone."

I reminded, "It was you who promised Connie's mother, not me."

"Oh, so now you can't go along with me on this?"

"I don't know, Vic. Give me some time to think about that one."

"We haven't got much time left, buddy. You know we're supposed to meet that Dr. Shapsmeir guy tomorrow at ten."

"I know, but I don't think I should keep Amy in the dark. Besides, don't you think she'll notice something's not right with Connie?"

"We don't know that for sure. Like I said, I'll find out from her mother if she's doing better, O.K.?"

"Alright, I'll leave it at that. You can call Connie's house first. I'll just wait to hear from you then."

Vic assured, "Right, I'll call you back in a little while, as soon as I know somethin'."

As soon as I put down the phone, it rang startling me a bit. When I picked up, it was someone I'd never spoken to, but hoped I would.

"Hello."

"Yes, hello. This is Harold Williamson from the Masonic Temple. Is Allen Williams there?"

"Yes, that's me. My mom said you dropped by today."

"Yes, Mr. Williams. May I call you, Allen?"

"Yes sir, that's fine."

Harold's strong deep voice resonated on the line.

"Allen, I dropped by because of the artifacts you found underneath the Old City Tavern."

"Yes sir, I have your number. I was going to call you tomorrow."

He replied, "I hope I'm not calling too late."

"Oh, no, that's fine", I said.

"I just wanted to ask you some questions about the artifacts."

"O.K., I guess that would be alright."

"Yes, well, have you shown them to anyone else besides *The Philadelphia Inquirer*?"

"Yes, my friend and I took the artifacts to the Historical Society to have the curator authenticate them."

Suddenly, Harold's tone of voice changed. He sounded a bit more anxious than before.

"If I may ask, did he hold the artifacts for you to authenticate them?"

I hesitated giving him an answer immediately sensing he was really after something else. Then, I decided to let the cat out of the bag informing him we were also awaiting a letter of assessment determining the value of the artifacts.

Innocently I told him, "Dr. Shapsmeir said he would write the letter so we could consider an offer for the artifacts tomorrow."

Now, I could detect an air of genuine concern in his voice as it rose in pitch.

"I see, so you are planning to sell the artifacts to them?"

"My friends and I are considering it, yes."

Now, he seized the moment responding quickly.

"I wonder if I might have some of your time before you make that decision. You see, there are certain items in your possession that our Temple would be most interested in having for our own museum's collection. I can't promise anything without examining the artifacts, although I am at liberty to offer a very attractive price if they are what we are looking for. Would you be interested in bringing them in for an assessment?"

"Well, like I said, I do have partners who would want to help make that decision. How soon do you need to know?"

Harold's voice became more genial.

"I would say after visiting hours on Saturday, if that's convenient. You could bring your partners along. I'd be happy to arrange a private tour of our Temple. I think all of you would find it most impressive and educational. The Temple is registered as a National Historical Landmark. Would you consider coming at say 2:30?"

Not wanting to sound over excited, I paused briefly. Catching my breath, I held my hand over the receiver looking up saying a short prayer. I took another deep breath, then removed my hand.

"Yes, Mr. Williamson, I will certainly be happy to extend your invitation to my partners. I'll call you back Saturday to confirm that appointment."

Harold seemed pleased saying, "Very well, I'll look forward to hearing from you soon. Thank you for your time and consideration, Allen. It's been nice talking to you."

"Sure, no problem; you, too, sir. I'll speak to you soon."

Easing down the receiver as if it were made of gold, I nearly jumped right out of my Keds when I heard my mother's voice behind me.

"Great job, Allen. You handled that call very well. I'm proud of you."

"Oh, Mom, I didn't know you were there. You startled me."

"I'm sorry, dear, I wasn't listening in, I was just passing down the hall when I heard you speaking. I bet that was Mr. Williamson. What did he have to say for himself?"

"He's invited me and the others to tour the Temple on Saturday. Best of all, I'm sure he wants to make us an offer. That is, if we have what his museum is looking for."

Mom clasped her hands together.

"Oh, that's wonderful, Allen."

"What do you think your friends will say if he offers to buy what you've found?"

"Well, I can't speak for all of them, but I'm going to suggest we let both parties bid for the artifacts. That way, I think we'll get the best offer."

Mom took on a serious expression. Then, she smiled in that gentle way I was used to seeing before she imparted words of wisdom.

"Allen, most young men stop maturing long before they start aging, but not you. You are truly something special. Whatever you choose to do with that money, I know it will be the right thing and you'll go far. I hope you do, too. I want you to go far away from all this and never look back. Just seek out the things that are meaningful to you and never let them go, my dear. Never take second best. You're better than that, believe me, I know."

I held my head high looking her straight in the eye.

"Thank you, Mom. You've always been there for me ready to say the right thing. You do make me feel special. Whatever happens, I won't forget you. You'll be a part of everything I do, always."

Just before she started to cry, she brushed past me in the hall speaking in a quavering voice. "That's the nicest thing a mother could ever want to hear. Goodnight son."

I just looked up saying another short prayer.

"Thanks, Lord, for taking an interest in me. You won't regret it, amen."

The phone rang. It was Vic.

"Hello."

"Listen up, Tonto. Now that you're finally off the line, I got good news. Connie is feeling better. I even talked to her for a while."

"Yeah, what did she say?"

"You know the usual stuff. I've missed you, when are you coming over, stuff like that. What are you going to say to those things, you know?"

I reminded, "The malt shop, Vic, what about the malt shop?"

"Oh yeah, she says she can't make it until eight-thirty. She says she's gotta wash her hair. Can you believe it?"

"Well, alright then, I'll call Amy. I'm sure her mom will let her go. Ever since we stepped out of that hole with treasure, I've been her golden boy."

"Yeah, same here. Funny how that works, ain't it? One day you're a bloody, butcher boy and the next you're sittin' on top of the world. How lucky can one guy get, huh?"

On a more serious note, I responded, "Let's don't be forgetting what we went through to get here, buddy."

"Don't worry, I ain't forgettin' that anytime soon. I'm just sayin' 'all's well that ends well' and 'ain't it grand', you know. Besides, if I need reminders, I have pictures of the closed coffin at Steve's funeral, thank you very much."

I let it go saying, "Just meet us at the malt shop, wise guy."

As soon as I hung up, I called Amy.

"Hello, Allen. I was wondering when you would call. What's new with you?"

I almost told her about Vic's decision to hold off telling Connie. Instead, I bit my lip figuring she would learn soon enough. I didn't want to jeopardize the chances of our meeting. I told her of Mr. Williamson's call and the idea of meeting with him Saturday.

"I think that's a great idea, Allen. This way, I can meet him when you do. The tour sounds interesting. Best of all, we've got two museums interested. That should lead to a better offer, don't you think?"

I answered, "Once again, our thoughts grow on the same tree, honey. That's exactly what I think. What's more important is what all of us decide. That's why I called. Vic wants us all to have a meeting at the malt shop at eight-thirty. Do you think you can make it?"

"Sure, I think so. Of course, I can't stay out too late. I must work tomorrow. Just think, Allen, it may not be long before I won't have to go to work at 'the house.'"

She laughed her soft laugh into the phone. It always got me going.

"Maybe it won't be too long before we have a house of our own, instead. You know, a real house with flowers, a yard, a cat, and a dog, and who knows what."

"Whoa, little lady, let's not get ahead of ourselves. Let's start with the meeting and go from there, alright?"

She sounded a little let down when she responded.

"I know, Allen; you always get to be the level headed one."

I reassured, "Hey, just because we're not kids anymore doesn't mean we can't hold on to a dream."

"Oh, thank you, Allen. That's very thoughtful. Together, I know we'll do the right thing. I'll see you at the malt shop, sweetheart."

She hung up, yet I lingered on the line imagining her face close to mine. Checking the clock, I saw I had plenty of time for a shower. I headed for my room with more than a few things on my mind.

Later, I stepped down the stairs of my apartment building two at a time. Remembering the heat of the day, I wore a loose fit button down blue and white striped shirt. I thought it matched well with my Levi's and black high topped tennis shoes. I was never a slave to fashion. That's one thing a slaughter house worker's son rarely has the wherewithal to become. Yet on the other hand, I wore what was tasteful. I enjoyed wearing clean outfits that matched right down to my thick white socks. I took to the sidewalk walking rapidly combing back my wet hair as I walked. By the time I reached the malt shop, my hair was clean, dry, and in place. Another pearl of Mom's wisdom ran through my mind as I entered.

She always said, "We may be poor, but soap and water are cheap."

Everyone else was there waiting. Amy waved from a booth at the back of the shop. I approached with my eye on Connie, not knowing how she was faring. Her disarming smile soon dispelled any misgivings I might have harbored about her state of mind. All things considered, she appeared her usual self. I sat down quickly next to Amy speaking to all of them immediately.

"Before we get started, I want you all to know the drinks are on me."

Vic quipped, "Give a listen to 'Diamond Jim' here."

At least, I made Connie laugh. Although, considering the source, I elected not to press my luck further.

Vic started in with a brief review of where we were now with our proposed sale of the artifacts. Taking a more serious tack than usual, he reminded we had little time to make our final decision.

I responded first.

"I'm sure you all know by now we have two appointments. As Vic pointed out, one is tomorrow at ten, the other at two-thirty on Saturday. I figured, since Amy has to work tomorrow, Vic and I will keep the appointment tomorrow."

I hastened to explain, mostly for Connie's benefit, that Vic and I already laid the groundwork. All we had to do was pick up the artifacts and the letter of assessment tomorrow. Therefore, I argued, it was unnecessary for Connie to go so long as she saw the letter before we concluded our Saturday appointment. In that way, Connie and Amy could go on the tour on Saturday and we could compare bids afterward.

Connie followed my line of reasoning like a bobble headed doll nodding silently in agreement with everything I said. At least, that was my take on it. However, when Amy interjected momentarily to assure, Connie understood. She just responded with her usual smile. It was the same one that made people wonder what, if anything, was going on behind those eyes.

Vic took charge leaning over the table looking her straight in the eye as he spoke slowly and deliberately.

"They want to know if you understand."

Connie appeared to pop out of her self-induced trance answering, "Oh, yeah, Vic, sure I understand."

Vic turned to us with an innocent smile shrugging his shoulders sympathetically as he spoke.

"So then, we're moving right along here."

Amy quickly shot him a sideways glance showing her disapproval of his condescension.

Vic returned the barbed look with a genuine look of unbridled innocence.

I decided it was time to make another point clear.

"When Vic and I meet with Dr. Shapsmeir, I think it would be a good idea if we sort of let it slip that we heard from the Masonic Temple's curator and they want to meet with us. Amy, quick on the uptake as ever, saw the connection immediately.

She added, "I see what you're after, Allen, but remember this is the real world so I wouldn't expect too much."

"I don't know. I think it's damn clever," said Vic. "Why not play one against the other? Maybe we can get a bidding war started."

Amy replied, "Maybe, on the other hand these guys are professionals who have to work within a budget. They know exactly what they're looking for, and I'd bet my bottom dollar they know exactly how much they will pay."

I asked Amy if she thought it was still a good idea. If not, then what else should we try?

"It's like this. We must know our buyer. We don't know the value of these artifacts beyond what they're willing to say they are worth. So, we remain dependent upon them to set the price. What we need to know, is which of the two is willing to pay the most?"

"You see, Vic, I told you she had a good head for business," I said. "I only wish you could be there with us tomorrow."

Amy admonished, "Just be clear about letting Dr. Shapsmeir know of the other curator's interest. It wouldn't hurt to drop his name. I'm sure they all know each other in this business. That would give you some credibility."

Vic asked, "What if they don't want all of the stuff we found?"

I assured, "I'm sure we can find a buyer somewhere. Or, better still, we could make it an all or nothing deal."

Amy agreed, "That's right, Allen, it could help to use the entire collection as leverage. Just because these guys work up town in suits doesn't mean they can railroad us."

I agreed, with a word of caution.

"We just need to be careful of cutting off our noses to spite our face."

Connie appeared perplexed, "What does that mean, Allen?"

Vic just leaned forward sucking through his straw at the bottom of his shake with a gurgling noise. Looking up from his glass, he smiled at Connie.

"Don't worry, sweetheart, nothing's going to happen to our noses."

Amy quipped, "That reminds me, I need to go powder mine. Do you wanna go with me, Connie?"

Both girls got up heading for the restroom leaving Vic and I to weigh the pros and cons of our sojourn in the world of acquisition and antiquities. One thing was painfully clear, we were amateurs dealing with experts. Like sheep amongst wolves, it was no time to rely upon the kindness of strangers. When the girls returned, there was one more revelation. Connie asked to be alone with Vic for a while. Since Amy had to leave early anyway, we said our goodbyes. When we had gone, Connie turned in her seat to address a bewildered Vic. He could not fathom why she wanted to be alone with him right then.

Connie started speaking slowly, methodically, "Vic, I know you don't really love me."

Vic leaned forward starting to protest, but Connie cut him off with a finger placed on his lips.

"Please let me finish cause this is hard. You and I have had some great times together. Some times were better than others, but mostly good. It's not your fault that I went with you down there. I remember you didn't want me going along in the first place."

Vic interrupted, "It was all for your own good, Connie."

"Please wait 'til I'm through. I know you don't love me the way Allen loves Amy. I just want you to know that's O.K. Only it's different with me, because I do. So, I want you to let me go so I can find someone else who does love me that way. Do you understand?"

Vic was completely flabbergasted. Connie was not only giving him an easy way out, she was holding the door for him. Dumbfounded, he struggled to conjure up an answer that seemed convincing in his confused state. Finding it impossible, he settled for the truth.

"Connie, I really do understand, but could you tell me one thing before I go?"

Connie held her breath trying not to cry. Up to that moment her bravery was barely sufficient to hold back the flood.

"Yes, Vic, what is it?"

"Did anyone tell you I didn't love you?"

Connie quietly lowered her head in thought then lifted her eyes to meet Vic's.

"No, not really. A girl just knows these things, I suppose."

With nothing left to say, Vic rose from his seat and walked slowly toward the door. Then with his special brand of bravado, he called back to her.

"It's been great knowin' ya, kid. I'll see you in the funny papers."

Connie held up a hand waving, smiling bravely, she said, "Not if I see you first," as the first tear drop fell.

The next day when I met Vic at the bus stop, it was the first thing he spoke about. He told me everything, then looked me in the eye. He had that look on his face. I knew exactly what he was going to say. Before he could even form the words, I cut him off.

"No, Vic, Amy didn't tell her. We talked about Connie on the way home last night and she swore she never said a word. She told me she wanted to, but she respected your decision. What's more she told me she couldn't bring herself to hurt Connie."

A true look of bewilderment came over him. He just sat like a stone not saying anything for the rest of the ride to the Historical Society. Finally, just before we entered the gray stone building, he spoke as if he were the only one there.

"I still can't figure how she knew."

I stopped on the steps turning to face him.

"Vic, did you ever stop to think maybe she really didn't know you were going to dump her. The same thing could have been on her mind ever since she got back. All I know is, she's probably better off in the long run."

Vic retorted, "Now, what's that supposed to mean?"

"You told me yourself, you weren't serious about her. You could have told her that. Oh no, instead you like to keep them guessing, don't you?"

"Give it some time, Vic. Someday you're going to notice there are other people in the world who count besides yourself."

I moved ahead through the large, heavy, oak doors leaving him to his thoughts on the steps. When I reached Dr. Shapsmeir office, I paused before knocking. Vic caught up and spoke again.

"I think you got me wrong, buddy, but for now it's strictly business. Afterward, you and I gotta talk."

"Alright, Vic, you're on. Now, let's do some business."

I knocked on the heavy oaken door. Beverly greeted us with a smile as she ushered us in.

"Good morning, gentlemen. Dr. Shapsmeir is waiting to see you."

The room we entered was the same as before. Yet, for the first time, I noticed it looked decidedly perfunctory. The drapes were one color and hung to the floor concealing the tall windows of the old building. There was no sign of luxury in the room. The imposing table in the middle was polished and clear of any object. The furniture around the room was mostly upholstered in leather, with a few exceptions being Queen Anne style fabric covered easy chairs. The vaulted ceiling and the spacious interior gave the room the look of largesse without seeming too over the top. The room itself was part of a working research library. As such, it was a functional meeting room reserved for those who had business or research to conduct in the Historical Society of Pennsylvania.

That is where Vic and I came in. Beverly led us to our chairs at the table.

She gestured, "Please do sit down. Dr. Shapsmeir will be with you shortly. Can I get you something to drink?"

Vic answered, "I'll take a Coke, if you've got any."

Beverly smiled patiently, "I think that can be arranged. What about you, Mr. Williams?"

"No, thank you. I'm fine. Please do call me, Allen."

She replied, "Yes, certainly, I'll be right back."

Vic leaned over with his hand covering his mouth confiding sarcastically.

"Allen, please do call me, Vic."

"That's enough out of you," I said.

He replied, "She sure looks hot today, doesn't she? How *does* a kid like that get a job like this?"

I answered, "You have to know somebody. Now, be quiet and stick to business. We've got to stay on the ball here."

Just then, a door in the back of the room opened. Professor Shapsmeir appeared dressed in a tweed suit again, this time wearing a bow tie. His steel rimmed glasses still hung precariously on the bridge of his nose making him look a bit like old Ben Franklin himself. As he padded across the thick Persian rug, he seemed to totter a bit.

"Good morning, gentlemen. It's truly good to see you both again."

After exchanging pleasantries, we got right down to business. He pulled a long envelope out of his right coat pocket sliding it across the table toward us.

"This is the letter of assessment, as promised. I hope you and your partners will find our offer satisfactory."

I picked up the envelope deciding then and there not to open it in his presence. Holding the letter in hand, I also decided it was time to do a little name dropping.

I began cautiously, "Dr. Shapsmeir, I know you recall our agreement was to allow the others to see the letter before making our final decision. Also, I feel it's only fair to tell you I have been contacted by another interested party. Recently, I spoke with the curator for the Pennsylvania Masonic Grand Lodge. I am to meet with Mr. Williamson this Saturday along with my partners. We are all in agreement that he should also have an opportunity to assess the value of our artifacts."

Silence befell the room. Having dropped the bombshell, I felt a distinct air of coolness coming from Beverly's position at the table. Vic didn't even look at her. Instead, he coolly took a sip of his Coke and looked back at me. The disappointment on Dr. Shapsmeir face was undeniable. He was clearly unsettled by my announcement. For a moment, I thought Vic and I might be ejected from the room by some Historical Society henchmen hidden behind the drapes. At long last, Shapsmeir spoke.

"We here at the Historical Society have a long reputation of fair dealing. Because we are servants of the public, naturally we are obligated to act in accordance with specific guidelines in the process of obtaining our acquisitions. Naturally, there are times when we are faced with competition in our duties to acquire and preserve the best representative examples of our nation's past. In so doing, it is our endeavor to showcase these exhibits in our collection for educators and researchers from all over the world. Unfortunately, we must act under the constraints of a governmental budget. Thus, at times, we find ourselves in a position less than favorable for obtaining the best acquisitions.

I understand your position is to gain the greatest amount possible for your discoveries. However, I would appeal to your sense of history when you consider the competitor's offer. They are a private concern with national standing. Frankly speaking, when it comes to acquiring artifacts, their pockets are much deeper than ours. Also, please keep in mind if you should sell your collection to the Masons it will not receive the public exposure we can offer. To be clear, the public is largely unaware of the Masonic Temple's fine collection. Because they are a private organization, many do not know they exist. For example, most tourists commonly mistake their headquarters building for a church because of its medieval style of construction.

All things considered, I urge you to think this through carefully. If you are interested in monetary gain only, then we may not be the right choice. However, if you want to see your important finds receive the notoriety and exposure they deserve, I would place them with us. Having said that,

I feel this concludes our meeting. If you should decide in favor of the Pennsylvania Historical Society, our offer stands as stated in the letter of assessment. Good day, gentlemen."

Before I could revive my foot from its sleep, I found myself limping out the door, tattered suitcase in hand.

Vic said, "Boy, talk about the bum's rush."

"Oh, give me a break, Vic. What did you expect? The Professor made a good point."

"Yeah, Allen, he made a good point, and we really busted our ass to get this stuff. We owe it to ourselves to get the most we can for it."

"I hear ya. It's just that he's probably right, you know? I had the same notion before I came here. When I first heard from Mr. Williamson, I knew our stuff would not be seen by as many people. I remember when I was twelve we went by that Temple across from City Hall. At the time, I thought it was a church, too."

Vic maintained, "Well, I say one down, one to go. It all depends on what that guy with the Masons says now. We sell to the highest bidder, right?"

"Yeah, yeah, I hear ya, Vic", I said feeling a little disgusted with his mercenary tone.

On the bus ride home, I couldn't get what Dr. Shapsmeir said out of my head. Somehow, I felt cheap and low like we were selling out or something. I thought *why does it always have to come down to money?*

Soon, Vic turned his attention on me.

"About me and Connie, there are two sides to everything, you know?"

"Oh, really, Vic. Why don't you tell me about your side?"

"Look, I know what you're thinkin'. You think I just take advantage of girls like Connie. Well, the way I see it, I'm just looking for some fun. Nothing serious, you see. It's not my fault if a girl thinks she's in love with me."

"I think it's more than that, Vic. I think you saw her as damaged goods best disposed of before it got to be your problem."

Vic looked out the window, then back at me.

"I'm just not ready for anybody right now, Allen. I don't know, Mom's probably right. I'm too irresponsible. I'll change you know. I've got time to grow out of it, but for right now I only want a girl who is fun to be around. I can't see myself getting serious like you and Amy. You guys are different. I want a girl I can see when I want to see her not because she leans on me. Do you know what I mean?"

I replied sarcastically, "Yeah, I do, Vic, and I agree with your mom."

Vic offered, "If you think I'm taking advantage of her, I'll make our tour of the Masonic Temple the last time I see her. What do you say to that?"

"You still don't get it, do you? It's not me, it's her, or a dozen other girls like her, that you'll dump when they get too close to you. You've got to grow soon, Vic. You should see it's sharing, not taking, that's important. That's how you build a real relationship. You know, one with a little give and take, partner."

Vic sunk in his seat thinking over what I just said. Although I wasn't holding my breath for any big changes in his attitude, I decided to let up on him for the time being. The rest of the bus trip was muggy even with the windows down. The bus seemed to suck the grit right off the streets leaving it on our faces each time it accelerated.

When we reached our transfer point, we had to wait at the stop. While we stood there, I tried to appear inconspicuous with my suitcase. I was hoping some mugger would not notice there was something of value in it. The notion did seem a bit ridiculous, considering the outward appearance of my mom's battered black case. Nonetheless, I kept a constant vigil for any would-be assailants who might get too close.

Vic suggested, "Don't hold the suitcase that way, Allen. Somebody's going to think you got valuables in it."

I claimed, "That's exactly why I'm holding it this way. I don't want to give anyone a chance at grabbing it."

He just laughed, "You've got to act natural like there's nothin' but your dirty underwear in there. I'm telling you, otherwise, we'll both get jumped."

I decided he was probably right. Releasing my arms from the suitcase, I pulled it away from my chest forcing myself to let it dangle from my hand by its handle.

It felt so unnatural knowing my whole world was in that suitcase. By the time the transfer arrived, I was sweating bullets. Thankfully, the remainder of our ride was uneventful. Although, I could swear, some shady characters toward the back of the bus were sizing me up. Stepping off the bus I said, "Whew, now I know what those bank guards feel like."

Vic offered, "Come on, I'll walk you home."

Chapter 17

By the time Friday evening rolled around, all our plans were made for the tour on Saturday. First, we would meet at the malt shop, and then we would catch the bus to City Hall. After arriving home the previous day, I had made Vic wait to see the assessment letter from Dr. Shapsmeir. That really took some doing, but I insisted we all view the copy at once. Then, we could make our plans for the next showing. Vic suggested we all meet Friday night, so I met him right outside my apartment house at seven o'clock sharp. He, too, was adamantly insisting he escort the letter and me to the malt shop.

When we arrived, Amy and Connie were already there. Sensing the auspicious occasion ahead, they were discussing dresses and shoes to wear. Vic and I promised to dress in our best button down shirts and slacks. I even considered a tie, but decided against it when Vic said he refused to be caught dead in one. I figured we'd go as a group looking much the same, thus showing solidarity among us.

Both Amy and Connie seemed anxious about the upcoming tour. Amy asked, "Is there any ritual we have to perform to get in?"

Looking surprised I replied, "I don't know. I wasn't told of one."

Amy returned, "My uncle is a mason, and he says you have to know some password to get in."

"I think that's for members only, Amy. Otherwise, Mr. Williamson would have told me. Anyway, we are coming after tour hours so there won't be anyone else except the staff."

Vic could wait no longer.

"Let's see the letter of assessment, Allen."

I was happy to comply being anxious as the rest to know the figures. Looking around myself at the table, I reached into my pocket revealing the sealed envelope. Everyone leaned in slightly with anticipation. I looked around at all of them, then smiled.

"Now, we'll all know what our struggles are worth in dollars and cents."

Amy declared, "Oh, stop keeping us in suspense, Allen. Just open it, please."

I took out my pocket knife slicing open the letter. Then, I slid it out, unfolding it neatly on the table. I was facing the print with Amy, but the double-spaced entries were clearly visible to Vic and Connie. It was typed like an accountant's ledger.

The Pennsylvania Historical Society's Official Assessment:

The following items listed below are assigned a dollar value in accordance with state guidelines for acquiring same for the Society's collection located at: 1314 Locust Street, Philadelphia, Pennsylvania. The assessor's committee has adjusted each item's value for its connection with or ownership by certain historical figures of interest.

1. Parchment document, a unity pledge, signed by Benjamin Franklin, John Hancock, and George Washington...................... $225,000.00

2. A 1754 Hawkins' musket pistol with brass barrel in walnut case, owned by General George Washington. $100,000.00

3. A collection of 60 Spanish milled dollars dated April 4, 1771, in mahogany case, all in mint condition................................…....... $55,000.00

4. 3 Paul Revere silver goblets...
    $9,000.00

5. 1 silver and pearl magnifying glass...
    $1,500.00

6. 1 carved ivory letter opener...
    $300.00

Total Offer: - **$390,800.00**

There was a moment of silence as everyone took in what they saw. I noticed Vic shifting nervously in his seat. Then he broke the silence.

"Didn't Dr. Shapsmeir say we hit the jackpot? I mean that's what he said, right?"

No one else seemed ready to admit what Vic was already grousing about. The total split four ways came to $97,700.00. No doubt it was more money than any of us had ever seen and, while none of us wished to appear greedy, I must admit it seemed Vic did have something to grouse about.

Amy remarked, "You know, after all we went through to get these things, it does seem a bit of a letdown. I thought they paid much more for historical artifacts like these.

Vic scoffed, "I told ya I could have done better in a pawn shop."

I asked, "So, what are you going to do, take your things out of the collection? Let's don't get in a panic here. We've still got the Masonic Temple bid, you know?"

Connie looked stricken; apparently, she had some inflated notion about the value of our artifacts, too, brought on, no doubt, by Vic's imagination.

I reasoned, "We might as well face it. We're not the experts here. These things are worth more in my opinion, too. If Mr. Williamson even comes close to this, we'll have to accept his expert judgment. There's nothing more we can do."

Vic suggested, "We could try some other city like Washington, D.C., couldn't we?"

"Sure, we could, Vic, but you're missing the point. These articles are all about Philadelphia's history. Where else would they have such an interest in preserving and displaying them?"

Amy declared, "Allen's right, we're in the best market, right here. What we need to do is a little bit of old fashioned horse trading."

Connie asked, "What do you mean, Amy?"

Amy replied, "We need to create the impression in Mr. Williamson's mind that the Historical Society is willing to pay top dollar. You know, we need to drive up the price by playing one off against the other like we said before."

Vic asked, "Just how are we supposed to do that? Dr. Shapsmeir already told us they're on a tight budget. I think I believe him. This is probably as much as they can pony up."

Amy insisted, "Alright, that may be so. Mr. Williamson doesn't have to know that."

I said, "I think I see what you're getting at, Amy. If we let on that the demand is high, we might get more out of Williamson."

Amy acknowledged, "It could work, Allen. We just have to find a way to get the bidding started."

Vic asked, "Somebody answer me just how can we do that?"

We spent the next ten minutes hashing out different ideas, yet none seemed to surface until it came to me like an epiphany.

"I think I got the answer to our dilemma." I said.

"If we can convince Beverly to meet with Mr. Williamson and tell him how important it is to Dr. Shapsmeir to have these artifacts to prove out his theory about the mason's involvement in founding our government, we're home free."

Vic remained skeptical, "Just how are we supposed to pull that off?"

I said, "Look, we already know she wants to make a good impression on Dr. Shapsmeir. If she thought she might make the difference by meeting with Williamson, it would be a feather in her cap."

Vic seemed hesitant, "I dunno. What if it backfires and he decides to let Dr. Shapsmeir have the artifacts?"

Amy insisted, "It's possible, but I sincerely doubt it. These two are professionals. The acquisitions are a point of pride between them. I doubt Williamson is going to let the opportunity slip past because of Shapsmeir's wishes. By the same token, his knowing there's stiff competition could make him raise the bar."

I confirmed, "I agree, Vic. I think it's worth the risk."

Vic sat back in his seat giving me that cocky grin of his.

"Well then, Allen, let's vote on it."

"Alright, all those in favor of contacting Beverly, raise your hands."

Vic looked around noting he was the sole dissenter. He seemed disappointed in Connie, but realized things had changed between them.

"It's settled then. Since I suggested it, I'll call Beverly myself. We haven't got much time. I just hope I can persuade her to see Williamson before two-thirty tomorrow."

We left the malt shop and headed home. When I arrived at the top of the stairs at home, I felt exhausted. Perhaps it was the added burden I took on of convincing Beverly. That night I did not sleep well. Thoughts of the underground realm kept crowding into my dreams. I told myself it was the added strain of worrying how things would turn out on Saturday. Finally, in the wee hours, sleep did manage to overtake me.

When I awoke, it was late. I glanced at the alarm clock on my night stand shocked to see it was already 10:00 a.m. I leapt out of bed making my way to the kitchen. Mom had made coffee, but was already gone. Then, I remembered her saying they were going to the farmer's market Saturday morning. With the house empty, I had the perfect opportunity to call Beverly. Sitting down in the hallway, I dialed the number I wrote down the night before.

After two rings, a woman answered.

"Pennsylvania Historical Society, how can I help you?"

"Yes, good morning, I would like to speak to Dr. Shapsmeir's assistant, please."

"Please hold, I'll ring that number."

Nervously drumming my fingers on the phone table, I repeated the words I rehearsed the night before. There was a click, then I heard Beverly's voice on the line.

"Good morning, Dr. Shapsmeir's office. This is Beverly, how may I help you?"

I took a deep breath.

"Yes, Beverly, this is Allen Williams. How are you today?"

She sounded particularly cheerful.

"I'm just fine. Thank you very much. I didn't expect to hear from you so soon. Did you want to speak with Dr. Shapsmeir?"

"No, ah… actually I wanted to speak to you."

"Oh? Is there some way I might be of assistance?"

"Yes, there is something, actually. You see, Beverly, as you know, my partners and I are going to visit Mr. Williamson today at the Masonic Temple."

"Yes?"

"Well, if I may explain. My partners and I were discussing the Society's offer and we felt …well, that is, we hoped you might be able to do Dr. Shapsmeir a service."

"I'm not sure I follow."

I steadied myself trying not to let my nerves get the best of me.

"You see, my partners and I felt the offer was a bit low. However, we're not ready to make any firm decision until we meet with Mr. Williamson today at two-thirty. We were thinking, that is my partners and I, that perhaps you might help Dr. Shapsmeir by meeting with Mr. Williamson. You see, we felt if you could make him aware of the professor's desire to prove out his theory with our complete collection that perhaps he might allow Dr. Shapsmeir to make a counter bid."

There was a pause. Then her voice came back still cheerful as ever.

"Well, I don't know. I didn't really give that idea much thought. You see, I'm new here and I'm not sure about the bidding process. Do your partners really think it might help Dr. Shapsmeir's cause if I met with Harold Williamson?"

"Oh, yes, definitely. You see, we feel he deserves another chance before we finalize our decision. We think it's possible that if Mr. Williamson only knew what it meant to the professor, he might allow the professor an opportunity to acquire the articles that best support his theory."

"Well that's nice of you to think of us that way. What time did you say you were scheduled to meet?"

"We will be meeting with Mr. Williamson at two- thirty this afternoon, Beverly."

"Well now that you mentioned it, I'll consider meeting with him before that if his schedule permits."

"Oh, I'm sure he would be happy to meet with you anytime. I wish you luck. We do want the best for all concerned, you know."

"Thank you, Allen. Goodbye."

I hung up hoping I said enough to convince her. Then, I started dialing Amy's number.

"Hello, Martin residence."

"Hi, Amy, it's me. I just got off the phone with Beverly. I'm pretty sure she's going to meet with Mr. Williamson."

"That's great, Allen. Are we still having lunch together?"

"Oh sure, I'll be over around twelve."

"O.k., I'll see you then, keep your fingers crossed."

I hung up and went to my room to prepare for what would be one of the most important days of my life. Before I finished dressing, my family returned from the farmer's market. Each of the children moved around the kitchen busily putting up their individual bags of groceries. Mom usually made a point of shopping once a month at the open market. Each of the children knew part of their duties consisted of preparing the groceries for storage. Sister Ginny would also peel potatoes while the younger girls would shell peas, snap beans, or shuck corn. Whatever needed doing, they all pitched in. By evening, we knew we could expect either a roast chicken or a pot roast dinner with fresh vegetables. Mom knew I was excused from chores because of my important meeting. She, too, anxiously awaited the outcome that could literally change our lives forever.

"Allen, I pressed your slacks and shirt last night. They're hanging in the hall closet. Did you polish your shoes?"

"Not yet, Mom. I will do that soon."

Grandma smiled, "It's important to put your best foot forward."

"Yes, Grandma. Don't worry-, I will."

Ginny offered, "You can take my new fountain pen if you like."

"Thanks, Ginny, I'll take you up on that."

Mom added, "Just remember, son, let them do most of the talking. What you're bringing will speak for itself."

"Yes, Mom, I'll remember. I'm going to lunch with Amy. I'll need to hurry to get there by noon. I've got to go now."

Suddenly, the entire family dropped everything, forming up at the door for hugs and well wishes. I felt as though I were being sent off to slay some distant dragon. Breaking away from the last hug, I stepped out the door giving them all thumbs up.

"Wish me luck," I said.

I could hear their wishes echoing in the hallway as I descended the stairs for the street. With my hair slicked back, shoes shined, clothes pressed, and that black suitcase in hand, I could have been any business man off on a business junket. For once, I was glad I carried a dilapidated suitcase. It gave me a sense of security. After all, who would carry a fortune through the streets of Philly in a beat-up grip?

As I approached the Old Meeting House Restaurant on Arch Street, I was glad to see Amy sitting outside. I certainly didn't favor waiting out front for her looking conspicuous with a suitcase. She looked smart in her pleated white blouse and gray skirt. The shoes she wore were her best. I'd only seen them once before in church. Her hair was pulled back tight in a bun. Not the way I prefer it, but businesslike nonetheless.

Each of us ordered something unlikely to spill on our clothes. I settled for a chicken salad sandwich while she had a ham and cheese. The weather was pleasant with just enough breezes to take down the heat rising from the sidewalk. We both displayed our nervousness by eating quickly. When the check arrived, I left a generous tip hoping this would be the norm after today's meeting. I had just checked my watch when I spotted Vic and Connie walking up the crowded sidewalk. I waved my arm attracting their attention.

"Are you two ready to get rich," I called out?

Vic immediately cautioned, holding his finger to his lips.

"Quiet, Allen, somebody's ear might be hanging out."

I just chuckled rising with my suitcase in hand.

"Well, in that case, maybe we better get a move on."

In the meantime, across town, Beverly Compton decided to take my suggestion to heart. After speaking with me, she called the Masonic Temple and spoke with Mr. Williamson. When he learned of her connection with Dr. Shapsmeir, he agreed to meet with her at the Temple. She arrived at noon and was greeted by Mr. Williamson himself just inside the massive seventeen foot doors of the Grand Entrance Gate at North Broad Street. He stood on the inner steps between two colossal bronze sphinxes.

"I thought it best to meet you myself, Miss Compton. I felt it best for both us to keep this meeting discreet."

Beverly looked up in awe at the huge bronze statues guarding the entrance.

"These sphinxes are most impressive; do they have names?"

Harold replied, "If they do, they haven't confided in me." He gestured toward the main hall. "Would you care to walk along with me? That way, I can show you some of the splendor of the Temple while we talk. Have you visited us here before?"

"Yes, but it was some time ago during my freshman year. We took a field trip to see the Temple."

Once they past the great sphinxes, he led her into the Grand Foyer. It ran the entire length of the building from the entrance gate to the huge oak doors of the Benjamin Franklin room. The interior architecture was of the Norman period with oil portraits of past Grand Masters hanging from the walls on either side. When they reached the end of the cathedral-like hall, Beverly stole a glance behind her. The entrance way floor stretched backward one hundred fifty-feet in gleaming patterned black and white Carrara marble.

Harold ushered her forward and to the right to the Grand Master's Conference Room just ahead of them.

"I'm sorry time will not permit me to take you on a complete tour of the Temple today. I thought for our purposes, we might be more comfortable meeting in here."

He opened the heavy oaken door to the room where the Grand Master holds many meetings with his officers and staff. The room was decorated with some of the most interesting paintings and artifacts in the Masonic Temple. The center of the room was dominated by a long cherry wood table surrounded by plush high backed red leather chairs. The walls were adorned with more oil paintings than Beverly had seen in one place together. Clearly, the Pennsylvania Historical Society's conference room could not hold a candle to it. Beverly was so impressed she almost lost hope in making an argument for the Society's acquisition of the artifacts in question.

Harold sensed her awe, extending his hand toward a seat near the head of the table.

"Please do sit down, Miss Compton."

Beverly quickly regained her poise seating herself at the table near a venerable old grandfather clock encased in intricately carved black walnut.

"Please do call me, Beverly."

Harold replied amicably, "Yes, of course, and you may call me Right Worshipful Grand Master if you like."

Beverly seemed taken aback until she noticed his gentle laughter.

"That's just a little Masonic joke. Please do call me Harold."

Relieved at his breaking the ice, Beverly felt ready to pursue her cause. Taking a deep breath, she started in.

"Harold, I asked for this meeting to explain my boss's position. I'm doing so on my own accord because I know his sense of professionalism precludes him from doing so himself."

Harold leaned forward with genuine interest.

"Yes, do go on, please."

"Well, it is Dr. Shapsmeir's academic position that Freemasons historically exerted a great deal of influence over defining moments in the formation of our country's government. In fact, he sites critical junctures in the creation of our government as being the work of certain masons operating toward a common goal."

Harold replied, "Yes, I have read several of his papers on that very subject with great interest. I believe he centered his theory on the collusion of Benjamin Franklin, John Hancock, and George Washington as the, 'cabal of conspiratorial masons', if I'm not mistaken."

Beverly felt a sudden rush of relief in learning Harold was aware of Dr. Shapsmeir's theory. With a renewed sense of confidence, she proceeded with her argument.

"That is why I am here today. I have viewed the collection of artifacts presented by Mr. Williams and his partners and I am convinced they belong in the Pennsylvania Historical Society's collection. If so, they would not only underscore Dr. Shapsmeir's life time of academic research, but provide maximum exposure of the collection to the public. Therefore, I ask you to consider this when you view the collection before making your final decision."

Harold leaned back in his chair digesting the young intern's bold proposal, and then took what Beverly thought was a curious tone.

"Look around you, Beverly. Every portrait in this room is of a famous mason. We have had our share, you know. Believe me, the list is long and still growing. I truly believe we have been successful as the oldest living fraternity in the world for one reason. We all work toward a common goal. In fact, we are defined as 'a common brotherhood of man under the all-seeing eye of God'. That, by no means, suggests we are foolhardy dreamers.

In this very room, George Washington's Masonic apron resides alongside the trowel he used to lay the cornerstone of the Capitol Building. In short, Miss Compton, kings and kingdoms have all passed away, but the Masonic order lives on. You see it is my duty to act judiciously on behalf of countless others, even in distant parts of the world, to preserve the antiquity of masonry. In that vein, I am honor bound to seek the finest representative collections of masonry in the world. Therefore, I trust you will see my choice is clear. I cannot concede nor consign even part of my duty to the work of one man and his theory, not one scintilla of Masonic History. I hope you see my meaning."

Beverly rose uneasily from her chair feeling as though her legs were turned to jelly. At once, she realized she had out stepped her bounds. The cause was lost. Only the dignified trappings of historicity, in which she was immersed, prevented her from running out the door. Mustering all her courage, she stood facing the Grand Master. I'm afraid I've wasted your time, sir."

Harold offered stoically, "I'll show you to the door."

Beverly replied, "No, thank you. I'm sure anyone could find it."

With that, she departed the conference room quickening her pace toward the massive doors at the entrance. Pushing the six-inch-thick door open, she walked into the sunlight feeling pangs of guilt. She had come to help Dr. Shapsmeir's cause. Now, she was leaving defeated and worried she had only made things worse for him. Her stomach cinched up in knots. She never felt more alone on a crowded sidewalk as she passed City Hall. Heading south on Broad Street, she decided to walk back to the Historical Society. She believed it would give her time to think. Time enough, she hoped, to reconcile why she had acted alone and so brashly. She wanted to blame Allen, but knew it was her own blind ambition that drove her to gamble recklessly with her boss's reputation. Secretly, she hoped he would never find out.

Across town, my partners and I were on the bus headed for the Masonic Temple. I sat beside Amy holding tight to my suitcase full of dreams. Vic and Connie sat behind us barely speaking. The heat in the bus was making Vic chafe under his starched white shirt. Constantly dabbing his handkerchief at rivulets of sweat beading on his temples, he wished he had not given Connie the window seat after all. Meanwhile, Amy made small talk the whole way hoping to ease my nervousness.

By the time the bus pulled to the curb at the last stop on Broad Street, we were all grateful to get off. Connie stepped from the bus ahead of Vic. He thought she looked cute in her checkered black and white dress. He even liked her high heeled black patent-leather shoes which really made her legs look great. In his mind, however, that was as far as it went. He was more than ready to move on with no regrets.

We all formed up on the steps facing the imposing doors of the Masonic Temple. From the outside, the building really did look like a church with its gray stone Gothic architecture. It could have fit in perfectly in 12th Century France with its tall spires and castle-like towers and graceful arches. With a feeling of trepidation tugging at my heart, I took the first fateful step toward the impressive structure. We entered by the same heavy doors as Beverly had. Once inside, we were awestruck by the grandeur of the Norman Hall Entrance where the massive black-eyed sphinxes kept watch over us.

Connie expressed her impression of the Grand Hall in a single word. "Wowee."

The rest of us were too awestruck to add more. I glanced at my watch confirming we were on time. Then, as I looked up, I spotted a tall gentleman in his sixties approaching us in a business suit. The silver-haired gentleman smiled as he spoke.

"Welcome to the Masonic Headquarters of the Grand Lodge of Pennsylvania. My name is Harold Williamson. I am the Right Worshipful Grand Master of the Temple, but you can call me Harold. Allen stepped forward extending his hand.

"Hi, I'm Allen Williams. We spoke on the phone."

Harold replied, "Yes, of course, it's good of you all to come. I've been looking forward to our meeting. Please introduce me to your partners."

I made introductions all around then commented.

"This is a wonderful Temple you have here."

Harold seemed bemused by my observation.

"Oh, this is only the beginning. I'm prepared to take you on a guided tour of the entire building. First, I would like to ask you good people if you would allow my team of experts to properly evaluate your artifacts. I thought perhaps you could leave them in their capable hands while we take our tour. That way, they should have sufficient time to authenticate and assess their value by the time we've finished touring."

I turned toward the others receiving their collective nod of approval. Then, I proceeded to hand over the suitcase. Harold, in turn, asked us all to wait while he turned it over to the evaluators.

Harold smiled again, "I'll be right back. Then we can begin our tour."

As he walked away, Vic poked me in the back whispering.

"Isn't that somethin'? That means we'll have our answer today. That's what I call service with a smile."

I answered, "Yeah, well, I guess that's just the way they do business here."

As promised, Harold returned momentarily.

He announced, "As we go through, please don't hesitate to ask questions. We have plenty of time, since we are the only ones taking the tour this time of day. Please step this way and we will commence our tour. Now, when you entered the Temple, you came through the Grand Entrance Gate. The architectural style of the Grand Entrance Gate is Norman."

Connie asked, "Does that mean it's named after someone?"

Harold hesitated momentarily then answered, "Actually, it's named for a people. You see the Normans populated Northern France in the 10th Century, they migrated from Scandinavia."

Connie said, "Oh, I see."

Harold moved on ahead resuming the tour as I whispered over my shoulder to Connie.

"Stop with the questions, Connie, or this is going to be one long tour."

Connie shot me a pained look, then, tossed her head in the opposite direction.

Harold was making his way across the Grand Foyer speaking as he went.

"These oil portraits are of Past Grand Masters. The Grand Master is the elected leader of our fraternity, and he serves a two-year term. They are referred to as the Right Worshipful Grand Master of the Lodge. Before you get the wrong impression, we don't worship the Grand Master. He is called Right Worshipful, meaning he is "full of worship" which is a good quality for any leader. Now, before we leave this area, turn around and look back toward the entrance and the stairs."

We all observed beautifully patterned black and white alternating Carrara marble tiles shimmering beneath the cherry wood Norman arches over portraits hung along the walls for one hundred and fifty feet. The double staircase was heavy iron painted ivory with an ebony handrail flanked by wainscoting of Lisbon marble.

Harold spoke, "Next, we'll move on to the Grand Banquet Room."

As we crossed the threshold, Harold remarked, "This is the most used room of the Masonic Temple. It can seat up to five hundred people. The hall features the Composite style of architecture. As you can see, portraits decorate the walls while the white tile floor is laid in small black intricate patterns."

Next, we strolled on to Oriental Hall, one of seven separate lodges within the building. We were told it was decorated in 1896 in the Moorish style.

Harold added, "The colors and decorations were copied from the Alhambra in Granada, Spain. Looking directly at Connie before she could ask he said, "That's a 13th Century castle."

Connie responded, "Oh".

Amy looked up marveling at the beauty of the ceiling.

Harold noticed her, commenting, "The ceiling is divided into seven thousand panels of various shapes. Its design is copied from the Hall of the Ambassadors. The border surrounding the ceiling is a pattern of the lotus flower copied from the Salon of the Tribunals. The chandeliers are the original gas fixtures converted from gas to electric in 1889. Our Temple is one of the first buildings in Philadelphia to install electric lights."

Harold, then, led us up the massive staircase that represented the Doric School of Architecture. Our next stop was the Ionic Hall decorated in 1890. Harold informed us it took its name from the style of architecture from Ionia, where King Ion reigned in Asia Minor. He told us the Ionians were mostly Greek emigrants and refinement and elegance were characteristic in their buildings. The walls of the hall were painted light blue, with panels containing full-length portraits of Right Worshipful Past Grand Masters.

Vic leaned forward to whisper in my ear.

"There sure were a lot of these guys, huh?"

Without turning I answered, "Long history."

Harold was explaining, "The ceiling of Ionic Hall represents heaven. In the center, shines the noon-day sun, surrounded by signs of the planets and stars. The signs of the Zodiac were often used decoratively by the operative masons of the Middle Ages in Europe. The clock on the west wall is one of the oldest in the Temple. It was made in 1874 and is still keeping time. Next, we will go to Egyptian Hall."

Harold led the way. He seemed to take great pride in the works within the Temple. The rest of us were speechless. None of us had ever witnessed such opulent surroundings. Showing us to a giant chamber with purple carpeting, Harold began again.

"This, of course, is Egyptian Hall. It was finished in 1889. It is decorated in the style of the Nile Valley. Twelve huge columns stand on its four sides. Each row of columns is surmounted by capitals peculiar to the Temples of Luxor, Karnak, Philae, and others. The Worshipful Master's throne is gilded ebony with a pedestal flanked by sphinxes. The ceiling is blue, indicative of the heavens. A solar disk is placed in the East. Representations of the major Egyptian gods are accurate copies from Egypt, and the room is often used by students of the style for research because the hieroglyphics are that accurate."

On the same floor, Harold led us to yet another lodge at the same end of the building. He entered Norman Hall pointing out it was finished in 1891, in the Rhenish Romanesque Style.

Harold confided, "The term 'Norman' is often indiscriminately used for round –arch architecture such as is found here."

Around the room's walls there were several panels. Some were occupied by windows; others displayed life-sized figures on a gold mosaic background. The figures bore the working tools of Freemasonry: Plumb, Trowel, Square, Mallet, and Compasses. The ceiling panels were a deep blue with the outside tinted in chocolate brown offset by bright red patterned carpet throughout and furniture in red leather.

It seemed to me nothing could surpass the workmanship in this building. Each hall mesmerized us with its palatial grandeur. I was even more amazed when Harold told us that much of the beautiful moldings found throughout the temple were not really wood at all, but plaster. It was finished so finely that turkey feathers were used in painting the plaster to give it a wood grained look. It was all truly breathtaking. Now, we were headed to the opposite side of the building's second floor to see Renaissance Hall.

Harold led us in stating, "Renaissance Hall is where the Grand Holy Royal Arch Chapter of Pennsylvania and some subordinate chapters meet. The Hall is decorated in the Italian Renaissance Style, and was finished in 1908. Just outside the Hall you can see the twelve-foot lion's head fountain made of marble. In the ceiling are round-headed paintings of Moses and King Solomon and over to your right is the painting of St. John the Evangelist. Of course, as you can see, the prevailing color of the room is scarlet, the symbolic color of the Chapter.

Amy craned her neck upwards exclaiming, "It's all so breathtaking, isn't it, Allen?"

I could only reply, "Yes, indeed."

Then, it was Harold's pleasure to lead us on to the next hall.

He began, "Now we are entering the meeting place of the Grand Lodge of Pennsylvania: Corinthian Hall. The features of this room were completed in 1903. It is decorated in strict conformity with the principles of Grecian Classical Architecture. He also pointed out bas-relief medallions two feet wide over the entrance hall and on the pilasters on the north and south walls that were taken from ancient Greek coins and medallions.

He continued, "The room is decorated with mosaics representing fragments from Greek mythology relating mostly to spiritual life. After dark, the stars and subdued lighting gives an atmosphere of an open hall in an ancient Greek temple. Lastly, the west wall bears the inscription 'Fide et Fiduccia', which means by fidelity and confidence."

Next, Harold led us to the Grand Staircase that would lead us to the last hall on the third floor.

Harold noted, high above the Grand Staircase are four large paintings: Demeter of ancient Greek mythology, the goddess of vegetation; "Bringing in the Harvest", "Woodlands", and "Group Singers."

"Then you see surrounding the staircase are full-length portraits of Washington, Franklin, Lafayette, and Stephen Girard. In the ceiling, directly above the staircase is a circular skylight twenty feet in diameter. Also, throughout, the walls and ceiling are emblems of Royal Arch Masonry."

Next, we ascended the Tennessee marble stairway to the final hall.

Harold stepped through the entrance of Gothic Hall and, without missing a beat, continued the tour.

"Gothic Hall has all the characteristics of the architectural style for which it is named. The groins, pointed arches, pinnacles, and spires appear in every part of the room. The Cross and Crown emblem high above the Grand Master's chair is the emblem of the modern Knights Templar. His chair is known as the Commander's Throne. It is a replica of the Archbishop's throne in Canterbury Cathedral. The Latin inscription you see around the emblem means, 'In this sign you will conquer.' The pictures on the walls are of Past Grand Commanders. The wainscoting is of oiled pine, and all the furniture in this hall is hand carved."

Harold took a few steps beyond the entrance to the hall turning to face us.

"Well, ladies and gentlemen, this concludes our tour. Do you have any questions?"

Vic took a chance at asking a question.

"Ah, yes, Harold, how long would you say masonry has been around?"

He responded, "That's a good question. According to records discovered in ancient Jerusalem the oldest account of a Master Mason is that of one Hiram of Abif. The records say he was murdered by those who wished to avail themselves of his secret skills in masonry. At the time, he was one of many masons assigned by King Solomon to build the temple in Jerusalem. For the construction of King Solomon's Temple, three Grand Master Masons were chosen; Hiram of Abif was one of those. In addition, the records state there was 3,600 Master Masons, 80,000 Fellowcraft Masons, and 70,000 Entered Apprentice Masons employed to build the temple."

Vic whistled, "Wow, that's a lot of masons."

Harold added, "Yes, and that was a long time ago. Well, if there are no more questions, we can adjourn to the conference room and see what the assessment team has come up with."

Speaking for myself, I was duly impressed not only with the tour but the Masonic organization. I could scarcely contain my curiosity about the assessment team's findings. As I looked to Amy, I could see that same gleam in her eyes. Vic walked ahead of us just behind Harold. It was not hard to imagine what he was thinking. As we descended the stairs, Connie made it clear what was on her mind.

Tapping Amy on the shoulder she asked, "What are you going to buy first with your share?" She hesitated trapped between a sense of decorum and desire to share her feminine side then she replied, "I'm not sure, but it ought to be expensive."

Harold turned on the stairs to see what the two girls were tittering about only to find quiet concealment on their faces. Each was determined to remain lithe and graceful, with no telltale twitch in their manners. When we reached the main floor, Harold asked us to wait in the foyer while he checked on his fellow masons in the conference room. He found the seven appointed masons seated at the conference table. As agreed, they had a list of the items provided for evaluation with corresponding dollar amounts.

When he entered, Nicolas Fillmore, the great, great grandson of a cloth-maker's apprentice and thirteenth president of the United States, stood to present their findings.

Harold accepted the envelope, "I trust my brothers have had ample time to assess these artifacts."

Nicolas replied, "We have, Worshipful Master."

"That being the case, I will admit the sellers into our chambers for their final decision."

Without further ado, Harold came out to the foyer and spoke with us.

"Please do come in everyone. My committee has reached its decision."

We all filed in after Harold, seating ourselves at the large cherry wood conference table. Despite the twelve persons present at the table, it still seemed overwhelming in size. I sat at one end facing the group of seven masons with Harold seated in between. Once we were all settled, Harold had a few words for us all.

"As you are aware, there is at least one outside bidder. We have taken that into account. The figures we are about to present are not necessarily final. However, I feel it necessary to inform you the Grand Lodge of

Pennsylvania has rarely reconsidered a bid to acquire in its history. Therefore, I suggest you give this bid your utmost consideration. Having said that, I hope all of you will entertain our bid. In the meantime, we will leave the room so you may discuss it among yourselves privately."

When the last mason left the room, I reached for the envelope in front of me. We all huddled in close as I opened it. When I laid the paper out for all to see, there was a collective gasping sound. Amy was the first to respond in words.

"Oh, my Lord, I don't believe it! Vic let out a whoop I'm sure those outside could hear. Then he proceeded to dance around the room with Connie. I was completely flabbergasted; my mouth remained open in wordless wonderment. The figure at the bottom of the column of artifacts read 500,000 dollars. I thought, *"Such a beautiful round figure."* Immediately, I tried regaining my composure, but it was just too difficult. I jumped up grabbing Amy around the waist joining Vic and Connie in a dance about the room. When we finally did stop dancing, I asked the others needlessly.

"Well, is this a figure we can live with?"

Vic shouted, "Hell, yes, it is!"

Instantly, I put my finger to my lips.

"Quiet, you. Do you want them all to hear?"

Vic retorted, "Hell, yes!"

I looked at Amy and pulled her close in a crushing embrace.

"Well, honey, let's tell the nice men outside what we think."

We all joined hands and left the conference room together. I supposed the masons waiting in the foyer already knew our answer. Nevertheless, just to make it formal, I told them the others appointed me to speak on their behalf in acceptance of their generous offer.

Harold shook my hand, and that of the others, congratulating us all on our decision. He assured us we were making a fine addition to the collection of the Masonic Temple. Also, he extended a lifelong invitation to visit the items soon to be on display in the Temple. I only had one request of him.

Stepping aside I asked, "Do you suppose it would be possible to loan the articles for display at the Pennsylvania Historical Society someday soon?"

Harold appeared to be in serious thought for a moment, then, his face broadened into a tolerant smile.

"Yes, Allen, I'm sure we can arrange that in the space of my tenure."

The rest of our stay at the Temple was all business. I must say I was impressed once again. After congratulations, we went into the treasurer's office. Four checks were made out in our names for $125,000 each. Then, we were escorted to the door by Harold. I turned to shake his hand once more.

"Thank you for the wonderful tour, it meant a lot to us. I know I speak for all when I say we'll take you up on your invitation to return and see the articles on display. We didn't come by them easily, you know."

Harold stated, "I'm certain those masons who penned the agreement you found did not find their promises came easily either."

I replied, "Thanks be to God they had enough courage and commitment to stand by them."

As I look back, it was a remarkable experience in all our lives. It's been fifty years now and I remember like it was yesterday. Amy's gone now after forty-eight years of marriage. She left me with two beautiful daughters who graduated with honors from University of Pennsylvania, just as she and I. After a valiant battle with breast cancer, she succumbed two years ago. Tonight, I am being honored for these many years of teaching history at the same University I graduated from. It's hard to believe how far this butcher boy has come in these many years.

Over the years, I've tried keeping in touch with Vic and Connie by letter and Christmas card. That is, until recently, when I received news that Vic was shot trying to break up a fight in his pool hall. After that, I sort of lost touch with Connie. The last I heard, she married some low life in New Jersey and was living in a trailer park in New Brunswick.

Sometimes my writing takes me on research trips to that side of Philadelphia, where I visit my sisters and pay my respects to my parents and grandparents in Drexel Hill Cemetery. In the quiet stillness beneath the trees, I think about the life I have lived and the consequences of going on such a youthful adventure. I smile when I think of the good things that came of daring to go somewhere I shouldn't have been. I always tell my students this important quote I've lived by:

"Try living out your dreams, no matter what the consequences. Too often in life we regret the things we didn't do, more than the things we've done."